Thomas Wright

The Life of Daniel Defoe

Thomas Wright

The Life of Daniel Defoe

ISBN/EAN: 9783337123833

Printed in Europe, USA, Canada, Australia, Japan

Cover: Foto ©Raphael Reischuk / pixelio.de

More available books at **www.hansebooks.com**

THE
LIFE OF DANIEL DEFOE

BY

THOMAS WRIGHT

PRINCIPAL OF COWPER SCHOOL, OLNEY; AUTHOR OF "THE LIFE OF
WILLIAM COWPER," ETC.

"Defoe was always my darling"—CHARLES LAMB
Letter to Mr. Walter Wilson

CASSELL AND COMPANY, LIMITED
LONDON, PARIS & MELBOURNE
1894

PREFACE.

WITH the personality of no eminent man of letters of the seventeenth and eighteenth centuries is the public less familiar than with that of Daniel Defoe. " Robinson Crusoe " has been read to tatters, " The Shortest Way " even has been taken down and dusted ; but of the man who wrote them the great world knows nothing, except, perhaps, that he had a hooked nose and was put in the pillory. Biographers have been so occupied in gathering together facts concerning his writings, especially those of the obscurer kind, and in trying to discover fresh writings, and have devoted so much space to the consideration of his position as a politician, that the man himself and his inner life have been almost entirely lost sight of.

Defoe, to quote Heine's phrase, was a brave soldier in the war of humanity, but he was also an extremely interesting personality, and it is partly in order to reveal the secrets of the mine neglected

by my predecessors that this work has been undertaken; and I use the word "neglected" advisedly,
for though, thanks to the kindness of friends, I
have had placed in my hands a great mass of
material with the existence of which my predecessors were unacquainted, nevertheless, it is owing
quite as much to a careful study of Defoe's works,
and especially his novels, as it is to the new
material, that I am able to present, as I trust I do
present, not a mythical figure hardly discernible
behind a pile of half-forgotten pamphlets, but a
man of flesh and blood—the hero, Defoe. I wish
to show the man who is responsible for the immortal story of "wild, wicked Robinson Crusoe,"
or wild, wicked Daniel Defoe, if you like—for,
Bunyan-like, he flagellated his own back; and I
shall describe the painful travail which made that
great allegory possible; for "Robinson Crusoe," as
Defoe himself declares, and as I shall prove, is an
allegory of Defoe's own life. I wish to show the
man who wrote the moving scenes in "Colonel
Jack," the unapproached realism of "Moll Flanders,"
the truth-like "History of the Plague," and the
stirring and picturesque "Memoirs of a Cavalier."

I wish to show Defoe in the street, in the
meeting-house, in "Lob's Pound" (as Newgate was

prettily called), on his travels, in his parlour with his three beautiful daughters, whom he loved so tenderly and of whom he was so justly proud, to show him cultivating his garden of four acres (with adjoining close)—he was a mighty gardener before the Lord—superintending his tile-yard, writing his books, and (must we say it?) dodging his creditors.

As in my "Life of William Cowper," I have not despised trifles, and for the reason that I believe, with Sir Walter Raleigh, that "Even by trifles are the qualities of great persons as well disclosed as by their great actions, because in matters of importance they commonly strain themselves to the observance of general commended rules; in lesser things they follow the current of their own natures."

Another feature of this work is my venturing to submit what I believe to be the true key to "Robinson Crusoe."

Defoe not only declares, in his "Serious Reflections" ("Robinson Crusoe," Part III.), that Robinson Crusoe is an allegory of his own life, but that the correspondence extended even to minuteness. He averred that the fright and fancies that succeeded the sight of the print of the man's foot, the discovery in the cave of the goat with gleaming eyes, the incident of his annexation of Friday — everything, in short, that happened in Crusoe — had its counterpart with Defoe.

As a natural consequence, many persons have tried to find out the key—to discover which incident in Defoe's life corresponded with his shipwreck, which with the coming of the savages, etc. ; one of the most recent of these explorers being the late Professor Minto (author of the Handbook to Defoe, in the " English Men of Letters " series), who, not meeting with success, came to the conclusion that the story is not an allegory at all : that it merely suited Defoe's purpose to call it by that name *after* it was published, whilst previously he had thought nothing about the matter. To my mind, indeed, the chief blemish of Professor Minto's book, valuable as it is, and much as I am indebted to it, is his charging Defoe with lying—declaring that he was a story-teller in both senses of the word. That Defoe "at his worst," that is at the most trying period of his political career, " might," as S. R. B. says, "have taught Talleyrand the method of plausible dissimulation, and Pope the art of mystification " is undoubtedly true ; but that is a very different thing from saying that he told—that he was in the habit of telling—downright falsehoods, on all sorts of occasions, for the mere pleasure of telling them.

I have not set myself the Quixotic task to paint a perfect man, and I am aware that the business of a biographer is not to justify words and deeds, but merely to record facts ; nevertheless, I may, without being suspected of bias, throw out one or two suggestions. While it does not fall to my lot to lay down to what extent a man may pardonably practise dissimulation, I may observe that all men, without exception, take a good deal of pains to give their neighbours a different idea of the condition of their affairs from what is really the case. Is that more venial than Defoe's playing the *rôle* of a Jacobite as he did, and writing as if he were a Jacobite for a Jacobite journal, all the while he was in reception of Whig pay ? Is being a spy a crime ? Does England execrate the memory of Major André ?

I was first thrown on the right track respecting the connection between "Robinson Crusoe" and the life of Defoe by the discovery, a few years back, by Mr. G. A. Aitken, of the true date of Defoe's birth, which was 1659 and not 1661, as previously supposed, with the result of the disclosure that in order to get at the date in the life of Defoe which corresponds with the date in "Crusoe," nothing has to be done except to add twenty-seven years. As in the body of this book the subject is thoroughly gone into (*see* § § 2, 7, 50, etc.), the various parallels being pointed out, nothing further on it need be said here, except to notice how very particular Robinson Crusoe is regarding dates; over and over again he repeats a date, in order to engraft it in the reader's memory.

Thanks to the kindness of Mr. Richard Champion Rawlins, I am able to settle once and for ever the vexed question as to whence Defoe obtained the bulk of the material upon which "Robinson Crusoe" is founded, and I give a photograph of the house of Mrs. Damaris Daniel in Bristol where Defoe met Selkirk. Mr. Rawlins is a descendant of Francis Rogers, one of the twelve merchants of Bristol who fitted out the *Duke* and the *Duchess*, commanded by Captain Woodes Rogers, who brought Selkirk home. (*See* § 42 and Appendix.)

The interesting facts connected with Defoe's imprisonment for writing "The Shortest Way," related in § 19, are also new. My attention was drawn to these by Joseph Redington, Esq., of the Record Office.

Another feature of this book is its bringing out, more clearly than can be found elsewhere, that

Defoe was above all things—that it was his endeavour to be at all times—the man of God.
This, after referring to his dissimulation in matters
political, may perhaps startle. But what I mean is,
not that he never sinned, or that all which he did
was right, but that his aims and desires were right.
His was a great soul, and little souls should beware
of measuring him by their own standard. An
Achilles in the field who feared not the face of any
man, Daniel Defoe before his God was a humble,
tearful penitent. To use his own words, "he was
often heard to pray to God in his solitudes very
audibly and with great fervency." The prize of
fame he constantly coveted, and it has been awarded
to him; but above all things he valued "the prize
of the high calling of God in Christ Jesus."

I have endeavoured to write this book without
bias, and the task has been the more easy insomuch
that, staunch a Dissenter as Defoe was, few authors
have spoken with greater kindliness of the Church
of England (*see* his beautiful remarks in § 30 and
§ 63). The book is likewise politically neutral. I
have too much admiration for some of Defoe's Tory
opponents to allow the "Whig dogs" to have always
the best of the argument. To speak soberly, my
desire is for it to be felt that Defoe belongs not to

b

the Dissenter or to the Churchman, not to the Whig or to the Tory. He is the nation's.

The question as to the number of works actually written by Defoe need not trouble us. Mr. Lee's list being undoubtedly the most trustworthy, I have followed it, but the precise number of books that Defoe wrote, or whether some of the minor works attributed to him were by him, will never be known. Whether, however, he wrote 240, 250, or 260 does not greatly matter, for the doubtful works are of no intrinsic value; and the same may be said of the "recently discovered" newspaper "writings" of Defoe, many of which were probably not by him at all, published by Mr. Lee in 1869. Even of the vast number of productions that were certainly his, very many deserve, and will receive from us, no more than a passing notice. To run away with the idea that everything that Defoe wrote is bullion is a mistake, and the sooner the mind is disabused of it the better. Mr. Lee's list is not only the best yet made, but probably the best that ever will be made, for we are unlikely to see another man willing to spend so much time and trouble in trying to settle a question of so little real importance. In this list I have made only two alterations. No. 1—"A Letter containing some Reflections on His Majesty's

Declaration for Liberty of Conscience "—was discovered, subsequent to the publication of Mr. Lee's
work, to have been written by Dr. Burnet. So this
I have struck out, but have put in its place Defoe's
first known publication—a tract relating to the Turks
—which, as it was lost, Mr. Lee did not trouble to
include. The other alteration is the insertion of the
work " Due Reflections for the Plague " (*see* § 76),
which Mr. Lee accidentally omitted.

The material that has been made use of for the
present volume is of four kinds :—

The first comprises the labours of my predecessors in the biographical office, to wit, the " Life
of Defoe " by the Scotch antiquary George Chalmers
(1786), the life by Walter Wilson in 1830, that by
William Chadwick in 1859, and that by William Lee
(1869), valuable works all of them, but dry as the
very Sahara.

The second comprises the discoveries that have
been made by various persons since the publication
of Lee—*e.g.*, the letter of Defoe to Keimer sent to
Notes and Queries in 1869 by Mr. James Crossley ;
the letters of Defoe to John Fransham, which we owe
to Mr. Norgate (*Notes and Queries*, April 3rd, 1875,
and April 10th, 1875) ; the letter in *Notes and Queries*
for January 26th, 1884, furnished by Mr. Joy ; the

articles by Mr. Aitken in the *Contemporary Review* for February, 1890, and the *Athenæum* for April 30th; 1889, and August 31st, 1890; and the notes in "Lewis's History of Islington."

The third comprises the valuable critical writings of John Forster (Historical and biographical essays, 1858), Hazlitt, Charles Lamb, Mr. Saintsbury in the " Britannica" and his " Introduction to Defoe's Minor Novels" (1892), the valuable review of the last in the *Daily Chronicle* by Mr. A. B. Walkley, and Professor Minto's monograph.

The fourth comprises the unpublished material in the British Museum and other collections, my own discoveries, and the material placed in my hands by various ladies and gentlemen.

In the British Museum are six letters by Defoe's sons, all of which have been useful—namely, one from Daniel Defoe, *fils*, to his cousin, Miss Cornwall, one by Benjamin Defoe to Sir Hans Sloane, and four by Benjamin Defoe to the Duke of Newcastle. There are also in the Museum some printed pamphlets relating to Defoe which my predecessors could not have seen.

In the " Calendar of Treasury Papers" (1702 to 1717), preserved in the Record Office, are two very interesting notices of Defoe and his arch-enemy the

Earl of Nottingham. My attention was most kindly called to these by Mr. Joseph Redington, of Church End, Finchley.

The Rev. Henry Defoe Baker, Rector of Thruxton, Hants, who very kindly entertained me at Thruxton, placed in my hands a great mass of materials, the most important of which consisted of a volume of letters written by Sophia, Defoe's youngest daughter, and Henry Baker, her betrothed, previous to their marriage, most of which contain allusions to Defoe; and seven unpublished letters of Defoe (one in Defoe's handwriting, and six copies made by Henry Baker). The Rev. W. Defoe Baker, Rector of Welton, Lincoln, was kind enough to send me copies of the four autograph letters of Defoe in his possession. One of them, a long and extremely beautiful letter, is given in its entirety in § 94; and from all I have made quotations.

Of no little importance was my discovery of the will of Defoe's grandfather—or rather the Rev. W. Sweeting's discovery of it, for it was found by him at Peterborough in the Consistory Court of North-ampton when he was making researches for me; and this disclosed, among other things, that the home of the Foes was Etton, not Elton, in Northamptonshire, and suggested an examination of the Etton registers which brought to light a number of other interesting facts.

I am under obligations to the Marquis of Bute for information concerning the so-called Kneller portrait of Defoe (*see* § 34); to Miss Mary Defoe (great-great-grand-daughter of the novelist) for in-formation conveyed during long conversations and by letter, and for the loan of a copy of "Wilson's Life of Defoe," with manuscript corrections; and to the aged and infirm Mr. James William Defoe (great-great-grandson of the novelist) for the indentures of Samuel Defoe, the novelist's grandson. I may observe in passing that the late Lord Tennyson, Poet Laureate, tried hard to get Mr. Defoe placed on the Civil List, and that, being unsuccessful, he joined cordially with me in establishing a fund for Mr. Defoe's assistance. This fund is still open.

I also wish to acknowledge my indebtedness, for various services, to the following ladies and gentle-men :—G. A. Aitken, Esq., Hornton Street, Ken-sington, to whom I have the honour of dedicating the book; Mr. John T. Page, Holmby House, Hampton Road, Forest Gate; Mr. W. H. Peet, of the firm of Longmans and Co., Paternoster Row, whose house of business occupies the site of the "Ship," whence "Robinson Crusoe" was issued;

Mr. Henry Gray, bookseller, of 47, Leicester Square, London, W.C.; the Rev. J. F. Kennard, Bury St. Edmunds; the Rev. F. Snape, Bury St. Edmunds; Mrs. Jennings, Cupola House, Bury; Rev. Evelyn White, Christ Church Vicarage, Chesham; the Rev. Dr. Anderson, Defoe Manse, Tooting; A. B. Walkley, Esq. (dramatic critic of the *Speaker* and the *Star*, etc., etc., and author of " Playhouse Impressions"); W. H. King, Esq., Leigh Hill, Leigh, Essex; the Rev. J. Lewis, College Road, Norwich; Mr. William George, St. Wulfstan's, Durdham Park, Bristol; Rev. J. R. Bailey, Craven House, Halifax; Rev. C. R. Durham, Rector of Etton, Northants; Messrs. George Bell and Sons (publishers of the useful edition of Defoe's works in seven volumes); Messrs. T. Nelson and Sons (publishers of the carefully edited " Household " edition of " Robinson Crusoe "); Mr. W. Wright, College Street, Westminster; Henry Gough, Esq., Redhill; W. W. Wainewright, Esq., 162, Portland Street, W.; the Rev. R. F. Whistler, Rector of Elton, Hunts; Alfred Double, Esq., F.S.S., C.C., Stamford Hill, N.; the Rev. W. D. Sweeting, Maxey Vicarage, Market Deeping; Mr. P. Soman, of the *Norwich Argus;* Mr. R. Batey, Halifax; Mr. Joseph Redington, Church End, Finchley; Miss Bessie Wright, Margery Hall, Forest Gate; Hyde

Clarke, Esq., St. George's Square, S.W.; J. G. Godwin, Esq., St. George's Row, Pimlico; Rev. F. C. Naish, Gravesend; E. Forbes Robinson, Esq., Aldeburgh House, Westcombe Park Road, Blackheath; W. H. G. Webb, Esq., R.N., The Firs, Warwick Road, New Barnet; H. Gough, Esq., Redhill; and my amanuensis, Miss May Burford.

THOMAS WRIGHT.

Cowper School, Olney.

        31 *May*, 1894.

CONTENTS.

CHAPTER IV.

In "Lob's Round" (about Eighteen Months).

CHAPTER V.

At Bury St. Edmunds.

CHAPTER VI.

Electioneering.

CHAPTER VII.

To and From Scotland.

CHAPTER VIII.

At Halifax (Autumn, 1712).

CHAPTER IX.

In " Lob's Pound " Again.

CHAPTER X.

Newington.

Book II.—NOVELIST AND HISTORIAN.

CHAPTER XI.

THE ADVENTURE SERIES.

CHAPTER XII.

CRIMINAL AND TOPOGRAPHICAL SERIES.

CHAPTER XIII.

Business and Magical Series.

CHAPTER XIV.

His Last Days.

LIST OF ILLLUSTRATIONS.

LIFE OF DANIEL DEFOE.

Book I.

PAMPHLETEER AND POET.

CHAPTER I.

CHILDHOOD AND YOUTH (1659—1678).

To narrate the career of Daniel Defoe is to tell a tale
of wonder and daring, of high endeavour and marvellous success. To dwell upon it is to take courage,
and to praise God for the splendid possibilities of life.
Defoe's incessant activity of itself excites astonishment. It can be said of him, even with greater truth
than of Dryden, "His chariot wheels got hot by
driving fast." Defoe is always the hero; his career
is as thick with events as a cornfield with corn; his
fortunes change as quickly and as completely as the
shapes in a kaleidoscope—he is up, he is down, he is
courted, he is spurned; it is shine, it is shower, it is
couleur de rose, it is Stygian night. Thirteen times
he was rich and poor. Achilles was not more audacious, Ulysses more subtle, Æneas more pious. The
tasks he set himself, the way he performed them, how

B

he struggled, and the meed that he won, it is the object
of these pages to set forth; and with a full sense of
the importance of our mission we proceed merrily.

I.—THE FOES OF ETTON IN NORTHAMPTONSHIRE.

The ancient home of the Foes—the village of Etton
—is a diminutive place of fewer than one hundred inhabitants, situated about five miles from Peterborough,
in Northamptonshire; and that it was this spot, and
not Elton in Northants (a place that does not exist),
or Elton in Hunts, as stated by previous biographers,
we are able, as the result of research at the Probate
Office, Peterborough, and in the Etton registers, to
lay down for certain. This, it may be urged, is a
small matter (which, for the sake of peace, we will
grant); but at the same time it may be submitted that
there is something decidedly cheering, when a long
journey has to be performed, in the knowledge that
one is right at starting.

Foe, Faux, Vaux, and Devereux—all variations of
the same—are old Northamptonshire names, and were,
there is not the slightest doubt, Flemish importations,
brought over, to use Chadwick's expression, "with
the straw-plat of Dunstable and the bobbin-lace of
Northampton." It is also almost certain that Defoe
himself was aware of his Flemish extraction, as may
be judged from his "Giving Alms no Charity," where
he lauds the wisdom of Elizabeth in encouraging the
Flemings, and mentions the names of a number of
Flemish families, though, for reasons best known to
himself, he does not give his own.

What we have unearthed concerning the earlier

Foes is as follows :—In the Court of the Archdeaconry of Hunts, 1616—1739, the name does not occur, nor is there anything like it; in the earlier books of the Consistory Court of Ely (1449—1618) there are none, but the later books (1683—1690) have Few, Fiew, and Faux, and once occurs a De Few (Edward), whose executor would not swear, because he was a Quaker. It is not, however, till the inquirer arrives among the Northants books that he finds himself in clover. In these, between the years 1608 and 1723, are eleven Foes, all of them of Etton or the neighbouring villages : — Foe, Margaret; Fooe, Henry; Foe, Robert; *Foe, Daniel;* Foe, Thomas;* Foe, Mathews; Fow, Thomas; Foe, William; Foe, Daniel, Foe, Luke (or Lucy); Foe, Godfry.

The first Daniel was the novelist's grandfather. He was in good circumstances, and, according to his grandson, kept a pack of hounds (*Review*, vol. vii., Preface).

Mr. Foe's dogs, owing to a whim of his huntsman's, bore names suggested by the Civil War. There was a Roundhead and a Cavalier, a Goring and a Waller; in fact, " all the generals of both armies were hounds in his pack."

Mr. Daniel Foe's will, preserved in the Consistory Court of Northampton, at Peterborough (E. 65), is dated 3rd March, 1630, and was proved 28th April, 1631. The first date we should now write 3rd March, 163$\frac{0}{1}$; therefore the will was proved only eight weeks after it was signed. The testator leaves to a Mr.

---

* Of Peakirk, three miles from Etton. Will dated 19th Nov., 1632.

Temple, 10s.; to the church, 10s.; "to the poore of
the parish, 10s."; to "Daniel ffoe," his eldest son,
"foure score pounds" at age of 21 ; to Mary Foe, his
daughter, £50 at marriage or at age of 21 ; to Henry
Foe, his son, £50, at age of 21 ; to James ffoe, his
son, £50, at age of 21. Residue to his "loving wife,
Rose Foe," whom he appoints sole executrix. The
portions of any child or children who died before they
received their legacies were to be equally divided
among the survivors.

It may be urged that the money left by "Daniel
ffoe" does not look like keeping a pack of hounds,
but let it be noted that we are not told the amount of
the "residue" left to his "loving wife," or whether
the testator earlier in life was in better circumstances.
From his having left a trifle to Etton Church, we may
presume that Daniel Foe was a Churchman.

Of James Foe (father of the novelist), who, having
been baptised May 13, 1630, was probably not more
than twelve months old on the death of his father, we
learn nothing more till many years later.

Daniel, James's eldest brother, continued to live
at Etton, where he died in 1647, leaving an only
daughter, Mary.

There is in Etton parish, a mile from the village,
a handsome old moated, thirteenth-century fortified
house, called Woodcroft, historically noted as the
scene of fighting in the civil wars (1643). This was
the principal house in the parish, but the Foes were
not "of Woodcroft," as all entries in the register from
there are so entered. From this, and from the fact
that no Foe was a churchwarden, we may judge that

the Foes were not squires of the place, but merely well-to-do yeomen, and that their residence was some substantial farm-house.

Although the name of his family was Foe, a name which the novelist did not change to Defoe till he had reached middle life, nevertheless, in order to avoid confusion, we shall call him Defoe from the beginning. To the great world that honours his name he will always be Defoe, and nothing else; consequently, it would be mere pedantry to persist in calling him Daniel Foe, or Mr. Foe, during the first forty years of his life.

2.—THE BUTCHER'S SHOP IN FORE STREET.

James Foe, after leaving school, was sent to London, and placed as an apprentice with John Levit, citizen and butcher. Subsequently he is found in business for himself as a butcher in Fore Street, parish of St. Giles, Cripplegate. To the Rev. Samuel Annesley, LL.D., minister of St. Giles's, Mr. Foe, and his family, who worshipped there, were, and always continued to be, very much attached.

In 1658, or early in 1659, a daughter was born to James Foe—Mary; and late in 1659 arrived his next child, Daniel, who was destined to become so famous. It is generally stated that Daniel Defoe was born in 1661, but Mr. G. A. Aitken, in the *Athenæum* for August 23, 1890, shows this to be a mistake, and proves that Defoe was born either in the latter part of 1659 or early in 1660. Probably it was in the latter part of 1659.

Mr. Aitken's discovery of the time of Defoe's birth

has been of the utmost importance to me, for it has
furnished one of the two clues which have enabled me
to discover what has so long baffled the search of
students of Defoe—the key to Robinson Crusoe.
Crusoe, as Defoe himself declares (in "Serious Reflections"), is an allegory or emblem of his own life,
and every important event in the story (Part I.) had,
as Defoe also declares, its counterpart in Defoe's life.
Robinson Crusoe is made to be born in 1632, twenty-
seven years before the birth of Defoe; and one has
only to add twenty-seven to every date in Crusoe (and
Crusoe was wonderfully careful about dates) in order
to arrive at the year that corresponds to it in the life
of Defoe.   To the other, and more important, clue I
shall refer later on (§ 7).

The names of James Foe's other children have not
transpired.   Crusoe, be it remembered, had two elder
brothers.   One of them was killed at Dunkirk, but
what became of the other, neither Crusoe nor his
father or mother ever knew, and it is noteworthy that
Defoe in all his writings refers only once to a "brother,"
who was living in 1705. (Letter to Lord Halifax. *See*
§ 30.)

In 1662, rather than submit to the Act of Uniformity, over two thousand ministers of the Church of
England quitted their livings, among them being Dr.
Annesley, who, taking with him a part of his congregation, including the Foes, founded a meeting-house
in Bishopsgate Street.   Of the persecution to which
Nonconformists were then subjected, Defoe could, of
course, know little, being much taken up about that
time with his whip, his "troop horse," and his "card-

board windmill at the end of a stick," but he often in after years heard his parents talk about it; and in his Reviews, and elsewhere, he has many a scathing word for the iniquitous times of Charles II.

Of his father and mother Defoe always spoke with studied respect. Robinson Crusoe describes his father as "a wise and grave man," who often gave him "serious and excellent counsel." At an early age Defoe was well-grounded in the Scriptures, but his parents, though Presbyterians, were free from asceticism and austerity, consequently his childhood was a happy one. To Presbyterianism, indeed, amid which he had been nurtured, Defoe clung with tenacity all his life; and to Scotland, the cradle of Presbyterianism, and to the Scottish people, he always felt himself bound by the cords of love.

In 1665 occurred the dreadful Plague of London, of which Defoe was destined, many years after, to write so graphic an account. To his own memory, however, he could have been indebted for very little, seeing that he was only six years old; nevertheless, the creepy tales of the cross-marked houses, of the fires in the streets, of the maniacs at large, of the dust-rakers with their horns, of the death-tumbrils with the eternal cry of " Bring out your dead!" must early have made an impression on a mind instinct with so strong a bias for the wild, the weird, the monstrous, and the *bizarre*.

Like other small boys he was sometimes naughty, and he used to say to his mother, " If you vex me, I'll eat no dinner"; but, commented he, long after, "my mother taught me to be wiser by letting me stay till I was hungry." He was of a light and buoyant disposition, and very courageous. In a boxing match which he had with another boy, he learnt the "piece of generosity" never to strike an enemy who is down —a rule that he adhered to throughout life—though, when he himself was down the compliment was not always returned.

Among the tasks that his parents set him, or that he set himself, one was to copy out the Bible! and he worked at it like a horse; but by the time he had finished the Pentateuch, he got so tired that he was obliged to acknowledge himself defeated. His acquaintance with the Scriptures in after years was phenomenal, scarcely less so, indeed, than that of his celebrated contemporary, John Bunyan. Among the delights of his childhood was to stand at a basket-maker's near his father's house, and watch "them make their wicker-ware." Being officious to help, as boys usually are, he sometimes lent a hand, and himself became an expert. Nor did he forget to turn his knowledge to account when, many years afterwards, he told the story of Robinson Crusoe.

In 1668, when about eight or nine, Defoe was taken, probably on a visit to some relation, to Ipswich, which he described as "a town of very good business; particularly, it was the greatest town in England for large colliers or coal-ships employed between New-castle and London," and these ships were built "prodigious strong." Fifty years later, however, when he wrote his "Tours," much of the trade had gone, and the town had considerably decayed.

When about fourteen, Defoe was placed by his
father, who intended him for the Dissenting ministry,
at a well-known academy at Newington Green, conducted by "that polite and profound scholar," Mr.
Charles Morton.

Mr. Morton, styled by those who did not love him,
"a rank Independent" had formerly been rector of
Blisland, in Cornwall, and was one of the two thousand ejected in 1662. To the goodness and learning
of his tutor, with whom, apparently, he stayed about
five years, Defoe pays many a tribute; and he also
looked back with gratitude to the liberality of his
father, who spared nothing that might qualify his
son to make a good scholar. Besides theological
knowledge, Defoe was grounded in Latin, Greek,
French, Spanish and Italian. But that which was of
much greater benefit to him in after life was the pains
Mr. Morton took to drill his pupils in good English.
Very wisely, though contrary to the custom of the
times, Mr. Morton read his lectures in English, the
consequence being that no academy of the time
turned out so many scholars that were adepts in their
mother tongue. Mr. Morton's discourses were not
stale or studied, but always new and occasional; no
matter what the subject started, he always had ready
some pleasant and pat anecdote for it. Other items
in the curriculum of the academy were mathematics,
natural philosophy, logic, geography, and history,
especially ecclesiastical.

In the year 1676, while Daniel Foe was grinding theology, mathematics, and languages at Newington, or strolling among the cornfields with which the academy was surrounded, an event, exterior to his knowledge though of no small import to him, occurred, to use a Crusoeism, on the other side of his island : the arrival, in the house of John Selcraig, a thriving shoemaker of Largo, Fife, of a seventh son, and not only so but with no intermediary and obtrusive daughters to break the charm; on the strength of which, together with the fact that Euphan Selcraig, the mother, Sarah-like, had "waxed old," her husband "being old also," more than one gossip prophesied great things ; and Alexander (familiarly Sandy) Selcraig, did, as we shall show, under the altered name of Selkirk, live to some purpose. Meantime, the infant Selcraig, who is understood to have been fortunate in that the lenity of his mother was nicely balanced by the sternness of his father, dribbled and cooed in his cot at Largo, comparatively in seclusion, the outside world not having as yet been apprised of his importance.

Daniel Defoe, who devoured every scrap of print he could set eyes on, may, in his desultory reading at Newington, have come across the saying of the Caliph Omar, " Thy place in life is seeking after thee," but he could have little thought just then that it was his destiny to become one of the greatest masters of fiction the world has seen ; yet here was young Selcraig, in Largo, doing his best to grow up and render the conjuncture possible. That Defoe would have been a great story-teller without the accident of

Selkirk, is very probable, but that he would have been among the greatest of story-tellers is open to question. The event at Largo, moreover, is still further suggestive. If the destinies of man, as Homer supposed, depend on the wills of the gods, the deity that took Defoe in tow must have had Scotland very much on the brain, for though Defoe was a Cockney born, of a Northamptonshire stock, yet, from beginning to end, as we shall see, he was always finding himself mixed up with Scotland and the Scottish.

Another contemporary event, though unconnected with Defoe, may here, not inappropriately, be noticed. It was in 1677, while Defoe was still tussling with languages and mathematics at Newington, that John Bunyan, another great Puritan, wrote his " Pilgrim's Progress " in Bedford Jail.

Defoe mentions four of his fellow-students by name, to wit, Kitt, Battersby, Jenkyns, and Hewling. Others who were educated at the academy were Mr. John Shower, Mr. Timothy Cruso, Mr. Hannot, of Yarmouth, Mr. Nathaniel Taylor, Mr. Owen, Mr. Obadiah Marriot (uncle of Dunton, the bookseller), and Samuel Wesley, father of the celebrated founder of Wesleyanism, all of whom obtained more or less distinction in their day as preachers of the Gospel. The one that rouses our curiosity most is, of course, Mr. Cruso, for it is impossible to disassociate him in our minds from a certain " Robinson Crusoe, of York, mariner," who, later on, made considerable bustle in the world.

Mr. Morton wrote several works, one of which, " Eutaxia," was a system of politics, drawn up in

imitation of More's "Utopia," and he published
several treatises upon religious and philosophical
subjects. In 1685, about seven years after Defoe left
him, Mr. Morton, owing to persecution, emigrated to
America, and became pastor of a church at Charles-
town (July, 1686), and vice-president of Harvard
College.

Despite the careful training at Newington, Daniel
Defoe did not enter the ministry after all. The
principal reasons for his change of mind were, first,
because it would make him less independent than he
wished to be, and, secondly, because, owing to the fact
that by no means the most gifted men were chosen
for the principal pulpits, there seemed to be in the
ministry very little scope for the exercise of the talents
of which he believed himself to be possessed. This
good opinion which he had of himself (and we blame
him not) was always a conspicuous element in Defoe's
composition. In prosperity, in adversity, in every up
and in every down, he always rode the high horse,
and it is doubtful whether any other quadruped could
have borne him through all his difficulties.

The exact date when Defoe left Newington is not
known. At some of the Nonconformist academies
students usually remained no longer than three years
(see Defoe's "Present State of Parties," etc., p. 319),
but the course at Newington, according to Wilson,
was five years. He may, therefore, have left in 1678.

That he did not throw up the ministry without a
rare tussle with his parents is certain, and, considering
the expense they had been at with his education, we
can find it in our heart to sympathise with them. It

is also certain that this quitting of Newington corresponds with Robinson Crusoe's running away to sea. Crusoe (as we learn from a passage in the middle of his history) was born on September 30, 1632, and ran away to sea on September 1, 1651, when he was eighteen years and eleven months old; and Defoe, assuming that he was born in 1659, would in 1678 be thereabouts the same age.

Defoe himself speaks of his abandonment of his ministerial career as a "disaster." "The pulpit," * he says, "is none of my office. It was my disaster, first to be set apart for and then to be set apart from the honour of that sacred employ," and we may well believe that often in the broils of his tempestuous life he must have looked back and reflected on what a clear, unruffled stream it might have been, had he, when a lad of eighteen, bowed to the will of his father. Not that this feeling could at any time have lasted long. With all his protestations, Crusoe is never able to convince us that, even had the opportunity offered, he would have quitted his island and returned to England for good and all. He was a born rover.

For the rest, the influence of Defoe's training at Newington can be traced all through his life ; like Mr. Stevenson's Long John Silver, he was always "a kind of a chapling," and was quite as capable of preaching a sermon as those who wore a Geneva gown.

In 1678, the year that, in all probability, Defoe

* *Review*, vi., 341.

left Newington, all England was in terror owing to
the abominable lies of Titus Oates. Everybody went
in fear of the " Papishes."

" I remember," says Defoe, "in the time of the
Popish plot, when murthering men in the dark was
pretty much in fashion, and every honest man walked
the streets in danger of his life, a very pretty invention
was found out, which soon put an end to the doctrine
of assassination, and the practice, too, and cleared our
streets of the murthering villains of those days; this
was a Protestant flail. Now, a Protestant flail is an
excellent weapon—a pistol is a fool to it; it laughs at
the sword or the cane; for you know there's no fence
against a flail. For my part, I have frequently walked
with one about me in the old Popish days, and though
I never set up for a hero, yet, when armed with this
scourge for a Papist, I remember I feared nothing."*
Though Defoe firmly believed in the reality of a
Roman Catholic plot, yet, when folk "ran up that
plot to general massacres, fleets of pilgrims, bits and
bridles, knives and handcuffs," and a thousand other
scares, he only shrugged his shoulders. It was impossible, he said, that the Papists, who in England
were not five to a hundred, could be contemplating a
general massacre of the Protestants.

No lie against the " Papishes" seemed too huge
to be swallowed. One day when Defoe was in a
tavern, a fellow entered and gravely told the gaping
audience that six Frenchmen had attempted to run
away with the Monument—even before it was quite

* *Review*, viii., 614.

finished, too, "and but for the watch, who stopped them as they were going over the bridge, and made them carry it back again, they might, for aught we know, have carried it over into France." Perceiving some to be incredulous, up jumps Defoe, and with a twinkle in his eye, begs the audience, if they have any doubts, to satisfy them by going to the spot "where they'd see the workmen employed in making all fast again." The simpletons, Defoe would have us believe, swallowed the joke, "and departed quite satisfied."

In the next year, 1679, Defoe's sister, Mary, was united to Mr. Francis Bartham, a shipwright, the following being the licence for her marriage :—

"Bartham, Francis, jun., of St. Mary, Whitechapel, shipwright, bachelor, about 30, and Mrs. Mary Foe, of St. Swithin, London, spinster, about 20, with her father's consent; at St. Mary Magdalen, Bermondsey, co. Surrey. 20 May, 1679."

I do not think Defoe anywhere mentions his sister. There are, however, very few allusions in his writings to any of his relations. His brother, as we have seen, he mentions only once. Other relations he speaks of are a schoolmaster of Martock, in Somersetshire, with whom he maintained a friendly intercourse ("Tour Through Great Britain," vol. i., let. 3); a near relation at Sherborne, in Dorsetshire ("Use and Abuse," etc., p. 99), and a cousin, who seems to have resided in London, a good man of business, but otherwise disreputable ("Hist. of Apparitions," p. 316).

CHAPTER II.

THE MERCHANT OF CORNHILL (1678-1694).

4.—AT THE SIGN OF THE CIVET-CAT.—HIS MARRIAGE WITH MARY TUFFLEY (JAN. 1, 1683).

WORK: 1.—A Tract on the Turkish Question. (Lost.)

SOON after leaving college, Defoe set himself to learn the hosiery business, and, as can be gathered from his marriage licence, he was already a merchant in the parish of St. Michael's, Cornhill, in 1683, his office or shop being in Freeman's Yard, nearly opposite the entrance to Change Alley. Defoe's enemies spoke of him as the civet-cat merchant, and Mr. Saintsbury suggests that " The Civet-Cat " was the sign of his place of business, and this is extremely likely, for the sign was a common one.

To his life at this period Defoe makes few allusions. In one of his Reviews he denies that he had ever been a hosier, but admits having been a trader. Perhaps what he means is that he had never stood behind the counter. In his " Tour Through Great Britain" (iii. 22), he speaks of being at Aylesbury once at the time "when there was a mighty confluence of noblemen and gentlemen at a famous horse-race, at Quainton Meadow, not far off," Among those present was the Duke of Monmouth, then very popular, who, contrary to custom, rode his own horses.

The interesting facts concerning Defoe's marriage, were first made known by Mr. G. A. Aitken, in the *Contemporary Review* for February, 1890, and the *Athenæum* for August 23 of the same year. Among other things, Mr. Aitken was able to prove that the oft-repeated statement that Defoe married twice is a mistake. The maiden name of the girl—for she was only twenty—whom Defoe made his wife, was Mary Tuffley. The licence was taken out on December 28, 1683, the wedding being solemnized four days after, on New Year's Day, 1684, at St. Botolph's, Aldgate. The following is the marriage licence allegation, which can be seen in the Vicar-General's Office :—

"28 December, 1683. Charles Lodwick, of St. Michael, Cornhill, applies for Daniel Foe of the same parish, 24, and a batchelor, marchant, and Mary Tuffley, of St. Botolph, Aldgate, 20, spinster, with consent of her father. At St. Botolph, Aldgate, St. Giles, Cripplegate, or St. Lawrence, Jewry."

The entry of the marriage in the parish register of St. Botolph's runs thus :—

"Jan. 1, 1683 [O.S.]. Daniel Ffoe, batchellor, and Mary Tufflie, spinster, married by Mr. Hollingworth."

During the next two or three years arrived his three eldest children, Hannah, probably the firstborn ; Mary, who died a child ; and Daniel, born probably in 1685.

How soon Defoe began to meddle with politics we are not told, but in 1683, the year of his marriage, we find not only that he is an ardent politician, but that he is using his pen. The occasion was the invasion of Austria by the Turks, who, having overrun Hungary

C

and surrounded Vienna, seemed not unlikely to be about to spread themselves over the whole of Europe. The Whigs in England, being very bitter against the Popish house of Austria, wished well to the Turks; but Defoe, though a staunch Whig, took in this matter the opposite view, considering that it was better the Catholics of Austria should ruin the Protestants of Hungary than that the infidel Ottomans should crush both Protestants and Papists by overrunning the continent. Whether his denunciation of the "unspeakable Turk" was ever published we know not, but no copy has come to light. The fact, however, that he wrote it is in itself interesting, for we have no record of anything earlier from his pen. Apparently, however, it would have been just then to Defoe's own interest to have let the Turk and everybody else alone, and to have paid a little more attention to his hosiery business.

5.—HE TRAVELS IN SPAIN AND PORTUGAL.—AN AFFAIR OF HONOUR.

Before proceeding further, it will be necessary to refer again to " Robinson Crusoe." The ship that Crusoe had embarked in at Hull on 1st September, 1651, was, a few days later, destroyed by a storm, Crusoe and the rest of the crew having the good luck to escape by means of a boat and to land at Yarmouth. From Yarmouth Crusoe proceeded to London, whence he set out on his first real voyage—to Guinea. Having returned in safety, he shortly after went out on another voyage, during which he had the misfortune—on September 1 (1653), his unlucky day,

the day he quitted Hull—to be taken prisoner near
the coast of Spain by a Sallee rover; and at Sallee he
was kept in captivity for two years, escaping on December 19th (1655), his lucky day, with the boy Xury.

What events in Defoe's life coincided with these
adventures we have no means of ascertaining, but it is
noteworthy that during the early days of his merchant
career, he voyaged, like Crusoe, about the coasts of
Spain and Portugal. Unfortunately, however, though
he mentions a number of incidents that occurred in
these travels, he does not give dates. In the "Essay
on Projects," speaking of the goods which in the
course of his business he imported from abroad, he
says that he sometimes paid more in insurance premios
than he had cleared by a voyage. But not only did
he voyage to Spain, for a time he took up his residence there. On one occasion he cleverly defeated an
attempt to outwit him over a consignment of brandy,
and in one of his Reviews he gives an account of the
loss on the Spanish coast of a vessel in which he was
a shareholder, and records the inhospitable treatment
the crew received from the natives, in retaliation for
barbarities they themselves had experienced when
wrecked on the coast of England. Defoe often had
occasion to denunciate the cruelty of the inhabitants
of English coast towns, especially Deal, to poor shipwrecked mariners.

In his *Review* for January 27, 1711, he alludes to
an old Spanish proverb, which, says he, "I learnt
when I lived in that country." The proverb is, "Let
the cure be wrought, though the devil be the doctor."

Among both the Spanish and the Portuguese,

Defoe must have found many admirable characters;
for the Portuguese captain who saved Crusoe and
Xury is a model of humanity and magnanimity; and
the Spaniards left by Crusoe on his island acted like
real Christians and perfect gentlemen.   Says Crusoe,
" I never met with seventeen men of any nation
whatsoever, in any foreign country, who were so
universally modest, temporate, virtuous, so very
good-humoured, and so courteous as these Spaniards."
On the other hand, Defoe must have met with both
Portuguese and Spaniards who were much less agreeable.   Speaking of the crew he found himself amongst
in his first voyage, Bob Singleton, the hero of Defoe's
story, " Captain Singleton," observes, " Thieving,
lying, swearing, forswearing, joined to the most
abominable lewdness, was the stated practice of the
ship's crew; adding to it that, with the most insuffer-
able boasts of their own courage, they were, generally
speaking, the most complete cowards I ever met with."
Singleton, indeed, entertained so settled an abhorrence
of the abandoned vileness of the Portuguese that he
could not but hate them most heartily from the beginning, and all his life afterwards.   The devil and a
Portuguese were equally his aversion.

Some time in early manhood Defoe was concerned
at least once in " an affair of honour," but we have no
particulars, and only know of it through an allusion
in a paragraph in the *Review* (vii. 451), where, in
compunctious mood, he says, " I am an enemy to
duelling, as it is a sin against God, and therefore
never speak of it but to declare *my own penitence
upon that subject.*"

6.—WITH "KING MONMOUTH."

In 1685 (February 14) terminated the "lazy, long, lascivious reign"* of Charles II.; and the accession of his brother James was speedily followed by the Rebellion of the Duke of Monmouth, who landed at Lyme-Regis on June 11th with about a hundred followers. Like many other Dissenters, Defoe sympathised with Monmouth; and, to his misfortune, took part in the rising. The peasantry of Devon and Somerset were so powerfully attracted, that, on June 15th, when Monmouth marched out of Lyme, his following amounted to 3,000, and by the time he had reached Bridgewater, where he assumed the title of King, to as many as 7,000, though they had but indifferent arms. In a skirmish at Philip's Norton Lane, near Bath, to which Defoe particularly refers, and at which he may have been present, "the Duke had the decided advantage, which, if he had pushed further, would have amounted to a complete victory."† Foiled of expectations from Bristol, and repulsed at Bath, Monmouth fell back to Sedgemoor, where he was defeated, July 6, 1685. Ten days later he was beheaded at Tower Hill. Then raged Jeffreys and Kirke. Defoe happily escaped them, but three of his friends, Battersby, Jenkyns, and Hewling — all of whom had been students at Mr. Morton's—found their way to the scaffold.

Among those brought before Jeffreys, we are to notice one in particular, a handsome, fearless young

* Defoe.   † Defoe's "Consolidator," p. 135.

fellow, whose opinions on social and political matters
were, and continued to be, as like to Defoe's as one
pea to another, though with Defoe himself he could
rarely agree. Brave to temerity, fearless even of
death, a wit and a master of sarcasm, John Tutchin,
subsequently of the *Observator*, and one of the
staunchest champions of the liberties of the people,
will, later on, be seen—such freaks have the fates—
sticking his spines into the man with whom he was
politically at one with as great a delight as he was
accustomed to stick them into those with whom he
was by nature at variance.

That Tutchin had taken an active part in the rebellion could not be proved, but he pleaded guilty to
having been intimate with friends of Monmouth, and
to having used a fictitious name; for which the up-
right judge thought it would be sufficient punishment
if the accused were "to remain in prison seven years,
once in every year to be whipped through all the
market towns in Dorsetshire, to pay a fine of one
hundred marks to the King, and find security for his
good behaviour during life."

Conceiving his situation to be worse than death,
John Tutchin, who describes himself as "of Lyming-
ton, now a prisoner in the county jail of Dorset,"
humbly petitioned his Majesty King James—not to
reverse the sentence—but to mercifully "grant him
the favour of being hanged with those of his
fellow-prisoners that are condemned to die"; to
which request the King, with whom mercy was not
exactly a speciality, declined to accede, thus putting
it into the power of the poet Pope, who disliked

Tutchin, to write, years after, spitefully, but truth-
fully :—

"And Tutchin flagrant from the scourge below."

7.—THE COMMENCEMENT OF THE LIFE OF SILENCE (PROBABLY
30TH SEPTEMBER, 1686).—CRUSOE IS WRECKED ON HIS ISLAND
(30TH SEPTEMBER, 1659).

The battle of Sedgemoor had been fought and
lost on July 6th, 1685, but of Defoe's movements
during the next two or three years we know little
that is definite. Probably he had to lie low. For a
time he resided at Mickleham (Surrey), near the
Thames (see "Tour Through Great Britain," vol. i.,
letter 2), and afterwards, as we shall presently see, at
Tooting, in the same county.

The arbitrary proceedings of King James after
the defeat of Monmouth are a matter of history : how
he gave commissions in the army to Papists, dis-
pensed with tests, erected mass-houses ; how, in short,
he fondled everything connected with the Holy See,
and frowned down all things Protestant. To believe
in the doctrine of the divine right of kings was only
what was expected of one. Says Defoe, "I have
heard it publicly preached, that if the king commanded my head, and sent his messengers to fetch
it, I was bound to submit and stand still while it was
cut off."

We come now to the point in Defoe's life which
corresponds with the moment in which Robinson
Crusoe was thrown on his lonely island ; and we are
to ask ourselves what Defoe meant when he solemnly
declared that the twenty-eight years odd months which

Crusoe spent in solitude corresponded with a great period of his own life. For this clue or key to Robinson Crusoe previous biographers searched in vain, but Chadwick, one of those who did not search, accidentally stumbled upon it, or rather upon the principal key, handled it and played with it, and then put it down without understanding its value.

The following is the key referred to, and it occurs in Defoe's " Serious Reflections " :—

" I have heard of a man, that, upon some extraordinary disgust which he took at the unsuitable conversation of some of his nearest relations, whose society he could not avoid, suddenly resolved never to speak any more. He kept his resolution most rigorously many years; not all the tears or entreaties of his friends, no, not of his wife and children, could prevail with him to break his silence. It seems it was their ill behaviour to him at first was the occasion of it; for they treated him with provoking language, which frequently put him into indecent passions, and urged him to rash replies; and he took this severe way to punish himself for being provoked, and to punish them for provoking him. But the severity was unjustifiable: it ruined his family and broke up his house. His wife could not bear it, and, after endeavouring by all the ways possible to alter his rigid silence, went first away from him; and afterwards away from herself, turning melancholy and distracted. His children separated, some one way and some another way, and only one daughter, who loved her father above all the rest, kept with him; tended him, talked to him by signs, and lived almost dumb, like her father, nearly twenty-nine years with him; till, being very sick and in a high fever, delirious as we call it, or light-headed, he broke his silence, not knowing when he did it, and spoke, though wildly at first. He recovered of the illness afterwards, and frequently talked with his daughter, but not much, and very seldom to anybody else.

" Yet this man did not live a silent life with respect to himself. He read continually, and wrote down many excellent things which deserved to have appeared in the world; and was often heard to pray to God in his solitudes very audibly, and with great fervency; but the injustice which his rash vow, if it was a vow of silence, was to his family, and the length he carried it, was so unjustifiable another way that I cannot say his instructions could have much force in them."

Chadwick's comment is as follows :—

"Now, this is very likely to have been taken from his own life, for *he read continually*, and *wrote down many excellent things ;* which is true of De Foe: *he read continually.* He was as a man always conversing with the dead ; he made his bed among the tombs ; his family would be comparatively strangers to him ; and the feelings of the one would be alien to the other. He was a poet, a writer, and a philosopher ; and his family felt this, and they made him feel it too ; for he, their father, was not like other fathers ; he wrote, and read, and ran away. . . . This poetic life must have involved misery to all—father, mother, and children."

More, Chadwick does not say. He perceived that in the extract from " Serious Reflections" Defoe was referring to himself; but that there was any connection between the almost twenty-nine years in the paragraph and the twenty-eight years odd months spent by Crusoe on the island did not strike him.

That the paragraph had reference to Defoe is evident from the opening sentence, even without taking into consideration the conclusive statements that follow it ; " I have heard of a man," " I know a man," and the like, being favourite prologues of Defoe's when he was about to introduce bits of personal history. Take, for example, the incident of his writing to the judge (" Vision of the Angelic World "),* which commences, " I know a man who made it a rule to obey these silent hints," etc., where it is absolutely certain that he meant himself.

The idea having struck me that the "nearly twenty-nine years" had reference to the twenty-eight

* *See § 52.*

years odd months Crusoe was on the island; and having noticed how extraordinarily particular Crusoe is about dates, I argued that at the time Defoe had his great illness, and broke his silence, he would be precisely the same age that Crusoe was when he left his island. Now, Crusoe, who left his island on December 19, 1687,* was born September 30, 1632, consequently he was fifty-five years two months nineteen days old. Defoe's great illness, which is fully recorded by all his biographers, commenced in the middle of December, 1714. That is an admitted fact. I assumed that the actual day it commenced was December 19; and counting back fifty-five years two months nineteen days, brought me to September 30, 1659, the very time (late in 1659) that, according to Mr. Aitken's discovery, Defoe in all probability was born. It may be urged that twenty-eight years two months nineteen days is not "nearly twenty-nine years," but it must be remembered that in saying "nearly twenty-nine years" Defoe is speaking roughly, and that had he been more exact he would have let the cat out of the bag, which was not his intention.

The following, then, are the dates of the four leading events of Crusoe's life, and our deductions from them :—

Crusoe was born 30th September, 1632; adding twenty-seven years, makes Defoe to be born 30th September, 1659; and, as we said, it is next to certain

---

* In most editions of Robinson Crusoe this date, by a printer's blunder, is put 1686, but of course, twenty-eight years, two months, nineteen days, added to 30th September, 1659, brings us to 19th December, 1687.

now, owing to Mr. Aitken's discovery, that Defoe was born late in 1659.

Crusoe (aged eighteen years eleven months) left Hull 1st September, 1651 ; adding twenty-seven years, makes Defoe to have left Newington 1st September, 1678; and it is always said that Defoe, who entered Newington at about fourteen, stayed there till he was nearly nineteen.

Crusoe was wrecked on his island (on which he stayed twenty-eight years two months and nineteen days) 30th September, 1659; adding twenty-seven years, makes Defoe's life of silence to commence 30th September, 1686; and from this date to the date of the commencement of his great illness, when, as we presume, he resumed his speech, is *twenty-eight years two months and about a half.*

Crusoe left his island 19th December, 1687; adding twenty-seven years, makes Defoe's silence to be broken 19th December, 1714; and that at this time Defoe's character underwent a great change I shall hereafter prove (§ 50).

To the minor parallels between Crusoe and Defoe we shall refer in their right order. For the present we are contented to state that the belief is forced upon us that Defoe, provoked on account of the irritating conduct of his wife, made a kind of vow to live a life of silence. That beyond maintaining this rigid silence he ever acted unkindly to her is improbable. No doubt, as Chadwick suggests, the reason of her " provoking language" was the fact of Defoe neglecting his business for poetry and politics. We can sympathise with Mrs. Defoe to a certain extent, for, above

all things, it is necessary that a housewife should have
the wherewithal to provide dinners; and she could,
no doubt, see, what Defoe couldn't see, that everything
was going to the dogs.   But we sympathise more with
him.   He lived in a high plane; he had the literary
temperament, the ideas of a man of genius, the ambition of Lucifer.   His wife couldn't understand him;
they were unequally yoked.   His reply to her taunts
was a vow of silence—that great silence, that extraordinary isolation, which made possible in after years
the marvellous realism of " Robinson Crusoe."

That Defoe was not unkind to his wife appears
to me to be proved by the will of Samuel Tuffley,
Mrs. Defoe's brother.   In this document, drawn up
in October, 1714, while Defoe was yet in silence,
occurs a very curious passage.   Mr. Tuffley leaves
all his property to his sister " absolutely and independently of her husband, or of any claim or demand
which he or anyone claiming by, from, or under him
by right of marriage or otherwise, might have or
make to the same."   Further on he enjoins her, " if
she should think fit to bestow any part at any time on
her children, to give the greatest share to such as
behave with the greatest tenderness, duty, and affection, both to their father and to herself," and further
on occurs the clause, " declaring that it is not from
distrust of or disrespect to their said father that this
my will is made in this manner."

In short, as I interpret it, though there had
been unpleasantness between Mr. Tuffley and Mr.
Defoe, Mr. Tuffley wished bygones to be bygones;
at the same time, knowing not only Defoe's original

methods of finance, but also his peculiar character, he was resolved that Defoe should have no opportunity to try experiments or play freaks with the Tuffley money. The phrase, " That it is not from distrust of," etc., is, of course, only the coating of gilt on the unpalatable pill.

At first sight it may appear monstrous that a man should for so long a time abstain from speech with his own family, but Defoe's conduct is, perhaps, extenuated, when we remember that for the earlier part of that period he could have seen very little of his wife or children at all, for, from the time of his bankruptcy (1692) to the year 1706, he was continually being hunted by his creditors. He had been in retreat, he says, August 23, 1706, fourteen years, with jeopardy, broils, and most of the time in banishment from his family (*see* § 32).

Despite his extraordinary vow, and despite, too, his nomadism, Defoe took great interest in the welfare of his children. All of them were well educated, the daughters noticeably so. He had always held that children are creditors to the father of a family ; that " he cannot be an honest man that does not discharge his debt to them, any more than he could if he did not repay money borrowed to a stranger "; and that the first and foremost item in that debt is education, by which he meant " not only putting children to school, which some parents think is all they have to do with or for their children," but several other additional cares, as—(1) Directing what school, what part of learning, is proper for them ; (2) studying the genius and capacities of their children in what they teach

them ; (3) the debt of instruction, the debt of government, the debt of example. But in this last, owing
to his vow of silence, as he himself admits, he in part
failed.

Another feature of Defoe's character, which may
here fittingly be mentioned, was his love of fine
clothes and ostentation. No matter how he is circum-
stanced, we always find him "gorgeously apparelled."
In prosperity or adversity, in shine or shower, Daniel
Defoe was always what, in his "Complete English
Tradesman," he so heartily condemns, "a tradesman
dressed up fine with his long wig and sword."

8.—DEFOE AT TOOTING.—HE VISITS THE OTHER SIDE OF HIS
ISLAND.—ORANGE EVERYWHERE (1687—88).

In April, 1687, King James, solely on his own
authority, and therefore illegally, published a Declaration of Indulgence permitting all his subjects to
worship in their own way. "Was anything ever
more absurd," asks Defoe, "than this conduct of
King James and his party in wheedling the Dissenters ; giving them liberty of conscience by his own
arbitrary dispensing authority, and expecting they
should be content with their religious liberty at the
price of the Constitution ?" From a passage in
Review viii., 442, it has been conjectured that
Defoe wrote some tracts on these proceedings of
King James, but it is more likely that he declaimed
against them only by word of mouth. In his opinions
Defoe stood almost alone. The "grave, weak, good
men" of his party were as much annoyed at the

THE DEFOE WINDOW IN BUTCHERS' HALL.

(From photograph by R. W. Thomas, 41, Cheapside.)

course he had taken as if they had been his adversaries. They called him a youth. But, says Defoe, " He that will serve men must not promise himself that he shall not anger them." The second and more important Declaration of Indulgence was proclaimed on April 27th, 1688. A few weeks previous, Defoe had sent in his claim to have his name inscribed on the roll of the Butchers' Company, and he was admitted a liveryman of the City of London on the 26th of January, 1688. The entry in the Company's book runs as follows :—" At a Court held in Pudding-lane, Daniel Foe, son of James Foe, citizen and butcher, of Fore-street, Cripplegate, attended to apply for his admission by patrimony, and was admitted accordingly, and paid, in discharge of serving all offices, £10 15s."

Thus, though his business was hosiery, he was a member, not of the Mercers' or the Haberdashers' Company, but of the Butchers' Company. " Probably," says Mr. Hyde Clarke, "the Haberdashers, or perhaps the Mercers, granted him leave to enroll himself as a butcher." A few years ago, consonant with the suggestion of Mr. Clarke, a stained-glass window to Defoe was placed in Butchers' Hall, Bartholomew Close.

Defoe now (1688) resided at Tooting, where he formed the Dissenters of the neighbourhood, chiefly Independents and Presbyterians, into a regular congregation, and there is no doubt that occasionally he preached among them. The church founded by Defoe met at first in a private house, and afterwards in a temporary wooden building, which in 1765-6 gave place to the Defoe Presbyterian Chapel, erected in the main street a few yards north of the "Angel Inn."

Tooting, which in Defoe's time was only a village, is to-day a populous and wealthy suburb of London; and the congregation of the old chapel are now intent on another move—namely, the erection of a large and handsome Defoe Memorial Church, with a spire and a statue.

DEFOE'S HOUSE AT TOOTING.

These years spent at Tooting correspond with the early period of Crusoe's stay on his island. The events in "Crusoe" of this period are, September 30, 1659, the shipwreck; October 1 to 24, voyages to and from the wreck; April 16, 1660, the earthquake; June 19 to 27, serious illness, Crusoe reads his Bible; spring, 1661 (eighteen months after the shipwreck), he visits the other side of his island.

Knowing so very little of Defoe's doings in 1686 and the two following years, it is impossible to say

to what events in his life all the above refer. It is
probable, however, that the illness, succeeded by a
devotional spell, corresponds with the period of his
religious activity at Tooting. Crusoe's visit to the
other side of his island (he was shipwrecked on the
south side) points to a visit of Defoe's to Scotland at
this time. This visit not being mentioned by previous biographers, was, I feared, unrecorded; but to
my very great satisfaction I found it described by
Defoe very precisely in "The Great Law of Subordination." He says: "As I made myself master of the
history of the ancient state of England, I resolved in
the next place to make myself master of its present
state also; and to this purpose I travelled, in three or
four several tours, over the whole island, critically
observing, and carefully informing myself of everything worth observing in all the towns and countries
through which I passed." . . . Before setting out
on this tour Defoe studied Camden's "Britannia,"
"and some other books too, which treat of the natural
history, as well as the antiquities, of every country."
He noticed, however, that while the books he perused
contained much about the gentry, "very few take
notice of the common people, how they live, and what
their employment, etc." To treat of the common
people, he resolved, should be his task. Defoe, in
short, was to topography something what J. R. Green
in our own day has been to history. He dealt with it
not as it concerned a few aristocrats, but as it concerned the people in general. "I took this journey,"
he says, "at the unhappy time when this change or
revolution in manners and temper of the common

D

people was in the height of its operation—namely,
in the years 1684 to 1688, for I was near four years
before I finished my travels." Unlike Crusoe, however, he did not go alone. "I took with me an
ancient gentleman of my acquaintance, who I found
was thoroughly acquainted with almost every part
of England, and who was to me as a walking library,
or a movable map of the countries and towns through
which we passed." Defoe often made tours through
England and to Scotland subsequently. For geography he had an extraordinary passion, so much so
that some of his works, as we shall see, are quite
spoilt by the superabundance of geographical detail.

We may notice, too, that Crusoe was wonderfully
smitten with the north side of his island ; indeed, he
would have taken up his abode there for good, only
the south side afforded greater facilities for keeping
a look out after ships ; and Defoe was not only vastly
enamoured of Scotland, but made preparations at least
once to remove his wife and family thither, and to
settle there.

9.—BANKRUPTCY AND BRISTOL (1692).—DEFOE'S DAEMON.—
TE DEUM LAUDAMUS.

WORKS : 2.—A New Discovery of an Old Intrigue. 1691.
3.—The Englishman's Choice and True Interest. 1694.

The arbitrary conduct of James II. had by this
time thoroughly alienated the hearts of the majority
of his people, and the eyes of all lovers of liberty
were turned towards the Netherlands. The day of
the nation's deliverance—November 4th, 1688, when
William of Orange arrived in Tor Bay—was ever

after commemorated by Defoe, who, as long as he kept up the *Review*, made this event, on each returning anniversary, the subject of a paper. He calls it, in *Review* iv., 453, " A day famous on various accounts, and every one of them dear to Britons who love their country, value the Protestant interest, or have an aversion to tyranny and oppression. On this day William the Third was born ; on this day he married the daughter of England ; and on this day he rescued the nation from a bondage worse than that of Egypt —a bondage of soul as well as bodily servitude—a slavery to the ambition and raging lust of a generation set on fire by pride, avarice, cruelty, and blood."

Defoe, who was among the many citizens who hastened to meet William, joined the second line of the Prince's army at Henley-on-Thames. On December 18, William made his public entry into London, Defoe one of the most handsomely dressed and one of the proudest in his train. The weather was squally, but an enthusiastic people neither sleet nor wind can subdue. It was orange everywhere. Bosoms and hats, cane-handles and sword-knots, all flamed with the popular colour. Protestant bells were rung backwards in the steeples, Protestant throats shouted until they were hoarse, and when night came half a million Protestant candles did their devoir in order that even then the jubilations might not cease.

Defoe was present during the debates of the Convention, and heard, with inexpressible joy, delivered at the bar of the Lords' House, in a message from the Commons, by Mr. Hampden, of Buckinghamshire, " That it is inconsistent with the Constitution of this Protestant kingdom to be governed by a Popish prince."

In due time, with "all the fantastic pomp of heraldry," William and Mary were proclaimed King and Queen of Great Britain and Ireland, with France, as the pleasant custom was, thrown in. This on February 13th. Then the land gave itself up to a saturnalia, which for deep, hearty enjoyment could scarcely have had an equal. One hears of "cavalcades of gentlemen and yeomen, processions of sheriffs and bailiffs in scarlet gowns, musters of zealous Protestants with orange flags and ribands, salutes, bonfires, illuminations, music; balls, dinners, gutters running with ale, and conduits spouting claret." Your true-born Englishman has often drunk more wine than is good for him; but rarely, it is to be supposed, with more excuse.

On the 29th of October (1689), when King William and his consort accepted the Lord Mayor's invitation to the City Feast, a regiment of volunteers, composed of the chief citizens and commanded by Charles Mordaunt, Earl of Peterborough, attended their majesties from Whitehall to the Mansion House; and among these troopers, "gallantly mounted and richly accoutred," Oldmixon noticed Daniel Defoe.

For the next fifteen months we know of Defoe's doings absolutely nothing. When he appears again it is in the character of a poet, the subject of his effusion being the recent Jacobite plot of Lord Preston and others, who were tried and found guilty in January, 1691. The title runs :—

"A New Discovery of an Old Intrigue: a Satyr level'd at Treachery and Ambition; Calculated to the Nativity of the

Rapparee* Plot, and the Modesty of the Jacobite Clergy. Designed by way of Conviction to the CXVII Petitioners, and for the Benefit of those that Study the Mathematics. *Unus Nobis Cunctando Restituit.*—Ennius."

A certain amount of interest attaches itself to this pamphlet, first, because it is the earliest production of Defoe's pen that has been preserved ; and, secondly, because, as he himself states, it was his first attempt at satire ; but its intrinsic value is *nil.*

As already intimated, Defoe's attention to politics and the muses was doing little good to his business. He found it more to his taste to argue upon the treacheries of the Jacobites, and to discuss Horace and Virgil at the coffee-houses, than to attend to his journal and his ledger ; and unlike—to use his own apt illustration—the carrier's waggon, " which keeps wagging and always goes on," he seems in his business to have attempted to go too fast, and to have injured himself by over-rashness in speculation. This we gather from certain remarks in his " Complete English Tradesman," where, however, with customary vanity, he gives the reader to understand that there are tradesmen and tradesmen, and that he himself was none of your petty pedlars, but a great merchant who did business beyond sea.

Finally, in 1692, came bankruptcy, with a deficit of £17,000. He hints in one of his Reviews that this misfortune was brought about by the frauds of swindlers, but persons who neglect their business are precisely the persons upon whom swindlers find it easiest to prey. The war, too, he considered had

---

* Rapparee : Irish plunderer.

done him harm.   Probably it had, but when attri·
buting his misfortune to these things, he never
speaks quite convincingly, and he always seems to
have had an inward conviction that Daniel Defoe's
worst enemy had been Daniel Defoe himself.

In order to escape his creditors he took refuge at
Bristol, where he lived at the Red Lion Inn, kept by

OLD HOUSE IN CASTLE STREET, BRISTOL, FORMERLY THE RED LION INN.

Mark Watkins, in Castle Street, now Nos. 80, 81.
Here he got the name of the Sunday Gentleman,
" because of his appearance on that day, and that day
only, in fashionable attire—a fine flowing wig, lace
ruffles, and a sword by his side—being kept indoors
during the rest of the week by fear of the bailiffs " ;
but after some parley with his creditors, " a composition was agreed to," though what that precisely means
it would puzzle a Dutchman to determine ; certain it
is that it was no impediment to his creditors hunting

him from pillar to post during the next dozen years,
though he was trying heart and soul all that time to
pay them back in full. The composition, however,
saved him from one thing—a debtor's prison.

It was not likely that a man of Defoe's buoyant
temperament would long remain down. Like his
Robinson Crusoe, he was one who could turn himself
to anything. Several business offers were made him,
and he could have had a remunerative post at Cadiz ;
but " Providence," as he afterwards said, " which had
other work for him to do, *placed a secret aversion in
his mind* to quitting England."

This is the first intimation we have of that curious
belief of Defoe's that, like Socrates and other ancients,
he was accompanied by a daemon or good spirit which
afforded him wise counsel on all trying occasions. To
this subject we shall often recur as this book proceeds,
and in the sections devoted to his works on magic deal
with it exhaustively. There can be little doubt that at
this time Defoe experienced many dark and distressing
hours, that he reviewed and reviewed again his whole
life, and that he prayed to God " in his solitudes very
audibly, and with great fervency." It may have been
in the midst of this great wrestling with Heaven that
the idea of the daemon first came to him. He had read
in his Bible that God had sent forth " ministering
spirits to minister to those who should be heirs of Salvation," and the belief, either at this time or before,
came into his mind that God had sent a special spirit
to him. In the Bible ages, Defoe insisted, instances of
such spirits accompanying men were numerous, whereas latterly " men, by a differing conduct and a way of

life too gross for so excellent and sublime a converse, have rendered themselves unworthy and unqualified; so that the angelic train seem to have forsaken the earth, and only communicate themselves to such as render themselves acceptable and worthy by a life of earnest application to the study of divine science, and who seek after the high illumination."

This brings us to another accompaniment of Defoe —the great refrain, *Te Deum Laudamus*, which bursts upon us at every turning of his career. When that intense belief in the wisdom of God which enabled him to offer these words of fervent praise at all times, whether in prosperity or adversity, first took possession of him, we cannot say; but it stands out as one of the most marked characteristics of his life. To bow the head and murmur submissively, "Thy will be done," is not always easy; but to cry aloud at all times and in all seasons, and in such times and seasons as Defoe experienced, "*Te Deum Laudamus!*" marks a confidence in the wisdom of the Almighty which but few have attained unto.

Entering again into politics, Defoe became, in 1694, "concerned with some eminent persons in proposing ways and means to the Government for raising money to supply the occasions of the war just begun"—the war with France. He also wrote a pamphlet entitled, "The Englishman's Choice and True Interest; in the vigorous prosecution of the War against France; and serving K. William and Q. Mary, and acknowledging their right"; and this pamphlet and other services were so appreciated by the Government that, "without the least application" of his own, he was sent for and appointed Accountant to the Commissioners of the Glass Duty—a post which he held till the duty was abolished in 1699.

It was probably during the year 1694 that he had the happiness of becoming personally known at Court. The Queen was about to lay out Kensington Gardens ; and Defoe, who, life through, was passionately fond of horticulture, "had the honour to attend her Majesty when she first viewed the ground, and directed the doing it." *

Queen Mary died of small-pox on December 28 of the same year (1694).

* "Tour through Great Britain,' vol. ii.

CHAPTER III.

10.—THE PANTILE WORKS AT CHADWELL (1694).—DEFOE
CHANGES HIS NAME (CIRC. 1697).

DEFOE gave up his hosiery business in Cornhill in
1794, and then, or soon after, took up his residence in
Hackney, where several of his children were born.

In the Hackney parish register are the following
entries :—

"Sophia, daughter to Daniel Defoe, by Mary, his wife, was baptised December 24th, 1701. Martha Defoe, a child, was carried out
of the parish to be buried in 1707."

We next find Defoe acting as secretary to a
manufactory of bricks and pantiles at Chadwell, near
Tilbury, in Essex, where a hundred labourers were
employed. It is possible that the estate the tile-yard
was situated in belonged to some of Defoe's kin. At
any rate, a branch of the Foe family resided at Chadwell, and had property both there and in the adjoining
parish of West Tilbury. In the parish register we find
the following : —

"1605. Edmund Foe, married man, was buried yᵉ 28 March."
"1621. Robert Smith, son of George Smith, of Welleborne, in
Wiltshire, and of Joane his wife (both deceased), and Katherine foe,

daughter of Edmond foe (deceased) and Lucie his wife, were married
the 13th day of February, 1621."

The connection between Edmond Foe and Defoe's
family I have not been able to find out ; but it would
indeed be an extraordinary coincidence—the name
being an uncommon one—if in so small a place as
Chadwell one family of Foe should have held property,
and 'another Foe (Defoe) have lived there, and yet
that the two should have been unconnected.   The site
of the brickyard is unknown.

What with one thing or another, Defoe had a second
time become prosperous, and by unwearied diligence
he punctually paid the composition on his bond ; but
he did more, he paid—of his own accord, as even his
antagonist Tutchin testifies—some of his old creditors
who had fallen into distress to the full amount, and
made the declaration " that, as far as God should
enable him, he intended to do so with everybody."

Defoe now set up a coach, and at Tilbury, where
he had a house " near the river's edge," he kept a
pleasure boat, which figures in his account of the prodigious flight of ants which fell about that time on the
marshes of Essex and in the Thames.   The ants fell
so thick that the water was covered with them, and
near two pecks were taken out of the boat.

About 1697, Defoe changed his name from Foe—
which, like his father, he had hitherto been called—to
De Foe.   He was now nearly forty.   Why he tacked
on this foreign prefix is uncertain.   Oldmixon declares
that it was because he had stood in the pillory ; Dr.
Browne that he did it at the suggestion of Harley :

"Have I not changed by your advice my name?"
Mr. Lee suggests that it was in order to be distinguished from his father, and scouts the idea that
personal vanity had any share in bringing about the
change. I am myself not so sure about that. As
already shown, Defoe had always a large share of
personal vanity. We noticed his rather uncalled-for
assertion that he had never been a common tradesman, and that though he did formerly engage in trade,
it was only in a superior sort of way; and also his
pleasure in telling us that his grandfather was a country
gentleman and kept a pack of hounds. Then again,
he always carried a seal with his coat of arms cut on
it, and he liked to see this coat of arms underneath
his portraits. But if you want to know what he thought
of himself, the "Divino" portrait will tell you precisely.
Is he not sitting "like a lord in Parliament"? Does
he not seem to be saying, "Here you behold me, the
great Daniel Defoe"? Few men of letters put forward
greater pretensions, and few with more justification.
He was a king in literature, and he knew it, and he
was resolved that everybody else should know it too.
His father's name could not have been sounding
enough for him. Writing for posterity, he would
naturally wish something more important than Foe.
But vanity was not his only reason. The word itself
was a constant thorn in his side. It is not surprising
that a man who plumed himself upon his patriotism
should dislike to be called a Foe—better almost such
a culling from the directories as Badman or Swindler
—and we know that our author's name often subjected
him to banter. He tells one of his annoyers (in his

Review) that he is a foe in name only, not by nature, to anybody. Before 1703 Defoe generally signed himself only " D.F." In that year he is " Mr. De Foe," and " Daniel De Foe"; but, curiously, even afterwards, and right on until the year before his death, he occasionally put " D.F.," with a full stop after the D.

II.—THE POET DEFOE AND HIS "ELEGY ON DR. ANNESLEY" (1697).

WORK : 4.—The Character of the late Dr. Samuel Annesley.

We are not accustomed to think of Defoe as a poet, yet nothing is more certain than that during the first forty years of his life he plumed himself more on his skill in writing verse than on anything else. And not only so, but his claim to the title of poet was very generally allowed. (*See* Gibbon's " Life of Watts," p. 346.) Indeed, at a time when Nahum Tate was Laureate, and such swans sang in Caystor as " Mr. Motteux and Mr. Richardson " (not the novelist), Defoe cut quite a respectable figure ; and if doggerel can be poetry, doggerel expressed in terse language, "full of earnest, weighty sense," every word of which hits like a hammer, it will be impossible even now to deny that he has gained a footing on Parnassus.

Born in the parish of Milton, whom he early learned to admire, though without adulation ; a close student of Dryden and Rochester, as well as of the great Latins, Virgil and Horace ; and the possessor of a consciousness of certain undeveloped powers within himself, he was already, in his own opinion, one of the great poetical brotherhood. But " the sweet and lovely dreams " that in early life " walk the waves of our sleep" rarely come true. There was a great future for Defoe; but it was not as a poet. Nevertheless, it must be admitted that he has written quite a respectable amount of verse that will live; and, at least, one passage, the quatrain beginning —

"Wherever God erects a house of prayer"

—to which we shall again refer by-and-by—has been quoted as often as anything else in rhythmic literature.

In 1697, when occurred the death of Dr. Annesley (the minister of the Meeting-house in Little St. Helen's, Bishopsgate), Defoe, at the request of Dunton, the bookseller—who had married one of Dr. Annesley's daughters—"improved" the event with a poem, entitled, "The Character of the late Dr. Samuel Annesley by way of Elegy"; and to praise this good man, under whom he and his father had so long sat, whom, moreover, everyone that had known him, remembered with love and reverence, must have been a congenial task.

Although the poem, as a whole, is of but little value, it contains several excellent passages; as, for example, the following, which reminds of the Good Parson in Chaucer:

"His native candour, his familiar style,
Which did so oft his hearers' hours beguile,
Charmed us with godliness; and while he spake,
We loved the doctrine for the preacher's sake;
While he informed us what those doctrines meant
By dint of practice more than argument."

This poem, and the poems by other writers that were published with it, are described by Dunton as "made by the chief wits of the age; namely, Mr. Motteux, Mr. De Foe, Mr. Richardson, and, *in particular*, Mr. Tate, now poet-laureat." Among them, too, was Swift, who, however, was as yet too small a warbler to be specially named.

One of the daughters of Dr. Annesley married Samuel Wesley, and became the mother of John and Charles Wesley, the founders of Wesleyan Methodism.

The following is an alphabetical list of the longer poems of Defoe—seventeen in number:—

Annesley, Dr., Elegy on	1697
Athenian Society, Ode to the	6th May, 1703
Caledonia	28th Jan., 1707
Compleat Art of Painting	1720
Double Welcome to the Duke of Marlborough	9th Jan., 1705
Good Advice to the Ladies	3rd Sept., 1702
Hymn to the Mob	14th July, 1715
Hymn to the Pillory, The	29th July, 1703
Hymn to Peace	10th Jan., 1706
Hymn to Victory	29th Aug., 1704
Jure Divino (in 12 books)	20th July, 1706
Mock Mourners, The	May, 1702
New Discovery of an Old Intrigue	1691
Pacificator, The	20th Feb., 1700
Spanish Descent, The	Nov., 1702
Storm, The	17th July, 1704
True-Born Englishman, The	Jan., 1701

Defoe, indeed, apart from his other labours, wrote far more poetry, such as it was, than even Milton or Dryden. "By his printing a poem every day," says Dunton, "one would think he rhymed in his sleep."

In 1697, when the war with France was brought to a close by the Treaty of Ryswick, all England got in commotion on the question of a standing army. The enemies of William were anxious that the army should be disbanded, and John Trenchard and others wrote pamphlets to show that a standing army was a menace to domestic liberties. Rushing into the fray, Defoe replied to Trenchard in a tract entitled, "Some Reflections on a Pamphlet," &c., &c., which reached a second edition the same year (1697) ; and, encouraged by his success, he produced in the following year a second pamphlet on the same controversy, entitled, "An Argument Showing that a Standing Army, with consent of Parliament, is not inconsistent with a Free Government." Upon this, Defoe's first great tract, Professor Minto writes thus eulogistically :—

"He was now in the thirty-ninth year of his age, his contro- versial genius in full vigour, and his mastery of language complete. None of his subsequent tracts surpass this as a piece of trenchant and persuasive reasoning. It shows at their very highest his mar- vellous powers of combining constructive with destructive criticism. He dashes into the lists with good-humoured confidence, bearing the banner of clear common-sense, and disclaiming sympathy with extreme persons of either side. He puts his case with direct and plausible force, addressing his readers vivaciously as plain people like himself, among whom as reasonable men there cannot be two opinions. He cuts rival arguments to pieces with dexterous strokes, representing them as the confused reasoning of well meaning but

dull intellects, and dances with lively mockery on the fragments.
If the authors of such arguments knew their own minds, they would
be entirely on his side. He echoes the pet prejudices of his readers
as the props and mainstays of his thesis, and boldly laughs away
misgivings of which they are likely to be half ashamed. He makes
no parade of logic ; he is only a plain freeholder like the mass
whom he addresses, though he knows twenty times as much as
many writers of more pretension. He never appeals to passion or
imagination ; what he strives to enlist on his side is homely self-
interest, and the ordinary sense of what is right and reasonable.
He wrote for a class to whom a prolonged intellectual operation,
however comprehensive and complete, was distasteful. To persuade
the mass of the freeholders was his object, and for such an object
there are no political tracts in the language at all comparable to
Defoe's."

The result of the pother was that Parliament
granted a standing army, though not so large a one
as the king wanted.

Defoe was now surrounded by numerous and influential friends, who respected his genius and took a
delight in the vivacity of his conversation and the
readiness of his wit. Among them was Sir John
Fagg, M.P., at whose noble seat at Steyning Defoe,
in the summer of 1697, was hospitably entertained;
and Dalby Thomas, afterwards knighted, one of the
commissioners of the Glass Duty.

13.—THE OCCASIONAL CONFORMITY SQUABBLE.—PLAYING BO-PEEP
WITH GOD ALMIGHTY (1769).

WORK : 6.—An Enquiry into the Occasional Conformity of Dissenters, &c.
25th Jan., 1698.

We are now to concern ourselves with that precious
piece of business, the Occasional Conformity squabble,
which, despite its contemptibility, was to rack all
England for over a dozen years.

E

That the oppressive laws against the Dissenters ought never to have been made ; and that it is unjust and tyrannical to disqualify anybody for a public office merely on account of religious differences is readily conceded ; at the same time, although the squabble reflects very little credit on the High Church Party, or " High-fliers," as the age called them, one cannot see that the Dissenters showed themselves in it to the best advantage. The practice of occasionally taking communion with the Established Church as a quali- fication for public office had grown up gradually, and had been in vogue during most of the reign of William, without attracting much notice ; but on 27th September, 1697, Sir Humphrey Edwin, a Dissenter, who had been elected Lord Mayor, thought fit, after attending church one Sunday morning, to go in the afternoon, with all the insignia of his office, to his meeting-house, Pinner's Hall. That was the signal for a very fine hullabaloo. The whole question of Occasional Conformity was raised ; and every weapon that bitterness, spite, jealousy, and tyranny could devise was brought out, furbished, and wielded. The High Church party were wrong ; for they should not have endeavoured to put into force laws that ought never to have been made. The Dissenters were wrong ; for they ought not to have taken upon themselves to receive the Lord's Supper in a manner which, but for the particular end of obtaining office, they would not have consented to. Such, at any rate, was the view that Defoe took, and, in consequence, he issued a pamphlet, entitled, " An Enquiry into the Occasional Conformity of Dissenters," in which he argued that occasional conformity was a sinful act, or else Dissent itself was sinful.

To receive the sacrament of the Lord's Supper at the table of the Church of England merely as a qualification for civic honours, and the privilege of playing at long-spoon and custard on Lord Mayor's day, was, he argued, "a scandalous practice, and a-playing at bo-peep with God Almighty"; and upon this ground Defoe stood for years, to the great annoyance of his co-religionists.

The din of this squabble, will again from time to time, assail our ears. For the present we turn thankfully to another subject.

14.—THE ESSAY ON PROJECTS.—"WOMAN, LOVELY WOMAN"
(MAY, 1698).

WORKS: 7.—An Essay upon Projects. 29th May, 1698 (Printed in 1697).
8.—The Poor Man's Plea, &c. 31st March, 1698.

For some time, as we have seen, Defoe had employed his pen in promoting objects that were pleasing to the king; and in January, 1696-7, he published his "Essay upon Projects," dedicated to his friend, Dalby Thomas. In this work he advocated a number of enterprises—some praiseworthy, others Quixotic.

Among the former was a College for the Education of Women. No other writer of the time regarded woman in so chivalrous and respectful a manner as Defoe, saving and excepting Steele. To Defoe a woman was not a doll, a fool, or a mere adjunct of man. She was a human being with a soul; and with man's training would be man's equal.

E 2

The only training that women had at that time was beneath his contempt. He did not believe, he said, that God made them so delicate, so glorious, to be only stewards of our houses, cooks, and slaves ; and then comes a passage which, for truth and beauty of expression, is among the very finest things that any man ever wrote of the other sex :—

"A woman well bred and well taught, furnished with the additional accomplishments of knowledge and behaviour, is a creature without comparison : her society is the emblem of sublimer enjoyments ; her person is angelic, and her conversation heavenly ; she is all softness and sweetness, peace, love, wit, and delight ; she is every way suitable to the sublimest wish ; and the man that·has such a one to his portion has nothing to do but to rejoice in her, and be thankful."

And then Defoe draws the picture of the same beautiful woman without education, showing that the chances are that she will degenerate "to be turbulent, clamorous, noisy, nasty, and the devil." A woman's ornaments and beauty, without suitable behaviour, are, he declares, "a cheat in nature; like the false tradesman, who puts the best of his goods uppermost that the buyer may think the rest are of the same goodness." ●

'Ware of the uneducated and uncultured but beautiful woman!

In verse Defoe is no less chivalrous to women than in prose. Whoever vituperised "The True-born Englishman," it is not to be supposed that the ladies did—

"Nor shall my verse the brighter sex defame,
For English beauty will preserve her name ;

Beyond dispute agreeable and fair,
And modester than other nations are ;
For where the vice prevails, the great temptation
Is want of money more than inclination."

And then follows a little couplet which rolls very deliciously round one's tongue—

" In general this only is allowed,
They're something noisy, and a little proud."

Among the other public improvements that Defoe suggests in this valuable book are a royal or national bank ; assurances against shipwreck, fires, etc, ; friendly societies ; savings banks for the poor ; a commission of inquiry into bankruptcy ; and the establishment of a society " for encouraging polite learning, for refining the English language, and for preventing barbarisms of manners," the last being also a favourite dream of Mat Prior and Jonathan Swift. Of these improvements several have since come into vogue ; and perhaps the time is not far distant when we shall even see a society formed for preserving the purity of the language, and the realisation of Mr. G. A. Sala's suggestion of an *Index Expurgatorius,* and the revival of the pillory for those miscreants who sully the waters of the pure well of English with such accretions as " talented," " preventitive," and " reliable." The only difficulty, apparently, would be to find pillories enough. The " Essay upon Projects " had no inconsiderable share in moulding the mind of Benjamin Franklin.

Among the commendable actions of William's Government, one was an attempt at the reformation of manners ; and in 1697 an address was voted by Parliament asking his Majesty to see that wickedness was discouraged in high places. To this good work Defoe lent his assistance in a pamphlet entitled " The Poor Man's Plea," in which the poor man pleaded the uselessness of passing laws and making proclamations for the reform of the people so long as persons in high places were themselves corrupt, the argument being spiced with some amusing anecdotes to show the prevalence of swearing and drunkenness among members of the judicial bench.

15.—HIS POEMS, " THE PACIFICATOR " AND " THE TRUE-BORN
        ENGLISHMAN."—DEATH OF DRYDEN.

WORKS: 10.—The Pacificator, a Poem. 20th Feb., 1700.
        11.—The Two Great Questions Considered, etc. 2nd Dec., 1700.
        12.—An Enquiry into the Occasional Conformity of Dissenters, etc.
        20th Nov., 1700.
        13.—The Two Great Questions further considered. 2nd Dec., 1700.
        14.—The Six distinguishing Characters of a Parliament Man. 4th Jan., 1701.
        15.— The Danger of the Protestant Religion considered, etc. 9th Jan., 1701.
        16.—The True-Born Englishman. Jan., 1701.
        17.—Considerations upon Corrupt Elections of Members. Jan., 1701.
        18.—The Freeholder's Plea against Stock-Jobbing Elections of Parliament
        Men.
        19.—A Letter to Mr. Howe. 24th Jan., 1701.
        20.—The Villany of Stock-Jobbers Detected. 11th Feb., 1701.

In his satirical poem, " The Pacificator," Defoe describes an imaginary war among the leading authors of the day. After recommending a cessation of hostilities, he advises each to choose only the part he can do well, and to confine himself to his own province—

> " *Dryden* to Tragedy,—let *Creech* Translate,
> *D'Urfey* make Ballads,—Psalms and Hymns for *Tate ;*
> Let *Prior* flatter kings in Panegyric,—
> *Ratcliffe* Burlesque,—and *Wycherley* be lyric ;
> Let *Congreve* write the Comic,—*Foe* Lampoon,—
> *Wessley* the Banter,—*Milbourn* the Buffoon."

" The Pacificator " was published on 20th of February, 1700; ere two months were fled Dryden, the
greatest in Defoe's list, had gone to his long home. He
died on May Day that year. Wycherley, aged sixty,
had fifteen more years to live; Prior, aged thirty-seven,
twenty-one more; Congreve, aged thirty-one, twenty-
nine more. Pope, who had not yet blazed into the
firmament, was a boy of twelve, living with his father
and mother at Binfield.

The death of Charles II. of Spain, in October
(1700), and the bequest of his throne to the Duke of
Anjou (grandson of Louis XII.) now caused trouble
on the Continent. By Charles's will Spain, Italy, and
France would be virtually one country, and this after
all William's endeavour, by sword and treaty, to limit
the power of France! The fiat then went forth from
the Court that there must again be war; but Parliament would none of it, and the people, tired of war,
stood by them. Defoe, taking the King's part, was
ready, as usual, with a pamphlet, which he entitled,
" The Two Great Questions Considered. I. What
the French King will do with respect to the Spanish
Monarchy. II. What measures the English ought
to take "—in which he contended that to allow the
French to obtain the upper hand in Spain was to
court the ruin of England. But even the eloquence
of a Defoe was unavailing. The people did not
want war, and war they would not have. The King
became unpopular, and every brazen-throated true-
born Englishman shouted, " Down with the Hugger-
muggers!" (Dutch). An anonymous writer, replying
to Defoe's pamphlet eight days later, accused him

of place-hunting, with the result of a rejoinder by Defoe entitled, "The Two Great Questions further considered" (2nd December, 1700).

In the meantime the Occasional Conformity caldron, which for a time had quieted down, had lately received a new ingredient; again the fire was stirred, and the nauseous liquor was now steaming and bubbling again with all its old virulence.

Three years had passed since the commotion about Sir Humphrey Edwin, and now another Dissenter, Sir Thomas Abney, Lord Mayor of London, and one of the congregation of the celebrated John Howe, had, upon induction to office, received the Sacrament according to the Church of England, with the result of reopening the whole question.

The High Church pamphleteers were of opinion that "Sir Tom" would have been much better employed singing "psalms at Highgate Hill," and "splitting texts of Scripture with his diminutive figure of a chaplain" (Dr. Watts), than in "running the hazard of qualifying himself to be called a handsome man, for riding on horseback before the city train-bands," or venturing damnation "to play at longspoon and custard for a transitory twelvemonth."

Defoe, whom chance, for the nonce, had put on the same side, reprinted his tract on "Occasional Conformity," cancelling, however, the former preface and substituting one to Howe, in the hope of eliciting "from so influential a minister some expression of approval or disapproval of the practice" (20th November, 1700).

Over and over again, Defoe maintains that the

ordinance of the Lord's Supper cannot be converted
into a civil action; and he repeats what he had before
advanced, that to take the Sacrament as the Occasional
Conformists did was "nothing but a bantering with
religion and playing bo-peep with God Almighty."

Howe lost his temper—persons who were confronted
with the exasperating coolness of Defoe generally did
—and, good man as he was, wrote a not very christian-
like reply. Defoe, who did not know what it was to
lose *his* temper, followed up with a pamphlet written
with even more than his usual imperturbability, "A
Letter to Mr. How," etc. (24th January, 1701), in
which he insists on the wrongfulness of "doubling
and shifting in points of religion," and sums up his
argument in one of those beautiful sentiments with
which all his works are so plentifully sprinkled :

> "Sincerity is the glory of a Christian. The native lustre of an
> honest heart is impossible to be hid ; 'twill shine through all his
> life in one action or another, in spite of scandal ; and it wants
> no artifice to set it out."

Mr. Howe made no reply, and so for a time the
matter again rested.

In January and February, 1701, besides the letter
to Mr. Howe, Defoe published five political pamphlets:
" The Six Distinguishing Characters of a Parliament
Man " (January 4), showing that the chosen of the
people should be loyal, religious, sensible, mature,
honest, and moral ; " The Danger of the Protestant
Religion considered " (January 9), advocating an
alliance with Austria (the natural rival of France)
and a defensive union of all Protestant States ;

"Considerations upon Corrupt Election of Members
to serve in Parliament," a tract directed against bribery
at elections; "The Freeholders' Plea against Stock-
Jobbing Elections of Parliament Men," exposing the
practice of buying and selling of seats in Parliament
upon the Stock Exchange; and "The Villany of
Stock-Jobbers detected" (11th February, 1701), a
denunciation of Stock Exchange gambling.

Far and away, however, the most important production of this period was his famous satirical poem,
"The True-Born Englishman." (January, 1701).

The unpopularity of the King has already been
touched upon. Among those who attacked him was,
for some reason or other, the Whig writer, John
Tutchin, the same who was brow-beaten by Jeffreys
and whipped through Doncaster, and who afterwards
bestowed a grudged compliment on Defoe's honesty.
Mr. Tutchin, in an effusion called "The Foreigners,"
styled delicately by Defoe "a vile, abhorred pamphlet,
in very ill verse," had taken upon himself to belabour,
not only King William, but the whole Dutch nation.
The chivalrous and loyal soul of Defoe smelt the
battle afar off. He rushed among the trumpets, and
his "True-Born Englishman" is the voice, "Ha, ha!"

This famous satire opens deliciously with the
following oft-quoted quatrain :—

> "Wherever God erects a house of prayer,
> The devil always builds a chapel there ;
> And 'twill be found upon examination.
> The latter has the larger congregation."

The author then goes on to mention the vices of
the various nations, coming at last to the English,

whom he shows to be the most mongrel race under heaven, derived from Roman, Gaul, Greek, Lombard, Saxon, Dane, and a host of others, continuing—

> " From this amphibious, ill-born mob began,
> That vain, ill-natured thing, an Englishman."

Englishmen, in short, are the offspring of foreigners, and what is more, of the scum of foreigners, consequently the term a true-born Englishman is an absurdity. The true-born Englishman does not exist. The history of our nation is then continued to his own time, with particular reference to the foreign elements that grafted themselves upon our stock in the reigns of Henry V., Elizabeth, and Charles II. Why, asks Defoe, need the English, seeing that they are themselves so composite, be so bitter against King William and the Dutch. The English did not grumble when William was assisting them against Stuart tyranny ; but

> " Wise men affirm it is the English way,
> Never to grumble till they come to pay ;
> And then they always think—their temper's such—
> The work too little, and the pay too much."

" The True-born Englishman " contains many fine breezy lines. Take, for example, the following :—

> " Titles are shadows, crowns are empty things,
> The good of subjects is the end of kings."

Defoe's opinions, too, on our legislators are worth remembering—

> " Statesmen are always sick of one disease,
> And a good pension gives them present ease ;
> That's a specific makes them all content,
> With any king and any government."

And with equal vigour he chastises the national sin of
drunkenness—

> " In English ale their dear enjoyment lies,
> For which they'll starve themselves and families.
> An Englishman will fairly drink as much
> As will maintain two families of Dutch."

What excited his detestation the most, however,
was undue influence of the priesthood. A ruling
priesthood he held to be as dangerous as a priest-rid
king—

> " And of all plagues with which mankind is curst,
> Ecclesiastic tyranny is worst."

But what most astonishes is the extraordinary
audacity of the whole thing. He strikes right and
left and in every direction, and no party or degree is
spared. " The lines run on from beginning to end
in the same strain of bold, broad, hearty banter," and
the piece was doubtless written off at a heat. To
sum up—

> " For Englishmen to boast of generation,
> Cancels their knowledge, and lampoons the nation ;
> A true-born Englishman 's a contradiction,
> In speech an irony, in fact a fiction."

As Defoe was of Flemish extraction, there was, in
addition, at the back of the trenchant arguments in
" The True-born Englishman," a strong personal
feeling.

The publication, fortunately for Defoe, was taken
by the public in the light that was intended. All
London laughed, and the name of its author was on
every tongue. Again and again it was reprinted by

Defoe himself; and of pirated copies alone it is estimated that over 80,000 were sold. Henceforth Defoe describes himself in his title-pages as the author of " The True-born Englishman." The poem being brought under the notice of the King, Defoe was welcomed to Court, employed in the Royal service, and rewarded " above his capacity of deserving."

The similarity between the King and Defoe, both in their moral temperament and their physical aspect, has been noticed by more than one, and it is sufficiently striking. Both were sincerely religious men, both inflexible of purpose, each led a life of comparative solitude. In physical aspect, too, men marked the similarity. The King was Defoe's senior by ten years, "but the middle size, the spare figure, the hooked nose, the sharp chin, the keen grey eye, the large forehead, and grave appearance were common to both,"* and as a rule the manner of each was cold.

16.—THE KENTISH PETITION.

WORKS: 21.—The Succession to the Crown of England considered. About 1st March, 1701.
22.—Legion's Memorial to the House of Commons. Presented 14th May, 1701.
23.—The History of the Kentish Petition. Aug., 1701.
24.—The Present State of Jacobitism considered. Before Oct., 1701.
25.—Reasons against a War with France. Oct., 1701.
26.—The Original Power of the Collective Body of the People of England, examined and asserted. 27th Dec., 1701.
27.—Legion's New Paper. 1st Jan., 1702.

The death of the Duke of Gloucester, son of the Princess Anne, in July, 1700, had drawn people's thoughts to the subject of the succession, and the eyes of Protestants were turned towards Hanover. In a

* Forster.

tract, printed about 1st March, 1701, entitled, " The
Succession to the Crown of England considered,"
Defoe examines the pretensions of all claimants, and
finds that the House of Hanover had the only in-
disputable title.

On the 8th of May, 1701, the grand jury of Kent
presented to the Commons a petition, which desired
them "to mind the public business more, and their
private heats less," a procedure which had the effect
of landing four of them in jail. Defoe, taking their
part, wrote a Remonstrance, his celebrated " Legion's
Memorial," which he had the boldness to deliver—
according to some, in the guise of a woman, or, as
others say, muffled in a cloak—to Harley the Speaker
as he entered the House of Commons. To quote the
" seductive page " of " Tory Hume," " The Commons
were equally provoked and intimidated by this libel,
which was the production of one Daniel De Foe, a
scurrilous party-writer in very little estimation."
When the Kentish petitioners were liberated, and
feasted at Mercers' Hall, Cheapside, by the citizens
of London, Defoe sat among them as an honoured
guest; and in the August following he published
his " History of the Kentish Petition," which came
out about the same time as the " Jura Populi Angli-
cani" of Lord Somers, a tract which also defends
the subject's right of petitioning—

> " Somers by nature great, and born to rise ;
> In counsel wary, and in conduct wise." *

The next tract of Defoe's, " The Present State

* Defoe's " Jure Divino."

of Jacobitism considered," etc., was suggested by
the death of James II., and the offensive action of
the French king in championing the cause of James's
son, the Pretender. .

The object of the pamphlet was to quiet the
animosities of the contending British parties, and to
advocate moderation and peace—a line of argument
which Defoe often afterwards took up. It was reserved, indeed, for Defoe, the most combative of
all our political writers, to be at the same time the
most persistent and eloquent of the preachers of
the gospel of peace. He was perpetually sticking
spikes into persons, and recommending them to keep
quiet. Nor did the incongruity of the thing ever
once occur to him. His next tract, " Reasons against
a War with France" (October, 1701), is styled by
Chalmers "one of the finest, because it is one of
the most useful, tracts in the language." Professor
Minto comments :—

" As Defoe had for nearly a year been zealously working the
public mind to a warlike pitch, this title is at first surprising ; but the
surprise disappears when we find that the pamphlet is an ingenious
plea for beginning with a declaration of war against Spain, showing
that not only was there just cause for such a war, but that it would
be extremely profitable, inasmuch as it would afford occasion for
plundering the Spaniards in the West Indies, and thereby making up
for whatever losses our trade might suffer from the French privateers.
This trick of arresting attention by an unexpected thesis, such as this
promise of reasons for peace when everybody was dreaming of war,
is an art in which Defoe was never surpassed."

Towards the end of 1701 two pamphlets—one a
vindication of the rights of the House of Commons,
by Sir Humphrey Mackworth, and the other a reply

vindicating the rights of the House of Lords, probably by Lord Somers —obtained considerable notice, where- upon Defoe, who perceived that neither of the disputants had properly taken into consideration the rights of the people, issued on December 27 his pamphlet, " The Original Power of the Collective Body of the People of England, examined and asserted " — a work of great merit which, in Mr. Chalmers' opinion, " vies with Mr. Locke's famous tract in power of reasoning, and is superior to it in the graces of style."

On January 1, 1702, the day after Parliament opened, Defoe was to the fore again with another pamphlet, " Legion's New Paper," etc.—" the nervous eloquence, the power of invective, and the lofty scorn " in which reminded Mr. Lee of "some of the finest passages in Junius." Its object was "further to expose the errors of the Parliament." " Legion," says Defoe's opponent, Dr. Davenant, "is come out again, more impudent and inflaming than he was last year."

17.—DEATH OF KING WILLIAM (8TH MARCH, 1702).

WORKS: 28.—The Mock Mourners, a Poem. May, 1702.
29.—Reformation of Manners, a Poem.
30.—A New Test of the Church of England's Loyalty. June, 1702.
31. Good Advice to the Ladies. 3rd Sept., 1702.
32.—The Spanish Descent, a Poem. Nov., 1702.

Defoe was now to receive a very severe blow in the death of his great friend and benefactor, King William. The King's health had for some time been failing ; nevertheless, but for a serious accident, he might have lived years. Whilst hunting near Hampton Court, on February 21st, his horse's foot caught against a mole-hill, and he fell and broke his collar-bone. The injury, acting on a frame reduced by asthma, brought on a fever, and on March the 8th he died.

Whoever felt distress at the death of William, the Jacobites did not; and some even went so far as to drink to the little "gentleman dressed in velvet"—meaning the mole that had occasioned the accident—and to the horse, Sorrel, from which the King had been thrown,

"Illustrious steed, to whom a place is given,
Above the Lion, Bull, or Bear, in heaven,"

a favourite Jacobite toast being—

"Well, then, my friends, since things you see, are so,
Let's e'en mourn on; 'twould lessen much our woe
Had Sorrel stumbled thirteen years ago,"

the thirteen years having reference to the length of William's reign.

These effusions naturally cut Defoe, and in a poem—"The Mock Mourners" (May, 1702)—he both expresses his indignation on their account and gives vent to his own affectionate sorrow. Many of its lines are well worth remembering. as, for instance, those recounting William's noble qualities—

"He knew that titles are but empty things,
And hearts of subjects are the strength of kings."

Defoe never after spoke of William without some affectionate or laudatory epithet, such as "Great King William," that "noble prince" William, or "that good and great man." In "Jure Divino" he breaks out—

"Wonder no more new raptures fire my pen,
When William's name I chance to write, and when

F

I search the lustre of his memory—
The best of monarchs and of men to me."

"The Mock Mourners" was followed by "Reformation of Manners," a satirical attack on the vices of the age, in which the taste of the nation is summed up with :
"One man reads Milton, forty Rochester."

This poem contains, among other things, an exposure of the knavery of company promoters, and a noble denunciation of the slave trade.

Defoe's next productions were an attack on the High Church party, entitled "A New Test of the Church of England's Loyalty" (June, 1702), and a poetical satire entitled "Good Advice to the Ladies," showing that as the world goes, and is like to go, the best way for them is to keep unmarried.

Louis of France having supported the claims of the Pretender to the sovereignty of England, Queen Anne, in deference to popular feeling, declared war both against France and its ally, Spain. An armament of fourteen thousand men, under Sir George Rooke and the Duke of Ormond, sailed for Cadiz, but returned to England without having effected a landing, a proceeding which filled the nation with disgust and gave origin to many lampoons, among them being Defoe's "Spanish Descent," a poem of twenty-seven pages, which castigates the English commanders for flying "scared with walls, and not with men," for bravely re-embarking when none pursued, and for quitting "the Andalusian shores," not covered with glory, but "drenched with Spanish wine and Spanish ——," what we need not name.

The poem, however, is not all vituperation, for on his way home past Vigo Bay, Sir George Rooke had swooped down on some Spanish galleons laden with bullion, for which Defoe gives him fair measure of praise.

18.—THE SHORTEST WAY; *DELENDA EST CARTHAGO*
(1ST DECEMBER, 1702).

WORKS: 33.—An Enquiry into Occasional Conformity. Nov., 1702.
34.—The Shortest Way with Dissenters. 1st Dec., 1702.

Now bubbles and boils again the detestable Occasional Conformity caldron, the origin of the new outburst being the introduction into the House of Commons, on November 4th, of a Bill to make occasional conformity illegal. Then ensued a battle of pamphlets, among them, of course, being one by Defoe—"An Enquiry into Occasional Conformity" —showing that Dissenters are in no ways concerned in it. The measure, he insisted, far from injuring the Dissenters, would, by weeding out time-servers, consolidate their true interests. The Court being for the Bill, the Tories anticipated success. Among others, they had won over fat and easy Lutheran Prince George, whose conscience salve, "My heart is vid you," said to Lord Wharton against whom he was about to vote, will for all time be a respectable jest. The decision of the Lords, however, drove, for the nonce, this absurd Bill out of the field.

The next production of Defoe's was his famous tract, "The Shortest Way with Dissenters," written, it is now generally conceded, if not at the suggestion, at any rate with the hearty approval of the Whig leaders,

F 2

among whom Harley was *facile princeps*.   But Defoe
did not at this time know Harley personally, and the
precise nature of his connection with the Whig leaders
cannot now be ascertained, for, as we shall see, he
kept his secret.   The object of the pamphlet was
undoubtedly to render odious to the people, and to
oust from office, Lord Nottingham and the Tories,
and to smooth the way for the succession of Harley.
In the "brief explanation" of the pamphlet which
he afterwards gave, Defoe declared that it had no
bearing whatever upon the Occasional Conformity
Bill, but that it was intended as a banter upon the
High-fliers, putting into plain English their furious
invectives against the Dissenters, and so, "by an
irony not unusual," answering them out of their own
mouths.

To use the words of Professor Minto :

"Its whole merit and its rousing political force lay in the
dramatic genius with which Defoe personated the temper of a
thorough-going High-flier, putting into plain and spirited English
such sentiments as a violent partisan would not dare to utter except in the unguarded heat of familiar discourse, or the half-
humorous ferocity of intoxication."

To use ●Tutchin's expression—for in this matter
Tutchin was on Defoe's side—Defoe came with a
lanthorn, and all the dark deeds of High-flyingdom
were revealed to the eye.   "Have done," cried Defoe,
addressing the Dissenters, "with this cackle about peace
and union, and the Christian duties of moderation.
We heard none of this when we were huffed and
bullied under your friend King William; but your day
is over, your power gone, and the throne of this nation

possessed by a royal, English, true, and ever-constant member of and friend to the Church of England. . . . Now that the tables are turned upon you, you must not be persecuted ; 'tis not a Christian spirit." What persecution had the Dissenters to complain of in the past ? If under the Jameses and the Charleses they did get a few buffets, they got no more than they deserved. Under King William they had insulted the Church, and now they must be rooted out. " 'Tis vain to trifle in this matter. We can never enjoy a settled, uninterrupted union in this nation till the spirit of Whiggism, faction, and schism is melted down like old money. Here is the opportunity to secure the Church and destroy her enemies. I do not pre-scribe fire and faggot, but *delenda est Carthago.* The light foolish handling of them by mulcts, fines, etc., 'tis their glory and their advantage. If the gallows instead of the counter, and the galleys instead of the fines, were the reward of going to a conventicle, to preach or hear, there would not be so many sufferers —the spirit of martyrdom is over. They that will go to church to be chosen sheriffs and mayors would go to forty churches rather than be hanged." " Now let us crucify the thieves," he concludes ; " and may God Almighty put it into the hearts of all friends of truth to lift up a standard against pride and Anti-christ, that the posterity of the sons of error may be rooted out from the face of this land for ever."

CHAPTER IV.

IN LOB'S POUND (18 MONTHS).

19.—IN THE CLUTCHES OF DON DISMAL (NOTTINGHAM).—"THIS DAMNED SATIRICAL WAY OF WRITING."—THE SHY INFORMER.

WORKS : 35.—A Brief Explanation of a late Pamphlet, entitled "The Shortest Way."
36.—King William's Affection to the Church of England. 25th March, 1703.
37.—An Ode to the Athenian Society. 6th May, 1703.

DEFOE'S trick was perfection; the High-fliers were hooked like so many gudgeon. They took it for granted that the writer of the pamphlet was a High-flier like themselves, only more enthusiastic, more out-spoken, more audacious. One clergyman declared that in his estimation, the "Shortest Way" came next to the Bible (*Review* ii., 277) ; and others were equally complimentary. Indeed, it "was so like a brat of their own begetting, that, like two apples, they could not know them asunder."*

But if the High-fliers were jubilant, the Dissenters, or rather the more timorous of them, shook like aspen leaves. Then the truth leaked out, that it was the work of a Dissenter. The Whigs held their sides with laughter. The Tories raged like Sirius. "This damned satirical way of writing," as they called it,† was more than the everyday stomach could endure. Nothing would suit now, but that the author of the

---

* Defoe.   † Defoe's "Consolidator."

pamphlet should be unearthed and brought to justice;
and—the Tories being in power—shrewd persons
hazarded guesses as to which side justice would lean.
We likened Defoe to a child catching gudgeon ; but
a more pertinent simile would be that of an over-
venturesome sailor presenting his blandishments to a
sea of sharks, with the result that both are caught, fish
and fisherman, the huge and savage beast pulling both
line and sailor into the uncomfortable sea. Rather
than Defoe should want a pass out of the world, one
" honest gentleman, a colonel," undertook to be hangman ; and another declared that if he could find the
villain he would deliver him up and abate the promised £50. Churchmen and Dissenters, all were
offended. The whole world "flew at him like a dog
with a broom at his tail." *

They tell us that the first to track the pamphlet
to Defoe was the "tall, sable-complexioned" High
Church Daniel Finch, Earl of Nottingham, Swift's
" Don Dismal," then one of the secretaries of State;
and this is not unlikely. At any rate, it is certain,
from a recent discovery, presently to be dealt with,
that Nottingham — who, as long as he lived, was
Defoe's bitter enemy—had Defoe's case in his hands ;
and it was Nottingham, doubtless, who worded the
famous proclamation issued by the Government,
offering a reward of fifty pounds for the discovery
of Defoe's retreat, advertised in the *London Gazette*,
for January 10, 1702-3. It runs—

"Whereas, Daniel De Foe, *alias* De Fooe, is charged with
writing a scandalous and seditious pamphlet, entitled, 'The Shortest

* Defoe.

Way with Dissenters.' He is a middle-sized, spare man, about forty years old, of a brown complexion, and dark-brown coloured hair, but wears a wig; a hooked nose, a sharp chin, grey eyes, and a large mole near his mouth; was born in London, and for many years was a hose-factor, in Freeman's Yard in Cornhill; and now is the owner of the brick and pantile works near Tilbury Fort in Essex; whoever shall discover the said Daniel De Foe to one of Her Majesty's principal Secretaries of State, or any of Her Majesty's justices of the peace, so he may be apprehended, shall have a reward of £50, which Her Majesty has ordered immediately to be paid upon such discovery."

Meantime, the pamphlet was burnt in New Palace Yard by the common hangman, and the printer and the publisher were taken into custody. From his hiding-place Defoe then put forth, "in order to remove the veil from the eyes of those who were too blind to perceive the drift of his argument," "A Brief Explanation of a late Pamphlet, entitled, 'The Shortest Way with Dissenters,'" in which he insists that the pamphlet that had caused so much excitement was nothing more than "a banter upon the high-flying Churchmen." He was also in hopes that his explanation might "allay the anger of the Government," and that the "poor people" (the printers) in trouble on account of "The Shortest Way" would be pardoned or excused.

That the Dissenters continued to misunderstand him particularly hurt his feelings. How could they suppose, he wanted to know, that he wrote with a design to have them all hanged, banished, or destroyed; and that the penalty of going to a conventicle should be the gallows or the galleys; or that he, a Dissenter like them, desired such treatment for

his wife, for his six innocent children, for his father,
and for himself? The only misfortune about the
matter was that the public were so chuckle-headed
that they couldn't understand him. Had he, when
he painted his picture, acted "like the Dutchman"
with his man and his bear, and "written under which
was the man and which the bear," all would have
been well.

But if the Dissenters were thick of hearing, the
Tories were deaf as adders. For years he had been
fulminating against the High-fliers, and doing everything in his power to render them odious to the nation;
and now they had him, as they supposed, so nicely in
their power, was it likely they were going to let him
off—the man who had vindicated the Revolution, pane-
gyrised King William, who had defended the rights
of the collective body of the people, who had lampooned High Torydom in the persons of Sir Edward
Seymour and Sir Christopher Musgrave? It was too
much to expect; for, after all, your High-flier is only
human nature.

Some of Defoe's enemies took the trouble to
forge against him more thunderbolts in the form of
pamphlets, as, for example, "The Fox with his Fire-
brand Unkennelled," and the "Shortest Way with
Whores and Rogues," the author of which wanted to
fight. "Accept this gentle dedication and seasonable
warning," he says, "from one that neither loves nor
fears you, and, were it lawful, dares meet you at any
time with a brighter weapon than a pen"; but seeing
that just then Defoe was being hunted like a hare,
this challenge savoured not so much of the heroic

as of the ridiculous. Into the fray, too, rushed Mrs.
Mary Astell—the Camilla of the strife—who held
that the Dissenters, if deprived of their political
rights, would be not only none the worse, but in the
enjoyment of a sempiternal pudding-time.

It is generally stated that Defoe, finding the
Ministry would not listen to him, "surrendered himself in order that others might not suffer for his
offence." This, however, as a recently discovered
document proves, was not the case. Defoe was found
out by, and arrested at the instance of, a person who
afterwards claimed and got the promised £50 out of
the secret-service money.

The shy informer, not caring to appear himself to
lay in his claim, the Earl of Nottingham was kind
enough to manage the dirty business for him.

"The person," says Lord Nottingham (writing to
the Lord High Treasurer), "who discovered De Foe,
for whom a reward of £50 was promised in the
Gazette, sends to me for his money, but does not care
to appear himself. If, therefore, your Lordship will
order that sum to be paid to Mr. Armstrong, I will
take care that the person shall have it who discovered
the said Defooe and upon whose information he was
apprehended.

"Dated May 25th, 1703."*

The 25th of March saw the issue of Defoe's tract,
"King William's Affection to the Church of England

---

* "Calendar of Treasury Papers from 1702 to 1717," lxxxv. No. 154.

examined," the object of which, like that of its predecessor, "The Mock Mourners," was to chastise the
calumniators of the late King, and to vindicate his
memory.

20.—THE "TRUE COLLECTION OF THE WRITINGS OF DEFOE."—
DEFOE AT THE OLD BAILEY.—BULLIED BY SIR SIMON HARCOURT.

WORKS : 38.—A True Collection of the Writings of the Author of "The True-Born
Englishman." July, 1703.
39.—A Second Volume of the Writings of the Author of "The True-Born
Englishman." Spring, 1705.

Whilst in a state of suspense awaiting his trial,
Defoe prepared for publication the first volume of his
works, under the title of "A true Collection of the
Writings of the Author of the 'True-Born Englishman,'" to which he had been chiefly prompted by the
issue a short time previous of a spurious edition.
The volume contains twenty-two pieces, including
"The Shortest Way"; and its frontispiece was a
portrait of Defoe engraved by M. Vandergucht from
a painting by Taverner.
Says Hazlitt :—

"No portrait can have more verisimilitude, to say the least of it.
It exhibits a set of features rather regular than otherwise, very determined in their outlines, more particularly the mouth, which expresses
great firmness and resolution of character. The eyes are full, black
and grave-looking; but the impression of the whole countenance is
rather a striking than a pleasing one. Daniel is here set forth in a
most lordly and full-bottomed wig, which flows down lower than his
elbow, and rises above his forehead with great amplitude of curl. A
richly-laced cravat and fine loose flowing cloak complete his attire,
and preserve, we may suppose, the likeness of that civic 'gallantry'
which Oldmixon ascribes to Daniel on the occasion of his escorting
King William to the Lord Mayor's feast."

M. Vandergucht, the engraver of the picture, figures in Bryan's Dictionary (Stanley's edition) ; but, singularly, the list of portraits by him in this book includes none of Defoe.

Taverner's name does not occur in Bryan; but there is the following notice of him in " Redgrave's Dictionary of Artists of the English School "—

" Taverner, Jeremiah, *portrait painter.* Practised early in the first half of the eighteenth century. There is a portrait by [*sic*, but query *of ?*] him, mezzo-tinted, by J. Smith. He was the author of several plays."

Defoe's trial at the Old Bailey came off in July (7th, 8th, and 9th).

The prosecution was conducted by Sir Simon Harcourt, the Attorney-General (afterwards Lord Chancellor), "a man without shame but very able." Who had charge of the defence we are not told, but there was small honour to him.

Conscious that his case was a weak one, Harcourt had recourse to violent bullying, and talked as if Defoe was guilty of a crime almost without parallel; and, unfortunately for the prisoner, this high-faluting and rowdy system had just the desired effect. Everybody, with the exception of Defoe, seems to have got frightened—bar, and bench, and jury; and Defoe, in a moment of weakness, listening to the advice of his counsel, quitted his defence, and threw himself upon the mercy of the Queen. Whether, subsequently, Defoe considered his counsel a knave, a traitor, or a fool, does not appear, but in his " Hymn to the Pillory," written shortly afterwards, he calls himself a fool very plainly for listening to his counsel's advice.

DEFOE IN THE PILLORY.

(From the picture by Eyre Crowe, A.R.A.)

He only regretted, he said, that he did not make a vigorous defence. It is doubtful, however, whether the best of defences would have availed him anything. One thing is certain, that he had been led to believe, both by his own counsel and by his adversaries, that he had nothing to fear if only he would throw himself upon the mercy of the Queen. The Court, having obtained its object, turned round and gave him about as stiff a sentence as they were able. He was to pay two hundred marks, stand three times in the pillory, be imprisoned during the Queen's pleasure, and find sureties for his good behaviour for seven years. That was one to Don Dismal.

21.—THREE DAYS IN THE PILLORY (JULY 29—31, 1703).

WORK: 40.—A Hymn to the Pillory.

Conformably to his sentence, Defoe stood in the pillory on the last three days of July, 1703—on the 29th before the Royal Exchange in Cornhill, on the 30th near the Conduit in Cheapside, and on the 31st at Temple Bar. Pope, with whom Defoe afterwards quarrelled, wrote spitefully—

"Earless on high stood unabashed Defoe;"

but Defoe's ears were not cropped, and he had more reason to be elated than abashed, for a crowd of admirers assembled around the "hieroglyphic state machine," and instead of garbage were flung bunches of flowers. The pillory itself was adorned with garlands, and tankards of ale and stoups of wine were drunk in honour of "the darling of the Whig mob." In the words of the High-fliers, said through their mouthpiece, Ned Ward—

> " The shouting crowds their advocate proclaim,
> And varnish over infamy with fame."

The daring " Hymn to the Pillory " which Defoe had written, and which was hawked about at the time, added to the enthusiasm. It begins—

> ," Hail, hieroglyphic state machine,
> Contrived to punish fancy in.
> Men that are men in thee can feel no pain,
> And all thy insignificants disdain."

Defoe said that he accounted it no dishonour to stand where Prynne, Burton, and Bastwick had stood, and where it had been intended to put even the " learned Selden," and he adjured the " bugbear of the law " to proclaim to the world that he, Daniel Defoe, was raised on high not for his crimes, but for his honesty—

> " Tell 'em the men that placed him here
> Are scandals to the times,
> Are at a loss to find his guilt,
> And can't commit his crimes."

To think of Defoe's dauntless courage in such a situation makes one proud of being an Englishman. The nature of his punishment, however, naturally excited much mirth in his enemies, who in lampoon and satire endeavoured to hold him up to ridicule. Among these productions were " The True-Born Huguenot " (anonymous), " A Pleasant Dialogue between the Pillory and Daniel Defoe," by Thomas Brown, and " The Dissenting Hypocrite," by Ned Ward. Tutchin, however, so often inimical to Defoe, on this occasion, in his "Observator," spoke out boldly against the scurvy way in which his fellow author had been treated ; so boldly, in fact, that he brought prosecution upon himself.

22.—AT "NEWGATE, HORRID PLACE."—*TE DEUM LAUDAMUS.*

WORK: 41.—More Reformation, a Poem.

From the pillory Defoe was taken back to Newgate, that "horrid place," as Moll Flanders calls it ; but in the face of so much popular feeling the Government did not dare to treat him as a common prisoner. He had liberty to write, and found means to convey his manuscripts to the printer ; and not only so, but in place of the conciliatory tone adopted before his conviction, he now breathed against the Government nothing but defiance. Brave as Defoe always was, he would scarcely, perhaps, at this moment have been so audacious had he not believed that there was a wily and powerful sympathiser outside watching his interests—Robert Harley.

Successful as had been the game, nevertheless, Don Dismal was not satisfied. How could he be, when, with all his endeavours, he had signally failed to connect with Defoe's affair the slippery and dangerous Harley ? So desirous was he of doing this, that he and another of his party called on Defoe, in Newgate, and offered a pardon on condition of the betrayal of the one "who set him on to write "The Shortest Way." A deep game of chess had long been playing between Nottingham and Harley; and as "The Shortest Way" was, on the face it, written with a view to pave the way for the Whig ascendency, Nottingham took it for granted that Harley had been the instigator of it. Two words would have made Defoe a free man. He had only to say "Robert Harley." But Defoe, to use his own expression ("Appeal to Honour and Justice"), had never up to this time had the least acquaintance with, or knowledge of, Harley, "other than by fame or by sight, as we know men of quality by seeing them on public occasions." Nor do we call Defoe's veracity into question; nevertheless, that he had been encouraged by some of the Whig leaders—and indirectly by Harley—is certain ; and he could, had he wished to do so, have made awkward revelations. But Defoe was mum. Neither by promises of reward, nor threat of punishment, could they prevail upon him to reveal anything.

There likewise visited him in prison two other peers, whose names are not given us, and his friends the five Kentish gentlemen concerned in the famous petition of two years previous.

Though as a political prisoner Defoe was able to separate himself when he wished from the herd of thieves, highwaymen, coiners, and pirates who thronged the prison, yet, that he did not keep himself at all times from them is certain. The man who was educated by a Morton, who worshipped under an Annesley, who founded a Christian church at Tooting, who ever upheld a high tone of Christian morality to his own hurt, who in later years wrote so much for the benefit of the poor and helpless, such a man, to use the words of Wilson, would improve "the opportunity

for conveying to the ignorant and the wicked that
moral and religious instruction which he knew so well
how to adapt to their capacities." But if some of these
miserable wretches got good from him, what he got
from them—though he did not know it—was incal-
culable. His insatiable curiosity would delight to
learn their histories. He would be as much at his
ease with Moll Flanders, Moll's "old governess," the
three Jacks, and the North-country highwayman as
he had been at a *tête-a-tête* with King William. Your
skilful physician, enamoured of his profession, perhaps
finds even more delight in a hospital full of hideous
diseases than in my lady's parlour. Truly, my lady
could tell no stories comparable with those of our
Newgate birds; and how soon Defoe began story
writing or biography writing—for with him, as with
all good artists, it was much the same thing—is
uncertain; but we know that he was accustomed to
withhold manuscripts from the press for many years.

In short, it is no exaggeration to say, that if Defoe
had not been put in durance the world would never
have heard of Colonel Jack, or of Roxana; and " Moll
Flanders "—the "most remarkable example of pure
realism in literature"—would never have been written.
Even "Robinson Crusoe" would have lacked some of
its most valuable touches had Don Dismal been less
malicious.

In short, what Bedford Jail, some thirty years
previous, had been to Bunyan, Newgate was to Defoe.
It taught him how to become immortal. Our most
bitter enemies are sometimes our best friends.

Before his confinement, as we have seen, Defoe

G

had published a poem on "Reformation of Manners."
This he followed up with another poem, entitled
"More Reformation : a Satyr upon himself," published July 16, 1703, about ten days after his trial.
In the preface he refers to "The Shortest Way," and
confesses his grand mistake to have been a too
favourable opinion of the discernment of the public,
as to the real intention of that work. Referring to
the ill-feeling that had been exhibited towards him
on account of his "Reformation of Manners," and
the troubles that had ensued, he declares he had
already discovered to his cost,

> "That he who first reforms a vicious town,
> Prevents their ruin, but completes his own."

It had been urged against him by his enemies
that he was none too good himself, and that he would
be benefiting society very much more if he would let
other people alone and reform the man Daniel. To
which he replies : "As I am far from pretending to be
free from human frailties, but forwarder to confess the
errors of my life than any man could be to accuse me,
I think myself in a better way to reformation than
those who excuse their own faults by reckoning up
mine—

> "Confession will anticipate reproach,
> He that reviles us then, reviles too much ;
> All satire ceases when the men repent,
> 'Tis cruelty to lash the penitent."

He says that he will not hide his infirmities ;
but, on the other hand, he does not consider himself
under obligation to confess sins he never committed.
At any rate, he has many negative virtues ; and he

declares that if negative virtues can be of any comfort, he has not been a man of vice. It is disagreeable to him to flaunt his religion; but says he: "If I must act the Pharisee a little, I must begin thus: 'God, I thank Thee I am not a drunkard, or a swearer, or a whoremaster, or a busybody, or idle, or revengeful; and though this be true—and I challenge all the world to prove the contrary—yet, I must own, I see small satisfaction in all the negatives of common virtues; for though I have not been guilty of any of these vices —nor of many more—I have nothing to infer from thence, but *Te Deum laudamus.*"

Te Deum laudamus, that, as before intimated, is the key-note to Defoe's life, and no careful student thereof can help being struck with the frequency with which these three words occur. His whole life was one long cry, "We praise Thee, O Lord." There was nothing of the pessimist in Defoe; and optimism beatified, and that only, could have carried him safely, as it did, through the surges that unceasingly broke upon him. He believed, as few men have believed, that the steps of a good man are ordered by the Lord; or, rather, the steps of a man whose meaning is good, whose intention is good, who strives after good; and when from time to time he looked back at what he had gone through, he could only say, "*Te Deum laudamus.*" But was the finger of God in every turning of Defoe's life? In no record of a human being that one knows of was the hand of the Deity more manifest. It is as if you were standing at the great Potter's elbow, and could see him gathering up the clay, pressing it into shape, passing it into the

G 2

furnace seven times heated, and drawing it out a vessel
for mankind to admire, and look on with wonder, and
to take courage from: to suggest, in short, to the
most thoughtless that of all cries to Heaven, the
most appropriate is "*Te Deum laudamus.*"

It has been said, and with much truth, that Defoe's
"whole life was a scene of dash and difficulty, bankruptcy and improvidence"; and that despite his great
wit, and his industry in cultivating that wit, he was
wanting in common prudence and stability.* His
fines, his imprisonments, the treachery of his friends,
the malice of his enemies, the troubles of his private
life, are not these here chronicled? Where, then,
was the finger of God? The answer is in the
question, "What did all this lead to?" We say
nothing of Defoe's benefits to his country, and
indirectly to the world, by his staunch advocacy of
the liberty of the subject; we point only to the great
work that subsequently gave him fame, and to the
cluster of satellites, some of them emulating their
planet itself in brilliancy, which, for want of a better
name, have been called his secondary works; and
then we think of the tens of millions who have
derived pleasure and profit from them, whose lives
have been brightened by them, whose courage has
been strengthened by them, whose religion has been
deepened by them. Who among the readers of
these pages, remembering all this, would not willingly
go through all the trials and misfortunes that Defoe
experienced in order to reach the high eminence that

* Chadwick.

he did, and to sit among the gods? O men and brothers, go forward, look upward! There are thousands of heights to be gained, there are thousands of victories to be won, not in literature merely, but in every department of life. Nerve yourselves for the struggle, gird up your loins, take courage. Every incident in your life, every misfortune, can be made a boon; every misfortune is a boon to the man who is nothing daunted. Ambition, and ambition only, makes the world go round; for even love without ambition were a vapid and valueless insipidity. Above all, cry as you go, "*Te Deum laudamus.*" Such is the moral of Defoe's life, and precisely as a biographer who neglected to lay stress on it would be a traitor, so the reader who took not the lesson to heart would be only a trifler, and might just as well have cast this book on the fire. A book is valuable only for the good one can get out of it. This book being the life of a man who *Went*, is, by necessity, a book of *Go*, and he who reads it and does not "go," what on earth use can it be to him?

Defoe had complained that his friends misunderstood him, but now that fate had "clothed his tenement in walls of stone," they went a step further and held aloof from him. The Dissenting ministers could visit highwaymen, thieves and murderers in Newgate, could "freely visit" even Witney there; but three of them, including John Howe, though invited, declined to see Defoe.

> "Yet three petitioned priests have said thee nay,
> And vilely scorn'd so much as but to pray."

Hurt as Defoe apparently was, and indignant as

he seems to have been against the "three petitioned priests," yet one cannot help heartily laughing when remembering how unmercifully the man in the "stone doublet" had trounced these same gentlemen only a few months previous. Of a forgiving temper himself, he was quite incapable of understanding how another person could nourish resentment, especially a parson. Combined with his astuteness, there was in Defoe's character a simplicity compared with which the simplicity of a little child is positive cunning. Who else, having in boisterous mirth flung clods at John Howe, and fluttered the Dissenting dovecotes by "The Shortest Way," would, immediately after getting into Newgate, have invited John Howe and other "topping Dissenters" to pray with him, and then felt aggrieved because they did not come! The thing is too absurd.

We may sympathise with Defoe in Newgate, and ought to do so, but let it be remembered that clapping political opponents in prison and making life generally uncomfortable for them was just then very much *comme il faut*. If Defoe was put in the pillory by the High-fliers, so, later, was the High-flying publisher, Nathaniel Mist, put in the pillory by the Whigs; if Defoe was cooped up eighteen months in Newgate, did not a two years' imprisonment in the Tower await Robert Harley; if Defoe's "Shortest Way" was burned by the common hangman, so, too, were High-flying Dr. Drake's "Memorial of the Church of England," and High-flying Dr. Sacheverell's famous sermon. In Anna's golden days it was *vae victis*, and the devil take the hindmost.

23.—THE FAILURE OF THE PANTILE WORKS (1704).

The long imprisonment of Defoe proved the ruin
of the pantile works at Chadwell, and with their ruin
departed what had for some time been his chief source
of income.   Not only had he been secretary for
the works, but it is evident from what he says about
the affair that he was the principal shareholder.
His losses by the abandonment of this undertaking
amounted to £3,500.   To use his own words, "Violence, injury, and barbarous treatment demolished him
and his undertakings" (*Review*, March 24, 1705).
Among other things that his enemies said was that he
"required bricks without paying his labourers."
Perhaps this accusation arose from the dispute, in
June, 1703, relative to a bill for beer which had
been supplied to Defoe's workmen.   The dispute ended
in a Chancery suit, and Defoe's defence is preserved
in the Record Office.   It is dated July 3rd, 1703,
three days after Defoe was last pilloried.   How the
suit ended we do not know, but possibly a com-
promise was agreed to, for Defoe, though he "denied
that he owed Chapman (the publican) £53 6s., or
near that sum," expressed his willingness "to come
to a fair account with Chapman."*

When hard pressed for lack of men, Defoe would
sometimes invite into his tile-yard any loafers or
beggars who happened to be in the neighbourhood,
though with ill-success.   "I affirm of my own knowledge," says he, "when I have wanted a man for
labouring work, and offered nine shillings a week to

* *See* Mr. G. A. Aitken's paper in the *Athenæum* for April 13, 1889.

strolling fellows at my door, they have frequently told me to my face, they could get more a-begging; and I once set a lusty fellow in the stocks for making the experiment." *

"One incident that occurred at Chadwell very much tickled Defoe's fancy, and he subsequently made use of it in order to illustrate what might happen if the High-fliers persisted in the persecution of the Dissenters. One day two of his brickmakers, who had quarrelled, fell to boxing. One got the other down and beat him unmercifully; thereupon the prostrate man cried out, "Pay me, Peter; pay me, Peter—'twill be my turn by-and-by." Peter did his best, and being a strong fellow laid on sufficiently; but presently the other, seizing the opportunity of Peter's being out of breath, suddenly sprang up, and, Peter being below, "used him accordingly." This anecdote Defoe, with his compliments, commended to the study of the High-fliers.

For his first bankruptcy, in 1692, Defoe has had little sympathy; but for this second, when his pantile works went wrong, he was at any rate not mainly to blame. To his prosperity before this crash he makes many allusions. In one place he says : "I had once a tenant in Westminster (though the world has since taken care I shall have no tenant anywhere) who was a butcher."

24.—THE COMMENCEMENT OF THE *REVIEW* (19TH FEBRUARY, 1704).

It was whilst in Newgate that Defoe commenced the most voluminous work of his life—his newspaper,

* " Giving Alms no Charity."

the *Review*, which in its first stage was a sheet of eight small quarto pages. After the first two numbers, it was reduced in size to four pages of smaller print. ⸒At first the issue was weekly; after four numbers it became bi-weekly, and so remained for a year.

The *Review* had a double mission. It sought both to instruct and to amuse. There was a serious department, and a department devoted to nonsense, gossip, and scandal. The design of the former was to give a true picture, drawn with " an impartial and exact historical pen," of the affairs of all the States of Europe. He was writing a history, sheet by sheet; and the brilliancy of his method, the vivacity of his style, and above all, his pugnacity " and his manifest delight in the strife of tongues," at once made him *facile princeps* among the journalists of his day. He exasperated his enemies to the very last degree. " The insolence of the *Review* is intolerable!" writes Lesley in No. 124 of the *Rehearsal.* " He studies to provoke in the most affronting manner he can think of. And then he cries Peace and Union, Gentlemen, and lay aside your Heats!"

To Louis and the French the *Review* continued, throughout its whole career, consistently antagonistic. Nothing was to be avoided that would thwart their plans—any stick to beat a Frenchman. At the same time, as in everything else that he did, Defoe was always a free-lance; and Dissenters as well as Highfliers, Whigs as well as Tories, often felt its keen point. On all occasions the Ishmael would out. The annoyance he had caused the Dissenters by " The Shortest Way" did not prevent him from indulging in more

jeux d'esprit of the same kind. As has been pertinently
said, " He had no tenderness for the feelings of such of
his brethren as had not his own robust sense of humour
and boyish glee in the free handling of dangerous
weapons." What other Protestant, for example, would
have had the cool audacity to extol the Grand Monarque
for the revocation of the Edict of Nantes ? But Defoe
tossed knives about as if they were gingerbread.

The non-serious portion of the *Review* was entitled
" Mercure Scandale ; or Advice from the Scandalous
Club, being a weekly history of Nonsense, Imper-
tinence, Vice, and Debauchery." Under this heading
current scandals are noticed, the club being represented
as a tribunal before which offenders were brought, their
cases heard, and sentence passed upon them ; but, unlike their successors, the inimitable light papers in the
Tatler and the *Spectator*, these effusions, nowadays,
utterly fail to interest. In its own day, however, the
Review was enormously popular. It was stolen, pirated,
and hawked about everywhere.

The rivals of Defoe's *Review* were Tutchin's
Observator (organ of the extreme Whigs), begun
April 1, 1702, and Lesley's *Rehearsal* (organ of the
extreme Tories), begun August 2, 1704.

25.--EIGHTEEN NEWGATE PAMPHLETS.—THE FALL OF "DON
DISMAL."

WORKS: 42.—The Shortest Way to Peace and Union.
 43.—The Sincerity of the Dissenters Vindicated.
 44.—An Inquiry into the Case of Mr. Asgill's General Translation.
 45.—A Challenge of Peace.
 46.—Some Remarks on the First Chapter in Dr. Davenant's Essays.
 47.—The Liberty of Episcopal Dissenters in Scotland truly stated.
 48.—Peace without Union.
 49.—The Dissenter's Answer to the High Church Challenge.
 50.—An Essay on the Regulation of the Press.

WORKS: 51.—A Serious Inquiry into this Grand Question : Whether a Law to prevent
Occasional Conformity, etc.
52.—The Parallel.
53.—The Layman's Sermon upon the late Storm.
54.—Royal Religion.
55.—Legion's Humble Address to the Lords.
56.—More Short Ways with the Dissenters.
57.—The Dissenters Misrepresented and Represented.
58.—A New Test of the Church of England's Honesty.
59.—The Storm.

During the eighteen months he was in Newgate,
Defoe, besides starting his *Review*, wrote no fewer
than eighteen pamphlets. In "The Shortest Way
to Peace and Union" (29th July, 1703) he endeavours to convince Dissenters that there ought to be
an established religion in connection with the State;
and that the Church of England is not only the most
fit, but the only capable institution for that supremacy.
Defoe had no quarrel with the Church of England
as the Established Church; it was only the High-
flying section of that body that he found so much
fault with. "The Sincerity of the Dissenters Vindicated" (18th September) is the answer to a pamphlet defending Occasional Conformity, by the Rev.
James Owen, a Dissenting minister of Shrewsbury.
Then, for a change, comes an answer to "the most
exquisitely and accomplishedly-whimsical Mr. Asgill,"
a Barrister in the Temple, who had written a pamphlet
to prove that it is possible for men to go to Heaven
without dying. Defoe's rejoinder, "An Enquiry into
the case of Mr. Asgill's General Translation," easily
shatters Asgill's arguments, but at the same time
deals gently and respectfully with Mr. Asgill and his
innocent delusion, at which, twenty years after, we
still find Defoe poking fun.*

* *See* "System of Magic."

In his "Challenge of Peace," dedicated to the
Queen (23rd November, 1703), Defoe (peaceful man!)
begs people all round to avoid heats and divisions.
It's those bad High-fliers, he tells her Majesty, "those
church vultures, ecclesiastical harpies," who make all
the pother.   The Dissenters were always content, and
ever will be pleased to have the power rest in the
hands of the Church."   But as we read these words
a murmur seems to arise from a thousand meeting-
houses, "Speak for yourself, Daniel."   Instead, however, of paying heed to the exhortations of Defoe or
anyone else for peace, the Tory House of Commons
set the occasional conformity pot a-bubbling again by
reviving the Bill for making occasional conformity
illegal, and not only so, but on the 7th of December
(1703) passed it.   It was happily, however, once more
rejected by the House of Lords.   On December 10th
Defoe published " Some Remarks on the First Chapter
in Dr. Davenant's Essays," a confutation of the argument in a recent tract by Dr. Charles Davenant, that
it is dangerous to appeal to the people ; though with
Davenant personally—"a very cloudy-looking man,
fat, of middle stature "—Defoe was on excellent terms.
Defoe's pamphlet was subsequently re-issued with a
new title : " Original Right ; or the Reasonableness of
Appeals to the People."   His " Liberty of Episcopal
Dissenters in Scotland truly stated " is an attack on
the aggressiveness of Episcopalians in the North.
Wherever appeared the cloven foot of the High-
flier, there was Defoe to hoot at him.   "Peace
without Union " (December, 1703) is a reply to a
pamphlet by Sir Humphrey Mackworth, who, like

Mr. Astell, supposed that if the Bill for Preventing
Occasional Conformity were passed, and the Dissenters were bound hand and foot, everything in England
would be *couleur-de-rose*. That, declares Defoe, is
not the way to obtain peace at home, and he who
thinks it is must imagine that "the Dissenters are
very blind, ignorant people." In short, though Defoe
disapproved of occasional conformity, he objected to
the Bill that would prevent it. If those High-fliers
would only be less bigoted and let the Dissenters
alone, all would be well! Then the learned and
dangerous Lesley, the High Church St. Dominic, dealt
his blow : " The Wolf Stript of his Shepherd's Clothing." The mildest he can say is, " For God's sake,
ye scoundrelly schismatics, tell us what you will conform to ? Give us a list of 'such indifferent things'
which, if granted, will bring you back to mother
church." Whereupon Defoe, ignoring the intolerant
tone of his adversary, replies (" The Dissenter's Answer to the High Church Challenge ") 5th
January, "Get the Convocation to pass it into an
Act, that the Church will not quarrel with us about
habits, ceremonies, liturgies, and ordinations — the
schism be upon us if we do not conform." In January these pestilent High-fliers are again at their
tricks. This time they would gag the Press. Daniel
is at them in a moment, and with his " Essay on
the Regulation of the Press " mangles their argument
like a bull-dog. Another pamphlet on the occasional
conformity question (" A Serious Inquiry into this
Grand Question, etc.") is tripped up by " The
Parallel : or Persecution of Protestants the shortest

way to prevent the growth of Popery in Ireland," in which Defoe shows that a recent Act of Parliament "requiring all Protestant Dissenters in Ireland, holding any office under Government, to conform to the Established Church," was, owing to its certainty to create disunion among the Protestants of Ireland, only playing into the hands of the Papists. Those High-fliers again! Always at it!

On the 27th of November, 1703, had occurred perhaps the most violent and destructive storm of modern times. The Great Storm, as it is called, swept the country from Trent to the Channel. Houses were unroofed, steeples blown down, stacks of corn scattered to the winds, vessels wrecked, and upwards of eight hundred persons drowned. Altogether, it is estimated that eight hundred houses, four hundred windmills, and a quarter of a million timber-trees were thrown down, a hundred churches unroofed, and twelve hundred vessels destroyed. Over fifteen thousand sheep perished by the overflowing of the Severn alone. On the whole, probably it was pleasanter that night in Newgate than outside. On the 24th of February Defoe improves the occurrence with "A Layman's Sermon on the Late Storm," which he thinks a severe animadversion upon the feuds and storms of parties, kept up with such unaccountable fury in the nation. This was followed by another panegyric on his late beloved master—"Royal Religion : being some Enquiry after the Piety of Princes. With Remarks on a Book entituled, 'A Form of Prayers us'd by King William ' "; the book referred to being a small pamphlet lately issued by

Dr. Moore, Bishop of Norwich. From personal knowledge, Defoe is able to state that William was a prince "of the greatest piety, sincerity, and unfeigned religion." In " Legion's Humble Address to the Lords " (April, 1704) the House of Lords is applauded as a bulwark of English liberty, in that it had thrown out the Bill against occasional conformity. The despotic conduct of the Tory House of Commons is denounced in the plainest language ; and the Lords are urged to persevere. " We resolve," it concludes, "as one man to live and die with you : our name is Million, and we are more." The exasperated Tories offered a reward of one hundred pounds for the apprehension of the author, and fifty pounds for the printer ; but though suspicion fell on Defoe, nothing further was done. It must be distinctly understood that the House of Commons did not at this time represent public opinion. Thanks to bribery, rotten boroughs, the high qualification for voters, and a hundred other abuses, the Commons no more represented the people than the Lords did ; and it was fortunate for England that just then bigotry and intolerance were confined to the lower house. Defoe was of opinion that the Lords had saved the nation.

At the end of April, 1704, a beam of bright light flashed into Defoe's " dungeon." The object for which he had so long intrigued, and for which he had written his " Shortest Way," had been attained. The Earl of Nottingham and his Tory friends, the Duke of Buckingham and Sir Edward Seymour, having offended the Queen, were put from power, and Robert Harley reigned in their stead—changes of ministry in those days being effected by the mere word of the sovereign, without consideration for the strength of any party in the House.

Unlike the "chief butler" who forgat Joseph, Robert Harley had no sooner returned to office than he sought to benefit the man to whom his party had been so greatly indebted, and who—let that be said too—might be able to render still further services. "While," says Defoe, "I lay friendless and distressed in the prison of Newgate, my family ruined, and myself without hope of deliverance, a message was brought me from a person of honour, who, till that time, I never had the least acquaintance with or knowledge of, other than by fame, or by sight, as we know men of quality by seeing them on public occasions. The message was by word of mouth, thus: 'Pray, ask that gentleman what I can do for him?'" In return to "this kind and generous message," Defoe took up his pen, and wrote, in the words of the blind man in the gospel, "Lord, that I may receive my sight!"

A mild and amiable man—"the Dragon," as by contraries his friends Swift and Pope called him— Robert Harley, notwithstanding the milk of human kindness which permeated him, was bent, above all things, on the attainment of one object, namely, the elevation of Robert Harley. In small things as well as big, everything that he did was done with a view to bringing about that sweet consummation. If he himself went to church, he was careful to send his family to the meeting-house; if a High Churchman sat on this side his dinner-table, a churchman "of another sort" sat on the other. If he was anxious to serve and secure the services of the radical Defoe, he was equally desirous of securing the services of the High-flying Dean Swift, whom he would carry "in his coach to country ale-houses," and with whom he would "play games of counting poultry on the road," or "who should first see a cat or an old woman." He even learned dancing—homely, and even clownish, as were his habits—in order to make himself more acceptable at Court. When it did not clash with his schemes, Harley was everything that a lover of liberty could wish. When it did clash, Harley was very sorry, but liberty had to give him the wall.

Thanks to Harley's representations, the Queen at once sent assistance to Defoe's wife and family; but beyond this nothing was done for four months.

In " More Short Ways with the Dissenters " (28th April, 1704), Defoe meets the recent attacks against Dissenting academies made by the Rev. Samuel Wesley, father of the great Wesley, and defends the character of his old tutor, the Rev. Charles' Morton. "The Dissenters Misrepresented and Represented" (May, 1704) and "A New Test of the Church of England's Honesty" (July 15) are two more buffets administered to the High-fliers. Defoe next took upon himself to write a history of and a semi-political poem on the late dreadful "Storm" (15th August), in which he contrived to knock a little more flour out of the wigs of the High-fliers. The account of the storm itself is "a most minute and circumstantial record, containing many letters from eye-witnesses of what happened in their immediate neighbourhood,"

H

and there is not the least doubt both that the letters
are genuine and that the other facts were obtained
from his numerous friends; for he had friends—and
staunch ones—in many parts of the country. This
work is particularly valuable as being the first of that
fine series of authentic narratives by Defoe, which
includes " Mrs. Veal," the " Journal of the Plague,"
and the " Memoirs of a Cavalier," all of which are to
all intents and purposes truth and fact, Defoe's share
in them being merely that of the consummate artist.

26.—DEFOE, SWIFT, ADDISON, AND STEELE.—DEFOE'S RELEASE FROM NEWGATE (AUG., 1704).

During the first half of 1704 the four greatest
prose writers of the period—Defoe, Swift, Addison,
and Steele—were all in London. Defoe's age was
forty-five ; Swift's, thirty-seven ; Addison and Steele
were thirty-two.

Defoe, who was still cased in his " stone doublet,"
we may for the moment leave.

Jonathan Swift, chaplain to the Earl of Berkeley
and Vicar of Laracor, in Ireland, had already distinguished himself with his pen, having this year written
and published " The Battle of the Books " and the
" Tale of a Tub." He paid several visits to London,
one extending from November, 1703, to 1704, and
another in April, 1705. With Addison, Swift was
at this time both intimate and friendly, as witness
the following entry in his note-book :—

" Tav^{rn} Addison 2s. 6d. Tav^{rn} Addison 1s. Tav^n Add^{sn} 1s. 6d.
Tav^{rn} Addis^n 4s. 9d. Tav^n Addis^n 2s. 6d."

Addison sent Swift a copy of his " Travels in Italy," with the inscription—

" To Dr. Jonathan Swift, the most Agreeable Companion, the Truest Friend, and the Greatest Genius of his Age, this Book is presented by his most Humble Servant, the Authour."

Joseph Addison had been in England since September, 1703, and it was in August, 1704, that, at the request of Lord Halifax, he wrote the poem on the victory of Blenheim (" The Campaign," published 14th December, 1704), which brought him fame and proved the stepping-stone to his greatness.

Richard Steele was as yet known only as a play-writer. His *Funeral* had appeared in 1701, *The Lying Lover* in 1703, and now in 1704 he was to produce *The Tender Husband.*

With none of his three great contemporaries was Defoe personally connected. He was not of their circle. He may be compared to the island of Great Britain, they to the Continent, which comprised, besides themselves, such fair territories as Gay, Congreve, and Pope. And as the dealings of Great Britain with the Continent were mostly of a belligerent nature, so, when Defoe did pay attention to his literary peers, it was usually to cross swords with them.

At Addison he again and again discharged the shafts of his wit. In the " Consolidator "—presently to be dealt with—he jeers at the man who had refused to write " The Campaign " " till he had £200 a year secured to him "; and the " Double Welcome to the

H 2

Duke of Marlborough" has the same thing in
verse—

> " Mecænas has his modern fancy strung—
> You fix'd his pension first, or he had never sung."

Between Defoe and Steele there were also
several lively skirmishes; and Swift, as we shall
subsequently see, hated Defoe as only he knew how
to hate.

It is, however, when we turn from personal
questions to a study of the writings of these four
great masters that we most see the necessity of taking
some notice of the other three, although dealing particularly with only one. Defoe's *Review* was the
forerunner, and probably the suggestor, of the *Spectator* and *Tatler*; and if Defoe had not written the
"Consolidator," Swift, much as he affected to de-
spise Defoe, would never have written "Gulliver."
Other interesting connecting links among these
head-and-shoulder men will be pointed out as we
proceed.

Four months had now passed since Harley had
sent to Defoe "in his dungeon," to inquire what could
be done for him; and the time was at last come when
it was safe to act. His own pieces on the great chess-
board being well placed, especially his queen, and
one or two important outworks of his enemy having
been taken, Harley was now able to make the risky
move of delivering Defoe from his prison-house. Had
he done so before, all Torydom would have openly
branded him as the abettor of the writer of the
"Shortest Way"; and even as it was, innuendoes were

not wanting. But clever, wily, tricky, shilly-shallying
—but say, too, cultured and good-hearted—Harley
minded not these; a knight—at the present juncture
one of the most useful pieces on the board—had been
freed from an awkward position, and the only thing
to do now was to make use of him.

CHAPTER V.

AT BURY ST. EDMUNDS (AUG., 1704—OCT., 1704).

27.—HIS FRIEND JOHN FRANSHAM.

WORKS: 60.—An Elegy on the Author of "The True-Born Englishman." 15th
Aug., 1704.
61.—A true state of the Difference between Sir George Rooke, Kt., and
William Colepeper, Esq. 22nd Aug., 1704.
62.—A Hymn to Victory. 29th Aug., 1704.
63.—The Protestant Jesuit Unmasked. 12th Sept., 1704.

IN order to avoid the public gaze, and also to re-
cuperate, Defoe repaired in August, 1704, to Bury St.
Edmunds, where he took up his abode in a handsome
residence called Cupola House. The ancient town
of Bury, even in Defoe's time, had many interesting
associations. Defoe himself, years after, eulogistically
described it as "a town famed for its pleasant situation and wholesome air, the Montpelier of Suffolk,
and perhaps of England; famous also for the number
of gentry who reside in the vicinity, and for the polite
and agreeable conversation of the company resorting
there."* In short, it was a fashionable health-resort.
The most conspicuous buildings were the magnificent
and unique Abbey gate of 1327, the beautiful churches
St. James's and St. Mary's, the Angel Inn, the Guildhall, the Abbot's Bridge, and the Town Hall.

Being a Presbyterian, Defoe naturally fraternised

* "Tour thro' Gr. Brit.," i.

CUPOLA HOUSE (DEFOE'S HOUSE AT BURY).

(From a photograph by W. S. Spanton, 16, Abbeygate Street, Bury St. Edmunds.)

with his co-religionists in the town. The Presbyterians of Bury, who worshipped in a house, or rather
a house that had been converted into a chapel, in
Churchgate Street, were ministered to by the Rev.
Samuel Bury, a very popular preacher, and the re-
cognised leader of Nonconformity in the district.
Owing to the great increase in the number of Mr.
Bury's hearers, the old meeting-house subsequently
became inadequate ; so it was pulled down, and a new
edifice, which still stands, was erected on its site.
This, however, was in 1711, seven years after Defoe
had quitted the town.

Shortly after his arrival in Bury, Defoe published
a poem which had been written during his confinement, "An Elegy on the Author of the True-born
Englishman," in the preface of which he complains of
the ill-usage he was still receiving from his enemies.
" Had the scribbling world been pleased to leave me
where they found me," says he, " I had left them and
Newgate both together ; and as I am metaphorically
dead, had been effectually so as to satires and pamphlets. 'Tis really something hard that, after all the
mortification they think they have put upon a poor
abdicated author, in their scurrilous street-ribaldry and
bear-garden usage, some in prose and some in their
terrible lines they call verse, they cannot yet be quiet."
" Their terrible lines they call verse," is one of those
delicious innocencies that constantly crop up in Defoe's
writings. When one remembers that no man inflicted
on the world a greater number of terrible lines called
verse than Defoe himself, the feeling of sympathy gives
place to one of amusement.

What the restrictions placed upon Defoe when he was released from prison were we do not know. All we can learn from his own pen is as follows :—

> " Memento Mori here I stand,
>   With silent lips but speaking hand ;
>   A walking shadow of a Poet,
>   But bound to hold my tongue and never-show it.
>   A monument of injury,
>   A sacrifice to legal t(yrann)y."

and

> " To seven long years of silence I betake,
>   Perhaps by then I may forget to speak."

But we must remember that on leaving prison he obtained an appointment with a pension from the Queen, and was employed on secret services; which has led to the suggestion that in writing these words he was only throwing dust in the eyes of his enemies. In the same poem he proclaims his hardship in that he had been "abandoned" by the Whigs; and he had reason to complain, seeing that they had permitted him to lie so many months in prison; nevertheless, in writing that, too, he was probably throwing dust, for it is certain that he was now working for Harley.

In respect, however, to another hardship of which Defoe complains he has our real sympathy. Not content with pirating the works of "The True-born Englishman," the mercenary printers of London, with a view to pecuniary advantage, now annoyed him by affixing his name to works with which he had no connection.

> " The mob of wretched writers stand,
>   With storms of wit in every hand ;

They bate my mem'ry in the street,
And charge me with the credit of their wit.
I bear the scandal of their crimes ;
My name 's the hackney title of the times.
Hymn, song, lampoon, ballad, and pasquinade,
My recent memory invade ;
My muse must be the whore of poetry,
And all Apollo's bastards laid to me."*

Defoe had nourished the hope that whilst he was at Bury his political enemies would let him alone ; but in that he was disappointed.

Dyer, the news-writer, spread it abroad that he had fled from justice. Fox, the bookseller, published that he had deserted his security. Stephen, a state messenger, everywhere said that he had a warrant for his seizure.

Defoe notices the slander that he had absconded and fled from justice in his *Review* for the 7th of October, in which he said that the Government knew where he was, and that he should be always ready to show himself to the faces of his enemies. In an unpublished letter to a friend at Shrewsbury, dated 11th October, 1704, he mentions that the malice of Dyer and the others made him think it necessary to come up to town and show himself—which he did ; and having informed the Secretary of State where he was, and when he would appear, obtained answer that there was no need to fear—that he had not transgressed.

From Defoe's pen about this time came a tract, written in the interest of his friend, Mr. Colepeper

* Elegy on the Author of " The True-born Englishman."

(known to us as one of the Kentish petitioners), who
was engaged in a political quarrel with Sir George
Rooke, a man whom the very soul of Defoe abhorred.
The title is, "A True State of the Difference between
Sir George Rooke, Kt., and William Colepeper, Esq."

While in prison Defoe had commenced, and made
some progress with, a poetical work on government,
"Jure Divino." He gave the finishing touches to it
at Bury St. Edmunds, and now (September, 1704)
advertised it to be published by subscription in near
one hundred sheets folio, at the price of ten shillings.
Among those who got him subscribers was his friend
John Fransham, of Norwich. The letters between
Defoe and Fransham, written about this time, were
first published in *Notes and Queries*, April, 1875.

Besides the works already enumerated, Defoe also
wrote at Bury "A Hymn to Victory" (August 29),
and a pamphlet, entitled, "The Protestant Jesuit
Unmasked" (12th September). The former is in
praise of the successes of Marlborough, which he
attributes, under God, to the change of government,
nor does he miss the opportunity to well lash the
leading members of the late ministry, Seymour,
Nottingham, and Rochester, to whom he owed his
imprisonment and his great losses.

"The Protestant Jesuit Unmasked" (12th September) is a reply to High Church Lesley, who had
endeavoured, with his pamphlet "Cassandra" (in
allusion to the famous legendary prophetess of evil),
to frighten people "with the fatal consequences of
moderation in church and state."

More malicious reports were now spread about

concerning Defoe ; and to what had been said before was added the declaration that he had been searched for by messengers but could not be found.

On his return to London Defoe inserted a notice in the *Review* of November 4th, declaring that what had been said about him was false, and offering a reward of twenty pounds for the discovery of " the author or publisher of any of those written news-letters, in which those reports were printed."

Said Mr. Fransham, in his letter to Defoe, 10th November, 1704 :—

" It was with no small Sattisfaction that I read your Justification in your *Review* wch I doubt not on the other hand prov'd as great a Mortification to Dyer. I had read it to several Gentlemen (before I receiv'd your Letter) in the chief Coffee-house here, where we have it as oft as it comes out and is approv'd of as the politest paper we have to entertain us with."

CHAPTER VI.

ELECTIONEERING.

IN November, 1704, Defoe plunged into a controversy with Sir Humphrey Mackworth, who was introducing into the House of Commons a Bill for the employment of the poor, the principal object of which was "to establish in every parish a parochial manufactory, and to provide a fund for its support." Convinced that Sir Humphrey's proposal was a mischievous one, Defoe penned his well-known " Giving Alms no Charity," in which he insists :—1st, That there is in England more labour than hands to perform it, and, consequently, a want of people, not of employment; 2nd, No man in England, of sound limbs and senses, can be poor merely for want of work ; 3rd, All workhouses for employing the poor, as now they are employed, serve to the ruin of families and the increase of the poor; 4th, It is a regulation of the poor that is wanted, not a setting them to work. What we want laws for, he says, is to make the people industrious, sober, and thrifty. There is plenty of work for all if they will do it ; and everyone would be comfortable if he would only take care of his earnings instead of running with them to the ale-house. " I once," he said, " paid six or seven men together on a Saturday night—the least ten shillings, and some thirty shillings—for work, and have seen them go with it directly to the ale-house, lie there till Monday, spend every penny, and run in debt to boot, without giving a farthing to their families, though all of them had wives and children. From hence come poverty, parish charges, and beggary." What is wanted, Sir Humphrey, is to apply proper remedies to these evils, and not to set up in every parish manufactories for which there is no occasion whatever. Thus, the question of the poor laws agitated politicians in the days of Queen Anne much as it does politicians in the reign of Queen Victoria ; and the worst of it is, we don't seem much nearer a solution to the difficulty.

McCulloch (" Lit. of Polit. Econ."), whilst granting that "Giving Alms no Charity" is written with considerable cleverness, insists that Defoe's arguments are not so conclusive as some have supposed : " The truth is, that in matters of this sort Defoe was quite as prejudiced and purblind as the bulk of those around him."

The Tories now introduced into the House of Commons, for the third time, the Occasional Conformity Bill ; and, in the hopes of forcing it through the Lords, they endeavoured to tack it to the Land-Tax Bill, which, owing to their being in the majority, they would have done but for the resistance of the Whig Ministry. The effort to deprive the Lords of their legislative authority, by tacking an obnoxious measure to a Money Bill, brought great unpopularity upon the one hundred and thirty-four Tackers. They were ridiculed and lampooned, and speedily became "a bye-word and a hissing to the whole nation."

Defoe, who had left Newgate with shattered health, had been in hopes that the rest at Bury would set him up. But such was not the case; and towards the end of October, shortly after his return to London, he was prostrated with an illness which lasted over two months. The *Review*, however, went on as usual, his own contributions being dictated, no doubt, to an amanuensis.

Defoe had already sung the praises of the Duke of Marlborough in "A Hymn to Victory," and he now heaped more praise on the victorious general in a congratulatory poem entitled " The Double Welcome to the Duke of Marlborough," published 9th January, 1705. In his *Review*, vol. ii., p. 233, he alludes to the national rejoicings which the Duke's victories had evoked: the Church kept holyday, the Queen made a procession to St. Paul's, the clergy sang anthems, and the people gave thanks. Apparently it was in this great public function that Robinson Crusoe took part ("Serious Reflections"), though he was not favourably impressed by it.

We have seen how, spite of drawbacks, Defoe pressed on with his work; but the most indomitable spirits are quelled by illness, and Defoe now announced that the *Review* would cease at the end of the first yearly volume. Yielding to the solicitations of his friends, however, he consented to continue it; and it was kept up for seven more years.

An anonymous admirer sent him a large sum of money to distribute at his discretion among the poor. This also gave him encouragement, and in the number for February 20th, 1705, he describes his mode of distribution. Henceforth it was to be *A Review of the Affairs of France* with observations on affairs at home, and a tri-weekly instead of a bi-weekly. About the same time he published a second volume of his collected works, with a few new pieces.

29.—THE MEN IN THE MOON.—A BEAUTIFUL LETTER (TO FRANSHAM).

> WORKS : 66.—Persecution Anatomised. 22nd Feb., 1705.
> 67.—*Review*, vol. 1. 24th Feb., 1705.
> 68.—The Consolidator. 26th Mar., 1705.
> 69.—A Journey to the World in the Moon.
> 70.—A Letter from the Man in the Moon.
> 71.—A Second Journey to the World in the Moon.
> 72.—The Experiment (Abraham Gill). 27th Mar., 1705.

In " Persecution Anatomised " (Feb. 22), another discharge at the High-fliers and their persecuting Bill for the Prevention of Occasional Conformity, Defoe shows that he is still smarting under a sense of the cruel injuries that so recently had been inflicted upon him. He was not a man of a revengeful spirit ; but when he remembered Newgate, it took no sting out of his utterances.

It then occurred to him to satirise the times by the medium of a pretended account of the Men in the Moon ; and in March 1705 appeared " The Consolidator : or Memoirs of Sundry Transactions from the World in the Moon. Translated from the Lunar language, by the author of ' The True-born Englishman.' " Its passages of well-pointed satire, and the exuberance of imagination that it displays have found admirers ; but the " Consolidator " has now lost most of its interest. In the Lunar language Defoe shoots his arrows at the follies of the times, and chastises individuals. Poets, wits, metaphysicians, and free-thinkers, all feel his heavy hand. He spares neither Dryden nor D'Urfey, Addison nor Prior, Malabranche nor Hobbes. Perhaps the chief interest of the " Con-solidator " to us lies in the fact that from it Swift got a good many of the ideas which he subsequently embodied in " Gulliver."

Shortly after the appearance of the " Consolidator,' Defoe issued several papers which may be regarded as appendices to it—namely, " A Journey to the World in the Moon," " A Letter from the Man in the Moon to the Author of the True-born English-man," and " A Second and more Strange Journey to the World in the Moon," all three of which consist partly of fresh matter and partly of extracts from the " Consolidator." The subject of the men in the moon is also dealt with in several of the *Reviews.*

A good deal of commotion had about this time been caused in the religious world by the case of Abraham Gill, a clergyman of the Church of England, who had ceased to use the Liturgy, and had become to all intents and purposes a Dissenter. As the place in which he conducted his services was a " privileged chapel," exempt from ecclesiastical jurisdiction, Gill did not think he was called upon to renounce his living. The rector of the parish, however, endea-voured to evict him, and a clerical magistrate charged him with being "an idle vagabond," and forcibly impressed him as a soldier.

The London Dissenters then took the matter up, and Defoe wrote a pamphlet entitled "The Experiment : or the Shortest Way with the Dissenters exemplified. Being the case of Mr. Abraham Gill, a Dissenting minister of the Isle of Ely, and a full account of his being sent for a Soldier by Mr. Fern (an Ecclesiastical Justice of the Peace) and other Conspirators. To the eternal honour of the temper and moderation of High Church principles."

Twenty copies of this tract were sent to Mr. Fransham for the "topping Dissenters" of Norwich, and Fransham's acknowledgment of the receipt of them drew from Defoe a letter which reveals a beauty of character that his critics have rarely given him credit for. It bears the very stamp of sincerity, and shows its author to have been a true Christian, seeking above all things the furtherance of the interests of his Master.

"You can give me no greater pleasure," he tells Fransham, "than to hear that anything I can do or have done in this world is useful and helps to forward that good which every honest man ought to wish, and which I believe I was brought into the world and am suffered to live in it only to perform."

That his work was of God, "whose immediate hand by wonderful steps" had led him through wildernesses of troubles, Defoe felt assured.

"This," he continues, "is the glory of his infinite wisdom that brings to pass the great ends appointed by his foreknowledge by the agency of us his most despicable instruments and the interposition of the minutest circumstances.

I

"To him be all the praise both of his own work and our little, little, very little share in it, and let the success of his service encourage all the lovers of truth to stand up for the Lord against the mighty."

The High Church party attempted to justify their proceedings against Gill by bringing forward charges against his private character.   Here was Gill's chance, and all he had to do was to vindicate himself in a court of justice.   Very unwisely (for the evidence is that the charges were trumpery) Gill neglected to do so, the consequence being that Defoe and the other London Dissenters, feeling they could no longer contend for a man so blind to his own interests, reluctantly left him to fight his own battle.

30.—LORD HALIFAX, THE ENGLISH MECAENAS.—DEFOE'S LETTERS
TO HIM (APRIL AND JULY, 1705,.

WORKS: 73.—Advice to all Parties.
74.—The Dyet of Poland, a Poem.

The thoughts of the country being now turned to the approaching General Election, Defoe, as usual, raised the cry of "Peace!"   Churchman and Dissenter, strive after peace!   He would do anything, he said, to promote peace.   "This is my ultimate end,—ought to be every Christian's wish,—and if an angel from Heaven preached any other doctrine to us, to me he shall be accursed."   In furtherance of his great desire he published a tract entitled, "Advice to all Parties" (30th April, 1705), written before the election of three years previous, which contains at least one very beautiful thought that all should treasure who have any wish for Christian reunion :—

"The Church of England and the Dissenters have but one interest, one foundation, and but one end. The moderate Church-men and the charitable Dissenters are the same denomination of Christians, and all the difference which now, looked at near the eye, shows large, if viewed at the distance of Heaven, shows not itself."

Concerning Popery, he says amusingly—

"Popery and slavery will never go down with this nation. Popery is so formidable a thing, that the very name of it would set the whole nation in an uproar. Those who do not understand it hate it by tradition; and I believe there are a hundred thousand plain country fellows in England, who would spend their blood against Popery, that do not know whether it be a man or a horse."

"The Dyet of Poland" (May, 1705), a poem of sixty pages, is merely English politics in Polish guise. The names of persons are throughout the poem obscured under Polish forms and terminations, but the characters are easily distinguishable. Halifax, Russell, Somers, Harley, and Godolphin are praised, Nottingham, Rochester and Seymour castigated, and, as in almost everything else in the political way of Defoe's, William III. (Sobieski) is held up to love and honour.

Among the very few letters of Defoe that have been preserved (twenty-four) are three written to Lord Halifax in April and July, 1705.

Charles Montague, Earl of Halifax, poet and statesman, was born at Horton House, four miles from Olney, his most important poetical achievement being "The Town and Country Mouse" (1687), of which he was joint author with Prior. To the robust-

ness of his intellect and the smoothness of his verse
Defoe pays a tribute in " Jure Divino " :—

"So sweet his voice, and all his thoughts so strong,
So smooth his numbers, and so soft his song."

We owe no thanks to Halifax for having been the
chief factor in the establishment of the National Debt,
but balanced against that is the fact that he was one
of the originators of the Bank of England.   In 1697
he obtained the Premiership, which, however, he was
obliged to relinquish shortly after.   In 1699 he was
created a peer, but during the whole of Anne's reign
he remained out of office.   From his liberality in
of patronising literature he won for himself the title
the English Mecaenas.   All the literary men of his
age sang his praises, except Swift and Pope, "who
forebore to flatter him in his life, and after his death
spoke of him, Swift with slight censure, and Pope, in
the character of Bufo, with acrimonious contempt." *
As Pope says, "he was fed with dedications," and
Tickell affirms that no dedication was unrewarded.

Defoe's first letter (5th April, 1705), the object of
which was to thank Halifax for favours, is chiefly
interesting because it contains the only existing
reference to any brother of Defoe's :—

"The proposal your Lordship was pleased to make by my
brother, the bearer, is exceeding pleasant to me to perform. . . .
But my misfortune is, the bearer, whose head is not that way, has
given me so imperfect an account that makes me your Lordship's
most humble petitioner for some hints to ground my observations
upon."

* Dr. Johnson.

Defoe would also be glad of "the name again of some book which his dull messenger forgot." Though not necessarily a fool, Defoe's brother does not appear to have been a genius.

Lord Halifax, though not in office, was evidently on the best of terms with the Whig Ministers, and Defoe expresses his desire to serve him. In the second letter, 16th July, 1705, with which were sent six copies of "The High Church Legion," an answer to the pamphlet of Dr. Drake, Defoe again thanks Lord Halifax for benefits.

The third letter (without date) refers to an interview, at the close of which his lordship placed in Defoe's hands a handsome sum of money, but without information from whom it had come. It was, of course, a reward from the Government for services rendered.

31.—EXETER AND THE WEST.—1,100 MILES ON HORSEBACK.—DOWN
WITH THE TACKERS (MAY, JUNE, 1705).

WORKS : 75.—The High Church Legion.
    76.—A Declaration without Doors.
    77.— Party Tyranny (Carolina).
    78.—An Answer to Lord Haversham's Speech.
    79.—Hymn to Peace.
    80.—Reply to a Pamphlet, entitled, "Lord Haversham's Vindication.
    81.—*Review*, vol. ii. 1st Jan., 1706.
    82.—The Case of Protestant Dissenters in Carolina.

In the British Museum is a long autograph letter (Birch's MSS., 4291) from Defoe to Harley, written the day after one of their meetings. It contains a request that Mr. Christopher Hurt (Defoe) may have leave to be absent on his private affairs for two months or more. The writer requests instructions,

and also a certificate to prevent his being questioned
or detained by meddlesome country justices. From
its reference to Defoe's poem, " The Dyet of Poland,"
the date of this letter is fixed for May, 1705, and,
shortly after, we find Defoe paying a visit to the
south-western counties, where he runs as much danger
of his life "as a grenadier upon a counterscarp," his
object being to promote by every means in his power
the election of such candidates as would support the
Ministry. His election cry, as we should expect, was
Peace, but Down with the Tackers (see § 28), and at
the Tackers and the High Church party he girded
perpetually. On this journey, undertaken on horseback, he was accompanied by "a friend and his
friend's servant," and he met with more insults, and
experienced more indignities than even he himself had
anticipated. High Churchism in the West did not
take to him kindly. At Weymouth, his letters, being
delivered to a wrong person by mistake, were shown
about the town, and one of them happening to contain
a scrap of news to the effect that somebody had
declared that the Queen had broken her coronation
oath, the booby of a mayor smelt sedition, and caused
all the persons he found had conversed with Defoe to
be hauled before the judges at Dorchester, where the
assizes happened to be going on, declaring that he had
discovered a " phanatick plot and a bloody design to
persuade folks to a peaceable rebellion," with the result
however, of being sent " home with a flea in his ear."
    At Exeter, this story being magnified and coloured,
certain persons misled the judge to the extent that
he was occasioned to remark in his charge to the jury,

that, to use Defoe's words, "a great party of *two men* are gone forth into the country to raise rebellion against the High Church, by earnestly pressing all the well-meaning people of England to adhere to the Queen's sober and healing admonitions and exhortations to peace and union," and he gave directions to apprehend them. Defoe happened then to be at Bideford, where he was unmolested; but on arriving at Tiverton, discovered that a Mr. Justice Stafford, of Crediton, had granted a warrant for his apprehension, which, however, was not utilised. But the most sapient magnate of all was a certain "Esquire S——," who, after having carefully issued a warrant for Defoe's capture, very thoroughly searched every house in the town except the one at which Defoe was known to have put up; and when he found that the dangerous intruder had left the neighbourhood, sent his warrant the contrary way. Such a character of Defoe was spread abroad, that when he showed himself, and the country people knew who it was, they began to look for the "cloven foot, the head, and the horns." On one occasion he "had the honour, with small difficulty, of convincing some gentlemen, over a bottle of wine, that the author of the *Review* was really no monster, but a conversable, sociable creature."

In all, Defoe had done 1,100 miles on horseback; and, spite of "Weymouth Gothams" hostile High-fliers and officious justices, arrived safely again in Cockaigne. But his dangers were not at an end, for owing to the freedom with which he had spoken his mind against the tactics of the enemy, he was not only subjected in London to scandal and abuse but even threatened with violence. Thirty letters were sent threatening his life. In reply, Defoe inquired in his *Review* whether the game was worth the candle? Everybody knows the fate of murderers.

"Indeed, gentlemen," he continues, "the mean, despicable author of this paper is not worth your attempting his correction at the price : goals, fetters, and gibbets, are odd melancholy things ; for a gentleman to *dangle out of the world in a string* has something so ugly, so awkward, and so disagreeable in it, that you cannot think of it without some regret ; and then the reflection will be very harsh, that this was for killing a poor mortified author, one that the government had killed before."

Despite these threats, Defoe moved about unguarded and unarmed, carrying nothing more formidable than a "little stick, not strong enough to correct a dog." Mr. Tutchin, who, as the author of the Whig "Observator," also came in for some threats, carried a "great oaken towel" (cudgel). But bullying threats of murder were not the only inconveniences Defoe had to put up with. He complains, among other things, of "crowds of sham actions and arrests; sleeping debts in trade of seventeen years' standing revived ; debts put in suit after contracts and agreements under hand and seal ; and, which is worse, writs taken out for debts without the knowledge of the creditor, and some after the creditor has been paid; diligent solicitations of persons not inclined to sue, pressing them to give him trouble"; the whole, could particulars be descended to, "too moving to be read." Defoe, however, had just then at least one satisfaction, for at the election the Tories were very badly beaten, with the result of a further weeding of them out of high places in the Administration.

Then arose the high cry of "The Church in Danger." Gird yourselves, ye High-fliers, for the Church is about to be given over to the tender mercies of the Dissenters! Nothing but the political extinction of Whigs and Dissenters can save her! So the Tory Dr. Drake and a host of others. Dr. Drake's pamphlet, published just before Defoe started on his Exeter tour, gets burnt by the common hangman, and a reward is offered for the discovery of the author and printer; but owing to insufficient evidence against him, Drake is unmolested. Defoe took a copy of it with him on his tour, mangled it in his Reviews, and on July 16th wrote a direct reply, "The High Church Legion," an "admirable defence of the Queen and Ministry," which, to quote Lee, "must have highly recommended him, for shortly after his return from the West he was introduced by Harley, became an attendant at his lordship's levées, was honoured by his confidence, and retained his friendship many years." From July to October Defoe published nothing but his Reviews. "A Declaration without Doors" (24th of October) is a pamphlet containing the substance of recent numbers of the *Review* dealing chiefly with matters relating to the Press. "Party Tyranny" is an exposure of the High-flier and his malpractices in Carolina, where Lord Granville, the Governor, was worrying the Dissenters just as his brother Fliers had done in England; and, thanks to the efforts of Defoe and others, the Queen declared Lord Granville's law null and void. Defoe *triumphans* !

Next comes the pen-and-ink duel with Lord

Haversham. His lordship, who since the change of
Ministry had joined the Tories, thought fit to make
a speech in the House of Lords on the state of the
nation, and in November, 1705, he printed it anonymously as a pamphlet. Defoe attacked it in his
Review, and subsequently published " A Complete
Answer to the Lord Haversham's Speech," in which
he observes : " The anonymous author "—Defoe knew
very well who the author was—" is nothing to me,
be he a lord or a tinker." This sent his lordship's
blood—only lately blued—up to boiling-point, and in
return he calls his antagonist "a mean and mercenary
prostitute"—a slave of the ministry, from whom he
received "both his encouragement and instructions.'
Now was Defoe's chance, and he belabours Lord
Haversham as only he knew how to belabour. But
notice how it all came about. Defoe first gives the
passer-by a sting with his whip (we find no fault with
him), the passer-by returns the compliment, and then
Defoe sets upon his antagonist in hearty style and
gives him a thorough good thrashing. That was his
way, but he never seemed aware that he himself was
always the aggressor. Among other things, he tells
his lordship, I had the honour to be trusted, esteemed,
and, much more than I deserved, valued, by the best
king England ever saw, and yet whose judgment I
cannot undervalue, because he gave his lordship "
(*i.e.*, Lord Haversham) "his honour and his dignity ;
which was, some time before, as mean as mine. But
Fate, that makes footballs of men, kicks some men
upstairs and some down ; some are advanced without
honour, others suppressed without infamy ; some

are raised without merit, some are crushed without crime; and no man knows by the beginning of things whether his course shall issue in a peerage or a pillory." Which nobody can deny. But it is much better that things were as they were; that John Thompson, who was nobody in particular, should be made Baron Thompson of Haversham, and bask in the smiles of prosperity; and that his antagonist, instead of blossoming into Lord Defoe, or Baron Defoe of Newington, should have done his term at Newgate.

"The Hymn to Peace" (Jan. 10, 1706) is a long Pindaric suggested by the movement in both Houses of Parliament against the faction cry of the Church being in danger. To us it is chiefly interesting on account of the peeps it gives into Defoe's personal history. The following, for example, is distinctly touching, and reminds, in respect to substance, of the well-known gem "My Mind to me a Kingdom is." Peace never visits Defoe. Says he:

> " When to the world thou mak'st a short return,
>   Me only thou hast scorned to shun ;
>   Me thou revisitest not ; but storms of men,
>   Voracious and unsatisfied as death,
>   Spoil in their hands and poison in their breath,
>   With rage of devils hunt me down,
>   And to abate my peace, destroy their own.
>   Brought up in teaching sorrow's school,
>   In peace and patience I profess my soul ;
>   Am master of my mind,
>   And there the heaven of satisfaction find. "

CHAPTER VII.

TO AND FROM SCOTLAND.

32.—THE "MELANCHOLY STORY" OF DEFOE'S EMBARRASSMENTS.
—HE PLACES HIS AFFAIRS IN THE HANDS OF THE BANK-
RUPTCY COMMISSIONERS.

WORKS : 83.—Remarks on the Bill to Prevent Frauds committed by Bankrupts.
      84.—An Essay at Removing National Prejudices against a Union with Scot-
          land. Part I. 4th May, 1706.
      85.—Ditto. Part II.
      86.—An Essay at Removing National Prejudices against a Union with
          England. Nov., 1706.
      87.—A Fourth Essay at Removing National Prejudices. Dec., 1706.
      88.—A Fifth Essay at Removing National Prejudices.
      89.—Two great Questions considered. Being a Sixth Essay at Removing
          National Prejudices. Jan., 1707.

EARLY in 1706 was brought into Parliament a
Bill entitled "An Act to Prevent Frauds committed by Bankrupts"; the acceptance of which,
both by his writings and personal solicitations, Defoe
did all in his power to bring about, and for one
reason, because he hoped himself to be largely bene-
fited by it. In his *Review* he pointed out the imperfections of the law as it at present stood, describing
the imprisonment without bail, or distinction of circumstances, and the power of creditors to punish a
debtor with life-long imprisonment for claims which
could never be paid, as barbarous and inhuman. He
also alludes to his own grievous losses from fraudulent
debtors, and insists that a distinction should be made
between those who are fraudulently bankrupt and those

who become bankrupt through no fault of their own.
To Defoe's gratification the Bill passed, and, on April
18th, he published an able pamphlet dealing with
the whole subject, and entitled, "Remarks on the
Bill to Prevent Frauds committed by Bankrupts."
His enemies said this was all very well, but why
did he not practise what he preached ; to which he
replied that he had practised what he preached, and in
the following letter to Mr. Fransham (May 24, 1706),
who inquired how these objectors were to be best
answered, he describes the ground upon which he
took his stand :—

"I am sorry to see you assaulted about my Integrity, and wonder
you should expect any man can be persuaded to believe a man
honest whom they lose by.

"I appeal to all the World, and in it to my worst Enemies for
these articles of my Honesty, and let any man in Trade shew better
if they can.

"1ˢᵗ If my Disaster was not from plain known inevitable causes
wᶜʰ human wisdom could not foresee nor human power prevent.

"2ᵈˡʸ If I did not first leave off early according to my advice now
to others, nay while my Estate was sufficient to pay all men their full
demand.

"3ᵈˡʸ If I did not immediately ofter a full surrender of all I had
in the World in Satisfaction to my Creditors.

"4ᵗʰˡʸ If after they had driven me to all extremities till all was
consumed and I had not 5ˢ in the World but by Providence and my
own Industry in the World I began to rise again I did not pay every
one according to my utmost ability.

"5ᵗʰˡʸ It notwithstanding this it has not cost me £5000 since I
have been in these Troubles to maintain my Liberty to work for
them and to defend myself against such as would have all their Debt
before others and indeed before I could get it."

Fransham having asked whether, besides reducing
his debts from £17,000 to £5,000, as declared in
his letter to Lord Haversham, he had likewise paid

some people at Yarmouth in full, as had been re-
ported, he answers :—

"As to people paid at Yarmouth I cannot but admire you should
suffer yourself to be prevail'd upon to bring that as a proof of my
honesty wch is a snare laid for me that finding some people paid
more than others they may haue room to complain and pretend to
take out a Commission of Bankrupt to recover it again.

"The thing is true in Fact, and as true that these people to
whom I have been so particular are now the only people who pursue
me so close that *I must at last I doubt quit the kingdom unless
reliev'd by this late Act of Parliament in wch I am not yet sure that I
shall find neither.*

"I have not time to enlarge on *this melancholy story, wch is
perhaps the severest ever you heard.* I desire to submit, but methinks
people that call themselves protestants should be content to take all
a man have and not pursue him to death."

Defoe's case was, indeed, a hard one. He had
been in retreat (as he tells us in his *Review* for
August 23, 1706) fourteen years—that is, from 1792,
the year of his bankruptcy—with jeopardy, broils,
and most of the time in banishment from his family.
They have since seen him, he says, "stripped naked
by the government, and the foundations torn up on
which he had built the prospect of paying debts and
raising his family; and yet now, when by common
reasoning they ought to believe the man has not bread
for his children, have redoubled their attacks, with
declarations, executions, escape warrants, and God
knows how many engines of destruction; as if a
gaol and death would pay their debts; as if money
was to be found in the blood of the debtor, and
they were to open his veins to find it."

Taking advantage of the new Act, Defoe now
surrendered to the commissioners who had been
appointed under it.

He gave up all he possessed, with full accounts
of the balance of his affairs ; beginning at his first
business misfortunes, fourteen years previous, and including the completion of his ruin in prison. After
four severe examinations on oath—in which the
bitterness of the lawyer opposed to him was so
great, that Defoe told him it had "in it all the
Villainy of abstract Malice"— the commissioners
appear to have been fully satisfied with his conduct,
as they refused to listen to a witness who proposed,
on payment of expenses only, to prove that Defoe
was then possessed of an estate of £400 per annum.

The question now began to be discussed as to the
advisability of the union of the Parliaments of England
and Scotland, a project that had always been caressed
by William III. ; and commissioners empowered to
examine the question were appointed by the Queen.
They first met on 16th April, 1706 ; and the 4th
of May Defoe, who heartily favoured the project,
was ready with "An Essay at Removing National
Prejudices against a Union with Scotland"; and
between that date and January, 1707, five other
essays dealing with the subject of the Union came
from his pen.

33.—MRS. VEAL AND THE "JURE DIVINO."—BENJAMIN BRAGG,
HIS SMARTNESS (5TH JULY, 1706).

WORKS: 90.—A Plea for Nonconformists. By Thomas de Laune. Preface by
Defoe.
91.—A Sermon preached by Defoe.
92.—Mrs. Veal.
93.—"Jure Divino," a Poem.

On the 6th of June, 1706, Defoe reprinted, with a
preface by himself, a work entitled "A Plea for the

Nonconformists," written twenty-three years previous
by Thomas de Laune, a Baptist schoolmaster, who for
its production had been tried by Judge Jeffreys, and
had died in prison.

Next we find him writing a *jeu d'esprit* on the
subject of a benefit night at Drury Lane on behalf of
a fund to renovate a building, recently a meeting-
house, to be used as an Episcopal chapel of ease.
This performance was advertised in the *Daily Courant*
of June 18, 1706, as the tragedy of *Hamlet, Prince of
Denmark*, with singing and an entertainment. An
article in the *Review* ridiculing the incongruity of
linking church and playhouse having tickled the town,
Defoe decided to reprint it, which he did, under the
title of " A Sermon preached by Mr. Daniel Defoe, on
the fitting up of Dr. Burgess's late Meeting House."
Defoe would have had no quarrel with plays or play-
houses had the stage been pure ; it was the immoral
character of the performances that so excited his indignation. Later on, when the Universities of Oxford
licensed a company to play in that city, Defoe attacked
the theatre a second time.

We are now to consider that toothsome morsel,
" The Apparition of Mrs. Veal," published 5th July,
1706, concerning which, perhaps, more nonsense has
been talked than of any other of Defoe's productions.
One ridiculous notion concerning it has been knocked
on the head by Mr. Lee, and I hope to be able
myself to give its quietus to another. First, as to
the story itself.

Mrs. Veal, " a modern gentlewoman of about thirty
years of age," subject to fits and an unkind father, had

an intimate friend named Mrs. Bargrave, who was afflicted with an even more common complaint, a worthless husband; and the two ladies would "often condole each other's adverse fortunes, and read together 'Drelincourt upon Death'"—a popular religious work that was in its third edition— 'and other good books." Owing to the removal of Mrs. Bargrave to Canterbury, and other circumstances, the two friends did not meet for two years and a-half; but on the 8th of September, 1705, just as "the clock struck twelve at noon," a knock came to Mrs. Bargrave's door, and who should the visitor turn out to be but Mrs. Veal, "in a riding habit." Asked in, Mrs. Veal "sat her down in an elbow chair," and then ensued a friendly conversation, amid which she reminded Mrs. Bargrave of old times, "and what comfort, in particular they received from Drelincourt's Book of Death, which was the best, she said, on that subject ever written." At her friend's request, Mrs. Bargrave went up stairs and fetched "Drelincourt," whereupon, said Mrs. Veal: "Dear Mrs. Bargrave, if the eyes of our faith were as open as the eyes of our body, we should see numbers of angels about us for our guard. The notions we have of heaven now are nothing like what it is, as Drelincourt says; therefore be comforted under your afflictions, and believe that the Almighty has a particular regard to you; and that your afflictions are marks of God's favour; and when they have done the business they are sent for, they shall be removed from you. And, believe me, my dear friend, believe what I say to you, one minute of future happiness will infinitely reward you for all your sufferings."

J

After more in a similar strain, spoken in so pathetic and heavenly a manner that Mrs. Bargrave wept several times, Mrs. Veal requested her friend to write a letter requesting Mr. Veal, her brother, to give funeral rings to such and such, and two pieces of gold to her cousin Watson. This extraordinary request led Mrs. Bargrave to imagine that Mrs. Veal was about to go into a fit, consequently she drew near, in order to be able, if necessary, to render assistance; and with the desire to get rid of the morbidity of the conversation, took hold of Mrs. Veal's "gown-sleeve several times, and commended it." After observing that it was a "scowered silk and newly made up," Mrs. Veal returned to the subject of the previous conversation, and renewed her request, adding, "though it seems impertinent to you now, you will see more reason for it hereafter"; and a few minutes later Mrs. Veal took her departure.

This all occurred, as we said, on the 8th of September, Saturday, but a few days after, upon making inquiries for Mrs. Veal, Mrs. Bargrave discovered, to her surprise, that Mrs. Veal was dead, and that her escutcheons were making; that, in fact, she had died on Friday, the 7th of September, at noon, exactly twenty-four hours before she had appeared to Mrs. Bargrave. That Mrs. Bargrave actually had seen the deceased, Mrs. Veal, and talked with her, and that it was no fancy of hers, is proved, first, by the ingenuousness of Mrs. Bargrave, and, secondly, from the fact that no one, as it transpired, except Mrs. Veal and Mrs. Watson, knew that the gown referred to was "scowered." In short, Mrs.

Bargrave had seen and conversed with the apparition of Mrs. Veal. The most striking feature of the narrative, however—its minute circumstantiality—it is impossible to convey in a brief summary. To enjoy that, recourse must be had to the original.

Never, perhaps, has a story been so misunderstood as this apparition of Mrs. Veal. The idle tradition that it was written to promote the sale of Drelincourt's work on "The Fear of Death," has been conclusively disposed of by Mr. Lee, who proves that when "Mrs. Veal" appeared "Drelincourt" was already a popular work in its third edition, and, furthermore, that Mrs. Veal's recommendation, contrary likewise to tradition, did not have any appreciable effect on the sale of "Drelincourt."

These traditions, which arose from the fact that the printer of "Drelincourt" was permitted to reprint Defoe's pamphlet in the fourth edition of "Drelincourt," deceived even so acute a critic as Sir Walter Scott. "Drelincourt," which long continued popular, was subsequently printed sometimes with and sometimes without "Mrs. Veal."

But there is another erroneous notion concerning "Mrs. Veal" that requires to be dealt with, and that is the assumption that the narrative is a fiction. Whoever will read the story, says Sir Walter Scott, "as told by Defoe himself, will agree that, could the thing have happened in reality, so it would have been told." But the extraordinary thing is that nobody should have inquired whether it was not true, that is to say, whether a lady of Defoe's acquaintance, to whom he gives the name of Mrs. Bargrave, did not

J 2

tell him, and in good faith, this story; and that such was certainly the case, no one who reads carefully Defoe's works on "Magic and Apparitions," can possibly doubt. Defoe, as we shall show, when dealing with those books, believed firmly in apparitions; he had had stories told him which there was no getting over, and this of Mrs. Bargrave's was one of them.

Says Defoe, " I asked Mrs. Bargrave several times if she was sure she felt the gown? She answered modestly, 'If my senses be to be relied on, I am sure of it.'" Moreover, Mrs. Bargrave had no interest in making anybody believe the story.

In other words, in order to understand "Mrs. Veal" we must, first of all, take into consideration Defoe's character, and, secondly, transpose ourselves into the early eighteenth century, a time when almost everybody believed in apparitions, for not only did Defoe believe in the apparition of Mrs. Veal but his readers believed in it too. A careful study of the seventeenth and eighteenth century writers on magic and spiritualism, such as Glanvil, Reginald Scot, Dr. Cotta, and Defoe himself, has forced upon me that this, and this only, is the correct interpretation of "Mrs. Veal," that, in short, it is a true story put in Defoe's inimitable style, and that the case of Mrs. Bargrave, whose veracity no one wishes to doubt, must be placed in the same category as Professor Huxley's well-known case of Mrs. A. (*See* §§ 88 and 89.)

On the 20th of July Defoe published his great satire, as some have called it, the " Jure Divino,"

I. Taverner. Pinx.

M. V.ⁿ Gucht. Sculp

Daniel De Foe
Author of the Trueborn Englishman

THE LOOKING-OVER-SHOULDER PORTRAIT.

(Frontispiece to "A True Collection of the Writings of the Author of the True-born Englishman."—2nd Edition, 1705.)

upon which he had been engaged on and off ever since his release from Newgate, and which apparently he always regarded as his masterpiece. To-day, however, this voluminous work—extending (like "Paradise Lost") to twelve books—is a thing forgotten. In connection with its publication occurred a scandalous piece of dishonesty. Benjamin Bragg, a London publisher, actually had the meanness as well as the unprincipledness to bribe a pressman in the office where "Jure Divino" was being printed to steal copies of the sheets as they were successively printed, by which he was able to issue the whole at the same time that the genuine edition was issued. That, in all conscience, was delicious enough, but now comes the coating of almonds. Bragg actually had the cool impudence to inform the public that this pirated edition of his was "to be sold for the benefit of the author." We cannot say that we feel much drawn towards "Mr. Benjamin Bragg, at the Black Raven."

Mr. Saintsbury happily describes the "Jure Divino" as "a poetical argument in some 10,000 terribly bad verses."

34.—THE "JURE DIVINO" PORTRAIT.—THE FIVE PORTRAITS OF DEFOE.

Of the word-portrait of Defoe that appeared in the *London Gazette* of 10th January, 1703, we have already spoken, but for convenience of reference we will again quote it. He is described as—

"A middle-aged, spare man, about forty years old, of a brown complexion, and dark-brown coloured hair, but wears a wig: a hooked nose, a sharp chin, gray eyes, and a large mole near his mouth."

Of portraits of him in the ordinary sense of the word, there appear to be in existence as many as five original ones,* namely :—

(1). The Portrait by Taverner, engraved by Vandergucht, prefixed to the collection of Defoe's works in July, 1703. (*See* § 20.)

(2). The Looking-over-Shoulder Portrait.

(3). The Laudatur et Alget Portrait, prefixed to "Jure Divino," fol. 1706 (also described as by Taverner and Vandergucht); 1706, age 47. This forms our frontispiece.

(4). The Oval, prefixed to the folio edition of Defoe's "History of the Union of Great Britain," engraved by W. Skelton; 1709, age 50.

(5). An Oval, by Medland.

No. 1 has already been described (§ 20). In respect to No. 3, Mr. Wilson observes :—

"It varies considerably from that prefixed to his works. Instead of his name it has the appropriate motto from Juvenal : *Laudatur et Alget*.† It is engraved by Vandergucht, and represents him in the costume of the times, but without the severity of countenance that distinguishes his former portrait. There is also a print of him before the spurious edition of ' Jure Divino,' but it is badly executed and without the engraver's name."

In his letter to Fransham of May 24, 1706, after mentioning that " Jure Divino " is ready, and asking how many copies Fransham will want, Defoe observes :—

"There is also a picture of your humble servant prepared at the request of some of my friends, who are pleased to value it more than it deserves, but as it will cost a shilling I shall leave it free for those that please to take or leave it."

---

* A portrait by Kneller, said to be of Defoe, is described in *Notes and Queries* for July 17, 1882. It now belongs to the Marquis of Bute, but there is doubt as to its authenticity.

† He is praised, yet not cherished.

Daniel De Foe

THE OVAL PORTRAIT.

Of recent portraits of Defoe, one of the best is that which forms the frontispiece to the "Life of Defoe," by Wilson.

The following interesting note is from Noble's "Continuation of Grainger," vol. ii., p. 305 (published 1806) :—

"I have a curious print of Defoe, one of George Bickham's medleys, which is entituled 'The False Brethren.' Defoe is represented in the pillory, with his face caricatured and his warts greatly enlarged. Below he is in his actual state, seated in his study with a book in his hand, in which is written 'Resistance lawful.' Before him is the Pope, *in pontificalibus*; behind him the devil, horned, with ass's ears, and his clawed hand upon Daniel's shoulder. The Knave of Clubs on one side, and the Knave of Hearts on the other. Below, Oliver Cromwell, and a Whig and Tory wrestling. Under the two last, as well as under the 'deformed head in the pillory,' are verses, as there are 'on the Calves' Head Feast,' and in a large oval at the bottom, in the centre. On the left side, at the bottom, is a card inscribed 'The Whig's Medley,' by G. B. [George Bickham], engraver, MDCCXII."

George Bickham died May 4, 1758, aged 74.

35.—SECRET SERVICE IN SCOTLAND.—THE UNION (OCT., 1706—DEC., 1707).—"YET ALIVE IN SPITE OF SCOTCH MOBS, SWEDISH MONARCHS, OR BULLYING JACOBITES."

WORKS : 94.—A Letter to a Friend.
95.—The Dissenters in England vindicated. Jan., 1707.
96.—Caledonia, a Poem.
97.—*Review*, vol. iii.
98.—A Short View of the present state of the Protestant Religion in Britain.
99.—A Voice from the South. May, 1707.
100.—A Modest Vindication of the Present Ministry.
101.—An Historical Account of the Bitter Sufferings of the Episcopal Church in Scotland.
102.—Defoe's Answer to Dyer's scandalous News Letter. Aug., 1707.

On the nomination of Harley and Lord Godolphin, Defoe now had the honour to be employed by the

Queen "in several honourable though secret services."
The nature of these services he never divulged; but
there is no doubt that one was his mission to Scotland
to promote the Union; and he had the happiness, he
tells us, to discharge himself in all these trusts to the
satisfaction of both Harley and Godolphin. Having
kissed her Majesty's hand, he set out in October for
Scotland.*

His two essays at "Removing National Prejudices
against the Union," written for the English people, were
now followed up by four additional essays for the same
purpose, addressed to the people of Scotland (Nos. 86,
87, 88, 89).

The Scots did not want the Union, and they
were encouraged in their opposition to it by the
English Jacobites, who possessed the people "with
a multitude of wild chimeras." The Duke of
Hamilton, who was the most conspicuous for his
opposition to the whole project, became the especial
darling of the Edinburgh mob, who followed his
coach every day "with blessings and prayers";
whilst the Duke of Queensberry, the leader of the
opposite party, was "insulted with stones, dirt, and
curses." They attacked the house of the Unionist
Sir Patrick Johnston with "sledges, or great ham-
mers," and but for the timely appearance of the
guard, he would have "been a second De Witt."†

In his letter to Fransham of 28th December,
1706, Defoe describes the Scottish Parliament as
going on with their work, "just as Nehemiah did

---

* *Notes and Queries*, 29 Oct., 1870.   † Defoe.

Daniel DeFoe

(*From Wilson's "Life of Defoe," published 1830.*)

with the wall of Jerusalem, with the sword in one hand and the mattock in the other."

The town was practically in the possession of the rabble, who went roving up and down, "breaking the windows of the members of Parliament, and insulting them in their coaches." "They put out all the lights, that they might not be discovered ; and the author of this" (Daniel Defoe) "had one great stone thrown at him, for but looking out of a window; for they suffered nobody to look out, especially with any lights, lest they should know faces and inform against them." In short, though the mob kept up high jinks, they didn't want any headaches in the morning; and Daniel, it is to be supposed, after that, kept his head away from the window.

At last matters got so bad that the Lord Provost was obliged to send out a battalion of guards, who took post in all the avenues of the city, with the result that the houses of the rest of the Unionists were saved. "The rabble were entirely reduced by this, and gradually dispersed ; and so the tumult ended."

The first article of the Union, which virtually decided the whole measure, was carried in the Scottish Parliament by a majority of 33 votes (116 for, 83 against), and Defoe saw "one significant omen of the future good success of the treaty," in that it "was voted on the most remarkable day for public deliverance that ever happened in this island"; that is to say on the 4th November (1706), the anniversary of William's landing at Torbay.

Then ensued a pamphleteering duel between

Defoe and Mr. James Webster, minister of the Tolbooth Church in Edinburgh, a divine who, after having been in favour of the Union, for some reason or other turned round and not only attacked it, but dealt some nasty thrusts at the English Dissenters. In "The Dissenters in England Vindicated" (Jan., 1707) Defoe "treated his opponent with the utmost tenderness and civility"; that is to say, he exasperated him almost to madness by his imperturbability, and the depth with which he made his incisions. Somehow, bodies of divinity never could get on with Defoe. Mr. Webster's answer was as fiery, rash, and abusive as Defoe's had been cool, feeling and polite.

Then it was Defoe's turn, and in his "Short View of the Present State of the Protestant Religion in Britain," he discusses all the points at issue between Webster and himself, deprecates the abusive language of his opponent, and poses in his favourite character of the blessed martyr. All this is amusing to a degree, but let not Defoe be suspected either of seeing through the joke himself, or of insincerity in advocating the Union. The completion of the latter was a thing very near his heart, and he believed that it would result in good for both kingdoms. Finding the Scots hard to convince in prose, he now tried the effects of his lyre, and broke out into "Caledonia: a Poem in Honour of Scotland and the Scots nation," a performance with which the indefatigable Orpheus, despite the unmelodiousness of his strains, seems to have quite charmed the land of cakes; but he who strives to please, generally does please, and soft blandishments are mostly acceptable, whether in a voice resembling the notes of a nightingale, or a voice that might have belonged to a brown bear or a peacock.

Despite the unpleasant habits of Edinburgh mobs, Defoe had quite a delightful time of it both in Auld Reekie and Scotland generally. By the Duke of Queensberry, Her Majesty's High Commissioner, who entertained him at Drumlanrig Castle, he was treated with every consideration and honour; and he contracted friendships with Lord Buchan, Lord Belhaven (an opponent of the Union), and other persons of distinction. Daniel Defoe was just then much in request.

The Union a *fait accompli*, Defoe writes and circulates in Scotland a pamphlet, reprinted from his *Review,* entitled "A Voice from the South"— a recommendation of harmony and "brotherly correspondence between all sorts of Protestants in the whole island." Meantime his reviews appear every other day with the regularity of clock-work, his essays consisting of all manner of subjects, from laudation of the Union to an inquiry ·as to the colour of the devil. Indeed, he is so taken with Scotland that in November he is considering the advisability of settling there altogether, with his wife and family.*

It passed the wit of the High-flying mind to understánd how a man in Scotland, 400 miles away, could write reviews published every other day in London; so it gave out in its malevolence that they were not written by Defoe at all, a libel which caused the latter

* *Review,* Nov. 16.

—always on the *qui vive*—"to assure the world, that no person whatever has, or ever had, any concern in writing the said paper, entitled the *Review*, than the known author D. F. That wherever the author may. be, the papers are wrote with his own hand, and the originals may be seen at the printers."

But, if his enemies gave him annoyance, his friends began to prick him up too. They had had Scottish affairs *ad nauseam*, and they complained "that the fellow could talk of nothing but the Union, and had grown mighty dull of late."

In February (1707), Defoe is lashing Lord Haversham again, in a pamphlet (published in April) called "A Modest Vindication of the Present Ministry; from the Reflections published against them in a late printed paper, entitled the Lord Haversham's Speech, etc."; and his lordship, who, besides vilifying the Ministry, had aspersed the memory of the man (William III.) to whom he owed so much, richly deserved all he got.* But Defoe did other work in Scotland besides helping to cement the Union, writing reviews, and fustigating blatant ingrates. He told the Scots how to improve their coal trade; he speaks of contracting for English merchants for Scots salt to the value of above £10,000 per annum; and he originated or gave an impetus to the Scotch linen trade, being the means of setting over a hundred families to work at it.

---

* Lord Haversham and those like him Defoe compared to dogs that bark at the moon: "They make a noise and look up; but the beauteous planet shines on, and suffers no eclipse from their rage. The glorious and immortal memory of the King will shine to the end of time."

His next publication was a refutation of the charge made by his old opponent Lesley, in his " Rehearsals," against the Established Church in Scotland, that they had cruelly persecuted Episcopal ministers there. Determined that it should be crammed down the High-flying throat, Defoe gave it a Jacobite title: " An Historical account of the bitter sufferings, etc., of the Episcopal Church in Scotland," with the result that your High-flier, smelling valerian, straightway possesses himself of it, when he finds to his infinite disgust that it is not valerian at all, and that the bitter sufferings of the Episcopalians exist only in the vapouring mind of one Lesley.

An article in the *Review* commenting on the unaccountable conduct of the King of Sweden (Charles XII.) in remaining "inactive in Saxony with an army capable of turning the scale of Europe," and also on the treatment of the Livonians by Sweden, having given offence to his Swedish Majesty, the Swedish ambassador received instructions to complain to the English Government. Dyer's News-Letter added gratuitously that the " Queen's messengers were in search of Defoe, who was to be bound hand and foot and surrendered to the Swedes," with the result of a spirited and defiant tract, entitled " De Foe's Answer to Dyer's Scandalous News-Letter," in which the fact is gloried in that no English subject can be punished except by a jury of equals.

As may be gathered from the last of the preserved letters to Fransham, Defoe left Scotland in the middle of December, 1707. The letter is dated Gainsbrough, December 20. In it he says:—

" I take this occasion to let you know that your old Friend and humble Servt is yet alive in Spite of Scotch Mobs Swedish Monarchs or Bullying Jacobites and is going to London to shew his Face to the worst of his Enemies and bid them defiance."

36.—"LITTLE LORD GODOLPHIN" (FEB., 1708, JUNE, 1708).—DEATH
OF DEFOE'S FATHER (FEB., 1706-7).

WORKS: 103.—The Union Proverb, "If Skiddaw," &c.
104.—*Review*, vol. iv.

In the meantime, Robert Harley, who, with a view to increasing his power, had been fomenting the discontents of the Whigs and coquetting with the Tories, had got himself into difficulties. The Duke of Marlborough was particularly incensed against him, and insisted upon his dismissal. At first, the Queen, whose chief *confidante* was now Mrs. Masham, Harley's friend, refused her consent, but, presently, owing to gross negligence on the part of Harley in the custody of his papers, the contents of some of which got to the French Court, she found herself compelled to yield. This was in February (1708), and Defoe now looked upon himself as lost, taking it for granted that "when a great officer fell, all who came in by his interest fall with him." Harley, however, hearing of Defoe's "resolution never to abandon the fortunes of the man to whom he owed so much," urged his follower to think rather of his own interest than of any romantic obligation. "My Lord Treasurer," said Harley, "will employ you in nothing but what is for the public service, and agreeably to your own sentiments of things ; and, besides, it is the Queen you are serving, who has been very good to you. Pray apply yourself as you used to do; I shall not take it ill from you in the least." To Godolphin—"Little Lord Godolphin," on account of his stature—Defoe accordingly applied himself, was by him introduced a second time to Her Majesty and to the honour of kissing her hand, and obtained "the continuance of an appointment which Her Majesty had been pleased to make him in consideration of a former special service he had done."

On the prospect of a threatened invasion from France at this time, Defoe published a short tract, entitled the "Union Proverb," viz. :—

> "If Skiddaw has a cap,
> Scruffell wots full well of that."

That is to say if Skiddaw in England is capped with clouds it will presently rain on Scruffell, just on the other side of the Solway, in Scotland. What is true of these mountains, argues Defoe, is true of the countries in which they are situated. What is bad for England is bad for Scotland. Whether in times of peace or times of war, they should be united.

As, on February 25, 1706-7, probate was granted to Defoe on the will of his father, it may be assumed that Mr. James Foe died early in this year. Mr. Foe, who was baptised on 13th May, 1630, would be seventy-six years of age. For a time he lived in Throgmorton Street, but during the last few years of his life he had been in lodgings at the sign of "The Bell," in Broad Street.

The will was executed on March 20th, 1705. Mr. Foe directed that all just debts were to be paid, and

that his body was to be buried at the discretion of his
executor, but at a charge not exceeding £20. He
left to his granddaughter, Elizabeth Roberts, £20; to
a Mr. John Marsh, £20; and to his cousin, John
Richards, such money as Richards owed him before
the 1st of November, 1704. His grandson, Benjamin
Foe, was to have the testator's gold watch, now in the
possession of his mother; and the silver watch, "now
in his possession," was left to his grandson, Francis
Bartham. A granddaughter, Anne Davis, was to
have a bed, furniture, and drawers. £100 was to be
paid to his grandson, Daniel Foe, at the age of
twenty-one. The remaining part of the estate was
given to this Daniel Foe's five sisters, to be divided
amongst them by their father, Daniel Foe, the
testator's son and sole executor; but in case Defoe
or his wife should by any accident be at any time so
distressed as to stand in need of any part of the legacy
hereby given unto their children for the subsistence,
education, or clothing of their said children, then
Defoe or his wife might make use of it for those
purposes, and it should be allowed by the children as
so much money paid to them on account of the
legacies.

Among the last recorded acts of James Foe is
his signing a testimonial, in 1705, to the character of
a servant girl, named Sarah Pierce, who had lived
two years in his service. He says he should not have
recommended her to Mr. Cave, "that Godly minister,
had not her conversation been becoming the Gospel."

Possibly towards the end of the same year in
which Defoe lost his father occurred the marriage of

Daniel, his eldest son, who could not have been older than twenty-one; all we know of the younger Daniel's wife is that her name was Dorothy, and that she bore her husband a son, named Daniel, christened at Clerkenwell, January 1, 1708-9. This child must have died young, as the father gave the same name to another child (by his second wife) sixteen years after. Dorothy Defoe died before 1720.

37.—HISTORY OF THE UNION, AND THIRD AND FOURTH VISIT TO SCOTLAND, &c. (JUNE—SEPT., 1708, AND AUG. AND SEPT., 1709).

> WORKS: 105.—The Scots Narrative examined. 19th Feb., 1709.
> 106.—*Review*, vol. v. 31st Mar., 1709.
> 107.—History of the Union.
> 108.—Answer to a Paper concerning Mr. De Foe.
> 109.—A Reproof to Mr. Clark.
> 110.—A Commendatory Sermon, preached 4th Nov., 1709.
> 111.—*Review*, vol. vi. 23rd Mar., 1710.

Early in 1708, shortly after the change in the Ministry, news came of the gathering of the French expedition under De Fourbin at Dunkirk, with a view, it was suspected, of trying to effect a landing in Scotland; and about the same time Defoe was despatched to Edinburgh on an errand which was "far from being unfit for a sovereign to direct or an honest man to perform." It is said that his object was to inquire, in behalf of the Government, "on what amount of support the invaders might rely in the bitterness prevailing in Scotland after the Union." The French expedition, however, made no attempt to land, and sailed back to Dunkirk without accomplishing anything.

Whilst on his way to Scotland (1708) his "travelling

K

occasions" led him to Coventry, where the horse of the gentleman who was travelling with him falling lame, it was substituted for another, obtained of one Mayo. The hire was paid down, and a further sum agreed upon for the purchase, in case the horse was not returned. Defoe's companion, having decided to keep the horse, remitted the money to Coventry, but Mayo, owing to a dispute about the price, declined to receive it. Defoe's enemies, ever on the alert for scandal, required nothing further; and, although Defoe was in no wise connected with the affair, issued some time after a pamphlet entitled, " A Hue and Cry after Daniel Defoe and his Coventry Beast . . . London, 1711," in which it was declared that Defoe had hired "a horse of one Mayo, which he took to Scotland; and that neither the animal nor the hire of it had been heard of since."

At the time the French fleet appeared, several persons who were known to be in the interest of the Pretender, and others whose loyalty was suspected, were ordered to be apprehended, among the latter being Lord Belhaven. The only reason for his lordship's arrest was that he had been a most bitter opponent of the Union, and as opponents of the Union were mostly rabid Jacobites, *ergo*, argued the Government, Lord Belhaven was a rabid Jacobite. In a letter to Defoe, written early in the year, his lordship showed that he took it greatly to heart in "that he should be suspected in a cause he had always abhorred"; and when Defoe visited him in the Castle of Edinburgh he complained still more bitterly. After pointing out that the misfortune in having been so ardent an opponent of the Union was the cause of the trouble, and that doves who consort with crows are likely birds to be netted, Defoe "endeavoured to calm his lordship's spirit," and declared that there would be no difficulty in establishing his innocence. Just before Lord Belhaven departed from Edinburgh, Defoe again waited on him to wish him good journey; but though his lordship was more cheerful outwardly, he suffered inwardly, and had resolved on self-destruction. This was on June 14th, and a few days later he was found dead. In the *Review*, v., 177—180, in compliance with the last request of the deceased, Defoe cleared his lordship's reputation.

In the autumn of the following year Defoe again visited Scotland, staying apparently about two months.

38.—" HIGH-CHURCH DARLING, SACHEVERELL" (FEB. 27, 1710).

WORKS: 112.—Letter from Captain Tom to the Mob. 11th Mar., 1710.
113.—A Speech without Doors. 19th Ap., 1710.
114.—Instructions from Rome in favour of the Pretender. 11th May, 1710.
115.—An Essay upon Publick Credit. 23rd Aug., 1710.
116.—A Word against a New Election. Oct., 1710.
117.—A New Test of the Sense of the Nation. 12th Oct., 1710.
118.—An Essay upon Loans. 21st Oct., 1710.

On the 5th of November, 1709, Dr. Sacheverell preached before the Lord Mayor and Aldermen, at St. Paul's Cathedral, his famous sermon upon "Perils Among False Brethren," in which he denounced the Revolution as an unrighteous change, maintained the duty of punishing Dissenters, and called on the people to defend the Church, which he declared to be in imminent danger. The sentiments in it were, in

K 2

fact, precisely those of Defoe's "Shortest Way."
Defoe had put into words what a High-flier thought,
and would have said had he dared; but now here
was a High-flier actually daring, and meaning what
he said. It matters not to us whether the sermon
was Sacheverell's own production, or whether, as
rumour said, it sprang from the brain of Dr. Atterbury. Its effect was extraordinary; the whole nation
was in a turmoil.

As a foil against the onslaught of Sacheverell,
Defoe had recourse to ridicule, a weapon which he
handled only clumsily, for the one thing needful to
make ridicule really effective—the gift of humour—
he sadly lacked. Nothing that Defoe ever wrote
made us laugh heartily, though he was a man who
was almost constantly in good humour, and often
tells what he is pleased to call "a merry tale"; but
these merry tales, even when they have a little
buffoonery in them, do not always provoke even a
smile. The merriest tale that Defoe ever wrote
might be read in church during a dull sermon without the slightest fear of being provoked to indecorum.
Very unwisely, the House of Commons resolved on
Sacheverell's impeachment. During the trial, which
took place in Westminster Hall, and lasted more
than a fortnight, the whole city, one might almost
say the whole country, was in an uproar. The mob
attended the doctor's carriage every day from his
lodgings in the Temple to Westminster Hall, huzza-
ing and pressing to kiss his hand; and during the
evenings employed themselves in wrecking meeting-
houses and hooting before the residences of the Whig

Ministers. On the 22nd of March (1710) Sacheverell was brought in guilty, and enjoined not to preach again for three years. This was considered by the mob and the High Church party as equivalent to an acquittal, and further riotings took place.

Nobody, as Defoe said, could think or talk about anything but the trial. Even the ladies, who, as a rule, were not particularly hot ver politics, caught the contagion. " Indeed, they have hardly leisure to live, little time to eat and sleep, and none at all to say their prayers. Even the little boys and girls talk politics. Little miss has Dr. Sacheverell's picture put into her Prayer Book, that God and the Doctor may take her up in the morning before breakfast."

Among the few letters of Defoe that have been preserved is one dated Newington, 7th April, 1710, warning Lord Wharton against a " scandalous priest of Leeds," named Cooper, who was soliciting preferment ; but if Lord Wharton took any notice of Defoe's " true account of ye morals and manners of this man," there wasn't much chance of his getting it.*

39.—THE SAVAGES ARRIVE.—"ET ERIT MIHI MAGNUS APOLLO."— "HEY, BOYS, UP GO WE!"

Those who had denounced Sacheverell went about in peril of their lives. No fewer than fifteen threatening letters were sent to Defoe ; three times he was beset and waylaid ; and his friends bade him remember Sir Edmundbury Godfrey, and stay

* This letter is in Wilson iii., 121.

indoors. But all this bullying had little effect on him. "My brief resolution," he says, "is this: while I live, they may be assured I shall never desist doing my duty in exposing the doctrines that oppose God and the Revolution : such as passive submission to tyrants, and non-resistance in cases of oppression. If those who are at a loss for arguments are resolved to better their cause by violence and blood, I leave the issue to God's providence; and must do as well with them as I can. As to defence, I have had some thoughts to stay at home by night, and by day to wear a piece of armour on my back : the first, because I am persuaded these murderers will not do their work by daylight; and the second, because I firmly believe they will never attempt it fairly to my face.

"Upon the whole, as I am going on in what I esteem my duty, and for the public good, I firmly believe it will not please God to deliver me up to this bloody and ungodly party; and, therefore, shall still go on to expose a bigoted race of people, in order to reclaim and reform them, or to open the eyes of the good people of Britain, that they may not be imposed upon. Whether in this work I meet with punishment or praise, safety or hazard, life or death, *Te Deum laudamus* "—the great refrain, notice : *Te Deum laudamus.*

The extraordinary peril in which Defoe found himself placed at this time seems to coincide with the arrival of the savages on Crusoe's island. The savages arrived just twenty-three years after Crusoe's landing; and the trial of Sacheverell occurred twenty-

three years after Defoe had taken his strange
vow of silence.

The opportunity appearing a suitable one, Defoe
now reprinted his "Shortest Way with Dissenters,"
adding to the title-page, "Taken from Dr. Sacheverell's Sermon and others"; and on December 15th
he re-issued "De Laune's Plea" with the following
title: "Dr. Sacheverell's Recantation; or, the Fire of
St. Paul's quickly quenched by a Plea for the Nonconformists. London, 1709." A pamphlet that appeared about this time, "The New Wonder; or, a
Trip to St. Paul's," which according to the title-page
is by Defoe, was probably only passed off as his by
the printer to make it sell—a trick that was then but
too common. Nor had Defoe any hand in another
contemporary pamphlet that has been attributed to
him—"The High Church Address to Dr. Henry
Sacheverell."

Tracts which about this time he did write were:
"A letter from Captain Tom to the Mobb now raised
for Dr. Sacheverell" (11th March, 1710), the object
of which was to prevent further destruction of property by the wild followers of the Doctor; "A Speech
without Doors," combating the Doctor's arguments
re non-resistance; and "Instructions from Rome in
favour of the Pretender" (11th May), a tract with the
same object, only written with more violence. In the
Review, he taunted the Doctor with being unable to
answer him. "Let him do this," said Defoe, "*et erit
mihi magnus Apollo.*" The efforts of Defoe, however, did little good; "even if he had possessed a pen
like Juvenal, to sting with the keenest satire," it

would have been used in vain; for the Whigs were unpopular, and in June the Queen, who bore no love to them either, dismissed the Earl of Sunderland.

When the news flew through the country that Sunderland had fallen, people comprehended that "the Sacheverell jig" had led to something. It reached Harley when he was making merry with some friends at his place in Herefordshire. "The game is up!" he cried, springing from the table. Instantly the order was given for the horses to be got ready, and away he went for London. Nor were his expectations falsified. The fall of Sunderland was followed by that of Godolphin; and in August Harley and his friends once more entered upon the enjoyment of the sweets of office—all this, too, after poor Lord Cowper, as his diary records, had devoted his best tokay, "good but thick," to the much-to-be-desired Whig conciliation.

After Godolphin's displacement Defoe waited on him, and "asked his lordship's direction what course he should take," with the result of a reply resembling the one Harley had given on a similar occasion: "That he (Defoe) was the Queen's servant, and that what had occurred need make no difference to him." Thus Defoe "was providentially cast back upon his original benefactor," Harley, who had now, as we have seen, turned Tory, though in reality only a lukewarm Tory.

On 23rd August, 1710, Defoe published "An Essay upon Public Credit," a tract suggested by the financial depression that had been occasioned by the change of Government; and on October 21st a supplement with the title, "An Essay upon Loans."

Finding that Harley was bent upon moderation, Defoe thought that he could consistently support him, and in the elections that followed he counselled the nation to elect, not Whigs only, but moderate men of no matter which party—advice which brought on him the charge of being a turncoat. Apparently, however, he did what was best, considering the circumstances. That it happened likewise to be what was best for his own interests will be regarded by the charitable as only a curious coincidence. That affection for Harley, however, pulled him, if not a long way, a certain distance, may be taken for granted. In the great election fight that then ensued, Sacheverell was successful all along the line ; and it was now to be, as Defoe had feared, " a Tory Parliament, a Tory Ministry, a Tory peace, a Tory successor, and *Hey, boys, up go we !* "

40.—DEFOE'S FIFTH VISIT TO SCOTLAND.—A PASSAGE AT ARMS WITH SWIFT.—A TREATY TO ABSTAIN FROM SHYING MUD (NOV., 1710, TO MARCH, 1711).

WORKS : 119.—*Edinburgh Courant.* 1st Feb., 1711.
120.—Atalantis Major. Probably Feb., 1711.

In the month of November, 1710, Defoe left his home and family on another journey to Scotland, but whether on a mission from the Government or to escape his creditors we are not told. On December 13, 1710, as appears from the Public Records of Edinburgh, a contract was entered into " between David Fearn, advocate, and Daniel De Foe, about printing and publishing a newspaper called *The Postman.*" The *Review* was continued as usual, and the copy transmitted regularly to London for publication.

On the 1st of February, 1711, the Corporation of
Edinburgh empowered Defoe to publish the *Edinburgh Courant*, in the room of Adam Booge, deceased,
but probably this newspaper soon passed into other
hands.   The only pamphlet written by Defoe at
this time " is an amusing piece of banter," entitled
" Atalantis Major, Printed in Olreeky, the chief city
of the north part of Atalantis Major," the occasion
whereof being " the election of the sixteen Scotch
representative Lords, and their rage at the oaths they
had to take as members of the British Parliament."

Owing to the frequency of his visits to Scotland,
Scotch expressions, as might be expected, are often
in Defoe's mouth.   In the " Use and Abuse," for
example, he observes, " If men will defile themselves,
as the Scots say, no man can dight them "; and he
quotes the Scottish proverb—

> " Titty, Tatty, Kitty, Katty,
> False to ea man, false to au men ";

he talks of " muckle thief devil," and in his " History
of Magic " he describes the Scottish caude (drawer in
a tavern) as inquiring, " What's your honour's wull,
sir ? "   •

Defoe and Swift being on opposite sides in politics,
it is not to be expected that much love would be lost
between them, nor is it surprising, considering the
way warfare was carried on in the Augustan age, that
the attacks were of a very personal nature.   It is
more than probable, if all particulars of the fray were
known, that it was Defoe who struck first blow; but
the earliest notification we get that the two are at

loggerheads is in 1708, when Swift, in his pamphlet, entitled "A Letter from a Member of the House of Commons in Ireland to a Member of the House of Commons in England, concerning the Sacramental Test," observes, "one of those authors (the fellow that was pilloried, I have forgot his name) is indeed so grave, sententious, dogmatical a rogue, that there is no enduring him."

England in 1894 does not forget Defoe's name, but neither does it forget Swift's. That they fought on different sides—that they were not friends—is nothing to us. We love and honour both. Their very mention is pleasant music, and a welling-up of deep affection from the innermost recesses of the heart.

But we return to the fray. In No. 16 of the *Examiner* Swift adds more fuel to the strife by calling Defoe and Tutchin "stupid, illiterate scribblers and idiots." Defoe at first made no reply; but Swift, in subsequent *Examiners*, continuing in the same strain, Defoe took upon himself to reply, and (*Review* vii., 454, 455)* gave his adversary a little more than he had received. He was not so very ignorant, he said, seeing that he could speak five languages, though he did not write a bill over his door, or set up Latin quotations on the front of his paper. His father, it was true, had neglected one element in his education, for he had not taught him the language of Billingsgate. In the fine art of swearing and using the foul language of the street with the ease of a porter or a carman, he confessed himself Swift's inferior. He

---

* *Review* vii. was published 22nd Mar., 1711.

had no objection to fighting a rascal, but calling a man one was not in his line. Then follows a comment on Swift's expression, a " scurrilous gentleman," a heterogeneity which Defoe confessed he had never met with, and could not for the life of him form an idea of what it was like.

This taunt of lack of learning, however, continued all his life to give Defoe annoyance; and in one of his papers in *Applebee's Journal*, whilst dealing with the subject of "learning," he shows his soreness by giving a very complete account of his attainments in languages, science, history, and geography, finishing up each sentence with the words, " Yet this man was no scholar." Even in his last important work, " The Compleat English Gentleman," written in 1729, the subject is again recurred to.

In 1711 Swift and others of the coterie to which he belonged were writing, like Defoe, on the side of Harley; but, according to Oldmixon, Harley "paid Defoe better than he did Swift, looking on him as the shrewder head of the two for business. Writing on the same side, however, did not render the two authors a bit more amicable. Swift made several subsequent attacks on Defoe, which the latter as often replied to, dubbing him on one occasion, in allusion to the Wood's Copper Coinage affair, the " Author of brains and brass."

A curious letter of Defoe's, showing the literary manners of the times, which bears date Newington, 17th June, 1710, is preserved in the British Museum (Harl. MSS. No. 7001, fol. 269). The letter is written to Mr. J. Dyer, of Shoe Lane, who was then employed by the Tory leaders in circulating Tory literature; and in it Defoe declares his readiness to make with Dyer "a fair truce of honour," viz., "that if what either party are doing, or saying, that may clash with the party we are for, and urge us to speak, it shall be done without naming either's name, and without personal reflections; and thus we may differ still, and yet preserve both the Christian and the gentleman." Defoe concludes by wishing Dyer success in all things, "your opinions of government excepted."

Dyer, it is worth noting, conducted his News-letter on a rather ingenious principle. The copies, instead of being written quite alike, were varied according to the tastes of the persons they were meant for. Previous to sending to a fresh coffee-house, he used to inquire what sort of people frequented it, and, on getting an answer, "would send such news as would fit them." But in time so little credit got to be attached to what Dyer said that Addison made Honest Vellum, a character in one of his plays, believe his master to be living, "because the news of his death was first published in Dyer's Letter."

41.—GUISCARD STABS HARLEY (8TH MAR., 1711).—"NO MAN HAS TASTED DIFFERING FORTUNES MORE": *ACTEON.*

WORKS: 121.—*Review*, vol. vii. 22nd March, 1711.
  122.—Eleven Opinions about Mr. Harley. 14th May, 1711.
  123.—Secret History of the October Club.
  124.—Do., part ii.
  125.—Essay on the South Sea Trade. 6th Sept., 1711.
  126.—Reasons why this Nation ought to put a speedy end to this expensive War.

On the 8th March, 1711, occurred the daring attempt of the Marquis de Guiscard to assassinate Harley, an event that added very greatly to Harley's popularity. April 21st, 1711, saw the publication of Defoe's "Secret History of the October Club," a tract written for the purpose of holding up to execration a coterie of extreme High-fliers, who, under the name of the October Club, held their meetings at the Bell Tavern in Westminster; and on May 14th he published a defence of Harley, with the title "Eleven Opinions about Mr. H——y; with Observations."

On the 24th May, Harley, who had daily risen in favour of the Queen since the attempt at his assassination, and who enjoyed the support of most of the Tories, was raised by Her Majesty to the peerage by the title of Earl of Oxford and Mortimer; and on the 29th of the same month he was made Lord High Treasurer.

A letter written by Defoe on May 29th, 1711, to the Earl of Buchan shows that he was understood at this time to have considerable influence with the Ministers. Lord Buchan had requested Defoe to plant his interest with Harley. Nothing, however, could be done just then, owing to "the wound of the assassin"; but Defoe promised to watch for a favourable opportunity.*

In 1711 we first hear of the scheme for trading on a large scale in the South Seas, a concern that subsequently led people into such wild courses and involved half the nation in ruin. The scheme was suggested by Harley in the hope of its being able to provide funds required for carrying on the war, and Defoe, who even so early as the time of King William had had similar plans in his brain, not only gave the suggestion his cordial support, but embodied his opinions in a pamphlet, published on the 6th of September (1711): "An Essay on the South Sea Trade." The beginning of the South Sea scheme was honourable enough; the end of it—the South Sea Bubble, as it came to be called—is known of all men.

The great aim and desire of the Tories, now that they had got into power, was to bring about a peace with France; and, after certain preliminaries, M. Mesnager was sent privately to England empowered to ascertain the views of the English Ministers; and Matthew Prior, the poet, proceeded on a similar errand to France. The support Defoe gave to the Ministry, which he did both in his reviews and in pamphlets, caused those who were adverse to the Government to repeat the charge of inconsistency, and they "wondered what sovereign medicine had been since applied to his eyes, and by how much gold they had been rubbed"— an insinuation that he repelled with indignation. The

* See *Notes and Queries*, 26th Jan., 1884, where the letter is given in full.

first of his pamphlets in support of the peace is entitled
" Reasons why this Nation ought to put a speedy end
to this expensive War " (Oct. 6, 1711). This, falling
into the hands of M. Mesnager, so delighted him that
he had it translated into French and circulated in the
Netherlands. Moreover, in order to secure Defoe's
services for the future, he tried the effect of a bribe.
" To facilitate the thing," says Mesnager, " I caused
an hundred pistoles to be conveyed to him, as a compliment for that book, and let him know it came from
a hand that was as able to treat him honourably as he
was sensible of his service." Defoe, however, though
he kept the pistoles as a " compliment for the book "
he had written, was not to be bought; for, continues
Mesnager, " I missed my aim in the person, though
perhaps the money was not wholly lost; for I afterwards understood that the man was in the service of
the State, and that he had let the Queen know of the
hundred pistoles he had received ; so I was obliged
to sit still, and be very well satisfied that I had not
discovered myself to him, for it was not our season
yet."

On the 30th of October appeared " Armageddon ;
or, the necessity of carrying on the war, if such a
peace cannot be obtained as may render Europe safe
and trade secure," and two days later the tract "The
Balance of Europe," in which Defoe gives it as his
opinion that the peace of Europe would more likely
be secured by handing over Spain to King Philip.
About November 27th he issues " An Essay at a
Plain Exposition of that Difficult Phrase, a Good
Peace," in the introduction of which he defends his

own position; and on November 29th he could show "Reasons why a Party among us, etc., are obstinately bent against a Treaty of Peace." By-and-by John Howe, M.P. for Gloucestershire, rakes up an old grievance against King William, whose memory he reproached on account of the Partition Treaty—the Felonious Treaty, as he called it—which caused Defoe, ever tender on the subject of his late master, to enter the lists with "The Felonious Treaty," etc., etc., in which he defended the conduct of William in words which he had "from his Majesty's own mouth."

Up to this point Defoe had been able to sail with Harley and the Tories, for the watchword had been "Moderation," and he had hoped that, thanks to the prestige of Harley, moderation would continue to be practised; but it was not so. Finding themselves in power, the Tories and High-fliers were unable to resist the temptation of making use of it, or rather of abusing it, and on their first opportunity they brought in again their Bill for the Prevention of Occasional Conformity; and, in order to secure its passage through the Lords, took the novel step of creating twelve new peers in one day. Nor did Harley and the Whig members of the Government offer any particular opposition.

Deserted by their friends, the Dissenters, with the exception of a few, including Defoe, abandoned all hope; and even Defoe was sometimes despondent. He says in one of his reviews, "The measure will infallibly ruin many hundreds of Dissenting families, or cause them to act against their consciences for bread, which, I think, is one of the worst kinds of

L

persecution." Applications to Harley were useless. Harley wished to remain in power; the Tories only could keep him in power, *ergo* he must please the Tories. As a last effort against the Bill, Defoe, on the 22nd of December, published a pamphlet in which he begged the Queen to make use of her right of veto : "An Essay on the History of Parties," etc. But neither was that of any avail, for the same day she gave her assent, and the Bill became law.

Defoe's tract, " The Conduct of Parties in England," was followed on the 17th of May by " The Present State of Parties in Great Britain," a large work upon which he had been engaged at intervals over eight years. The last chapter consists of advice to the Dissenters "as to the best course to be adopted in their present depressed condition." To this succeeded a dissertation on the Peace question, his " Reasons Against Fighting " (June 7, 1712).

On July 29th, 1712, was finished the eighth volume of his *Review*. In the preface, which is of the greatest interest, he gives " a retrospect of the whole work, the treatment it has received during its progress of more than eight years, including many particulars of his past life, and the existing state of his circumstances." He had expected to make enemies, he said, by speaking plain, nor had he been deceived ; but it was certainly hard that he should so often have been ill-treated by his friends.

" I am now," says he, " hunted full cry, Acteon-like, by my own friends—I won't call them hounds—in spite of protested innocence and want of evidence, against the genuine sense of what I write, ، ، ، against fair arguing, against all modesty and sense ; condemned by common clamour as writing for money, for particular persons, by great men's directions, and the like ; every tittle of which, I have the testimony of my own conscience, is abominably false, and the accusers must have the accusation of their own consciences that they do not know it to be true."

After a careful examination of his own thoughts, desires, and designs, he found " a clear, untainted principle, and consequently an entire calm of conscience." And having looked *in*, he looked *up*. He would submit, "with an entire resignation," to whatever might happen to him. He fully believed that Heaven would yet deliver him " from the power of slander and reproach ; " but even if not, he would still say, as he had so often said, *Te Deum laudamus !*

"I have gone," he adds, "through a life of wonders, and am the subject of a vast variety of providences ; I have been fed more by miracle than Elijah when the ravens were his purveyors. I have, some time ago, summed up the scenes of my life in this distich :—

No man has tasted differing fortunes more,
And thirteen times I have been rich and poor.

" In the school of affliction I have learnt more philosophy than at the academy, and more divinity than from the pulpit; in prison I have learnt to know that liberty does not consist in open doors, and the free egress and regress of locomotion. I have seen the rough side of the world as well as the smooth : and have, in less than half a year, tasted the difference between the closet of a king and the dungeon of Newgate. I have suffered deeply for cleaving to principles."

By none was he so basely betrayed as by those whose families he had preserved from starving. " Fame," he says further on, " would talk me up for I know not what of courage.; and they call me a fighting fellow." But if he is bold, he says, it is because his cause is a just one : " Truth inspires nature ; and, as in defence of truth no honest man can be a coward, so no man of sense can be bold when he is in the wrong. He that is honest must be brave."

In defence of truth he could dare to die.

" I question whether there is much, if any, difference between bravery and cowardice, but what is founded in the principle they are engaged.for. Truth makes a man of courage, and guilt makes that man a coward.

" I have a large family—a wife and six children, who never want what they should enjoy or spend what they ought to save. Under all these circumstances, and many more, my only happiness is this : I have always been kept cheerful, easy, and quiet, enjoying a perfect calm of mind. If any man ask me how I arrived to it, I answer him, in short, by a constant, serious application to the great, solemn, and weighty work of resignation to the will of Heaven."

42.—THE ADVENTURES OF ALEXANDER SELKIRK.—THE MEETING IN BRISTOL OF SELKIRK AND DEFOE.

The memory now reverts to the child, Alexander Selkirk, whom we left crowing in his cot at Largo. Grown to be a youth, a desire possessed him to follow the sea ; but, although his mother favoured the idea, his father opposed it. Wild and restless of control, young Selkirk daily kicked against the authority of the home, and elsewhere his conduct was equally wild. In August, 1695, he was cited to appear before the kirk session for making a disturbance in church ; but when the kirk session met they found themselves powerless to do anything except to insert in their record.: " August 27th.—Alexander Selcraig called out ; but did not appear, having gone to sea." For six years he roved the ocean—probably in the company of some band of buccaneers—and then came home again, more reckless and boisterous than ever. A ridiculous incident that ought to have been passed over originated in the house a disgraceful quarrel. Andrew, a half-witted brother, having brought in a can full of salt water, Alexander took a drink of it through mistake, and then beat Andrew for laughing at him. The father and another brother, John, coming to Andrew's assistance, Alexander attacked them both; and John's wife, who had followed her husband, found Alexander gripping both old Selkirk and her husband; and in the scuffle she too received blows. For this, in accordance with a decree of the kirk sessions, Alexander was obliged to stand up in church in front of the pulpit, where he made "acknowledgment of his sin in disagreeing with his brothers, and was rebuked in the face of the congregation for it, and promised amendment in the strength of the Lord, and so was dismissed."

This was on Sunday, November 30, 1701. Selkirk remained at Largo during the winter, but in the spring of 1702 he again set sail, this time with the celebrated buccaneer, Dampier. Dampier's expedition, the object of which was to plunder French and Spanish vessels, consisted of two ships, the *St. George*, commanded by Dampier himself, and the *Cinque Ports*, commanded by Charles Pickering, with Thomas Stradling for lieutenant and Selkirk for sailing master. The second mate of the *St. George* was William Funnel, who wrote a narrative of the voyage. Before long, Pickering died, and Stradling, a man of ferocious and

quarrelsome temper, succeeded him. On the 10th
of February, 1704, the two vessels were off the coast
of Juan Fernandez, west of Chili in South America,
an island of cabbage-trees and pimentoes, sea-lions,
turtles, and wild goats. "The sea-lions, if hard
pressed, raise their bodies on their fore-fins and face
you with their mouths wide open; so that we used to
clap a pistol to their mouths and fire down their
throats." Juan Fernandez is about the size of the
island of Bute. Its hills, which have for soil a loose
black earth, besides being "very rotten," are honey-
combed with excavations made by "a sort of fowl called
the puffin." A sail coming in sight, the buccaneers
gave chase to it, but without success; and after a
fruitless attempt on Santa Maria, a town of Peru,
where they hoped to find a quantity of gold, and the
capture of a valuable prize laden with food, Dampier
and Stradling quarrelled and separated. Stradling
returned to Juan Fernandez, where, owing to a dis-
agreement with him, Selkirk now signified his intention of remaining; and no opposition being offered,
he and his effects were rowed ashore. When, however, he saw the boat returning, the horrors of his
situation vividly presented themselves; and, rushing
into the surf up to the middle, he stretched out his
hands towards his comrades, and implored them to
come back and take him on board again. The only
answer was a jeer. The boat reached the ship,
the ship spread her sails, and Selkirk was alone on
his island.

Unable to abandon the hope that Stradling would
relent and come back for him, the unhappy Selkirk

found himself chained to the beach ; and even when gnawed with hunger, rather than go in search of fruits and other products of the woods, he contented himself with shell-fish and seal's flesh, and whatever else he could obtain without removing inland. He hated even to close his eyes. Often he cursed the folly that had brought him to this terrible solitude, and sometimes, starting up in agony, he would resolve on suicide. Voices spoke to him both in the howlings of the sea in front and in the murmur of the woods behind. The shore was creatured with phantoms. Then—cooling his fevered brain—came sweet visions of his childhood, the home at Largo, his mother, the fields he had rambled in, the words he had heard in the old kirk, thoughts of God.

His mind more at ease, he now sought to render his residence on the island more endurable. Cutting down pimento wood, he built two huts, one a sleeping-room, the other a kitchen. He obtained fire Indian-fashion, by rubbing together two pieces of pimento. Overhauling his stores, he found clothing and bedding, a firelock, a pound of gunpowder, a hatchet, a knife, a kettle, a Bible, some other religious works, a book or two on navigation, and his mathematical instruments. To these must be added a flip-can, holding about two quarts, made of brown stoneware, glazed, with inscription and posy, of the kind with which your roaring old buccaneer delighted to decorate his belongings—

> " Alexander Selkirk, this is my one,
> *   *   *   *
> When you take me on board of ship,
> Pray fill me full with punch or flip."

This can, his firelock, his chest, and a cocoa-nut shell cup which he made, are still, or were until recently, in the possession of descendants of the family.

Every day he watched the horizon for sails. Every morning he read a portion of Scripture, sang a psalm, and prayed, speaking aloud in order to preserve the use of his voice. He had never before

A CAVE IN JUAN FERNANDEZ.
(From a photograph lent by Mr. W. H. G. Webb, R.N.)

been so good a Christian. Turtles, crawfish, turnips, parsnips, cabbage palm, goat-flesh, radishes, and water-cresses formed his food. When his powder failed, he chased the wild goats on foot, and by dint of practice became so fleet that he could run them down ; and he kept a small stock, tamed, round his dwelling. When his clothes wore out, he clad himself in skins. Annoyed by rats, which had taken to tasting his toes when he was asleep, he caught and tamed some cats. To

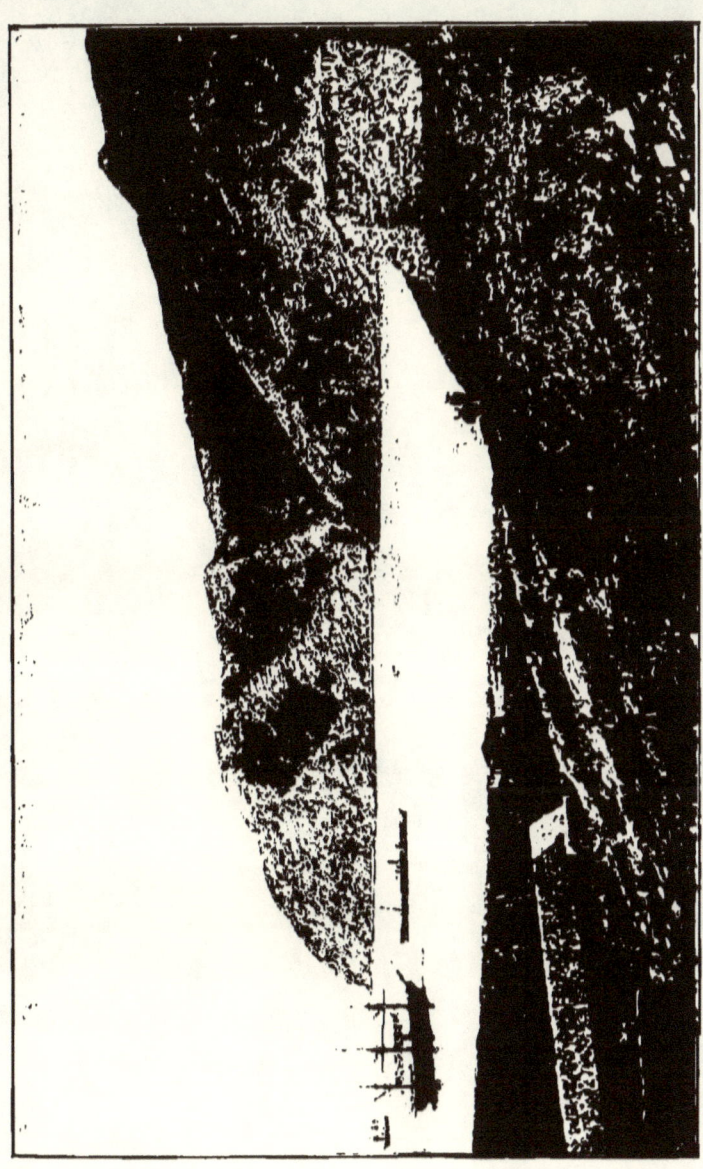

CUMBERLAND BAY, JUAN FERNANDEZ.

(From a photograph lent by Mr. B. H. G. Webb, R.N.)

amuse himself, he taught his cats and some of his goats to dance; and, anxious that, in the event of his dying in solitude, his having lived there might not be unknown to his fellow creatures, he carved his name on a number of trees.

Several times he saw vessels passing the island, and two anchored beside it; but discovering the strangers to be Spaniards, and therefore enemies, he feared to make himself known. Once when hunting the wild goat he fell down a precipice, and lay stunned for twenty-four hours; but though invalided for three days, he sustained no permanent injury. The whole island was now familiar to him, with its appearances and productions at various seasons. Though partly reconciled to his fate, he would nevertheless occasionally indulge in the sad reflections made familiar to us by Cowper's poem, in which the solitary buccaneer is represented as at first saying—

> " I am monarch of all I survey,
>   My right there is none to dispute ;
> From the centre, all round to the sea,
>   I am lord of the fowl and the brute ; "

but afterwards, when a full sense of his utter loneliness came upon him—a loneliness to which the loneliness of an anchorite was even the busy world—

> " O solitude ! where are the charms
>   That sages have seen in thy face ?
> Better dwell in the midst of alarms,
>   Than reign in this horrible place."

In the meantime, only ill-luck had attended the *Cinque Ports*, Selkirk's old ship, and its companion the *St. George*. The former was wrecked, and though

Stradling and a few of his crew escaped, they ultimately fell into the hands of the Spaniards, and out
of the knowledge of history.   The *St. George* was
taken by the Dutch, and " Dampier returned naked
to his owners, with a melancholy relation of his
misfortunes, occasioned chiefly by his own strange
temper."   The merchants who had employed Dampier
now prepared for another marauding expedition, and
fitted out two vessels, the *Duke* and the *Duchess*,
over whom they put Captain Woodes Rogers, a man
of ability and prudence.   Dampier, who could not
be entrusted with the command, sailed as pilot.   On
the 31st of January, 1709, after cruising along the
Brazilian and Chilian coasts, they bore for Juan
Fernandez in order to take in water, and here, to
their surprise, they found "a man clothed in goat
skins, who looked wilder than the first owners of
them."   At first Selkirk was so overcome with joy
that he could not speak, but after a time he tendered
explanations ; and, by Dampier's recommendation,
the post of mate having been offered him, he gladly
accepted it and came on board.   His feat of running
down the goats caused general astonishment.   " His
way of living," says Rogers, "and continual exercise
of walking and running, cleared him of all gross
humours, so that he ran with wonderful swiftness
through the woods and up the rocks and hills.   We
had a bull-dog, which we sent with several of our
nimblest runners to help him in catching goats, but
he distanced and tired both the dog and the men,
caught the goats, and brought them to us on his
back."   In the middle of February, 1709, the *Duke*

THE HOUSE OF MRS. DAMARIS DANIEL, IN WHICH DEFOE MET SELKIRK.

(*From a photograph by T. Protheroe, 35, Wine Street, Bristol.*)

and the *Duchess* set sail from the island, and in a short time took two prizes, to one of which Selkirk was appointed the command. The rest of the voyage of the *Duke* and the *Duchess* was chiefly taken up with sacking more coast towns, and in the beginning of 1711 these "good Christian pirates," as Defoe would have called them, who listened to the Church of England service regularly and piped to prayers before every action, set sail for England, which, however, they did not reach till October. Of the plunder— one hundred and seventy thousand pounds—taken during this successful expedition, the share allotted to Selkirk seems to have been about eight hundred pounds.

As soon as his singular story was made known in England, Selkirk became an object of curiosity, and was visited by a great number of persons. Defoe, ever on the *qui vive* for what was odd and unusual, and what he fancied could be turned to account, made a journey from London to Bristol apparently for the express purpose of seeing him. The date of this journey is not known, but it was probably late in 1711 or early in 1712. The interview occurred in the house of a friend of Defoe's named Mrs. Damaris Daniel, who lived in a corner house in St. James's Square (Bristol), the corner originally opposite the entrance from the Barton. St. James's Square, which contains some fine examples of houses in the Queen Anne style, and was occupied only by wealthy families, was begun about 1707, consequently Mrs. Daniel's house at the time Defoe visited it must have been only recently built. The result of the meeting was that Selkirk, as he subsequently told Mrs. Daniel, placed in Defoe's hands all his papers. When Defoe commenced his famous "Robinson Crusoe," which was founded on these papers, it is impossible to say, but the probability is that nothing was done, or very little, before his great illness of 1715, when his tongue was loosed, and when he would be struck with the remarkable analogy between the isolated life of Selkirk on his island in the Pacific and the isolated life of Daniel Defoe in the island of Great Britain.

For the charge that Defoe surreptitiously appropriated the papers of Selkirk, there is no foundation whatever. They were handed over by Selkirk simply as a matter of business. Not that it is likely that Defoe gave much for them. Defoe himself made no use of them, nor got anything whatever out of them, till eight years after.*

Selkirk was subsequently interviewed by another literary big-wig, Sir Richard Steele, who, on the 3rd of December, 1713, occupied the twenty-sixth number of the *Englishman* with an account of the information he had elicited.

In 1712 Captain Rogers published an account of the expedition with the title "A Cruising Voyage Round the World, . . . Containing," among other things, "An account of Alexander Selkirk's living alone four years and four months in an Island"; and several other accounts of Selkirk's adventures also got abroad.

* For the papers from which these facts are gleaned I am indebted to Mr. Richard Champion Rawlins, a descendant of Francis Rogers, one of the twelve merchants of Bristol who fitted out the *Duke* and the *Duchess*.

The subsequent history of Selkirk, though in no way concerning Defoe, may be briefly stated. In the spring of 1712 he returned to his native Largo, where he stayed about three years, when he ran away to London with a young girl named Sophia Bruce, in whose favour in 1717 he made a will. Apparently Sophia Bruce died shortly after, for

SELKIRK AND HIS FAMILY.
(From " Providence Displayed.")

Selkirk married a Frances Candis; who, after his death in 1723, laid claim to, and was awarded, his property. In 1885 a bronze statue of Selkirk was erected at Largo.

The original accounts of Selkirk are four in number—

(1) Captain Woodes Rogers's book, 1712.

(2) " A Voyage to the South-Sea Trade, and round the World; wherein an account is given of Mr. Alexander Selkirk, etc." By Cooke, 1712.

(3) " Providence Displayed: or a very surprising account of one Mr. Alexander Selkirk, etc. . . . Written by his own

hand." A quarto tract of twelve pages, compiled from
Rogers and Cooke. Selkirk had no hand in it.

(4) Further particulars concerning Selkirk are to be gleaned from
The Englishman, Dec. 3, 1713, and from the voyages of
Funnell, Shelvocke, Anson, and Ulloa.

Complete accounts of Selkirk's life, in which the
particulars of the foregoing are condensed, appeared
subsequently. Such are:—

(1) "Providence Displayed," etc. By Isaac James.
With a Map of the Island, and twenty-four Wood-cuts.
This work also contains accounts of other persons left
on uninhabited islands, as William the Mosquito Indian,
Serrano, and Ephraim How. Bristol, 1800.

(2) "The Life and Adventures of Alexander Selkirk,
etc." By John Howell. Edinburgh, 1829.

CHAPTER VIII.

AT HALIFAX (AUG. TO DEC., 1712).

43.—AT THE SIGN OF THE ROSE AND CROWN.

WORKS : 137.—Inquiry into the Real interest of Princes. 18th Sept. 1712.
138.—A Seasonable Warning and Caution. 1712.
139.—Hannibal at the Gates.
140. —A Strict Enquiry (The Hamilton-Mohun duel). 1713.

ALTHOUGH Defoe was so much occupied with literature, he still continued to be connected with commercial concerns; and about 1712 he was in partnership in some trading speculation with a Mr. Ward, mercer and draper of Coleshill in Warwickshire. But, like most other trading concerns that Defoe embarked in, it ultimately came to grief, and both Defoe and Ward lost considerably. We are reminded again by it, however, that Defoe was all his life connected with trade. He did not abandon the merchant when he put on the poet and the pamphleteer, or even when, long after, he stood forth as a full-blown novelist and an historian. We have proof that as late as 1726, seven years after Crusoe was published, he was engaged in mercantile pursuits. (*See* § 88.)

The course in politics which Defoe had taken had raised up against him, as we have seen, a host of enemies ; and had he been blamed only for what he did write, he would have had reason enough to feel uncomfortable. But that was not all; as on former occasions, he got blame, too, for things he did not write. He says: "Whenever any piece comes out which is not liked, I am immediately charged with being the author; and very often the first knowledge I have had of a book being published has been from seeing myself abused for being the author of it in some other pamphlet published in answer to it." At last he was so disgusted that he resolved not to set pen again to paper any more that year, except to write his reviews; and in order to put himself out of the reach of the malice of his enemies, he took a journey "to Halifax in Yorkshire," where he stayed till December.

We are told that he resided "in the Back Lane at the sign of the Rose and Crown"; and that he was known "to Dr. Nettleton, the physician, and the Rev. Nathaniel Priestley, of Ovenden, who had the charge of the then Trinitarian Presbyterian congregation assembling at the Northgate Chapel, Halifax."

Whilst at Halifax, observing the insolence of the Jacobite party, and how they insisted openly on the Pretender's rights, he "set pen to paper again" by writing "A Seasonable Caution"; and, to open the eyes of the poor ignorant country people, "gave away' this all over the kingdom, as gain was not intended." On the 30th of December he published another tract of similar tendency, entitled "Hannibal at our Gates"; and early in the next year he endeavoured to prove, in "A Strict Enquiry into the Circumstances of a late duel," that the quarrel between the High Tory Duke of Hamilton and the Whig Lord Mohun, fatal to both, had resulted from a private quarrel—politics, contrary to Tory insinuations, having had nothing to do with it.

44.—THE MAN THAT BLOWS HOT AND COLD WITH THE SAME BREATH (FEB. AND APRIL, 1713).

WORKS: 141.—Reasons against the Succession of the House of Hanover. 21st Feb., 1713.
142.—And what if the Pretender should come? 26th Mar., 1713.
143.—An Answer to a Question that nobody thinks of—viz., What if the Queen should die? 26th Mar., 1713.

In continuance of his purpose of circumventing the designs of the Jacobites, Defoe in February, March, and April wrote three more tracts :

1. "Reasons against the Succession of the House of Hanover."

2. "What if the Pretender should come?"

3. "What if the Queen should die?"

In the first, whose title, like the tract itself, is ironical, is an amusing picture of the national broils, which disturbed even the peace of the household :—

"You please to listen to your cook-maids and footmen in your kitchens; you shall hear them scolding and swearing and scratching and fighting among themselves; and when you think the noise is about the beef and the pudding, the dish-water or the kitchen-stuff, alas! you are mistaken ; the feud is about the more mighty affairs of the government."

It was the same in the storey above the kitchen— the shop—where the 'prentices, instead of posting their books, "fight and rail at the Pretender and the House

M

of Hanover." Even in the next storey—among the
family—it is no better : " the ladies, instead of their
innocent diversions, are all falling out one among
another " :—

> " If the chamber-maid is a slattern, and does not please, hang her,
> she is a jade ; or I warrant she is a High-flier ; or on the other side,
> I warrant she's a Whig ; I never knew one of that sort good for any-
> thing in my life. Nay, go up to your very bedchambers, and even in
> bed the man and wife shall quarrel about it. People !—people !
> What will become of you at this rate ? "

The following quotation, from this tract has been
supposed to contain the mainspring of most of Defoe's
political actions, and to explain the apparent want of
consistency with which he is often blamed :—

> " Learned men say some diseases in Nature are cured by anti-
> pathies, and some by sympathies ; that the enemies of Nature are
> the best preservatives of Nature ; that bodies are brought down by
> the skill of the physician, that they may the better be brought up ;
> made sick to be made well ; and carried to the brink of the grave in
> order to be kept from the grave. For these reasons, and in order to
> these things, poisons are administered in physic, and amputations in
> surgery ; the flesh is cut that it may heal; an arm laid open that it
> may close with safety ; and those methods of cure are said to be the
> most certain, as well as most necessary in those particular cases ;
> from whence it is become a proverbial saying in physic, ' Desperate
> diseases must have desperate remedies.' Now, it is very proper to
> inquire in this case, whether the nation is not in such a state of
> health at this time that the coming of the Pretender may not be of
> absolute necessity, by way of cure of such national distempers as
> now afflict us, and that an effectual cure can be wrought no other
> way. If upon due inquiry it should appear that we are not fit to
> receive such a Prince as the successor of the house of Hanover is,
> that we should maltreat and abuse him if he were here; and that
> there is no way for us to learn the true value of a Protestant suc-
> cessor so well as by tasting a little what a Popish Pretender is, and
> feeling something of the great advantages that may accrue to us by
> the superiority of a Jacobite party; if the disease of stupidity has

so far seized us that we are to be cured only by poisons and fermentations; if the wound is mortified, and nothing but deep incisions, amputations, and desperate remedies, must be used; if it would be necessary thus to teach us the worth of things by the want of them; and there is no other way to bring the nation to its senses; why, what can be then said against the Pretender? Even let him come, that we may see what slavery means; and may inquire how the chains of French galleys hang about us, and how wooden shoes are to walk in; for no experience teaches us so well as that we buy dearest and pay for with the most smart."

These tracts met with "so much approbation among persons sincere for the Protestant succession, that they were sent all over the kingdom," about seven editions being printed; and Defoe protests that even if the Elector of Hanover had given him a thousand pounds to promote the Protestant succession and to make the interest of the Pretender odious and ridiculous, he could have done nothing more effectual to these purposes than writing these pamphlets.

But, unfortunately, Defoe, by his efforts to cool the warlike spirit of the time, had offended the leading Whigs; and, "anxious to vent their malice on a writer who had now become the object of their hatred," they seized the opportunity to have their revenge on him.

William Benson, a Whig writer, commenced, at his own cost, a prosecution, and thus the most bitter opponent of the Pretender was charged with the worst kind of Jacobitism. The printer of the pamphlets being threatened, "gave information upon oath against Defoe as the author," and Lord Chief Justice Parker granted a warrant for his apprehension.

"Mr. Defoe," says the hostile *Flying Post*, written by Ridpath, "having taken precautions to make his house at Newington as secure

M 2

to him as was necessary for a man in his circumstances, his Lordship's officers were forced to take constables, and a great many
other persons to their assistance; and with much difficulty and
hazard got into the house, and secured him, and brought him from
thence to town."

This was on a Saturday, and Defoe remained in
the custody of the tipstaff till the following Tuesday, when bail to the amount of eight hundred
pounds being offered and accepted he was set at
liberty.

A spiteful contemporary pamphlet, written in
reference to these proceedings, and entitled "Judas
Discovered," calls Defoe "an animal who shifts his
shape oftner than Proteus, and that goes backwards
and forwards like a Hunted Hare; a thoroughpaced,
true-bred Hypocrite, an High Churchman one day and
a rank Whig the next: like the man in the Fable, he
blows Hot and Cold with the same breath."

Prompted by consciousness of innocence, Defoe
defended himself in the *Review*, where, however, he
made the mistake of referring indiscreetly to the
conduct of the Lord Chief Justice. When the case
came on, his lordship caused the reviews to be produced in court, and declared that they were "very
insolent libels against him in particular, and also
against the laws of England." The other judges
concurred in this opinion, and the court was unani-
mous that the books for which Defoe was bound over
were scandalous, wicked, and treasonable libels.

It was in vain that Defoe protested that the books
were written ironically. Sir Thomas Powis, one of
the judges, "with learned arguments," proved to the

satisfaction of himself and his brother dispensers of justice, that the books had not been written ironically; so Defoe was sent to Newgate to await his trial. His fate at this moment was indeed a hard one. To write pamphlets in the interest of the Hanoverian succession, and then to be put into prison for favouring the Pretender was enough to exasperate any man.

CHAPTER IX.

45.—TWO VIPERS TANGLED INTO ONE.—THE END OF THE
REVIEW.—THE SCRIBLERUS CLUB.

WORKS: 144.—Essay on the Treaty of Commerce with France. May, 1713.
145.—Considerations upon the Eighth and Ninth Articles of the Treaty of
Commerce and Navigation. 2nd June, 1713.
146.—*Review*, vol. ix. 11th June, 1713.
147.—Some Thoughts upon the Subject of Commerce with France.
148.—A General History of Trade. Aug. and Sept., 1713.

IN the meantime, on 11th April, 1713, the treaty
of peace, which had so long been under discussion,
was signed at Utrecht. In respect to the share
Defoe had in bringing it about, Mr. Lee observes:
"His attachment to the Earl of Oxford was a
snare, so far as his gratitude for past favours imposed silence on those points of policy which he
could not approve; and this forbearance brought
upon him all the odium of being retained to ex-
pound the views of ministers. He served them
by smoothing the way to peace; but he disapproved
of the terms upon which it was concluded, and expressed his disapprobation in the *Review*, even at
the risk of displeasing Lord Oxford. He acquiesced,
however, in the peace, when it was accomplished,
as a good subject bound by a national obligation."

But the truth is, Defoe was not satisfied with either of the political parties. Trimming, dodging, and intriguing were characteristic of both. To him they were only, to use Shelley's phrase, "two vipers tangled into one." If the Tories were bent on persecuting the Dissenters, and would have welcomed back the Pretender, the Whigs had acquiesced in the persecution of the Dissenters, and had persecuted the man who was the Pretender's most bitter opponent. Defoe had given up contending for parties ; now he contended only for principles.

In May appeared his tract " An Essay on the Treaty of Commerce with France," in which he shows himself to be on the topics of trade a century and a half in advance of general public opinion. " He believed that international reduction and abolition of duties would increase trade, cheapen commodities, promote national and individual prosperity, and become the most powerful guarantee of a lasting peace. To use the modern phrase, Defoe was the first and foremost advocate of ' Free Trade.' " *

The 2nd of June saw the publication of his pamphlet, " Considerations upon the Eighth and Ninth Articles of the Treaty of Commerce and Navigation."

On 11th June, 1713, after a publication extending over more than nine years, he relinquished his *Review*. As it had commenced in Newgate, so it finished in Newgate, for Defoe was still a prisoner. The later numbers had dealt less with French affairs, and more with English Trade and Politics ; his motto being : " England, bad as she is, is yet a

* Lee.

reforming nation."* When we remember that this
important and voluminous work was the offspring
not of an editor and a numerous staff, but of the
brain and pen of one man, who during those nine
years did so many notable things besides, the feeling uppermost is one of wonder. "There were
giants in the earth in those days."

Some allusion has already been made to several
of the more famous of Defoe's literary contemporaries. These had now formed themselves into
two coteries ; one the immortal Scriblerus Club, which
met in the rooms of Dr. Arbuthnot at St. James's
Palace, and the other that nameless circle that
worshipped at the shrine of Addison at Button's
Coffee House. Though not primarily political societies, the members of the first were all Tories, if
not Jacobites, those of the latter Whigs.

Of Addison and his satellites we have no occasion
to say anything, but the Scriblerus Club—owing to the
intense animosity of most of its members against
Defoe—requires some attention.

The heart and soul of the society was its founder,
the manly, learned, lovable, genial, humane, and witty
Dr. Arbuthnot, whose sweet face, if such an adjective
be permissible in connection with the male sex, would
alone have drawn folk to him. Shuffling in gait,
owing to a cruel internal malady, he " could do everything but walk." A more distinguished, but scarcely
more amiable, member of the fraternity was " Dr.
Martin," as they called him, because " a martin is a
sort of swallow, and so is a swift "—sharp-featured

* *Review* iii., 602.

and blue-eyed—one whom even his most intimate friend, Pope—another member—never quite knew how to take. To these were joined the Dragon (Harley), Lord Bolingbroke, Congreve, Dr. Parnell, too fond of claret—a complaint then rather common— who, before Pope arose, outdid all other bards "a bar's length"; Bishop Atterbury, with his head perpetually on the nod, too fond of the Pretender; and the Shaver, Erasmus Lewis, Under-Secretary of State, too fond of ombre, who, instead of turning up at our meetings, "sneeks off to some warm house, wins money and convinces the ladies from whom he wins it that they are highly obliged to him." Lewis's sight subsequently failed him, but he never grew so blind but that he could see "the pips on the cards." It will never be known how much the world owes to these meetings. The witty memoirs of Martin Scriblerus, chiefly from the pen of Arbuthnot, have not only great intrinsic value, but they divide with Defoe's "Consolidator" the palm of having suggested "Gulliver's Travels" Arbuthnot's "John Bull," many of Pope's poems, and some of Gay's, all owe improvements to criticisms in Dr. Arbuthnot's sanctum, and some pieces which we are in the habit of attributing to one man were, perhaps, more correctly, the work of three or four. The lovely ballad, "'Twas when the seas were roaring," for instance, may safely be attributed to the conjunction of Gay, Arbuthnot, and Pope. With the exception of Lord Oxford (Harley), the members of the club had an extraordinary animus against Defoe; partly, no doubt, because he was a Whig, more because he was a Dissenter, but most of all because they were so self-conceited as to believe that nothing was good outside their own narrow precincts. To Swift's hatred of Defoe we have already several times referred. Just before the termination of Defoe's great newspaper, Gay observed, " The poor *Review* is quite exhausted, and grown so very contemptible that, though he has provoked all his brothers of the quill, none will enter into a controversy with him. The fellow, who had excellent natural parts, but wanted a small foundation of learning, is a lively instance of those wits who, as an ingenious author says, will endure but one skimming " (" Present State of Wit," 1711). Gay, it will be noticed, attacks Defoe much in the same style as Swift had done; only he is patronising rather than spiteful. But Gay was a fat man, *ergo* more amiable. To the passage at arms between Defoe and Pope we shall refer later on.

Some time in June, 1713, Defoe delivered himself of " Some Thoughts upon the Subject of Commerce with France," and in the beginning of August he commenced another work, which presented itself in four fortnightly numbers, with the title of " A General History of Trade."

46.—MERCATOR AND DEFOE'S PARDON (NOV. 20TH, 1713—26TH MAY, 1713).—STEELE AND SWIFT AGAIN

WORKS: 149.—Whigs turned Tories. 1713.
    150.—Union and no Union. 1713.
    151.—A Letter to the Dissenters, 3rd Dec., 1713.
    152.—The Scots Nation and Union Vindicated. Mar., 1714.
    153.—A View of the Real Danger of the Protestant Succession. April, 1714.
    154.—Reasons for Impeaching the Lord High Treasurer. April, 1714.
    155.—The Remedy worse than the Disease. 9th June, 1714.
    156.—Mercator. 26th May, 1713—20th July, 1714.

For several years Defoe had desired to conduct a periodical that should be entirely taken up with the

subject of trade, and now that peace had been declared
the favourable moment seemed to have arrived ; so, in
conjunction with others, he started a paper called
Mercator, or Commerce Retrieved. Each number of
Mercator consisted of one leaf small folio, and it
was continued every Tuesday, Thursday, and Saturday until the 20th of July, 1714. Defoe denied
being the author—that is, conductor or editor of
this paper—and said that he had not power to put
what he would into it. But as Professor Minto
observes :

"Every number bears traces of his hand or guidance ; *Mercator*
is identical in opinions, style, and spirit with the *Review*, differing
only in the greater openness of its attacks upon the opposition of
the Whigs to the Treaty of Commerce."

The comments of Defoe's enemies on *Mercator*
are amusing.

"This paper"—*Mercator*—says Boyer, in his "Life of Queen
Anne," "was soon after discovered to be the production of an ambi-
dextrous mercenary scribbler, Daniel De Foe, employed by the Earl
of Oxford, who for this dirty work allowed him a considerable weekly
salary."

Oldmixon,* writing on the same subject, observes :

"Foe, as well as the Lord Treasurer, had been a rank Presbyterian, and their genius was so near akin that Harley could not but
take him into his confidence as soon as he got acquainted with him.
He was adored and caressed by that mighty statesman, who gave
him, as that mercenary said himself, to the value of one thousand
pounds in one year. Foe's business was only to puzzle the cause by
mercantile cant and bold sophistry."

But all this time, be it remembered, Defoe was
in prison. Harley, however, had not forgotten him,

* "History of England," vol. iii., p. 519.

and on November 29th (1713) there came for him
a pardon passed under the Great Seal.

The pamphlet "Whigs turned Tories" (1713) was
written with a view of inducing "all Whigs as well as
Hanoverian Tories" to lay aside their "uncharitable
heats," and to unite their forces in order to 'circum-
vent the plans of those "Jacobite, Popish, and
conforming Tories," whose chief aim and hope was
to bring in the Pretender. "Union and no Union,"
Defoe's next tract, was an inquiry into the grievances
of the Scots, who considered that by the imposition
of the Malt Tax and other violations of the Treaty
of Union, they had been unfairly used. Defoe
admits that they had some cause for complaint, but
insists that disaffection against the Union is confined
only to a few.

In "A Letter to the Dissenters" (3rd Dec., 1713),
he chastises his fellow religionists for uniting with
their political enemies, the "old Ministry," in order
to overthrow the Ministry in power, and warns them
that unless they desist further disabilities will be
forced upon them.

On January 19th, 1714, Steele published a pamphlet,
entitled "The Crisis," advocating the Hanoverian succession, for which—such was the bitterness of party
spirit—he was expelled from the House of Commons.
Swift replied to it, and ridiculed it in his " Pubilc Spirit
of the Whigs," described as "a very clever and bitter
reply to 'The Crisis'"; and in March Defoe, with much
warmth, answered the portions of Swift's pamphlet
relating to Scotland and the Union, in a tract called
"The Scots Nation and Union Vindicated,"

etc., followed shortly after by "A View of the Real Danger of the Protestant Succession," in which he insisted that the Ministry were to be trusted, and that those who desired the Hanoverian succession had no cause to fear—a tract whose natural successor was " Reasons for Impeaching the Lord High Treasurer, and some other of the Present Ministry," a production which, instead of being an attack on Harley, as its title suggested, was in reality a defence. Defoe is ready enough to admit that if Harley wished to endanger the Protestant succession he would deserve to be impeached, but insists that Harley did not wish it.

Your High-flier now brings in a Bill "to prevent the growth of Schism, and for the further security of the Church of England, as by law established "—a measure framed for the express purpose of persecuting Dissenters and bringing back the state of affairs that had existed under the Act of Uniformity. Having passed the Tory House of Commons, it was duly sent up to the House of Lords. Then the pamphleteers set to work. Steele had a tract against it, and on June 9th Defoe published another, " The Remedy Worse than the Disease ; or, Reasons against passing the Bill for preventing the Growth of Schism," etc.

Despite opposition, the Bill, which had passed the Commons on June 1st, was acquiesced in by the Lords on the 15th, and received the royal assent ten days afterward. It is only fair to Harley to say that he did his best to prevent his Tory colleagues from bringing in this Bill, and that, when brought in, he endeavoured to modify it; but he was powerless. A few months later, after the accession of George I., the Act was repealed.

To the *Tatler*, *Spectator*, and *Guardian* of Steele, side by side with whom we have just seen Defoe fighting, there are a number of friendly references in the *Review*—

"There is not a man in this nation," says Defoe (Vol. viii., No. 82), "that pays a greater veneration, to the writings of the inimitable *Spectator* than the author of the *Review*, and that not only for his learning and wit, but especially for his applying that learning and wit to the true ends for which they are given, viz., the establishing virtue in, and the shaming vice out of, the world."

There is also an interesting reference to Steele in *Mercator*, in which Steele's views on trade are opposed. Says Defoe :—

"The *Guardian* is now entered into the dispute; and who shall be able to stand before the *Guardian*? The *Guardian* has so many better talents that it can be no detracting from him to say that the knowledge of trade is not of the number of his acquisitions."

Addison, in his contribution to the same discussion, a pamphlet called "The Trial and Conviction of Count Tariff," adopted a very different style. He classed the *Mercator* and the *Examiner* together, hinted at the fear occasioned by the word pillory, and called *Mercator* "a false, shuffling, prevaricating rascal."

CHAPTER X.

NEWINGTON.

47.—DEATH OF QUEEN ANNE (1ST AUG., 1714).—SAMUEL TUFFLEY
MAKES HIS WILL (28TH OCT., 1714).

WORK : 157.—The Flying Post. 27th July, 1714—21st Aug., 1714.

THE cord that bound Harley and his followers to the
extreme Tories, which had so long been strained, at
last snapped, and the late nominal friends were now
open enemies. In the manœuvering that succeeded,
Bolingbroke and the Tories obtained the ascendancy,
and on the 27th of July Harley was ousted from office ;
but before the Tories were able to win to themselves any
real advantage, an event occurred which frustrated all
their plans—namely, the death of the Queen, on
August 1st (1714).

A few days previous, on July 20th, Defoe's paper,
Mercator, had been discontinued ; but a week later
we find him launching a new venture, *The Flying Post*,
written for William Hurt, the printer, who had
previously published Ridpath's paper of the same
name.

On the 22nd of October, 1714, Samuel Tuffley of
Hackney, brother of Defoe's wife, made his will.

To Daniel Defoe and his children one guinea each was left to buy
rings, and there were a few other small bequests; but the bulk
of the estate—lands, tenements, goods, etc.—was left in trust

for and to the only use of his dear sister Mary Defoe, the wife
of Daniel Defoe, and for and to her disposing and appointment
absolutely and independently of her husband, or of any claim or
demand which he or anyone claiming by, from, or under him by
right of marriage or otherwise might have or made to the same ; the
intent being that Mary Defoe after the testator's decease, notwithstanding her marriage, might fully receive and enjoy the effects of
the estate as universal heir, with full power to sell, dispose, and
transfer as far as the trust above mentioned would possibly admit.
The trustees were to account to her or to her assigns for all the profits of the estate and to none other, and to pay her or her assigns
every six months, or oftener if she required, all the profits ; and a
receipt under her hand was to be a sufficient discharge to the trustees,
without requiring a receipt under her husband's hand. The trustees,
or two of them, were at any time, at her request, given under her
hand and seal, to sell or make over for such considerations as she
agreed to, any part or all of the estate.   And if she affixed her hand
and seal to any deed of sale with the trustee, it should be a good
and sufficient sale although her husband were then living, and the
purchase money was to be paid to the trustees in trust for her.   If
Daniel Defoe died, then, and immediately after his death, this trust
was to expire, and Mary to enter upon all the estate in her own right
and name.   And as her children might suggest that the trust was
made in order to preserve the estate for them, Tuffley expressly
declared that his will was that the estate should be preserved for the
sole use of his sister, to be used and disposed of to such persons as
she thought fit; and if she thought fit to bestow any part on the
children, his will was that she should give the greatest share "to
such of them as behave with the greatest tenderness, duty, and
affection, both to their father and to herself, declaring that if any of
the said children shall behave undutifully, disobediently, or disre-
spectfully, either to their said father or mother, and continue obstinately to do so without humbling themselves to their parents and
obtaining their pardon, he requested that "to such not one shilling
of my estate shall be given, my desire being as much as in me lies
that the said children should be kept in an entire dependance upon
their said father as well as their mother, declaring that it is not from
distrust of or disrespect to their said father that this my will is made
in this manner."

Mary Defoe was to make a will or disposition of

all the estates within two months after Tuffley's decease.

48.—THE LORD ANGLESEY AFFAIR.—"THE WHITE STAFF" AND "FRIDAY."

WORKS : 158.—Advice to the People of Great Britain.   7th Oct., 1714.
159.—A Secret History of One Year.   1714.
160.—The Secret History of the White Staff.   Oct., 1714.
161.—   Do.   part ii.
162.—   Do.   part iii.

In his labours on the *Flying Post*, Defoe again came into collision with the law. Bolingbroke had recently despatched the Tory Earl of Anglesey on a mission to Ireland. But scarcely had the earl landed at Dublin when news came of the Queen's death, and he returned to act as one of the Lords Regent. In the *Flying Post* Defoe declared that the object of the journey to Ireland had been "to new model the forces there, and particularly to break no less than seventy of the honest officers of the army, and to fill up their places with the tools and creatures of Con. Phipps,* and such a rabble of cut-throats as were fit for the work that they had for them to do."

The allegation was probably true, but Anglesey at once took action against it as a scandalous libel. Brought before the Lords Justices in August (1714), Defoe was committed for trial, but shortly after liberated. Though again in hot water, Defoe did not allow his pen to be idle. His "Advice to the People of Great Britain" (7th Oct., 1714) is simply to be good Christians and to be loyal to King

* Sir Constantine Phipps.

N

George. His "Secret History of One Year," that is the first after the Revolution, is one more tribute to the memory of King William; a subject upon which Defoe, whenever hard up for copy, could always fall back. The "Secret History of the White Staff" (Oct., 1714)—a vindication of the policy of Harley—generally attributed to Defoe, has been the subject of a good deal of argument. Mr. George Chalmers says : " There can be no doubt that Defoe was not the author; for he solemnly asserts by his Appeal in 1715, that he had written nothing since the Queen's death." Mr. Walter Wilson, who avoids expressing any opinion of his own as to the authorship, says: "It is certain that Defoe had the credit of it at the time." Mr. Lee, who vainly endeavours to wriggle away from Defoe's renunciation of having written the work, declares that it affords "internal evidence " sufficient to justify the decision that he was the author. Perhaps the real truth is that it was written by his collaborator, the personage who in "Robinson Crusoe" is called Friday; for that Defoe had a collaborator, one who acted for him much as Maquet and others acted for Dumas, is pretty evident. Defoe, indeed, admits as much in his " Serious Reflections." He says—

"The story of my man Friday, and many more most natural passages observed here, are all historical and true in fact. It is most real that I had . . . such a servant, a savage, and afterwards a Christian, and that his name was called Friday, and that he was ravished from me by force, and died in the hands that took him, which I represent by being killed ; this is all literally true, and should I enter into discoveries many alive can testify them. His other conduct and assistance to me also have just references in all their parts to the helps I had from that faithful savage in my real solitudes and disasters."

As Professor Minto says—

"If Defoe had a real man Friday, who had learnt all his arts till he could practise them as well as himself, the fact might go to explain his enormous productiveness as an author."

This partnership between Defoe and Friday, however, must have closed before 1720, when were written the "Serious Reflections," in which Defoe speaks of Friday's death. It could therefore have been only in his political writings that Defoe had the help of a collaborator, or at any rate of this collaborator.

49.—SECOND LONG ILLNESS.—HOW DEFOE TURNED HIS FIT OF APOPLEXY TO ACCOUNT.—THE QUAKER PAMPHLETS.—AND KEIMER THE PRINTER (NOV., 1714—JAN., 1715).

WORKS: 163.—An Appeal to Honour and Justice. Jan., 1715.
    164.—A Reply to a Traitorous Libel entitled "English Advice to the Free holders of England." 29th Jan., 1715.
    165.—A Friendly Epistle, etc., from one of the People called Quakers to Thomas Bradbury.
    166.—The Family Instructor. 31st Mar., 1715. [*See* § 51.]
    167.—A Sharp Rebuke from one of the People called Quakers to Henry Sacheverell, the High Priest of Andrew's, Holbourn.
    168.—A Seasonable Expostulation unto . . the Duke of Ormond By the same Friend that wrote to Thomas Bradbury. 31st May, 1715.

About the 1st of October, 1714, was finished a pamphlet entitled an "Appeal to Honour and Justice. . . . By Daniel Defoe. Being a True Account of his Conduct in Public Affairs." His principal reason for desiring men to know precisely what his conduct had been was a presentiment that he had not long to live.

"By the hint of mortality, and by the infirmities of a life of sorrow and fatigue, I have reason to think I am not a great way

N 2

from, if not very near to, the great ocean of eternity, and the time
may not be long ere I embark on the last voyage. Wherefore, I
think I should have even accounts with this world before I go."

In this pamphlet he explains the principles upon
which he had acted during the whole of his political
life, dwelling particularly upon the much-criticised
course he had taken in respect to the Treaty of
Utrecht. He says that he had never liked the
Treaty ; but, he continues—

"When it was made, and could not be otherwise, I thought our
business was to make the best of it, and rather to inquire what
improvements were to be made of it, than to be continually ex-
claiming at those who made it. While I spoke in this manner,
I bore infinite reproaches from clamouring pens of being in the
French interest, being hired and bribed to defend a bad peace,
and the like."

A short time after—about the middle of December—he was struck down with a fit of apoplexy,
and for a time was in so dangerous a condition that
his life was despaired of. The illness lasted six
weeks. At the conclusion of the " Appeal," which
was issued the first week of January, the publisher
mentioned the circumstance of the author's illness,
explaining that the pamphlet was consequently in-
complete, and adding—

"If he recovers, he may be able to finish what he began ; if not,
it is the opinion of most that know him that the treatment which he
here complains of, and some others that he would have spoken of,
have been the apparent cause of his disaster."

But, as Professor Minto observes—

"There is no sign of incompleteness in the *Appeal ;* and the
conclusion by the publisher, while the author lay ' in a weak and

languishing condition, neither able to go on nor likely to recover, at least in any short time,' gives a most artistic finishing stroke to it."

The happy idea, indeed, had occurred to Defoe to turn the apoplexy to account.

"With grave anxieties added to the strain of such incessant toil, it is no wonder that nature should have raised its protest in an apoplectic fit. Even nature must have owned herself vanquished, when she saw this very protest pressed into the service of the irresistible and triumphant worker."*

Early in January had appeared a powerfully written pamphlet by Bishop Atterbury, entitled " English Advice to the Freeholders of England," written with a view to influencing the approaching elections. Among the numerous answers to this pamphlet, which has been described as "treasonable against the king," and libellous upon the whole body of the Whigs, appeared one by Defoe, " A Reply to a Traitorous Libel, etc.," published on January 29th, whilst, probably, he was still in his sick chamber. Atterbury's pamphlet is denounced as a " mixture of party fury with notorious slander and forgery."

During this illness Defoe was visited by a Quaker, whose kindness made a great impression on him, and he never after neglected an opportunity of speaking well of the religious body to which the good man belonged. And they deserved to be spoken well of, for at this exciting period, when all England was in a ferment, when even the pulpits were made to answer the purpose of hustings, the Quaker body alone advocated temperance and Christian charity. Like Defoe, they cried " Peace, peace ! "

* Professor Minto.

Among the pulpit fulminators was an eminent Dissenting minister named Thomas Bradbury, and in order to reprove Mr. Bradbury, without giving offence, Defoe wrote a pamphlet, in the style and manner of a Quaker, which he published on February 19th, a little after his recovery. It is entitled, "A Friendly Epistle by Way of Reproof from One of the People called Quakers, to Thomas Bradbury, a Dealer in Words"—London: S. Keimer; and in it Defoe tells Bradbury that preaching men like him ought rather to move their people and their brethren to forbear and forgive one another than to move and excite them to severities. Referring to Bradbury's recommendation of the new administration, which included the Duke of Marlborough and others, Defoe says, " I must lead thee by the hand, not by the nose, Thomas—others have done thee that office already."

The Quaker fraternity, however, afraid lest in the excited state of the nation this pamphlet might bring them into trouble, published, on March 5th, in the *London Gazette*, and on March 7th, in the *Daily Courant*, an advertisement disowning it, in which they stated their belief that it was written by an adversary of theirs, " whereby to vent his own invectives against the Government in our name, and to expose us to the displeasure thereof, and the censure of sober people." Nor is it surprising that the Quakers were anxious to be free from all suspicion of blame, for they had no desire for a repetition of the persecutions of the previous reigns.

Defoe, however, pleased with his new *rôle* as a child with a toy, still continued to play the Quaker,

and the same year published two more pamphlets :
" A Sharp Rebuke . . . to Henry Sacheverell" (no
date), and " A Seasonable Expostulation . . . unto
. . . the Duke of Ormond" (May 31st), both of
which, like the first, were printed by Samuel Keimer,
of Paternoster Row. In the former he charges "the
High Priest of Andrew's, Holbourn," as he calls
Sacheverell, with being in league with the Pretender ;
and in the latter, though with less warmth of language, he expostulates with Ormond, whose vanity
was leading him to encourage Jacobite mobs.

In reference to Defoe's partiality for the Quakers,
it may be noticed that there is a good Quaker lady in
" Roxana," and Quakers are much to the fore in
"Captain Singleton."

When a few years later (1718) Keimer, the printer
of these tracts, got into trouble, Defoe showed himself
a true friend. Keimer was printer of the *Weekly
Journal*, and on account of certain paragraphs in it
relating to the execution of Hall and Paul, he was
committed, by warrant from Lord Townshend, to the
Gatehouse, of the horrors whereof he gives a graphic
account in his tract, written while he was in prison, " A
Brand Pluck'd from the Burning," etc., which contains
the following reference to, and letter from, Defoe :—

" My outward wants encreasing, I wrote to several of my former
acquaintance for relief, but with little success except from one who
had known the different stations of life from the closet conversation
of a King and Queen to the fatiguing difficulties of a Dungeon, who
with his welcome kindness sent me the following lines :—

" ' Mr. Keimer,

" ' I have your Letter : The account you give of your hardships
is indeed very moving ; the relief I have been able to give you has

been very small; however, I have repeated it by the same kind messenger.

"'Of all your Letter, nothing pleases me so much as to find you hint something of your being touch'd with a sense of breaking in upon principle and conscience: God grant the motion may be sincere. Afflictions do not rise out of the dust: They seem to leave God himself no other room but that of vengeance to deal with them who are neither better'd by mercies or afflictions. The time of sorrow is a time to reflect, and to look and see wherefore he that is righteous is contending with you. Only remember that he is not mocked. Nothing but a deep, thorough, unfeigned, sincere humiliation is accepted by him. God restore you to your health, liberty, and prosperity, and, last of all, to his blessing and favour.

"'Shall I recommend a sincere prayer put up to heaven, tho' in verse, by one I knew under deep and dreadful afflictions? I'll write you but a few of them :—

"'"Lord, whatsoever troubles rack my breast,
Till sin removes too, let me take no rest ;
How dark soe'er my case, or sharp my pain,
Oh, let not sorrow cease and sin remain.

"'"For Jesus' sake, remove not my distress
Till thy Almighty Grace shall repossess
The vacant Throne, from whence my crimes depart,
And make a willing captive of my heart."

"'These are serious lines, tho' Poetical. It's a prayer I doubt few can make : But the moral is excellent ; if afflictions cease and cause of afflictions remain, the Joy of your Deliverance will be short.

"'I have sent you the printed paper you wrote for —— I should be glad to render you any service within my power, having been always perhaps more than you imagin'd

"'Your sincere Friend and Servant.'"*

The two stanzas Defoe quotes are a Christian paraphrase from Pliny (Ep. vii., 26).

Keimer subsequently emigrated to America, and mention of him occurs in Franklin's "Autobiography."

* Communicated to *Notes and Queries*, 8th May, 1869, by James Crossley.

50.—END OF THE LIFE OF SILENCE (19TH DEC., 1714).—CRUSOE
LEAVES HIS ISLAND (19TH DEC., 1687).

This great illness of Defoe's was the turning-point
in his life.   It marked the end of his period of silence.
As he lay helpless on his couch, and death stared him
in the face, his thoughts would naturally be led more
particularly to the world beyond the grave.   He
would review his past, and ask himself whether his
conduct had been such as could be defended.   In
summing up his political actions he would see little
to regret ; in business matters he would see that he
could easily have acted with greater discretion ; but
when he came to his wife and family a feeling of
uneasiness must have come over him.   He had been
guilty of no act of what could rightly be called cruelty
to them ; he had supplied them with the wherewithal
to provide themselves with the comforts of life ; he
had taken care that his children should be well
educated, but he had lived apart from them ; he had
not spoken to them, or scarcely spoken to them, for
many, many years—to his wife for more than twenty-
eight years.   To repeat again his words, "it was their
ill-behaviour to him at first" that "was the occasion of
it ; for they treated him with provoking language,
which frequently put him into indecent passions and
urged him into rash replies."   There is no doubt that
the cause of the vexatious conduct of Mrs. Defoe was
her husband's recklessness in business, and the great
losses that in consequence ensued.   Defoe himself
admits that thirteen times he was rich and poor.   What
did that mean to his family ?   Defoe nowhere admits

that any blame lay upon himself.   Mrs. Defoe would
see with other eyes.   Defoe heaped up fortune after
fortune.   His splendid genius, like the magician in
the Arabian tale, turned to gold everything it touched;
but, as happened in the tale too, it required nothing
more than the breath of some malignant afrit—whom,
with care, he could generally have kept at a distance—
to turn the beautiful yellow gold back again into dross.

Some light is thrown on Defoe's disastrous methods
of handling money by the conduct of his son-in-law,
Mr. H. Baker, with the manuscripts left by whom I
shall deal with exhaustively in their proper place.
Mr. Baker could never get at the bottom of Defoe.
"Your father," he tells his sweetheart, "loves to hide
himself in mists"; but the most significant passage is
this: "Ruin and wild destruction sport around him,
and exercise their fury on all he has to do with"—a
passage suggested by Defoe's refusal to come to terms
with Baker concerning Sophia's portion.   As the con-
text shows, the words "ruin and wild destruction" had
reference specially to the destruction of Baker's peace
of mind by Defoe's obstinacy; but they also point to
an intimate knowledge by Baker of Defoe's whole
history, for had Baker's knowledge of Defoe been such
as to warrant confidence in him, he would have
accepted Defoe's promise, married Sophia at once,
and been saved much heart-burning.   But the fact is,
Baker knew Defoe too well; he knew that in the great
Daniel's unsanded fingers the house at Newington, the
lands at Colchester, the gardens and the coaches, were
as slippery as so many eels, and that something more
was required than either Daniel's word or his bond.

But we go back to Defoe's reference to the great silence : " He took this severe way to punish himself for being provoked, and to punish them " (his wife and children) " for provoking him. But the severity was unjustifiable ; it ruined his family and broke up his house. His wife could not bear it ; and, after endea-. vouring by all the ways possible to alter his rigid silence, went first away from him and afterwards away from herself, turning melancholy and distracted. His children separated, some one way and some another way, and only one daughter, who loved her father above all the rest, kept with him ; tended him, talked to him by signs, and lived almost dumb, like her father, nearly twenty-nine years with him ; till, being very sick and in a high fever—delirious, as we call it, or light-headed—he broke his silence, not knowing when he did it, and spoke, though wildly at first. He recovered of the illness afterwards, and frequently talked with his daughter, but not much, and very seldom to anybody else.

"Yet this man did not live a silent life with respect to himself. He read continually, and wrote down many excellent things, which deserved to have appeared in the world ; and was often heard to pray to God in his solitudes very audibly, and with great fervency ; but the injustice which his rash vow, if it was a vow of silence, was to his family, and the length he carried it, was so unjustifiable another way, that I cannot say his instructions could have much force in them."

This great illness of Defoe's commenced, as we have said, in the middle of December, 1714, and,

according to my calculation in § 7, the exact date
when Defoe terminated his period of silence was
December 19th. Crusoe had left his island ! Twenty-
eight years two months and nineteen days he had
lived in his solitude. Twenty-eight years two months
and nineteen days Defoe had lived a life of silence.
And as, even after his deliverance, Crusoe did not
long content himself at home, so Defoe, even after
his tongue had been loosed, talked " not much, and
very seldom to anybody." Like his contemporary
Addison, he was, life through, more or less a silent
man ; though, in congenial circles, as we learn from
his own pen, he could be sociable; but the silence
of Addison was loquacity itself compared with the
silence of Defoe.

As a great change had come over the mind of
Defoe, we should naturally expect to see indications
of it in his next work ; and we do—indications of
the most marked character.

51.—THE FAMILY INSTRUCTOR, VOL. I, (31ST MAR., 1715).

This work was the first volume of his long-
popular book of dialogues for young people, " The
Family Instructor." He had sold the work during
his convalescence, with the stipulation that the name
of the author should be concealed, " lest some men,
suffering their prejudices to prevail even over their
zeal for public good, might be tempted to 'lay the
imperfections of the author of this book as a
stumbling-block in the way of those who might
otherwise receive benefit by it." Mr. Matthews,

the purchaser and publisher, employed the Rev. S. Wright, an eminent Presbyterian minister, to write an introduction. "The Family Instructor" is in three parts—" I., Relating to Fathers and Children; II., To Masters and Servants; III., To Husbands and Wives."

In the preface Defoe professes "to have a firm belief that he was not without a more than ordinary presence and assistance of the divine spirit" in the performance of the task, and there is no doubt that it has been the means of doing a deal of good.

No one should sit down and attempt to go straight through it. A better plan would be to read a portion out aloud to one's family once or twice a week, and no doubt that is how it has been most used. Not that we agree with all Defoe's opinions; nor would anyone. His illness, though it had loosed his tongue, had somewhat narrowed his soul. He had always been a man of religion, putting that before everything else. At all times the fear of God had been before his eyes; but now he was to go a step further, and his household was henceforth to be conducted on lines rigidly Puritanical. But times and customs have changed since then. I hope that in the nineteenth century we love and honour the Deity as much as they did in the eighteenth; but we no longer insist that our young people "shall not stir out of doors after church," that playbooks shall be burnt, and the playhouse tabooed.

Card-playing—the vice of the age—drinking, and swearing are sternly, and properly, condemned. It will be no alleviation to a parent's sorrow, observes

Defoe, to say, after a child is ruined, "I used those diversions moderately and kept myself within compass; it was but very seldom I used an ill-word; I played at cards but very moderately, and never for money; I seldom drank hard." In Defoe's own house there was family prayer every morning and every night, and the crucial importance of this institution is over and over again insisted upon. The converted father in the dialogue requires his daughter "to use more modesty in her dress and conversation," and "to wear no more patches," and to lay by her "foolish romances and novels," whereupon, having no intention of so doing, "she flings upstairs in a rage." This was very wrong, but one sympathises with her just a little when her mother took her "good collection of plays, all the French novels, all the modern poets, Boileau, Dacier, and a great many more," and flung them on the fire, especially as in place of them she was given the "Practice of Piety" and "The Whole Duty of Man," both very excellent reading, but of which, even on a Sunday, it is possible to have too much. Says the girl, "I have learnt a great deal of good from a play." Replies Defoe, with all the old Puritan narrowness, "But might you not have learnt more from the Scriptures?" On the other hand, it must be admitted that many of the plays then to be had were mixed with "much lewd, vicious, and abominable stuff." In the fifth dialogue we get a description of a Sunday in a strict household, such as Defoe's was: "The young ladies are obliged to be downstairs half an hour after nine in the morning, ready dressed." Then follow prayers, and soon after they all go away, either to the church or to the meeting-house; but whichsoever it is, they are almost sure to meet together after sermon, sometimes at the very door, and then, children and servants, not one stirs from home. In the evening the head of the family "calls them all together, reads to them in some good books, and then sings psalms, and goes to prayers; when that is over, they go to supper, then they spend an hour perhaps, or two, in the most innocent and the most pleasant discourse and conversation imaginable— it is always about something religious—and then everyone retires to their apartment, and the young ladies spend their time in their closet devotions, till they go to bed."

The feeling uppermost after reading this is pity for the "young ladies." It was religion gone mad. Still, better that than the profanity and utter careless-ness prevalent in so many households.

In dialogue six, it is mentioned prettily that while the family were at prayers, when there was any word that the mother thought the child ought to remember particularly, she would touch his cheek; and then, after prayers were over, she would tell him why she did so, and how that sentence was proper for him to remember and to make use of for himself. It is the little touches like this which render "The Family Instructor" so charming, and which show that with all its Puritanical stiffness, Defoe's religion was of the right sort—that it was genuine, and sprang from the heart. The chief blemish of the book is the excessive severity which the father shows to his unrepentant son. It was Nebuchadnezzar over again: "Their houses shall be made a dunghill." But that is human nature; and Defoe was nothing if not in earnest.

Some of the scenes in "The Family Instructor," which was, doubtless, written as well for the instruction of Defoe's own family as for the edification of the public, are laid in the grounds of his house at Newington, which, like the house in the narrative, had a fine garden, with a close behind, in which may or may not have been "a row of lime trees."

Defoe's youngest child, Sophia, was at this time fourteen, just at an age when the female mind was ensnared by millinery, plays, and patches. How old his other daughters, Hannah, Henrietta, and Maria were we do not know. It may be merely a coincidence, but it is noteworthy that while the eldest daughter in the narrative repents and becomes reconciled to her father, the eldest son continues in his obstinacy to the end; and it is painful to remember that both Defoe's sons caused their father a great deal of sorrow.

52.—CHARLES XII. OF SWEDEN.—THANKS TO A DREAM, OR HOW DEFOE GOT OUT OF THE ANGLESEY SCRAPE (JULY 12, 1715).

WORK 169.—History of the Wars of Charles XII. of Sweden.

Defoe's next publication, "The History of the Wars of His Present Majesty Charles XII., King of Sweden" (6th July, 1715), was compiled in part from the items of news in the *Review*. What the "Scots Gentleman in the Swedish Service," who figures on the title-page as the author, had to do with the book, beyond helping to make it sell, we have no means of ascertaining. That he was a myth is unlikely. As we have already shown, Defoe, whenever possible, got his information first hand, and the majority of the facts here dealt with may well have been derived from a " Scots Gentle. man in the Swedish Service." That Defoe was perfectly acquainted with all the tricks of the pro- fession, and that he did not neglect to avail himself of them; that indeed his own ingenuity invented some very pretty new ones, we readily admit; but he was far more scrupulous in such matters than some would have us believe. Five years later (21st May, 1720); after the death of Charles, Defoe republished this work with an appendix carrying the story on up to date.

Ever since the previous August, Defoe had been at large upon his recognisances for the article relating to the Earl of Anglesey. On the 12th July, 1715, he was brought to trial at the Court of King's Bench. As he had acknowledged the authorship, nothing remained for the court to decide but whether or not he had broken the law, and what punishment should be inflicted. But though brought in guilty, sentence was deferred. How at last he got out of this scrape, we are informed by himself in that portion of his " Serious Reflections" which relates to the phenomena of dreams, and the beliefs in premonition by dreams, and silent hints by God in the daytime—a very favourite subject of his, as we have already noticed. He says—

"I know a man who made it a rule always to obey these silent hints, and he has often declared to me that when he obeyed them,

o

he never miscarried ; and if he neglected them, or went on contrary to them, he never succeeded; and gave me a particular case of his own, among a great many others, wherein he was thus directed. He had a particular case befallen him, wherein he was under the displeasure of the Government, and was prosecuted for a misdemeanour, and brought to a trial in the King's Bench Court, where a verdict was brought against him, and he was cast; and times running very hard at that time, against the party he was of, he was afraid to stand the hazard of a sentence, and absconded, taking care to make due provision for his bail, and to pay them whatever they might suffer. In this circumstance he was in great distress, and no way presented unto him but to fly out of the kingdom, which, being to leave his family, children, and employment, was very bitter to him, and he knew not what to do; all his friends advising him not to put himself into the hands of the law, which though the offence was not capital, yet in his circumstances seemed to threaten his utter ruin. In this extremity he felt one morning (just as he had awaked, and the thoughts of his misfortune began to return upon him)—I say he felt—a strong impulse darting into his mind thus : WRITE A LETTER TO THEM. It spoke so distinctly to him, and as it were forcibly, that as he has often said since, he can scarce persuade himself not to believe but that he heard it; but he grants that he did not really hear it, too. However, it repeated the words daily and hourly to him, till at length walking about in his chamber where he was hidden, very pensive and sad, it jogged him again, and he answered aloud to it, as if it had been a voice, WHOM SHALL I WRITE TO ? It returned immediately, WRITE TO THE JUDGE " [Lord Chief Justice Parker]. "This pursued him again for several days, till at length he took his pen, ink, and paper, and sat down to write, but knew not one word of what he should say, but, *dabitur in hac hora*, he wanted not words: It was immediately impressed on his mind, and the words flowed upon his pen in a manner that even charmed himself, and filled him with expectations of success. The letter was so strenuous in argument, so pathetic in its eloquence, and so moving and persuasive, that as soon as the judge read it, he sent him word he should be easy, for he would endeavour to make that matter light to him ; and in a word never left, till he obtained leave to stop the prosecution, and restore him to his liberty and to his family."

53.—A GOVERNMENT SPY.—THE LETTERS TO MR. DE LA FAYE.

The country was now all in an upset on account of what is generally called " The '15," the attempt of the Pretender to seize the English throne; and Defoe's next three effusions, as might be expected, have reference to it. " A Hymn to the Mob" is a history of the mobs of all times, and a denunciation of those which just then were making the streets of London such scenes of disorder. The strains of Defoe did not get more dulcet as he advanced in years. Even the atrocities of Tate and Eusden are more tolerable than the " Hymn to the Mob."

On the 15th of October he very sensibly returns to prose again with " A View of the Scots Rebellion," in which he shows how the plans of the Highlanders could be circumvented; and on November 10th he poses once more as a Quaker, and addresses a pamphlet to the rebel Earl of Mar, with the title, " A Trumpet Blown in the North," etc.

We have seen that Lord Chief Justice Parker prevented further proceedings against Defoe; but he did more. He sought an interview with Lord Townshend, the Secretary of State, and represented to him that Defoe was a staunch supporter of King George.

Townshend received the deserter, or the supposed deserter, with open arms, and thus was Defoe restored to his old Whig love. Townshend's next thought was how to make the best of his new ally, and it occurred to him that it would be good policy if—the reconciliation with the Government being concealed—Defoe could remain in the enemy's camp as a Government spy.   Jacobite journals had of late published numbers of seditious and treasonable articles, which had done the Government damage.   If Defoe were to worm himself into the confidence of these journalists—which he could easily do, on account of his supposed antagonism to the Government—and counteract their designs by intercepting or taking the sting out of treasonable papers, it was evident that the Government could be materially assisted.   Townshend, therefore, inquired whether Defoe would do this—whether, in short, he would be a Government spy.   Defoe consented, and on these broad conditions engaged himself in Lord Townshend's service.   Whether he is to be blamed or not, different persons will have different opinions.   If it is dishonourable to be a spy, Defoe's conduct cannot be defended ; if it is not dishonourable, let no stones be cast at him.   He wrote during this period nothing "contrary to his conscience, or to the principles which had directed his whole life."   The arrangements with Lord Townshend are stated by Defoe in six letters written by him to Mr. De La Faye between April 12 and June 13, 1718.   Whether Defoe had at first any fixed remuneration does not appear ; but at the end of 1716, when Townshend went out of office, he received an appointment, "with promise of further allowance as service presented." Apparently this appointment was held till 1726.

About the end of 1715 Defoe published a prose satire, entitled, "An account of the Great and Generous actions of James Butler (late Duke of Ormond)," in which he shows that Ormond, who was the occasion of rioting at Oxford and other disturbances, and who had recently fled to the Continent to avoid the consequences of his treasonous actions—had attained popularity, not on account of his Jacobitism, but through his "vanity, ambition, and the prodigal squandering of a princely fortune." "Some Account of the Two Nights' Court at Greenwich" (published early in 1716) is a history of the frustration of the Jacobite plans at the time of the landing of King George.

This production Defoe—"that prostituted tool of the Ministry," as Boyer calls him—followed by two pamphlets (Nos. 175 and 176) in support of the measure for establishing Septennial Parliaments, which was introduced as a bulwark against the Jacobite agitations, and which passed both houses on the 10th of April, 1716.

54.—*MERCURIUS POLITICUS* (MAY, 1716, TO SEPT. 1720)—AND *DORMER'S NEWS LETTER* (JUNE, 1716, TO AUG., 1718).

WORKS : 177.—Mercurius Politicus.
        178.—Dormer's News Letter.
        179.—Memoirs of the Church of Scotland.
        180.—Count Patkul.

Previous to the time when Defoe linked himself to Townshend, he had announced his works as being written by the author of "The True-born Englishman", or the author of the *Review*; but subsequently, owing to the nature of his connection with the Government, he deemed it expedient to issue them either anonymously or pseudonymously. With two trifling exceptions, observes Mr. Lee, " Daniel Defoe never appeared again before the world, as an author, in his proper person, nor laid any public claim to productions of his own pen that were so popular as to have passed through half-a-dozen editions within less than a month." This is true, but the public rarely failed to recognise his hand ; for though he hid his name, he took no pains to disguise his style. Nor was he ever displeased at being detected. He took it as a compliment.

He now set himself in good earnest to fulfil his engagement with the Government, and as a commencement established (May, 1716) a monthly periodical, *Mercurius Politicus*, which was always to be kept (mistakes excepted) to pass as a Tory paper, and yet be so managed that it could give no offence to the Government. Each number of this periodical consists of an octavo pamphlet of nearly a hundred pages. Defoe was connected with it till 1720, and probably longer. In June (1716) we find him, with the approbation of Townshend, becoming part-proprietor and manager of the red-hot Tory and High Church *Dormer's News Letter*, a piece of business that was the more acceptable to the Government from the fact that News Letters were not printed or published in the usual way and openly sold, but were only transcribed by hand, and sent by post to all subscribers. He was connected with *Dormer's* till 1718, and perhaps later. It "still seemed to be Tory, so as to amuse the party, and prevent their setting up another violent paper." What time during the next nine months could be spared from bamboozling the Tories was devoted to writing a volume of four hundred and fifty pages, entitled "Memoirs of the Church of Scotland," a work which was published April 26th, 1717.

Early in 1717 the Government discovered that the Jacobites were making preparation for another rebellion, and in consequence of secret information a raid was made upon the residence of Count Gyllenborg, the Swedish Ambassador, with the result of the discovery of a damning correspondence between him and Baron Goertz, a distinguished Swedish Ambassador abroad. In consequence, there arose throughout England a feeling of intense animosity against the King of Sweden, and it occurred to Defoe to revive the account of the King of Sweden's barbarity nine years previous to a nobleman named Count Patkul, which he did, in a pamphlet published in April with the following title: "A short narrative of the life and death of John Rhinholdt, Count Patkul, a nobleman of Livonia, who was broke alive upon the wheel in Great Poland anno 1707. Together with the manner of his execution: Written by the Lutheran minister who assisted him in his last hours. Faithfully translated out of a High Dutch manuscript, and now published for the information of Count Gyllenborg's English friends." Mr. Lee is uncertain whether this is a translation or an original composition, but inclines to the latter, because it refers to, and quotes nearly four pages from, Defoe's former work on the "Wars of Charles XII."

55.—"FRIDAY" WRITES THE MINUTES OF THE NEGOTIATIONS OF MONSIEUR MESNAGER (17TH JUNE, 1717).

WORKS: 181.—Minutes, etc., of Mesnager.
182.—A Declaration of Truth to Benjamin Hoardley (another Quaker Pamphlet)

We have seen how, in 1711, M. Mesnager, the French ambassador, had endeavoured to corrupt Defoe with a hundred pistoles, and how the plot had failed. On the 17th of June, 1717, appeared a pamphlet entitled "Minutes of the Negociations of Monsr. Mesnager at the Court of England towards the close of the last reign," the object of which was to defend Harley, Lord Oxford, whose trial was to commence on the 24th of that month. Now the publication of this work is one of the most interesting events in the life of Defoe, for though the book contains abundance of evidence of Defoe's finger in it, yet, when charged with writing it by his enemy Boyer, he declares point blank in *Mercurius Politicus* for 1717 (pp. 471–3) that he was "not the author or the translator of the said book," that he had "no concern in it," and that he "did never see it, other than its outside, in the bookseller's shop." He further says—

"Mr. Boyer has also now published, the titles of a great many Books and Pamphlets, which he charges me with writing (no less than Fourteen in number), but is so unfortunate in his Spleen, that of all the Number, there is but one that I was sole Author of, not above three that I ever had any Hand in, and five or six that I never saw in my Life."—*Mercurius Politicus* for 1717, pp. 471–3 (July).

In a letter to *Notes and Queries,* February 12, 1870, Mr. Lee, after giving five proofs that Defoe was connected with " Mesnager," says :—

"If Defoe did not write 'Mesnager's Minutes,' who did? Had he a 'double,' or an imitator never heard of or suspected by himself, his friends, or his numerous enemies, and yet holding all his political principles, thinking the same thoughts, and clothing them in precisely the same peculiar phraseology, having the same gratitude towards the Earl of Oxford, and continuing faithful to him throughout his imprisonment?"

And Mr. Crossley, as great an authority on Defoe as Mr. Lee, inquires similarly—

"Who was the contemporary who imitates so well his style and manner of writing, as it cannot be denied that some of the tracts repudiated by Defoe bear strong traces of his pen?"

Mr. Lee inquires whether Defoe had a " double," but he forgets that Defoe himself declared that he did have a "double," a collaborator, a " Friday"; and it is impossible to get out of this difficulty respecting Mesnager except by assuming that " Friday" wrote it—and wrote it without Defoe's assistance, though, doubtless, at his suggestion.

Other works that Defoe disclaimed authorship of, and that contain the impress of his hand, are: " The Balance of Europe," 1711 ; " Armageddon," 1711 ; "Mercator"; "Secret History of the White Staff," 1714; and the two tracts on " Triennial Parliaments."

The Whig party were now having it all their own way : it was given out that the Occasional Conformity Act and the Schism Act were to be repealed. To smooth the way for this course, Dr. Hoardley, Low Church Bishop of Bangor, preached a sermon on

"The Nature of the Kingdom or Church of Christ," which caused Defoe, who approved the Bishop's doctrine, to write another Quaker tract, in which he roguishly advises the Bishop to go one step further—to come out from the Church, lay down his "painted vestments and profane trinkets," and unite himself with the Society of Friends.

56.—MIST AND HIS JOURNAL (24TH AUG., 1717).—DANCING OVER BROKEN GLASS.

WORK: 183.—*The Weekly Journal; or, Saturday's Post* (Mist's).

How Defoe worked *Mercurius Politicus* and *Dormer's News Letter* for the Government we have already seen. Lord Townshend, who went out of office in December, 1716, had been succeeded by Lord Sunderland, who "was pleased to approve and continue" Defoe's previous service; and with his lordship's approbation, Defoe put the Government under still further obligations by connecting himself, "in the disguise of a translator of foreign news," with the Tory journal of Mr. Nathaniel Mist, the organ of the Pretender's interest. Defoe had no share in the property of Mist's *Journal*, and "therefore no absolute power to reject improper communications; but he trusted to the moral influence he should be able to acquire and maintain over Mist, who had no suspicion that the Government was indirectly concerned in the matter." In his account of these various transactions, Defoe thus sums up his duties :—

"Upon the whole, however, this is the consequence, that by this management, the *Weekly Journal* (Mist's) and *Dormer's Letter*, as

also the *Mercurius Politicus*, which is in the same nature of management as the *Journal*, will be always kept (mistakes excepted) to pass
as Tory papers, and yet be disabled and enervated so as to do no
mischief or give any offence to the Government."

The correspondents and supporters of Mist's were
" Papists, Jacobites, and enraged High Tories, a generation whom," says Defoe, " I profess, my very soul
abhors." In the performance of his duty he was
compelled to hear traitorous expressions against the
King, and "to take scandalous and villainous papers,
and keep them by him, as if he would gather materials
from them to put into the news, but really with a view
to suppressing them. Thus," concludes Defoe, " I bow
myself in the House of Rimmon." He says that this
work was not only far from pleasant, but also dangerous; and dangerous it truly was, for the possibility
constantly stared him in the face that he might be
found out, and that Mist or his friends Atterbury,
Ormond, Bolingbroke, and Mar might discover how
the wind really lay, which, as we shall see by-and-by,
they in the end did. But, with all its dangers,
Defoe loved it. Ticklish business of one kind or
another he was engaged upon the whole of his life.
To dance over broken glass, on the edges of preci-
pices, on the thinnest of ice, were feats that his soul
revelled in; and though over and over again he came
to grief, yet he never could wean himself from the
delight. He was a sphinx, a jack-o'-lantern, a
mystery. He delighted to encircle himself in a mist.
He had as many faces as Garrick, and which was the
real Defoe none of his contemporaries could make up
their minds. Mist's *Journal*, with which Defoe became

connected about the 24th of August, 1717, consisted of
six pages small folio. In No. 68, published on the 29th
of March, 1718, an important improvement was effected
in the paper. Each number, in addition to its previous contents, presented an essay or communication
on some subject of public interest, written in the form
of a letter—generally by Defoe—and addressed to
Mr. Mist, but signed with any letter or name that
might, for the appearance of variety, occur at the
moment. This practice was presently adopted by
other papers, and the articles which were placed at the
commencement of each number shortly after became
distinguished by the title of "Letters Introductory."
The writers of such letters became dignified with the
title of Author, as, for example, "Mist's Author,"
"Applebee's Author." * Thus it may be claimed for
Defoe that he was the originator of that mighty
agency of modern times, "the leading article." For
his services on Mist's *Journal* Defoe was paid "after
the rate of twenty shilling a week." †

57.— *THE WHITEHALL EVENING POST.* —"THAT NOTORIOUS
INSIGNIFICANT ANIMAL. MIST AND· HIS SCANDALOUS
AUTHOR DANIEL FOE."

WORKS: 184.—Curious Little Oration.
    185.—Memoirs of Public Transactions in the Life and Ministry of his Graco
        the D. of Shrewsbury.
    186.—The Case of the War in Italy Stated.
    187.—Memoirs of the Rev. Daniel Williams, D.D.
    188.—The Family Instructor, vol. ii.
    189.—*The Whitehall Evening Post.*
    190.—A Friendly Rebuke to one Parson Benjamin. 10th Jan., 1719.

The death of the Duke of Shrewsbury, early in
1718, suggested an account of that nobleman's life, or

---

    * Lee.   † State Papers. See *The Athenæum*, 26th August, 1893.

rather of his public transactions (185) ; and scarcely was Defoe's ink dry before he was ready with " The Case of the War in Italy Stated "—a pamphlet dealing with the complications between Spain and Austria.

Between April and June (1718), Lord Stanhope having succeeded Lord Sunderland, Defoe addressed a series of six letters to Mr. Charles de la Faye, one of the secretaries under Lord Stanhope, to explain his connection with Mist's *Journal*, and it is from these that the facts in this singular episode in Defoe's life have been gleaned.

Early in 1718 Defoe had dealings with the famous and infamous publisher, Edmund Curll, who goes down to posterity as having added a new word to our language and invented a new sin—the sin of Curllicism, defined by Defoe as " writing beastly stories, and then propagating them by print." " In the four years past," added Defoe, " more beastly unsufferable books have been published by this one offender than in thirty years before by all the nation."

The tall, thin, white-faced figure of Edmund Curll, with its goggle-eyes and splay-feet, was a familiar sight in the streets of London ; and stories were told of translators in his pay " lying three in a bed at the ' Pewter Platter Inn ' in Holborn," " how he and they were for ever at work deceiving the public," of his penuriousness, which would never allow indulgence in drink, much as he craved it, and of the nauseous greed with which he did indulge at another's expense—" drinking every day till he was quite blind, and as incapable of self-motion as a block." Alongside with " the most filthy and ribald works that were ever issued," Curll, who had piously erected a Bible over his shop as a sign, kept a very large stock of religious works; and memoirs of celebrated divines was a speciality of his; consequently, upon the death of the Rev. Daniel Williams, D.D., a distinguished Presbyterian minister, he requested Defoe, a friend of Dr. Williams, to write the deceased clergyman's memoirs.

Defoe describes Curll as " odious in his person, scandalous in his fame; he is marked by nature, for he has a bawdy countenance, and a debauched mien, his tongue is an echo of all the beastly language his shop is filled with, and filthiness drivels in the very tone of his voice."*   An unsavoury man in an unsavoury den.   Defoe had dealings with a good many publishers, but with none whom he liked less than Edmund Curll.

The " Memoirs of Daniel Williams " was followed by a second volume of " The Family Instructor," which owed its origin to the popularity attained by the first volume, now in its fourth edition.   The first part of the new volume relates to family breaches and their obstruction of religious duties, the second, " to the great mistake of mixing the passions in the managing and correcting of children."   Says Defoe, " The same desire of doing good, which moved the first part, has been sincerely the occasion of a second"; and he believed that, as on the former occasion, he had had the presence and assistance of God.   The same remarks that were offered in respect to the first volume apply to this one.   It requires to be taken

* Defoe, in Mist's *Journal*, 5th April, 1718.

in doses. As in its predecessor, the prevailing vices of the time are unsparingly denounced. There is a whip for people who get "as drunk as a wheelbarrow," for those who in waspish moods unjustly beat their children, and for those who indulge in the fashionable "Poison me!" and other foolish expletives. Perhaps the most interesting figure in the book is the coloured man, Toby, who, like his more famous successor in "Robinson Crusoe," gets converted; and there is a sea captain in it.

"The Family Instructor" marks a stage in Defoe's development. At first he was a pamphleteer, then in "The Family Instructor" he ventures on a series of thin stories, with a huge amount of moralizing. The edifice was presently to be capped with such productions as "Robinson Crusoe," "Moll Flanders," and "Captain Singleton," with plenty of story and only just enough moralizing for the average sinner to take with comfort.

The change that had come over Mist's paper did not pass unnoticed by the contemporary press. The racy political articles against the Government that had been so palatable to the extreme Tories had now given place to tomfooleries about a "Floating Island," "The Destruction of the Island of St. Vincent," etc., papers bantering the customs of the day after the manner of the *Tatler* and the *Spectator*, or "diverting stories," such as Defoe delighted in, about a thief robbing a Quaker's house by way of the chimney and getting off scot free by representing himself as the devil; of a physician set upon by thieves, who, because he had no money, obliged him by way of punishment to take his own medicine, etc. etc.

Read's (Whig) *Journal* in particular rallied Mist on the change, concluding its taunt by declaring that Mist's wings were clipped and that he only fluttered about like a wounded bird ; and subsequently, when the secret as to Defoe's connection with Mist had leaked out, *Read's* had a good deal of abuse to heap upon " that notorious, insignificant animal Mist" and "his scandalous author, Daniel Foe."

But not only was Mist taunted by the Whigs; his friends the Tories were also exasperated against him, and, owing to the pressure they brought to bear, violent articles against the Government again began to appear in its columns. It was in vain that Defoe endeavoured to suppress these things, in vain that he represented that it was dangerous to do more than rally the Whigs and admit foolish and trifling things in favour of the Tories. " This," he told Mist, "is the only way to preserve your paper, and keep yourself from jail, and unless you will keep measures with me, and be punctual in these things, I will not serve you any further, or be concerned any more in your paper"—a serious threat enough, seeing that it was entirely owing to Defoe's skill that the large circulation of the paper was kept up. With Defoe pulling on one side and the Jacobites on the other, poor Mist led a dog's life of it; but the Jacobites pulled the strongest, and in October appeared in the *Journal* a letter signed Sir Andrew Politick, which gave offence to the Government. The premises of Mist were searched for the letter, "a seditious libel was found hid in the ceiling, all the persons on the premises were seized, and Mist on hearing the news surrendered and was taken into custody."* When examined on November 1st before Lord Stanhope and Mr. Craggs, Mr. Mist declared falsely that Defoe was the author of the offensive letter; but as his lordship was in Defoe's secret, no harm resulted. A few days later, owing to the influence of Defoe, Mist obtained a discharge; he was, however, none the more willing to agree to Defoe's terms, so they separated. *Read's Journal* on the 6th of December maliciously insinuates that the separation was owing to a quarrel about money.

> What strange adventures could untwist
> Such true-born knaves as Foe and Mist?
> They quarrelled sure about the pelf,
> For Dan's a needy, greedy elf.

But whatever else *Read's Journal* did, it never flattered the great Daniel. When the hawkers roared about the streets a dismal elegy which gave out that Defoe had lately hanged himself at Newington, *Read's* very kindly contradicted the report, but added "though that scurrilous fellow has no superfluity of grace, loyalty, and common honesty, yet has he just wit enough not to befriend the hangman, by becoming a *felo de se*, which he knows would be the 'Shortest Way' to the devil." No doubt in George's day the skins of

* See *Athenæum*, 26th Aug. '93.

P

journalists were thick and tough, but few . could
have been assailed with more virulence than Defoe.
Nor need it be wondered at, for he was provoking
to the very last degree. He took it for granted
that his antagonists were all rogues, knaves, or
thieves, and that he himself was Daniel Immacu-
latus. He was continually outwitting them, continually getting the whip hand of them; and while
they were swearing blue murder, he was either as
cool as a cucumber or as merry as a grig. If he
did at times have the "hippo," as he calls it, he
never let *them* see it.

The way, too, he talked of his own doings,
works, and sufferings, also riled them. Indeed, of
blowing his own trumpet and parading his own
experiences he was never tired. " He had all the
vaingloriousness of exuberant vitality,"* and the
recital of his own adventures exhilarated him as a
country walk on a fine day in April does a pent-
up student. That he outdistanced his fellow
penmen too in their own arts was also a source
of annoyance. When we hear of the sly methods
used nowadays by so many for puffing themselves
into notice, and for keeping their name before the
public, we are apt to think our own age contrasts
badly with that of the Augustans, who, we inno-
cently imagine, rose to eminence merely by virtue
of their greatness; but . it was not so. As a
master in the art of puffery, Defoe could give
points to any penman of the present day or to any
publisher. He wrote letters to himself, saying that

* Professor Minto.

his paper "was the best and most sensible of all newspapers";* he referred to himself as "the well-known Daniel Defoe"; he wrote books anonymously with a preface signed by his own name, recommending the books as all that was admirable, and praising them to the skies. If it answered his purpose, he corrected himself, quoted himself, vituperised himself. He never lost an opportunity of forcing down people's throats that he was a man of importance. He took care to keep them perpetually in remembrance that he had written " The True-born Englishman," and it was not his fault if the public forgot that he had hob-a-nobbed with King William and had been received into favour and rewarded by Queen Anne.

In short, if Defoe's literary contemporaries did not love him, we have not far to go to seek the reasons. The hind runners in a race do not usually make themselves hoarse with applauding the victor; the spectators do, however, and Defoe had his full share both of applause and roses.

In the meantime he had started another paper, *The Whitehall Evening Post*, a tri-weekly, consisting of two leaves small quarto. The first number appeared on Sept. 18th, 1718, and he continued to be connected with it until June, 1720.

Finding that the circulation of his paper had rapidly gone down, Mist now sought out and put himself again into the hands of Defoe who resumed the control of the paper, on his own

---

* *See* the attack on Defoe in *The Half-Penny Post* for 16th April, 1720.

P 2

absolute terms, in the beginning of January, 1719;
or, as *Read's* puts it, Daniel had "now again undertaken the dirty work of penning Mist's *Journal.*"

We have already seen that Defoe was intimately
connected with Norwich (§ 27), where resided his
friends John Fransham and other "topping Dissenters"; and the connection of the Defoes with
that city was now to be made stronger by the
marriage, with a Norwich person, of Benjamin, the
novelist's second son.

The following is the entry in the register of
St. Helen's, Norwich—

"Benjamin De Foe of Stoke Newington in the county of
Middlesex singleman and Hannah Coates of St. George of Colegate in the City of Norwich singlewoman were married the twenty-
second of Septembeʳ, 1718."

Benjamin Defoe and his wife appear to have
resided for a time at Norwich; for in the register
of the Octagon Chapel appears the following entry
of the birth of their first child—

" Benjamin son of Benjamin De Foe gent. and Hannah his wife,
of St. George of Colegate, was baptized 6 June, 1719."

No one of the name of De Foe was rated in
the parish of St. George of Colegate in 1718 or
1719, but that of the widow Coates occurs before
and after these dates.

Book II

NOVELIST AND HISTORIAN.

CHAPTER XI.

THE ADVENTURE SERIES.

58.—WILD WICKED ROBINSON CRUSOE (PUBLISHED 25TH APRIL, 1719).—DEATH OF ADDISON (17TH JUNE, 1719).

WORK : 191.—Robinson Crusoe (Part I.).

Defoe was now in his sixtieth year. He had already accomplished an enormous amount of work. He had written scores of pamphlets, conducted half a dozen newspapers, and published several books, some of them very voluminous — to say nothing of his exertions in other fields—but the work he had so far got through was as nothing compared with the labours he was now to commence. His output during his last decade is unparalleled in the history of literature ; and it now lies with us to unfold the chronicle of this enchanting period—to tell how he turned out story after story, and history after history, some of them of the highest, and all of very high, merit—three, four, and even five in a year. For the rate at which he worked, and the amount and value of the work he turned out, no author, English or foreign, can compare with him, save only perhaps Balzac ; and even Balzac, prodigious as were his toils, compares with him only feebly, for at the time Defoe was producing his wonderful series of novels he was also writing political pamphlets and conducting three or four newspapers— a monthly of nearly one hundred pages, a weekly, a tri-weekly, and, during part of the time, a daily. But nothing is more delectable to your dexterous charioteer than driving six horses abreast. Whether or not the great stories of Defoe which we have now to consider come within the bounds of fiction depends upon how the word fiction is defined. Defoe would not have it that any of them were fiction. ".Crusoe," he said, was an allegory; "Moll Flanders," "Colonel Jack," "Single-ton," the "Journal of the Plague," and the "Memoirs of a Cavalier," are declared to be true histories—that is to say, a collection of authenticated facts in an artistic setting. A novel or a romance, as the terms are usually accepted, he considered as not worth writing and a waste of time to read. In the "Family Instructor" "novels and romances" are categoried with plays and songs "and such like stuff."

The first, and thanks to his felicity in the choice of a subject, the greatest of his stories was the famous "Robinson Crusoe," founded on the adventures of Alexander Selkirk, from whom, as we have narrated, Defoe, about 1712, obtained papers. The resemblances between the adventures of Selkirk and those of Crusoe are so patent that no one reading the two narratives can help noticing them. To take only a few : Selkirk, like Crusoe, built two huts, employed himself " in reading, singing psalms, and praying ; so that he said he was a better Christian while in this

FRONTISPIECE TO THE FIRST EDITION OF "ROBINSON CRUSOE." 1

solitude than ever he was before." Selkirk cut on trees the time of "his being left and continuance there," and Crusoe had his post with notches. Selkirk, like Crusoe, was pestered with cats, some of which became tame, and "when his clothes wore out, he made himself a coat and cap of goat skins." There were no venomous or savage creatures either on Selkirk's island or Crusoe's, "nor any other sort of beasts but goats."

After Captain Woodes Rogers had taken Selkirk on board, the sailors persisted in calling him "the governour," in allusion to his government of the island where his "right there was none to dispute"; and Robinson Crusoe was called so when there were other Englishmen on his island.

These resemblances alone would suggest that Defoe had Selkirk's narrative in mind, but this is not all. Not only did Defoe get from Selkirk the idea of Crusoe, but there is every probability that he was indebted to him, or rather to him and Captain Rogers, for the idea of Friday, too.

"'Captain Dampier,' says Rogers, 'talks of a *Moskito Indian* (William) that belonged to Capt. Watlin, who being a-hunting in the woods when the captain left the island, lived here three years alone, and shifted much in the same manner as Mr. Selkirk did, till Captain Dampier came hither in 1684, and carried him off. . . . But whatever there is in these stories, this of Mr. Selkirk I know to be true.'"

But if there are resemblances between the narratives, there are also striking enough dissimilarities. Crusoe's island was in the Caribbean Sea, and Selkirk's in the Pacific; Selkirk went on his island voluntarily, Crusoe was shipwrecked; Crusoe's island, unlike Selkirk's, contained no cabbage-palms or pimento trees, which to Selkirk were so great a boon. No savages troubled Selkirk; he did not have a Friday; and he stayed on his island only four and a half years, whereas Crusoe's solitude lasted twenty-eight years.

These dissimilarities, however, are probably intentional; at the same time, it is quite possible that Defoe may have been indebted for some of his ideas to the adventures of others; for stories of shipwrecked mariners and marooned buccaneers were in those days by no means uncommon, and at least two persons have been put forward in rivalry to Selkirk as prototypes of Robinson Crusoe. The first of these is Peter Serrano, whose story is told in Garcilasso's "History of Peru," translated into English by Sir Paul Rycaut, and published in 1688—that is, about twenty years before the issue of "Robinson Crusoe." Mr. W. T. Lynn, however, in *Notes and Queries* for October 13, 1888, thus comments :—

"It is difficult, indeed, to see any connection between it and the story of 'Robinson Crusoe.' The shipwreck in both is really almost the only circumstance common to the two. The island on which Serrano is stated to have been thrown is one of the little islets called from him Serrano Islands, which are, indeed, in the Caribbean Sea, but in the western part of it, nearly midway between Jamaica and the mainland, and very far from the mouth of the Orinoco. They are, as Garcilasso describes Serrano's island, almost destitute of water, wood, or grass, and very different from the island imagined to have been tenanted by the immortal Robinson. Serrano, if the narrative be true, lived on this island seven years—three alone and four with another who was afterwards shipwrecked in the same way."

THE
LIFE
AND
Strange Surprizing
ADVENTURES
OF
ROBINSON CRUSOE,
Of *YORK,* Mariner:

Who lived Eight and Twenty Years,
all alone in an un-inhabited Ifland on the
Coaft of AMERICA, near the Mouth of
the Great River of OROONOQUE;

Having been caft on Shore by Shipwreck, wherein all the Men perifhed but himfelf.

WITH

An Account how he was at laft as ftrangely deliver'd by PYRATES.

Written by Himfelf.

LONDON:

Printed for W. TAYLOR at the *Ship* in *Pater-Nofter-*
Row. MDCCXIX.

TITLE-PAGE TO THE FIRST EDITION OF "ROBINSON CRUSOE."

Another writer in *Notes and Queries* (I.M.P., 31st March, 1888) urges the claims of the second pretender, the hero of a work by the German novelist, Grimmelshausen. He says :—

"Grimmelshausen does not work out his story in great detail, as Defoe did, but in many ways he anticipates him. The coincidences are interesting.

"His hero is wrecked on an uninhabited island in the tropics, rich in vegetation, with a warm climate and a periodical rainy season. He builds himself a house, and has, further, a cave to retire into. He makes clothes for himself of the skins of penguins and other birds. He keeps a register of time by cutting notches on a stick. He experiences an earthquake. He moralises on the uselessness of some money which he gets. The island is visited by a ship, the captain of which offers to take him away. There is a visit from savages in boats, who carry him off. There is a very strong religious element introduced into the story.

"In one point there is a marked difference. Grimmelshausen deals largely with the supernatural, which Defoe does not."

The title of Defoe's work was no doubt suggested by the name of one of his companions at Newington Academy, Mr. Timothy Cruso, who became a distinguished Dissenting minister. He is buried in Stepney Churchyard, but the stone, which had a Latin inscription, is gone. Mr. Cruso came from Norwich, with which city, as we have seen, Defoe himself was much connected.

Between 1610 and 1669 four members of the Norwich family of Cruso were admitted to Gonville and Caius College, Cambridge ; and it is interesting to note that there used to be a well-known family of the name at Leek, in Staffordshire, whose motto was —a play upon the name—" Sub Cruce."

The following is a brief outline of the story of

Defoe's great work, with all the dates, which I am careful to give, because I believe it to be, as Defoe said, an allegory of the life of its author. Born at York on September 30, 1632, Crusoe, at the age of nineteen, ran away from home and embarked on a ship bound for London. This was on September 1, 1651—his fatal day—and about a fortnight later the ship was wrecked in Yarmouth Roads. The crew escaped in a boat, and from Yarmouth Crusoe made his way to London, where he embarked with a Guinea captain. This, his first great voyage, was a successful one, and upon his return he found himself possessor of some £260. He now set out on a second voyage, but had the misfortune to be captured, on September 1, 1653, his fatal day, by a Turkish rover, and was carried to Sallee, where for two years he worked as a slave. On December 19, 1655, he escaped from Sallee with a Moresco named Xury, and was shortly after picked up by a Portuguese trader and carried to Brazil, where he resided for four years as a planter.

On the fatal 1st of September, 1659—exactly eight years after he had first left Hull, and six years after he had been taken to Sallee—he went on board a ship bound for Africa for the purpose of obtaining slaves to work in his plantations, but was shipwrecked and thrown on an uninhabited island near the mouth of the Orinoco. This was on September 30, 1659, his birthday. His age was twenty-seven. These coincidences of days struck Crusoe, and had he been superstitiously inclined he would, he said, have had reason to look upon them with a great deal of curiosity. Doubtless there were similar in

Vera Effigies
TIMOTHEI CRUSO.
Ætat 40. 1697.

THE REV. TIMOTHY CRUSO, DEFOE'S FELLOW STUDENT AT NEWINGTON
AND SUBSEQUENTLY A DISTINGUISHED DISSENTING MINISTER.

Defoe's own history; at any rate, he always had an
eye to coincidences of the kind, as witness the parallels
he adduces in his " History of the Plague." From the
wreck Crusoe obtains many useful things, including
provisions; and on his island he finds grapes and
turtles, and shoots goats. He makes chairs and other
articles of furniture; sets up a tent in front of a cave
and fortifies it, calling the place his castle; he experiences an earthquake, is taken ill, recovers; makes an
excursion into the interior of his island, indulges
in a "monarch of all I survey" soliloquy, and erects a
bower in the middle of the island. He next makes a
journey right across his island, where he finds innumerable turtles and also a vast number of fowls of many
sorts; whilst on the south side of the island he had
found only three turtles in the year and a-half he had
been there. Just as the north of the island was agreeable to Crusoe, so Scotland proved a land of clover
to Defoe. Says Crusoe: " I confess this side of the
country was much pleasanter than mine, yet I had not
the least inclination to remove; for as I was fixed in my
habitation, it became natural to me, and I seemed all
the while I was here to be as it were upon a journey,
and from home." So Crusoe's headquarters continued
to be at his castle in the south, just as Defoe's continued to be in London. He now grew corn, baked
pottery, and made a canoe, too big to be moved;
which brought him to the end of his fourth year.
Next he makes a smaller canoe, in which he attempts
a voyage round his island, and nearly loses his life.
Then occurred the incident of his astonishment at
hearing himself addressed by what appeared to be a

human voice, but which turned out to be that of his parrot. He rears goats, is alarmed at seeing a footprint in the sand, and fortifies more strongly his dwelling. The savages visit his island, and for two years he con- fines himself almost exclusively to his own quarters— namely, his castle, his bower, and his enclosure in the woods. He then discovers a cave or grotto, "which was *perfectly dark*," and in which he saw "two broad shining eyes" of a creature which turned out to be a dying goat—an Hibernianism that exposed him to the arrows of the critics. In the twenty-third year of his residence on the island—it was the month of December —the savages came; they departed, however, without troubling him. On the 16th of May of his twenty- fourth year occurred the second arrival of the savages, and the annexation of Friday. Later on, Crusoe and Friday slaughter many of the savages, and rescue Friday's father and a Spaniard. A mutinous crew of an English ship having landed on the island, Crusoe and his friends assist the captain, the mutineers are suppressed and left on the island, and Crusoe and Friday sail for England (19 Dec., 1687).[*]

In "Robinson Crusoe" there is no woman, nor do petticoats entrammel in any of Defoe's works except those in which a woman is the chief character, as "Moll Flanders" and "Roxana." There is no woman in "The Memoirs of a Cavalier," in the "History of the Plague," or in "Captain Singleton"—no woman, or none to speak of, even in "Colonel Jack," notwith- standing that he was married five times.

The book that was to bring such great fame to · · · · · ·

[*] *See* footnote in § 7.

Defoe was now ready for the press, but, according to tradition, it was with very great difficulty he got it published. The incident is thus pictured by Mr. Francis Espinasse, and with probable accuracy :—

" In the winter of 1719 there might be seen issuing from a large white house in Church-street, Stoke Newington, hurrying to the booksellers' shops, and bustling in and out of them, a 'middle-sized spare man ' of 60 or so, ' of brown complexion, with a hooked nose, a sharp chin, grey eyes, and a large mole near his mouth,' carrying an MS. in his pocket or in his hand. From Lombard-street to Catherine-street, Strand—from Little Britain to Westminster Hall (inside which in those days booksellers plied their trade)—the middle-sized spare man offered his 'copy' for publication, but in vain. The whole 'metropolitan trade' would have nothing to do with it, when in a lucky hour he turned his steps to the Ship, in Paternoster Row. Mr. William Taylor, more descerning than his neighbours, ' accepted the manuscript,' and on the 23rd of April, 1719, registered his right to the whole property in it, in the books of the Stationers' Company. Presently appeared a moderately-sized octavo volume of 364 pages, which the world still fondly cherishes, and the contents of its title-page ran as follows :—' The Life and Strange Surprising Adventures of Robinson Crusoe, of York, Mariner : who lived Eight and Twenty Years all alone in an Un-inhabited Island on the Coast of America, near the Mouth of the Great River Oroonoque ; Having been cast on Shore by Shipwreck, wherein All the Men perished but himself. With an Account how he was at last as strangely delivered by Pyrates. Written by himself. London. Printed for W. Taylor at the Ship in Paternoster Row, 1719.' "

The publisher cleared a thousand pounds by the venture ; whether Defoe got anything by it or not is unrevealed.

" Edition after edition was called for so rapidly, that several printers had to be employed to set up the new work. Spurious abridgements of it followed—in one of which, Mr. Thomas Gent, printer, of York, the author of the curious autobiography, has confessed to a share—and Mr. Taylor began a bill in Chancery against a certain 'T. Cox at the Amsterdam Coffee House,' who had printed another of them ; an angry controversy ensuing."

Indeed, even in this short time Crusoe was already "famed from Tuttle Street to Limehouse-hole " ; and there was not an old woman that could go the price of it, but bought it and left it "as a legacy, with the ' Pilgrim's Progress,' the ' Practice of Piety,' and ' God's Revenge Against Murther,' to her posterity." *

Dibdin, in the "Library Companion," 1824, says that " Robinson Crusoe " "first greeted the public eye in the sorrily-printed pages of *The Original London Post, or Heathcote's Intelligence*, from No. 125 to No. 289 inclusive, the latter" (error, it should be "*former*," not latter) " dated October 7th, 1719. Of this extraordinary periodical production, the only copy with which I am acquainted is in the library of the Right Hon. Thomas Grenville."

But this is incorrect. " Robinson Crusoe " was issued by Mr. Taylor six months before it appeared in the *London Post.* Heathcote was only one of the many who pirated it. That it did appear in this form, however, is exceedingly interesting—for, in all pro-bability, " Robinson Crusoe " was the very first novel that appeared as a serial or *feuilleton.*

Not long after the issue of " Robinson Crusoe," Mr. William Taylor died, leaving behind him two very desirable properties ; and, curiously enough, his executor, Mr. Innys, the bookseller in St. Paul's Churchyard, had an eye to one, and his other executor, Mr. Osborn, of Cornhill, an eye to the other. The

* Gildon.

one property, the business in Paternoster Row, Mr.
Osborn wanted for his prospective son-in-law, Thomas
Longman, the founder of the present firm of Messrs.
Longmans, Green and Co.; the other property, the
one that Mr. Innys wanted, was none other than Mr.
Taylor's widow, who was attractive, not only on
account of her portion (thirty thousand pounds), but
also on account of her personal charms, and her
amiable manners ; for to do Mr. Innys justice, though
he had no objection to a good round sum, yet, like
Ricardo, in Middleton's play, he liked a good round
widow better. And each had his desire. Tom Longman, in consideration of a sum of two thousand odd
pounds, got the shop, and presently married pretty
Mary Osborn ; and Mr. Innys led to the altar his
buxom widow ; so all, like a well-constructed fairy
tale, ended with bonfire and fireworks.

Few books have received more praise than
" Robinson Crusoe." " Was there ever anything
written by mere man," asked Dr. Johnson, " that
was wished longer by its readers, except " Don
Quixote," " Robinson Crusoe," and the " Pilgrim's
Progress ? " " Robinson Crusoe," says Marmontel,
" is the first book I ever read with exquisite pleasure ; and I believe every boy in Europe might
say the same thing." Sir Walter Scott could name
" no work more generally read or more universally
admired " ; and in the opinion of the Rev. Stopford
Brooke " it equals ' Gulliver's Travels ' in truth-
ful representation, and excels them in invention."
M. Alphonse Daudet puts Defoe at the head
of all the standard English writers of fiction,

pronouncing him to be England's national author.
" Even Shakspere," he asserts, " does not give
so perfect an idea of the English character as
Defoe. Robinson is the typical Englishman *par
excellence*, with his adventuresomeness, his taste for
travel, his love of the sea, his piety, his commercial and practical instincts. And what an artist
he is—Defoe! What effects of terror there are in
' Robinson '—the foot of the savage on the sand ;
and then his dramatic gift—the return of Robinson
to the island, and the parrot still screaming, ' Robin
Crusoe! Robin Crusoe!' If I were condemned to
a long period of seclusion, and were allowed only
one book to read, I would choose ' Robinson.' It
is one of the few works of fiction that may be
considered as nearly immortal as any written thing
can be." Equally enthusiastic in the praise of
" Robinson Crusoe " is another eminent Frenchman,
M. Zola, but it would be easy to fill volumes with
laudatory passages. Is not every reader of it its
panegyrist !

On the 17th of June, 1719, about two months
after the publication of " Crusoe," died at Holland
House, in his forty-eighth year, Defoe's celebrated
contemporary, Joseph Addison.

59.—THE DAEMON OF DEFOE.

The consideration of " Crusoe " brings again
forcibly before us that deep-seated belief of Defoe's
that he was accompanied, as Socrates and other fine
or devout souls are said to have been, with a good
spirit or daemon, which afforded him wise counsel

on all trying occasions. (*See* § 9.) It was Defoe's belief that on extremely great and important occasions, the Holy Spirit itself guided and directed him; but that in the multitudinous occasions of minor consequence he was indebted to the daemon.

Shortly after discovering that his island had been visited by savages, Crusoe fell into reflecting what his situation would have been if, when he discovered the print of a man's foot, he had "instead of that, seen fifteen or twenty savages," and found them pursuing him.

"This," says he, "renewed a contemplation which often had come into my thoughts in former times, when first I began to see the merciful dispositions of Heaven, in the dangers we run through in this life; how wonderfully we are delivered when we know nothing of it; how, when we are in a quandary, a doubt or hesitation whether to go this way or that way, a secret hint shall direct us this way, when we intended to go that way: nay, when sense, our own inclination, and perhaps business, has called us the other way, yet a strange impression upon the mind, from we know not what springs, and by we know not what power, shall overrule us to go this way, and it shall afterwards appear that had we gone that way which we should have gone, and even to our imagination ought to have gone, we should have been ruined and lost. Upon these, and many like reflections, I afterwards made it a certain rule with me, that *whenever I found those secret hints or pressings of mind, to doing or not doing anything that presented, or going this way or that way, I never failed to obey the secret dictate;* though I knew no other reason for it than such a pressure, or such a hint, hung upon my mind. I could give many examples of the success of this conduct in the course of my life."

The further instances to which he refers, there is no need to mention here; suffice it to say that the idea permeates the whole of the book. Nor were Defoe's critics slow to perceive it; Gildon, the most bitter of them, flourishing it as a proof of Defoe's irreligion.

Q

"These daemons which attend men, are not," argues Defoe, "the spirits of the departed; they are spirits that have never been embodied." Dealing, in his "History of Apparitions," with the communications of these spirits, he says—

"By this silent converse all the kind notices of approaching evil or good are conveyed to us, which are sometimes so evident, and come with such an irresistible force upon the mind, that we must be more than stupid if we do not perceive them; and if we are not extremely wanting to ourselves, we may take such due warning by them as to avoid the evils which we had notice of in that manner, and to embrace the good that is offered to us. Nor are there many people alive who can deny but they have had such notices, by which, if they had given due attention to them, they had been assisted to save themselves from the mischiefs which followed."

"And on the other hand," he observes, "people are forewarned of things which are for their good." And to clinch his argument, he says—

"Now by what agency must it be that we have directions for good or foreboding thoughts, of mischiefs which attend us, and which it is otherwise impossible we should know anything of, if some intelligent being who can see into futurity had not conveyed the apprehensions into the mind, and had not caused the emotion which alarms the soul."

Over and over again, in "The History of Apparitions," he reiterates this belief of his in "an appointed, deputed sort of stationary spirits in the invisible world." The spirits having given the hint —to speak plainly they are not able—then man has to do his part, namely to raise his eyes to Heaven and ask "for direction and counsel from that hand, who alone can both direct and deliver."

60.—BARON GOERTZ (MAY, 1716).

WORKS: 194.—Baron Goertz.
    195.—A Letter to the Dissenters.
    196.—The Anatomy of Exchange Alley.

Our eye now turns once more to the enchanted land of Sweden. The great Charles was back in his native land after his romantic and disastrous adventures in Turkey; but he had scarcely got home when a quarrel arose between him and George I. of England. George had in 1716 bought from the King of Denmark, the Duchy of Bremen, which Charles claimed as his own. The thoughts of the Swedish king turned towards war, and he instructed his minister to intrigue with the Jacobites in this country. (*See* § 54.) Then was suggested the mighty scheme, which suited only too well the vastness of Charles's ambition. Make terms with the Czar, said Goertz, by surrendering the Baltic provinces of Sweden, then conquer Norway. This done, land in Scotland and replace the House of Stuart on the Throne of England.

Charles resolved to carry it all through. He purchased peace with the Czar, he burst into Norway; but early in 1718, whilst, with all his characteristic impetuosity, besieging Fredrickshall, he was killed by a musket shot.

> "His fall was destined to a barren strand,
> A petty fortress, and a dubious hand.
> He left a name at which the world grew pale,
> To point a moral or adorn a tale."

When Baron Goertz heard of the fatal event, he exclaimed: "The bullet that has killed the king

Q 2

has killed me too." And his words were literal,
for he shortly after fell a victim to popular rage
and resentment. He was executed on the 11th of
February, 1719. Defoe comments on the event in
Mist's *Journal* for March 21, and a few weeks
later, about May, he enlarged this account into a
pamphlet, to which a portrait of the baron was
prefixed.

　　Two more tracts on other subjects followed in
quick succession, "A Letter to the Dissenters,"
deploring the spread of Unitarianism among the
Nonconformists, and counselling those who could not
agree in doctrine, at any rate to avoid unseemly
quarrelling; and " The Anatomy of Exchange
Alley," a denunciation of the wicked practices of
Stock-jobbers, a subject that he had often dealt with
both in journal and pamphlet.

61.—" ROBINSON CRUSOE," PART II. (20TH AUG., 1719).

WORK: 192.—Robinson Crusoe (Part II.).

　　The favourable reception accorded to " Robinson
Crusoe," which had run through four editions in the
short space of three months, encouraged Defoe to
continue the subject, and on the 20th of August he
published a second volume with the title of "The
Further Adventures of Robinson Crusoe; Being the
second and last part of his life, and of the strange
surprising accounts of his travels round three parts of
the globe. Written by himself. To which is added
a Map of the World, in which is delineated the
voyages of Robinson Crusoe."

It has been said, and truly, that the second part of "Robinson Crusoe" is inferior to the first; that when Crusoe peopled his island with Spaniards, English pirates and Caribbees, the charm of it was gone. But though there is nothing in the second part to correspond with the striking idea of Crusoe's isolation, let it not be imagined that the master had lost his hand. The fascination of style is the same, and passages quite as fine as those in the first, if not finer, are scattered up and down its pages. Take, for example, the golden words on idleness and industry. The English merchant says to Crusoe :—

"If you will put one thousand pounds to my one thousand pounds, we will hire a ship here, the first we can get to our minds. You shall be captain, I'll be merchant, and we'll go a trading voyage to China ; for what should we stand still for? The whole world is in motion, rolling round and round ; all the creatures of God, heavenly bodies and earthly, are busy and diligent : why should we be idle? There are no drones in the world but men ; why should we be of that number?"

The beginning of the book finds Crusoe married and settled down in England, where he and Friday dwelt contentedly for seven years. Indeed, finding his wife dead set against his going abroad again, Crusoe bought a farm in Bedfordshire and resolved to remain in England all his life. But in the midst of his felicity he had the misfortune to lose his wife ; and finding the only tie that bound him to England snapt, he, in his sixty-first year, took to roving again, and in company with Friday set out to visit his old island. On the way he rescues the shipwrecked crew of a French ship, one of the passengers of which, a French priest, accompanies him on the voyage.

The story of Crusoe's second stay on the island, however, which lasted but twenty-five days, takes up only a portion, considerably less than half, of the book. It was merely one episode in a series of adventures. After quitting the island, Crusoe visits Madagascar, where Tom Jeffry, one of the crew, met his end; Tonquin, where occurred the incident of the scattering of a party of enemies with hot pitch; China, for whose fortifications and army he had such a sovereign contempt; and Siberia, where he destroyed a great Tartar idol, and hob-a-nobbed with an exiled Russian prince. Nor does the interest anywhere flag, for even when almost home Crusoe runs a narrow escape of being killed by a party of Kalmucs; and one is heartily glad when, on the 10th of January, 1705, the hoary-headed old wanderer gets safe back to London.

The verisimilitude that is so prominent in the first volume of "Crusoe" is as much in evidence in the second. The thoroughly bad fellow, Will Atkins, who was "scarce worth hanging," does not meet with a violent end, as a less clever writer would have managed it, but by force of circumstances becomes a reformed character and an influence for good all round. When the five Englishmen choose wives, he who has first choice does not pick the best favoured.

"He that drew to choose first went away by himself to the hut where the poor naked creatures were, and fetched out her he chose; and it was worth observing, that he who chose first took her that was reckoned the homeliest and oldest of the five, which made mirth enough among the rest; and even the Spaniards laughed at it; but the fellow considered better than any of them, that it was

MAP OF CRUSOE'S ISLAND.

(Fac-simile from the Map in the "Serious Reflections."—Crusoe, Part III.—published in 1720)

application and business they were to accept assistance in, as much as in anything else ; and she proved the best wife of all the parcel."

And it did not turn out that the two good men had good wives and the three bad men bad ones. Oh no!

"As it often happens in the world (what the wise ends of God's providence are, in such a disposition of things, I cannot say), the two honest fellows had the two worst wives : and the three reprobates, that were scarce worth hanging, that were fit for nothing, and neither seemed born to do themselves good, nor any one else, had three clever, diligent, careful and ingenious wives."

Those prominent features in Defoe's character—a firm belief in, and trust in, the goodness of Providence ; and the idea of the daemon are as much to the fore as in the first part. Take, for example, Crusoe's remarks concerning the wisdom of the Spaniards in planting a grove round his old bower.

"This was excellently well contrived : nor was it less than what they afterwards found occasion for, which served to convince me, that as human prudence has the authority of Providence to justify it, so it has doubtless the direction of Providence to set it to work ; and if we listened carefully to the voice of it, I am persuaded we might prevent many of the disasters which our lives are now, by our own negligence, subjected to."

62.—THE ACRIMONIOUS ATTACK ON "ROBINSON CRUSOE" BY GILDON (28TH SEPT., 1719).—CRITICISMS ON "ROBINSON CRUSOE."

It was not to be expected that a work could reach the popularity that "Robinson Crusoe" did without arousing a good deal of jealousy, and provoking attacks from Defoe's multitudinous enemies ; for though the work was issued anonymously, the public instantly fathered it on the right sire. The most acrimonious of these critics was Charles Gildon, a gifted writer, who found out some very weak places in Defoe's armour. Gildon's pamphlet, published on the 28th of September, is entitled, "The Life and Strange Surprising Adventures of Mr. D—— De F——, of London, Hosier, who has lived above fifty years by himself, in the kingdoms of North and South Britain. The various shapes he has appeared in, and the Discoveries he has made for the benefit of his country. In a Dialogue between Him, Robinson Crusoe, and his man Friday. With remarks serious and comical upon the life of Crusoe. *Qui vult decipi, decipiatur.*" The title and dialogue occupy nineteen pages, then follows an epistle to Daniel Defoe, occupying twenty-nine pages, and lastly there is a postscript of nineteen pages referring to the second volume. Mr. Lee holds that this pamphlet has "nothing to recommend it but the title"; Defoe, however, evidently thought otherwise, for he made alterations in subsequent editions in deference to Gildon's criticisms.

"How could Crusoe," inquires Gildon, "fill his pockets with biscuits when he was naked?" So in the next edition Defoe was careful to put his *protégé* in breeches. But the enemy was not appeased even then. "The pocket of a seaman's breeches," said Gildon, "is no bigger than a tobacco pouch, it couldn't hold any biscuits."

Gildon also wanted to know how it was that Crusoe had no clothes, though he had brought great quantities from the ship; and how Crusoe was able to see the goat's eyes in the cave when it was pitch dark; and how the Spaniards were able to give Friday's father an agreement in writing, when they had neither paper nor ink.

These blunders and others like them, it may be urged, were mere oversights, which could easily be put right in subsequent editions, as, indeed, some of them were; but it is ridiculous to abuse the critic for laying his finger on them.

Then again, Defoe certainly made a mistake in causing Xury to speak broken English. As Gildon justly observes : " Crusoe might speak broken Arabic, but Xury would have no motive to speak broken English."

But Gildon's hardest hitting is when he finds fault with Defoe for representing going to sea as an act of wickedness, or, at any rate, of intense folly. "Our sailors," says Gildon, "are the nation's glory, yet here is this Defoe employing all the force of his little rhetoric to dissuade and deter all people from going to sea"; and Gildon would be glad to know " whether the profession of a Yorkshire attorney is more innocent and beneficial to mankind that that of a seaman."

" Duty to parents, too, is all right," he continues, " but blindly submitting to all their commands, whether good or bad, rational or irrational, is to make children slaves and exclude all manner of free agency. Crusoe was eighteen, and quite old enough to choose for himself." Gildon points out pertinently, moreover, that "storms are not sent to deter men from navigation," and that " you don't go to Guinea ' to see the world by travel' among negroes." A score of other criticisms are equally just, though, perhaps, Gildon need not have said them with so much spitefulness. A hornet, however, is always a hornet, and Gildon was a particularly vicious one.

But though many of his charges are just, on the other hand, a number of them are exceedingly frivolous, as when he finds so much fault with Crusoe for speaking so well of the French priest, which, it is argued, sounds ill in the mouth of a Protestant; and when he cavils about Crusoe's daemon, "who generally gave him notice and warning of any evil that threatened him." But in spite of these ineptitudes, in spite, too, of the malevolence of the author, or, perhaps, by virtue of it, this pamphlet is very delightful to read side by side with Crusoe, at the end of which it might, not inappropriately, be bound.* In fine, because we admire Defoe and Crusoe, we are not going to follow our predecessors in the biographical office, and call Gildon a carping fool.

63.—*THE DAILY POST* AND "DICKORY CRONKE" (14TH OCT., 1719).—
DEFOE AND THE CHURCH OF ENGLAND.

WORKS: 192.—*The Daily Post.*
198.—The Dumb Philosopher (Dickory Cronke): 14th Oct., 1719.

On the 4th of October (1719) Defoe was to the fore with yet another venture in the way of a newspaper: *The Daily Post*, which consisted of a single leaf small folio, one side news, the other advertisements. At

---

* Gildon's guess that Defoe's great story is an allegory is also interesting, especially as his tract was written twelve months before Defoe's declaration in "Serious Reflections."

the same time, be it remembered, he was conducting *Mercurius Politicus*—a monthly periodical, Mist's *Journal*—a weekly, and *The Whitehall Evening Post* —a tri-weekly. He seems to have used the *Daily Post* "for such occasional letters and communications, from his own pen, as he was desirous of placing before the public without any delay."* We noticed, some pages back, a treaty between Defoe and Dyer not to shy mud at each other; a similar compact was now made between Defoe and Read, each promising to raze out "scandalous epithets" relating to the other which occurred in letters of their correspondents.

The 14th of October was marked by the issue of " Dickory Cronke," a thick pamphlet, whose fuller title runs:—" The Dumb Philosopher, Or Great Britain's Wonder. Containing (1) a faithful and very surprising account how Dickory Cronke, a tinner's son in the county of Cornwall, was born dumb, and continued so for 58 years, and how some days before he died he came to his speech; with memoirs of his life and the manner of his death," etc. The isolated state of Cronke, who, through his malady, was shut out from intercourse with mankind has caused the book to be styled, " The Little Robin-son Crusoe." Mr. Lee interestingly remarks of the heroes of these two books :—

" Both were reflective, religious men, and wrote meditations. The first and second volumes of ' Crusoe ' were written in the same year as Cronke, and the latter is interposed, in point of time between the second and third volumes of ' Crusoe.' There is the same atmo-sphere of truth surrounding all the details of both, so that the reader lives in the reality of each story, and scepticism itself is set at

* Lee.

defiance. In 'Crusoe' the author has declared that the history of his own life is allegorically enclosed; and, though I will not positively affirm that portions of his inner life are contained in Cronke, yet I believe so. It is noticeable that Cronke's life is made to begin about the same time as Defoe's—to terminate at the author's age when writing this book; and that, like himself, Cronke had a fit of apoplexy."

To the veneration of Defoe for the Church of England several references have been made in these pages; but the following, which occurs in "Dickory Cronke," coming as it does from one of the staunchest of Dissenters, is noteworthy even among the utterances of so catholic a spirit as that of Defoe. I would observe, however, that it was written at a time when the Dissenters were disgracing themselves by unseemly quarrels, and when many were embracing Unitarianism. "The Church of England," says Defoe, "is doubtless the great bulwark of the ancient catholic and apostolic faith all over the world—a Church that has all the advantages that the nature of a Church is capable of. From the doctrine and principles of the Church of England we are taught loyalty to our prince, fidelity to our country, and justice to all mankind; and therefore I look upon this to be one of the most excellent branches of the Church universal. It stands, as 'twere, in a parenthesis, between superstition and hypocrisy."

On the 29th of March, 1720, occurred the second marriage of Defoe's eldest son, Daniel, which is thus entered in the register of Aske's Hospital :—

"1720.—Defoe and Webb. Daniel De Foe of St. Michael's, Cornhill, and Mary Webb of St. Mary, Aldermanbury, were married Mar. 29, 1720, in Esq. Aske's Chapel, at Hoxton, from the A.B. of Cant.

"P. HENRY VAUGHAN."

A child born to " Nathaniel " (evidently a mistake
for Daniel) Defoe and Mary his wife was buried in
November, 1720. Its name was Tuffley, after its
grandmother.

64.—DUNCAN CAMPBELL AND THE GHOST OF DOROTHY
DINGLEY.

WORKS: 199.—Charity still a Christian Virtue.
200.—The King of Pirates, Captain Avery.
201.—The Chimera.
202.—Duncan Campbell.
203.—Mr. Campbell's Pacquet.

On the ignorance, folly, and tyranny of Justices of
the Peace in those times Defoe is frequently found
pouring the vials of his wrath ; and he was never
more justified in doing so than when, on 16th October,
1719, in a tract entitled " Charity still a Christian
Virtue," he took up the cudgels against two of them in
behalf of a persecuted clergyman named Hendley.
Mr. Hendley had taken the children of St. Anne's
(Aldersgate) charity school to Chiselhurst, where he
preached a sermon and collected the alms of the congregation on their behalf, when lo ! our petty justices
" proceeded against the clergyman and those of the
committee who collected in church, as beggars and
vagrants, rogues and vagabonds, and committed them
them for trial, at the next assizes at Rochester, where
by a mockery of justice they were fined, and left to
seek a remedy by Writ of Error." Defoe, however,
castigates not only the justices of the peace, but also
the judge and jury ; and the names of all concerned are
recorded in full " for the admiration of posterity."
Proceedings were afterwards taken against the two
justices for disturbing and interrupting divine service

in Chislehurst Church; but owing to the death of Mr. Hendley they escaped the punishment which would certainly have been meted out to them, and their reckoning was left to be settled in another world.

"Captain Avery" (published 10th December, 1719) is one of those narratives of personal bravery, surprising encounters, and hairbreadth escapes which Defoe had now begun to take so much delight in describing. The full title is "The King of the Pirates; Being an account of the famous enterprises of Captain Avery, the Mock King of Madagascar. With his rambles and piracies." But, wild rover of the sea as he was, Captain Avery carried quite a respectable amount of the salt of religion in his constitution; he and his brother freebooters were strictly honourable among one another, and when asked who they were gave as a reply, "good, honest Christian pirates." Among Captain Avery's experiences was a visit to Juan Fernandez, where his men hunted goats, took in water, and remained twenty-two days; but no mention is made either of Alexander Selkirk or Robinson Crusoe.

Defoe's "Chimera" (end of 1719) deals with the Mississipi Scheme of John Law, and prophesies the crash, which ultimately came in July the following year, spreading ruin throughout the whole of France. To the "Chimera" succeeded "Duncan Campbell."

A celebrated fortune-teller of London, Duncan Campbell, professed to be, and probably was, deaf and dumb. He possessed rare natural powers, improved by habit and by practice; but his reputation was chiefly founded on his claim to the faculty of second sight. The *Spectator* (No. 560) says of him : " The blind Tiresias was not more famous in Greece than this dumb artist has been for some years past in the cities of London and Westminster." The quickness of his sight and the delicacy of his touch were extraordinary. He could play upon the violin with great exactness, and tuned it by putting the instrument between his teeth. He was an expert in the art of self-defence, and especially at fencing. On one occasion a pistol was fired close to his ear, but he neither started nor betrayed any symptom of surprise. He was so much resorted to by persons who desired him to tell their fortunes, that he gained a great deal of money ; but owing to his extravagant habits, it soon slipped from his fingers. Thinking this personage a suitable subject for his pen, Defoe composed, and published on the 30th of April, 1720, a work with the following title, " The History of the Life and Adventures of Mr. Duncan Campbell, a gentleman who, though deaf and dumb, writes down any stranger's name at first sight, with their future contingencies of fortune. Now living in Exeter Court over against the Savoy in the Strand."

The work was so successful, that a second edition appeared in the same year, with several illustrations, including a portrait of Campbell, engraved by Vandergucht.

On the 18th of June appeared " Mr. Campbell's Pacquet," consisting of three parts, the first two being poems by various persons with which Defoe had nothing to do. But the third, " An Account

of a most Surprising Apparition, sent from Launceston in Cornwall; attested by the Rev. Mr.
Ruddle,* Minister there," is certainly from his pen;
though why it was included in the "Pacquet" is a
mystery, for it has nothing whatever to do with
Campbell. The substance of this story, which
belongs to the same category as the "Apparition
of Mrs. Veal," is as follows: A Mr. Ruddle, after
preaching a funeral sermon over a lad who had
died under singular circumstances, was accosted by
a gentleman, who declared that he had a son who
was in the same strange way as the deceased had
been. Would Mr. Ruddle visit the lad? Mr.
Ruddle consented, and the boy, whose name was
Sam, declared that a woman named Dorothy
Dingley, who had "died about eight years since,"
had been in the habit of meeting him on his way
to and from school, morning and evening, in a field
called the Higher Broom-Quartils. "Then," continued the boy, "I changed my way, and went to
school the under Horse Road, and then she always
met me in the Narrow Lane, between Quarry Park
and the Nursery, which was worse." The thing
became a terrible trouble to him. Night and day,
sleeping and waking, the shape was ever running in
his mind, and he declared that his misery was
insupportable.

Mr. Ruddle then proposed that they should
go and see the "spectrum" together, which they

---

* Mr. Ruddle was of Caius College, Cambridge, M.A., 1662; Vicar
of Launceston, 1664-99; and Vicar of Altarnon, near Launceston,
1679-99. He died in 1699, and is buried in Launceston Church.

accordingly did next morning; but though both saw
the ghost, they had no communication with it.
The next three weeks a sickness in his family kept
Mr. Ruddle at home; but he "studied the case,
resolving by the help of God to see the utmost."
In subsequent visits to the field, though he often
addressed the spirit, he could get no reply; but
on Thursday, 28th of July, 1665, he persisted in
speaking to it "until it spake again," and gave him
satisfaction. "But," continues the reverend gentleman, "the work could not be finished at this time
wherefore the same evening, an hour after sunset,
it met me again near the same place, and after
a few words on each side, it quietly vanished, and
neither doth appear since, nor ever will any more,
to any man's disturbance." In short, the good
man had prevailed on Dorothy Dingley to keep to
her grave.

The same remarks that were made in respect
to Mrs. Veal apply to Dorothy Dingley. Defoe
evidently received the story from someone whose
word he thought could be relied on; and being a
firm believer in ghosts and apparitions, he put it
into writing without any misgivings. Several ver-
sions of the story got abroad. One appears in
C. S. Gilbert's "History of Cornwall," 1820, another,
"The Botathen Ghost," in the prose works of the
Rev. R. S. Hawker, of Morwenstow.

Another tract connected with Campbell's name
—that Defoe may have been the author of—is
"The Friendly Daemon," being an account of a
cure wrought upon "that famous deaf and dumb

R

gentleman, by a familiar spirit that appeared to him in a white surplice, like a cathedral singing boy." London, 1726.

65.---"THE MEMOIRS OF A CAVALIER" (20TH MAY, 1720).

WORK : 204.—The Memoirs of a Cavalier.

"The Memoirs of a Cavalier" has elicited admiration from critics of all opinions. "As a model of historical work of a certain kind," says Mr. Saintsbury, "it is hardly surpassable, and many separate passages —accounts of battles and skirmishes—have never been equalled except by Mr. Carlyle." Mr. Lee calls it "one of the finest military memoirs extant in any language."

The stupid notion that "The Memoirs of a Cavalier" is purely a work of fiction has now long been exploded. That Defoe was a very great man goes without saying, but he was not a god, and it would have required a mind with little less than divine powers to have invented so minute and circumstantial a narrative as "The Memoirs of a Cavalier." Of course, the fact that Defoe himself declared that the work was not fiction weighed little in the estimation of the sapient early critics. They had got it into their dense understandings that nothing that Defoe wrote was true; and when they came to the "Cavalier" they wondered, not how on earth a man could write such a production out of his own head, but how it was that Lord Chatham accepted it as genuine history. The fact, so obvious to us, that Lord Chatham was was right, and that the work is genuine history, never entered into their minds. History, thank Heaven, is not all written the same way. There's Macaulay's way and Carlyle's way, there's Froude's way and J. R. Green's way, and there's Defoe's way. Doubtless, moreover, there will be numerous other ways which time will bring to the birth—for the great subject admits of an infinite variety of treatment. Some extol Macaulay, others Carlyle, and so on; but the true and faithful student will find it in his heart to admire all. Defoe thought fit to write his great histories in the first person; and as the gain from an artistic point of view, and in verisimilitude, is very great, he was perfectly justified in so doing. The foundation of "The Memoirs of a Cavalier" was, as Defoe tells us—and we have no reason to doubt his statement—a manuscript that got among the plunder taken by a Parliamentarian cavalry officer, at or after the fight at Worcester. Defoe, to use his own expression, was very fond of "rummaging among old records."* The writer of the manuscript, who was likewise the hero of the book, is supposed to have been Andrew Newport, second son of Richard Newport (afterwards Lord Newport) of High Ercoll, Salop.

The work easily divides itself into two parts, the first detailing the service of the Cavalier on the continent under "Gustavus Adolphus, the glorious King of Sweden"; and the second, his adventures in the army of King Charles I. of England.

That Defoe took great liberties with his manuscript,

* See *Review*, iv., 513.

R 2

and that in order to heighten the lights and deepen
the shadows, he borrowed facts from other sources is
as certain as that he dished up the whole in his own
inimitable style. But notwithstanding the circumstantial character of the work and the minuteness of
its detail, or, perhaps we might say better, in consequence of it, Defoe was a great bungler; even
Shakspere was not guilty of more anachronisms.
For example, Defoe was exceedingly anxious that
the public should believe the Cavalier to be a real
personage, yet, whilst in the preface it is shown that
the manuscript could not possibly have been continued by the Cavalier after 1651 (the date of the
battle of Worcester), nevertheless the narrative itself
ends after the Restoration of 1660. Then, again, we
wonder where a Cavalier scribe of the time of
Charles I. could have got his information from about
"The Tale of the Tub," the "Observator," and
"Jure Divino." These phenomena would lend colour
to the opinion that the whole thing is fiction, only
they are more than counterbalanced by something
else. The Cavalier's great hatred of the Scots would
in itself be quite sufficient to prove that Defoe was
expressing not his own sentiments, but those of
another. Defoe would not have reminded the Scots
that by selling their king they had branded themselves
with eternal infamy, or have called them "these cursed
Scots." "In style and diction," observes Mr. Lee,
"there are occasionally whole paragraphs that scarcely
afford a trace of Defoe's pen. His mind as well as
his hand is much more perceptible in the latter part
of the book than the former; and, as he was better

acquainted with the geography and physical character
of his own country than that of Germany, this part
of the narrative is often very characteristic of his
genius." Possibly this is true, but the first half of the
" Memoirs of a Cavalier " is immeasurably superior to
the second. Fighting under the banner of such a
leader as Gustavus Adolphus is as joyous as the
inaction under so poor a creature as Charles I. is
dispiriting. Oh, one feels, to be trailing a pike again
under Sir John Hepburn! Oh, to be back at the
Lech, where Gustavus withstood Tilly—where the
gods hurled rocks at one another. If we are to read
about a battle, let it be one in which there is good
generalship and stubborn fighting on both sides.
And Defoe, as in imagination he frittered away his
time in King Charles's camp, felt it, too. " My old
hero, the glorious Gustavus Adolphus used to say
an enemy reduced to a necessity of fighting is half
beaten." Now and again, it is true, one gets cheered
up a bit, as, for example, by the deeds of the garrison
at Newark, "brave, old, rugged boys, fellows that,
like Count Tilly's Germans, had iron faces," or the
brisk reply of our intrepid commander, Sir Marmaduke
Langdale, " A soldier ought never to suppose he shall
be beaten." The courage, too, of Lord Fairfax,
though our enemy, we cannot but admire, and when
in the enemy's camp as a hostage we are generous
enough to compliment him on his actions, and
especially to compare him to Gustavus Adolphus,
whereupon " he would blush like a woman, and be
uneasy, declining the discourse," which reminds of
Gustavus even more.

Defoe now set about another story on something
the same lines as "Robinson Crusoe," entitling it,
"The Life, Adventures, and Piracies of the famous
Captain Singleton: containing an account of his being
set on shore in the Island of Madagascar," etc. Like
"Robinson Crusoe," "Captain Singleton" is in two
parts. In the first we read how little Bob Singleton,
who had been trepanned when a child, was sold to a
gipsy. At twelve he went to sea, and after several
adventures found himself in a Portuguese ship on his
way to Lisbon. His master dying there, he engaged
himself as cabin-boy in a Portuguese vessel bound for
India. Degraded as he had become, the wicked
conduct of his shipmates filled him with horror. At
Goa he escaped the Inquisition by turning Catholic,
being no less willing to suit his religion to circumstances than Crusoe was. When the vessel reached
Madagascar, on its homeward journey, a mutiny broke
out among the seamen, and twenty-seven of them,
including Singleton, were left on shore. After
various adventures, the mutineers embarked in a
paraguay and made for the mainland of Africa. A
description is then given of the marvellous journey
from Mozambique across the great unknown continent
of Africa to its western coast, a truly extraordinary
piece of work, for, though writing one hundred and
fifty years before the explorations of Livingstone,
Baker, and Grant, and one hundred and seventy
before the discoveries of Stanley, so carefully had

Defoe studied the geography of Africa and the reports of various adventurers that there is scarcely anything he says that modern discovery has been able to throw discredit on; this, too, at a time when the centre of Africa was to the generality of men unknown, and, when on their maps of it geographers, as Dean Swift has it, put "elephants for want of towns." He describes the great Lake Nyassa and its *entourage* as follows :—

"It was the ninth day of our travel in this wilderness, when we came to the view of a great lake of water. . . . The next day we came to the edge of this lake, and, happily for us, we came to it at the south point of it; so we passed by it, and travelled three days by the side of it, which was a great comfort to us, because it lightened our burthen, there being no need to carry water when we had it in view. And yet, though there was so much water, we found but very little alteration in the desert."

There were no trees, neither was there any grass or herbage, except a broad flat thistle, though without any prickle, which the buffaloes ate eagerly.

But Defoe's allusion to the mighty lake that feeds the Nile—the Victoria Nyanza—is more extraordinary still, for it was only a few years ago that the question of the source of the Nile was finally settled by Mr. Stanley. Defoe's account is as follows :—

"In three days' march we came to a river, which we saw from the hills, and which we called the Golden River; and we found it ran northward, which was the first stream we had met with that did so. It ran with a very rapid current, and our gunner, pulling out his map, assured me that this was either the river Nile, or ran into the great lake out of which the river Nile was said to take its beginning."

The river flowing north was the Lualaba, which, as we now know, thanks to the discoveries of Stanley,

does not, as Defoe supposed, and as, I believe, Mr.
Stanley himself once supposed, flow into the Victoria
Nyanza.   It is the commencement of the Congo or
Livingstone.

Having at length reached the western coast,
Singleton separated himself from the rest of his
companions, and, embarking at Cape Coast Castle,
returned to England with "a glorious sum of
money," thus ending the first part of his adventures.

In England he fell into bad company, spent his
money in "all kinds of folly and wickedness," and,
when it was gone, shipped on a voyage to Cadiz.
A plot to seize the vessel having failed, he transferred himself to a companion ship, where he again
plotted, and this time with success.   Having chosen
a man named Wilmot as captain, the mutineers put
to sea, and before long captured a Spanish sloop,
which they manned for a privateer and gave the
command to Singleton.   Success and riches followed,
and after two years the sloop was sold, and Singleton
and his crew transferred themselves to a Spanish
frigate of thirty-eight guns.   Again they took numerous prizes, on one of them being a Pennsylvanian
Quaker named William Walters, who henceforth
figures largely in the story ; but a difference having
arisen between Singleton and Wilmot, the two parted
company, and Wilmot carried off all the spoil, thus
leaving Singleton to go over all his labours again.
Nothing daunted, however, with his frigate carrying
four hundred men and forty-four guns he again
tried his luck, William the Quaker bearing him
company.   Once more fortune proved kind, and

again he grew rich. After a time Singleton, who, owing to the conversation of the Quaker, felt himself visited with prickings of conscience, entered upon the resolve to reform and to make reparation for some of his deeds of violence; and the story ends with the marriage of Singleton to a fair Quakeress, William's sister. As Mr. Lee points out, Defoe was quite justified in introducing a Quaker pirate. "Few men had better studied, or more highly respected, the body of Friends, called Quakers," than Defoe; "but there were undoubtedly in the reigns of Queen Anne and George I. professed Quakers, such as we know nothing of now. London had several who kept taverns, one who was an owner of race-horses, that ran for wagers on Banstead Downs; and several Quakers were transported for burglaries and highway robberies."

67.—*APPLEBEE'S JOURNAL.*—SUMMARY OF DEFOE'S JOURNALISTIC WORK.—THE BURSTING OF THE SOUTH SEA BUBBLE.

WORKS: 206.—*Applebee's.*
    207.—*The Director.*
    208.—Complete Art of Painting—a Poem.
    209.—A Vindication of the Honour and Justice of Parliament against the Speech of John A———, Esq.
    210.—A Collection of Miscellany Letters, selected out of *Mist's.*

In June, 1720, Mr. Mist was in trouble again. The Roman Catholic Elector Palatine had recently, owing to British interference, been induced to leave off persecuting his Protestant subjects. Mist's continental correspondents, who were Roman Catholics, having resented and reflected upon this interference, Mist was unwise enough, contrary to the advice of

Defoe, to insert their contributions, with the result
of the presentation of the matter before the House
of Lords; and Mist, being apprehended, was
committed to the King's Bench to await his trial.
Defoe, however, notwithstanding his vexation on
account of Mist's indiscretion, appears to have
carried on the paper during his colleague's imprisonment. The rupture between them, however, was
only doctored and not healed; for Defoe, though
he did not abandon *Mist's*, now joined himself to
another periodical, *Applebee's Original Weekly Journal.*
Applebee's, as it was familiarly called, which had
been established about six years, was published on
Saturdays, and consisted of three leaves small
folio. In principles, though loyal to the House of
Hanover, it was mildly Tory.

To the inauguration of the South Sea Scheme
we have already made allusion. That it became
popular, and that the success that attended it induced the formation of a number of rival companies
is a matter of history. Change Alley for many
weeks was a perfect babel with the cries of the
advocates of the various " Hubble Bubbles." Even
kitchen-maids, shoe-makers, and tavern-drawers had
caught the infection: everybody was puffing or
listening to the claims of this or that fraudulent
company; everybody was buying or selling stock.
But at the request of the South Sea Company,
Parliament now put its foot on all these petty
schemes; the Act for the suppression of which
came into operation on June 24, 1720. Defoe's first
contribution to *Applebee's* describes the changed

condition of affairs in town, owing to the enforcement of the Act. The cobbler had returned to his stall, the tavern-damsel to her customers, the small-coal man to his small coal, the chimney-sweep to his chimneys, and the barber to his stubbly chins. In short, equilibrium had been restored. The same number of the paper contained the following item of news: "Yesterday at noon, South-Sea Stock was 1,000." Shortly after, the chairman of the Company and some of the principal directors sold out. Then people grew suspicious, the stock began to fall, and those who had been so eager to buy were now more eager to sell. On August 27th it had fallen to 800, on September 12th to 400. It still fell, and thousands were ruined. A glance down the columns of the newspapers of the day sufficiently informs of the state of things that followed. A Suffolk knight hangs himself, a mercer in Bedford Street, Covent Garden, throws himself "out of a window two pair of stairs backwards," "a noted banker in the Strand, of great credit," fails and goes into the Mint, "a merchant in Crutched-Fryers shoots himself in his chamber"; but these were only a few out of tens of thousands of sufferers.

"At this juncture, Defoe and some with whom he acted, thought it desirable to commence a paper which should be devoted to the discussion of the financial evils under which the nation was suffering, and the best means of restoring public credit. The first number of this paper appeared on the 5th of October, 1720, with the title *The Director*. It was written by Defoe, and published by W. Boreham. every Wednesday and Friday; but had, probably, only a brief existence."*

* Lee

"The Compleat Art of Painting," by M. du
Fresnoy, which in 1720 Defoe translated into·English
verse, broken into short sections, for T. Warner,
the publisher, was probably intended merely as a
memoria technica for young students.

Applebee's Journal being the last newspaper to
which Defoe was a contributor to any great extent,
this is a fitting place to sum up his journalistic
labours.

He had relinquished his *Review* in 1713, after
a publication extending over more than nine years.

In May, 1716, he commenced *Mercurius Politicus*,
a monthly periodical, which he continued till 1720,
and probably much longer.

In June, 1716, he was offered, and accepted, a
share in *Dormer's News-Letter*, a manuscript paper.
His connection with it lasted till August, 1718.

His connection with Mist's *Journal* commenced
apparently in August, 1717, and continued till October,
1724, having lasted, with interruptions, over seven
years.

In September, 1718, he set on foot the *Whitehall
Evening Post*, with which he was connected till 1720.

In 1719 he established the *Daily Post*, his connection with which lasted till April, 1725.

His connection with *Applebee's Journal* commenced on June 25, 1720, and continued till 12th
March, 1726.

68.—THE "SERIOUS REFLECTIONS" (ROBINSON CRUSOE, PART III.)
(6TH AUG., 1720).

As the splendid reception of the first part of
"Robinson Crusoe" encouraged Defoe to write a

second, so the scarcely less flattering reception of
the second impelled him to write a third, with title-
page as follows : " Serious Reflections during the Life
and Surprising Adventures of Robinson Crusoe : with
his vision of the Angelic World.   Written by himself.
London.   Printed for W. Taylor, at the Ship and
Black Swan in Paternoster Row, 1720."

Besides a preface by Defoe, which is signed
" Robinson Crusoe," the book also contains a preface
by Taylor, the publisher.

"The success," says Mr. Taylor, "the two former parts have
met with has been known by the envy it has brought upon the
editor, expressed in a thousand hard words from the men of trade ;
the effect of that regret which they entertained at their having no
share in it.   And I must do the author the justice to say that not a
dog has wagged his tongue at the work itself, nor has a word been
said to lessen the value of it but which has been the visible effect of
that envy at the good fortune of the bookseller."

Nor, thought Mr. Taylor, could the success of
the third volume be less than that of its predecessors : "while the parable has been so diverting, the
moral must certainly be equally agreeable."   To the
biographer of Defoe, and the student of English
literature generally, this " Serious Reflections " is
a dish toothsome in the extreme, for it enables to
get closer to the writer than anything else that Defoe
penned ; but the general reader has seen nothing
in it to admire.   Where millions have read Crusoe
Part I., and thousands Crusoe Part II., only units
have ever even heard of Crusoe Part III.

The work consists "mainly of meditations on
Divine Providence in times of trouble, and discourses
on the supreme importance of honest dealing" ; but

by far the most interesting feature is its declaration that the story of "Robinson Crusoe" is an allegory of Defoe's own life. As, however, we have gone into this subject thoroughly in previous sections, we need do no more here than to repeat Defoe's declaration in it, that "Robinson Crusoe," even down to the minutest particulars, is a picture of his own experiences—

"The adventures of Robinson Crusoe are one whole scheme of a real life of twenty-eight years, spent in the most wandering, desolate, and afflicting circumstances that ever man went through, and in which I have lived so long in a life of wonders, in continued storms, fought with the worst kind of savages and man-eaters; by unaccountable surprising incidents, fed by miracles greater than that of the ravens; suffered all manner of violences and oppressions, injurious reproaches, contempt of men, attacks of devils, corrections from Heaven, and oppositions on earth; have had innumerable ups and downs in matters of fortune, been in slavery worse than Turkish, escaped by an exquisite management, as that in the story of Xury and the boat of Sallee; been taken up at sea in distress, raised again and depressed again, and that oftener perhaps in one man's life than ever was known before; shipwrecked often, though more by land than by sea. In a word, there's not a circumstance in the imaginary story but has its just allusion to a real story, and chimes part for part, and step for step, with the inimitable Life of Robinson Crusoe."

When asked why, if he had such a regard for the strict and literal, truth he did not tell his history in his own person, Defoe replied that he wrote for the instruction of mankind, for the purpose of recommending "invincible patience under the worst of misery; indefatigable application and undaunted resolution under the greatest and most discouraging circumstances," and that he did not believe that any other method would so well effect the purpose.

CHAPTER XII.

CRIMINAL AND TOPOGRAPHICAL SERIES.

69.—MIST IS PILLORIED.—HE IS VISITED IN PRISON AND CHEERED BY HIS "JUDICIOUS, LEARNED, AND MERRY FRIEND," DANIEL DEFOE.

WE now return to Mr. Nathaniel Mist, whom we left in prison awaiting his trial. Brought, on 3rd December, 1720, before Lord Chief Justice Pratt at Guildhall, "for having scandalously reflected on His Majesty's seasonable interposition in favour of the Protestants abroad," Mr. Mist was found guilty. The judgment pronounced upon him on the 13th of February, 1721, was as follows :—" That he stand twice in the pillory, at Charing Cross, and the Royal Exchange ; pay a fine of £50; suffer three months' imprisonment in the King's Bench, and give security for his good behaviour for seven years." Unable either to pay the fine or to give the required security, Mr. Mist remained in prison ; and, while there, aggravated his offence by permitting two articles, one reflecting on the King, and the other against Marlborough, to appear in his journal. Upon his refusing to mention the names of the writers of the articles, the House of Commons committed him to Newgate. He was to have been tried on the 9th of October, but owing to a severe illness, induced by the unhealthiness of his cell, the matter was postponed till the next sessions. In the meantime, Defoe, acting the part of a true friend, continued his oversight of the journal.

Downcast on account of his pecuniary difficulties, caused by the expenses of his prosecution, fines, fees, and absence from business, Mist looked about for sources of relief, and just as he was pondering the advisability of publishing selections from the *Journal*, by subscription, in came Defoe; or as Mist puts it, "a judicious, learned, and merry friend (as good luck would have it) made me a seasonable visit. The gentleman finding me in a very pensive posture, reproached my want of fortitude very frankly, and was very liberal in exhortations, supported by arguments drawn from history, philosophy, and religion, to bear my misfortune patiently." But Defoe was ready with something more than cheering words; he heartily endorsed Mist's proposal concerning the selections, and promised to write the dedication himself, and to superintend their publication. Of the articles in this work, published 9th January, 1722, thirty-two were by Defoe. In the meantime (9th December, 1721) Mist had been brought up for trial, but no evidence being offered against him he was discharged. "There can be little or no doubt, from his own words some years later, that the influence of Defoe with the Government had much to do with this merciful termination of Mist's imprisonment." *

* Lee.

70.—DEFOE'S SON BENJAMIN IN TROUBLE (14TH AUG., 1721).

The bursting of the South Sea Bubble had not only set all England in a ferment, but it had excited those who had been swindled to loud cries of vengeance on the directors. Parliament, however, though willing to mete out punishment, was inclined to act with clemency. This course provoked a yell of indignation ; and among the newspapers that censured the merciful proceedings of Parliament was the *London Journal*, in which, about the middle of August (1721), appeared "a scandalous and seditious libel."

On the same day "Mr. Wilkins, the printer, and Mr. Peele, the publisher," were taken up, but admitted to bail ; and on the 14th of August Benjamin Norton, Defoe's second son, who was author or responsible editor of the paper, and putative writer of the article, was committed to Newgate. At the same time that this libel appeared Daniel Defoe was writing eloquent pseudonymous articles in *Applebee's* in support of the proceedings of Parliament, from which it has been concluded that father and son were just then not on friendly terms.

Defoe had evidently foreseen that his son would get into trouble, for in one of his articles which dealt with libels he tried to show that the authors of libels were, as a rule, more foolish than malicious. He thought the law on libels ought to be amended, and observes :

"The indictment is loaded with the usual adverbs—seditiously, maliciously, or traitorously and seditiously, and the like—when

S

perhaps the unhappy scribbler has had no sedition, or treason, or malice in his head, and the indictment ought only to have said greedily, covetously, and avariciously, the man having had no design at all but merely to get a penny, and perhaps to buy him bread."

Apparently Defoe had warned and cautioned his son without effect : and this " Essay on Libel " seems to have been written in the hope that the punishment which, like Damocles' sword, hung over the young scribbler might be avoided.

By-and-by we learn from *Read's Journal* that Benjamin " was admitted to bail before Mr. De la Faye, himself being bound by recognisance in the sum of one thousand pounds, and his two sureties in the sum of five hundred pounds each, for his appearnce at the King's Bench Bar on the first day of the term." In *Applebee's Journal* of August 26 Defoe again attempts to help his son, and declares in respect to the publisher and printer of the *London Journal*—

"'Tis known that the young Defoe was but a stalking-horse and a tool, to bear the lash and the pillory in their stead, for his wages ; that he was the author of the most scandalous part, but was only made sham proprietor of the whole to screen the true proprietors from justice."

Of course it was not known at the time that the writer in *Applebee's* was the father, who indeed took every precaution possible to keep his connection with that journal secret. As " nothing is recorded in the public prints as to any further proceedings having been taken against B. N. Defoe," it is probable " that, out of consideration for his father, the Ministry forbore the preparation of any indictment and discharged the son from his recognisances."

71.—THE GREAT CRIMINAL SERIES.

Mr. Lee has been at considerable pains to explain Defoe's motives for writing that great series of stories of criminals which includes "Moll Flanders," "Colonel Jack," and "Roxana," and with which we have now to deal; and he considers it his duty to defend Defoe. But I do not see either that Defoe's motive requires any explanation, or Defoe himself any defence. Curious, prying, inquisitive; a never-tiring hunter after anecdotes which he is ever pouring from his full treasury; one who loved to wonder, and to make wonder; one who had studied life in the nealing-arches of Dallow's glass-house, in Rosemary Lane, and in the palace of King William of commendable but obtrusive memory, in the dungeons of Newgate and in the country-house of Sir John Fagg; a man whose passion for the odd, the wild, the *bizarre*, the startling and the marvellous, peeps out in everything he said or did; it was nothing but natural that he should dip his pen, in order to write the narratives of some of the extraordinary characters who had crossed his path; that he should have perpetrated: "Moll Flanders," "Colonel Jack," "Rob Roy," "Roxana," "Bizeau," "Jack Sheppard," and "Jonathan Wild." He wrote them because his imagination had been excited, and because he simply could not help writing them. It is very lamentable, no doubt, but the lives of great criminals are, as a rule, much more entertaining reading than the lives of great divines. That, however, is a law of nature for which Defoe is in no wise responsible. Nobody failed more miserably than Defoe himself when he tried to write the life of a good man; as for example, the Memoirs of Daniel Williams, D.D. Let it then at once be admitted that Defoe wrote these tales because they were extraordinary tales, because he had been excited by the recital of them, and because he enjoyed telling them. He told them, however, in the right way, one of their *raisons d'être* being his desire to lead the fallen and depraved to see not only the error but the folly of their ways, and to entice them to paths of virtue and honesty. Instead of treating sin flippantly, and presenting great rogues as heroes, as did so many writers, Defoe took upon himself to impress upon his readers how intensely wretched is the career of even the most prosperous rogue, and how vastly better it is to live in the narrowest circumstances, than to be surrounded with wealth gotten by wickedness. But he also points out that it is not sufficient for the criminals themselves to reform, the whole country must reform; and instead of upholding laws that tend to the manufacture of criminals and the spread of vice, a Christian people, such as the English plume themselves on being, should abolish those laws, and not rest satisfied till a far better state of affairs has been arrived at. That he exhibits vice in its native deformity, without being sentimentalised is perfectly true, and that his rogues get punished is true also; but Defoe feels for them. There is good in the worst character he draws, and when he is able to do so, as for · · ·

example when he describes characters under fictitious names, he not only spares them from the gallows, but, when he consistently can, considerately furnishes them—after repentance, of course—with a competency in their old age.

And if Defoe is not to be castigated for thinking fit to write the lives of thieves and harlots, neither is it fair to charge him with being coarse. "Moll Flanders," "Colonel Jack," and "Roxana" are not books for the drawing-room table, but neither are "Hamlet," "Gulliver's Travels" (unexpurgated), "Tom Jones," "Joseph Andrews," or "Tristram Shandy." Defoe belonged to an age when a spade was called a spade. Had he lived at the present day, he would doubtless have used a decent periphrasis. He did not wittingly offend: indeed, he prided himself on the purity of his page; and his contemporaries, ever ready as they were to pick holes, never once preferred against him the charge of coarseness.

Much of the material upon which Defoe based his stories, was no doubt obtained during his imprisonment at Newgate; where although, as he was confined only for having published a libel, he would not be compelled to associate with his fellow prisoners, the criminals, yet it is quite certain that he was not the man to lose such fair opportunities for studying a class in which he was always so much interested; and it is known that he often kept manuscripts, intended for the press, by him for years. His "Tours" lay in MS. nearly forty years; his tract "Advice to All Parties," three years (*see* § 30) ; and " Crusoe," probably four years. " The Present State of Parties in Great Britain " took him, on and off, eight years (*see* § 41) ; and "Jure Divino," three years. As Mr. Lee has shown, however, Defoe owed a great deal of his 'knowledge of the criminal classes to his connection with *Applebee's—*

" Mr. John Applebee, the proprietor of *The Original Journal,* carried on the general business of a printer in Water Lane, White· friars. He might also with propriety be designated the official printer of Newgate, for from his office were issued the printed papers of the ordinary—as to the conduct of the condemned felons under his spiritual care—and their confessions, if any. The last dying speeches of criminals were known to be correct if Mr. Applebee's name was printed on the papers ; and in any extraordinary case, with the consent of the condemned, the narrative of his life was taken from his own lips, or any paper he had written was given to Mr. Applebee, and embodied in a pamphlet, often printed before, but published immediately after, the execution. For these purposes, Mr. Applebee, or any one authorised to represent him, had access to the prisoners in Newgate during all the six years that Daniel Defoe was con nected with the management of *The Original Journal.*

" A short experience would suffice to convince Defoe that the largest proportion of these papers and books circulated among the criminal population, and were read with great avidity. An examination of the lowest class of thieves' literature of the time printed in other offices, shows that successful highwaymen and burglars were exalted into heroes, whose great deeds were more held up as examples of imitation than as warnings to be avoided ; and even those who had expiated their crimes upon the scaffold were objects of highest admiration when they ' died game.' If any such became penitents, they were execrated as sneaks and cowards. No point of morality was ever touched upon in these stories."

72.—MOLL FLANDERS (27TH JANUARY, 1722).

WORK : 211.—Moll Flanders. 27th Jan., 1722.

This extraordinary narrative, which is styled by Mr. Saintsbury " the most remarkable example of pure realism in literature," which is regarded by Charles Lamb as of no inferior interest to "Robinson Crusoe," and by Mr. A. B. Walkley, as a finer novel than "Crusoe," "because more subtle, more complex,"* was published on 22nd January, 1722. There is no doubt that almost all its features are taken from real life. The early scenes are laid in Colchester, a town with which Defoe was much connected.

Though born in wretchedness and thrown helpless on the world, Moll Flanders had the good fortune to get into a family where she was carefully brought up and educated, and all went well till her mistress's eldest son fell in love with her and ruined her. By and by Moll married her mistress's second son, who soon died. Her next husband was a Colchester draper with stylish tastes ; consequently, for a time they lived like the quality and indulged in such luxuries as a drive to Oxford and Northampton in a coach and six. When her husband went bankrupt and absconded, Moll removed to the Mint in London, where her supposed fortune and the charms of her person brought her a third time into wedlock. With her husband, a sea captain, she goes out to Virginia, only to discover, to her horror, that she has married her brother, or rather half-brother. She returns to England, and after an intrigue with a gentleman at Bath, unites herself to a north-country fortune hunter, who pretended to be a landed gentleman. The unimportant fact that two of her former husbands were still living, of course, did not weigh with her. Her new husband, the fortune hunter, on discovering that

* *Daily Chronicle*, 7th Feb., 1892.

Moll is possessed of only a few pounds, betakes himself
to his old calling, namely, the road, whilst his spouse,
after a few genuine tears, hies to London, and by and
by gets married, at Little Brickhill, in the lace country
of Buckinghamshire, to a respectable and well-to-do
bank clerk, with whom she lived happily till his death,
when, falling into poverty, she took to thieving. Her
exceptional run of luck lasted twelve years, but in
the end she was landed in Newgate, where she found
herself in company of her fourth husband, the highwayman. At Newgate she began to reform, and not
before it was high time. She and her husband
proceed to Virginia in the same vessel. In Virginia
they prosper and grow rich, and spend the remainder
of their years " in sincere penitence."

" Moll Flanders " was the Bible, the one book, of
an old apple-woman whom George Borrow (the story
is in " Lavengro ") found on London Bridge. The old
crone had, very literally, apotheosised Moll into " Our
Blessed Mary " Flanders. " There have been more
imposing religions," observes Mr. Walkley, " with far
less literary justification."

Professor Minto will have it that it is only
in some respects "that 'Moll Flanders' is, as a
novel, superior to ' Robinson Crusoe.' Moll is a
more complicated character than the simple, open-
minded, manly mariner of York ; a strangely-
mixed compound of craft and impulse, selfishness
and generosity—in short, a thoroughly bad woman,
but made bad largely by circumstances. In tracing
the vigilant resolution with which she plays upon
human weakness, the spasms of compunction which

shoot across her wily designs, the selfish after-thoughts which paralyse her generous impulses, her fits of dare-devil courage and uncontrollable panic, and the steady current of good-humoured satisfaction with herself which makes her chuckle equally over mishaps and successes, Defoe has gone much more deeply into the springs of action and sketched a much richer page in the natural history of his species than in 'Robinson Crusoe.'"

The weakness of the book, he points out, is that it " is not firmly organised round some central principle of life," and he complains that it has no " heart and members."

"Compared with ' Robinson Crusoe,' 'Moll Flanders ' is only a string of diverting incidents, the lowest type of book organism, very brilliant while it is fresh and new, but not qualified to survive competitors for the world's interest. There is no unique creative purpose in it to bind the whole together ; it might be cut into pieces, each capable of wriggling amusingly by itself."

Attention may here be drawn to a very common trick of Defoe's, practised for the purpose of giving verisimilitude to his narrative, and that is the trick of pretended ignorance. When Moll is sailing for Virginia, the ship, she says, "came to anchor in a little bay, near a river, whose name I remember not, but they said the river came down from Limerick, and that it was the largest river in Ireland." In "Crusoe," Book I., Xury shoots a creature "like a hare, but different in colour, and longer legs " ; and in "Crusoe," Book II., the hero refers to a certain seaport, the name

of which "I may perhaps spell wrong, for I do not
particularly remember it, having lost this, together
with the names of many other places set down in a
little pocket-book, which was spoiled by the water by
an accident."

Another interesting feature of the book is the light
it throws on the importance at that time of the lace
trade, the centre of which was Olney, or, as Defoe in
his "Tours" calls it, "Ouldney."

When Moll Flanders was married at Little Brickhill to her fifth husband, the bank clerk, "finding it
was a lacemaking town," she gave to her bridesmaid
"a good suit of knots, as good as the town would
afford," and to the girl's "mother a piece of bone
lace for a head"; and whilst she was at the inn at
Brickhill she heard that "the coaches were robbed at
Dunstable Hill, and £560 in money taken; besides
some of the lace merchants that always travel that way
had been visited too." But lace being a commodity in
much demand, and fetching high prices, it was often
carried off, not only by highwaymen but also by shop-
lifters and other petty thieves. Moll herself, after she
became an "artist," as she prettily terms it, "made
a venture or two among the lace folks," and once
"carried off a piece of bone lace, worth six or seven
pounds, and a paper of thread"; on another occasion
she filches a parcel of lace "worth nearly £20"; but
her greatest prize in the lace way was when she captured £300 worth of Flanders lace which was "lodged
in a private house." Flanders lace, however, being
prohibited, she on this occasion made a virtue of her
peccadillo, and divided her spoil with the custom-house

officer. Among Moll's captures were thirty-guinea watches, sixty-guinea periwigs, and once she even helped herself to a horse; these trifles, however, were by the way—the mainstay of her calling was lace.

To students, of course, expurgated editions are the devil; but it is desirable that others nowadays besides students should have the opportunity of reading Defoe's great work.

The nearest thing we know to an expurgated "Moll Flanders" is in the "Selections from Defoe's Minor Novels" (Percival and Co.), edited by Mr. George Saintsbury. This is a charming little book —a book to love—and should be in the hands of every admirer of Defoe. One could wish, however, that instead of two extracts from "Moll" four or five had been given; in fact, almost all of it.

As a proof that Defoe's time was now valuable, let it be noted that on the 10th of April, 1721, he paid a fine of five pounds to be excused from serving parochial offices in Stoke Newington.

73.—CHARACTERISTICS OF DEFOE'S STYLE.—THE AMORPHOUSNESS
OF HIS WRITINGS.

About "fame's great antiseptic style," as the term is usually understood, Defoe troubled himself but little. He put his thoughts into the same homely, unaffected dress when he wrote them as when he spoke them. Matter, he took it, was almost everything; manner but very little. If in his political pamphlets he could drive an argument home he was satisfied; if in his fictions he succeeded in proving to his reader that it was all true, there was an end of it.

But though he troubled himself so little about what may be called the trivialities of style, its great essentials he always endeavoured to bear in mind, and he tells us in his "Compleat English Gentleman" what his ideal style was. It should be "manly," he says, "and polite, free and plain, without foolish flourishes and ridiculous flights of jingling bombast, or dull meannesses of expression below the dignity of the subject." As an English man of letters, it is natural that he should have been proud of the medium in which he was privileged to express his thoughts.

"As in all languages," says Defoe, "there is a beauty of style, a cadence and harmony in the expression, so in the English much more than any other vulgar speech in the world. The late Earl of Roscommon, the most exact writer and the best judge of polite language in his time, confirms my opinion, and I need no better a testimonial. Speaking of the French, which was boasted of at that time as a polite and beautiful language, he says—

' For who did ever in French authors see
  The comprehensive English energy?
  The weighty bullion of one sterling line,
  Drawn to French wire would thro' whole pages shine.' "

In the article in the *Daily Chronicle* (17th February, 1892), already quoted, Mr. A. B. Walkley deals skilfully with a feature in Defoe's writings which some have disallowed, namely, their amorphousness.

"However much," says Mr. Walkley, "we may praise Defoe's writings, however much—which is not always the same thing—we may enjoy them, we cannot choose but regret that he had not more leisure to be brief. His great, his gigantic literary qualities, his gift of narrative, his verisimilitude, his racy vocabulary, his inimitable art of vivid presentation went hand in hand with a lack of all sense of proportion, measure, restraint, form."

Mr. Walkley traces this amorphousness of Defoe's to "two distinct causes—one external, and related to the workaday aims of Defoe the man ; one internal, and involved in the technical method of Defoe the artist. For artist, and great artist, as he was, Defoe was a born tradesman, always writing for the market, always keeping a steady eye on the main chance. Writing was with him a business before it was an art. Each of his books was intended to meet a certain demand."

When Defoe's hosiery business went wrong, and he found political pamphleteering more profitable, he took to pamphleteering. Subsequently, seeing a "good opening" in journalism, "he straightway became the most industrious, the most prolific of journalists." Believing that he saw a chance of making an honest penny "out of the demand for stories of adventure," he produced "Robinson Crusoe," and the success of "Crusoe" led to further stories.

One "might trace the same origin—the policy of 'put money in thy purse'—for all the rest of his novels. Obviously this principle—the principle not of saying something because he had something to say, but of selling something which the public wanted to buy—was fatal to anything like artistic form. The length of the work was conditioned, not

by its subject, but the state of the market.
Here, then, was the first cause of the amorphous
character of Defoe's writing.

"The second cause, if more subtle, is no less un-
mistakable.   The quintessence of Defoe's art was
its verisimilitude, the object of which he never lost
sight, and which no writer before or since has ever
so fully attained, was to 'lie like truth.'   Now
nothing gives the stamp of truth to art like a certain
artlessness, a trick of digression, prolixity, ends left
loose, and edges ragged.   Defoe's narrative is like
life itself; and life is, above all things, amorphous.
From the technical point of view, nothing could be
worse than the 'construction' of Defoe's novels:
they invariably neglect the Aristotelian precept that
a work of art should have a beginning, a middle,
and an end.   'Robinson Crusoe' does not end:
it tails off.   The conclusion of 'Moll Flanders,'
after the heroine's reprieve, is a miserable anti-
climax.   What could be more dilatory, more tediously
undramatic than the latter part of 'Roxana'?

"And yet one would not wish these books otherwise constructed, for their very artistic faults are, in
in a sense, qualities, their discontinuity, their décousu,
their alternate slackening and hurrying of pace,
their digressions, their garrulity, their level tracts of
commonplace give them the very air of truth.

"Defoe knew what his public wanted, and saw
that they got it.   The novel-reading taste of that
day, like the novel itself, was in its infancy.   What
is the question which the child, now as then, puts
to its nurse, on being told its first fairy tale?   'Is

it true? Did it really happen?' The reading public, under the first George (and, indeed, long afterwards) were as little children. They could not be induced to take an interest in a story unless they were persuaded that it was true. Indeed, it is highly probable that they would have thought a work of professed fiction an absolutely wicked thing. In Defoe's time theatrical audiences were prepared, no doubt, to swallow the lie for the lie's sake; but the theory of '*l'art pour l'art*' was as yet quite unknown to the novel-reader. Nor would Defoe himself—quite apart from any thought of his readers —have accepted it. For Defoe was essentially a man of his time: a true John Bull, an out-and-out Philistine, to whom the idea of art as an end in itself, as something purged of all moral purpose, would have seemed nonsensical affectation. The modern notion that the be-all and end-all of literature *qua* literature is to give pleasure, would have been scouted by him as immoral. ' The character of a good writer,' he says, ' wherever he is to be found, is this—viz., that he writes so as to please and *serve* at the same time.' In his ' Serious Reflections ' on ' Robinson Crusoe ' he has very plain language on story-telling merely to amuse. ' This supplying a story by invention is certainly a most scandalous crime. It is a sort of lying that makes a great hole in the heart, in which by degrees a habit of lying enters in.'

    '' There is no reason to doubt Defoe's sincerity in the utterance of these edifying sentiments : he supposed, in perfect good ·faith, that not only

'Robinson Crusoe' but his histories of 'Captain Singleton,' of 'Moll Flanders,' of 'Roxana,' and of 'Colonel Jack,' stood excused as conveying excellent moral lessons. For us they need, of course, no such excuse. We enjoy them for their splendid literary quality: their directness, their force, their naively unconscious glorification of the will-to-live. They describe the seamy side of things, the adroit expedients of adventurers, the essential humanity of rascals and demireps, with the hearty gusto of a man insatiably curious, determined to touch life at all points, calling nothing common nor unclean."

74.—"RELIGIOUS COURTSHIP" (20TH FEB., 1722).

"Twenty-four days," to use Mr. Lee's expression, "after the world had received the story of the coarse lewdness of 'Moll Flanders,' Defoe presented the world with the sweet domestic influences of 'Religious Courtship.'"

For this work both Mr. Wilson and Mr. Lee professed unbounded admiration. To say that I too enjoyed reading it would be untrue. A little of the powder of "admirable unsectarian morality," as Mr. Lee calls it, in a large spoonful of the preserve of fiction could be put up with; but when, as in the case of "Religious Courtship," there is a heaped-up spoonful of this "admirable unsectarian morality," relieved by only the thinnest streak of preserve, one makes wry faces.

The full title of the work is "Religious Courtship: Being Historical Discourses on the Necessity

of Marrying Religious Husbands and Wives only.
As also of Husbands and Wives being of the
same Opinions in Religion with one another."

The thin, weak story on which this huge mass
of morality hangs, is as follows : A merchant has
three daughters. The hand of the youngest is
asked in marriage by a rich young gentleman,
whom on account of his indifference to religion
the young lady refuses. The merchant is angry;
but the girl, believing herself to be in the right,
insists on breaking the match off, and tells her
lover the reason. The young gentleman, struck by
some words she had let fall, is led to make inquiries on the subject of religion, and after a time
becomes a professed and an actual Christian. Some
years later the young people are thrown into each
other's company again, and the one hindrance to
their union having been removed, the young man
is again allowed to pay his addresses, and they
marry with loud applause—so finishing Part I.
Part II. is the history of the second sister, who
unwisely marries a Roman Catholic, an affectionate
and a considerate husband, who, nevertheless,
owing to "his little idolatrous tricks and endeavours to win her over to his faith," causes her
continual pain, which is intensified when, after his
death, she discovers that, according to his will, her
two boys are to be brought up Roman Catholics.

With the lessons Defoe sought to convey one
finds little fault, though his views on this and kin-
dred subjects were narrow. A person of real Christian principles could scarcely expect to find much

T

happiness in the life-long company of one who neither
knows nor cares anything about religion ; and, as a
rule, no doubt, it is best for Protestants to mate with
Protestants.   But, unlike Mr. Lee, I did not, when
reading this book, " become interested in the welfare
of" the merchant's family, I was not "carried along "
—I forced myself—"through the history of its
members."   I did not "share their happiness," and
I was not "as a friend, touched with their cares and
anxieties."   Those I did sympathise with were the
numerous young persons of both sexes whose pious
parents have forced them to read it; and numerous
they must have been, for even so early as 1789 it
had reached its twenty-first edition, and there have
been many editions since.

Uninviting, however, as the book is as a story,
it is invaluable as throwing light on the character of
Defoe.   The merchant was Defoe himself, the three
daughters were his own three daughters, for whose
edification, as well as for the edification of others, the
book was written.   The youngest, Sophia, was then
nineteen.   Defoe ever had the welfare of these
lovable and lovely girls at heart, and perhaps it
was the very fact that he was so much in earnest that
caused him to make the book so dry.   Whilst reading
it, one can fancy Defoe himself talking to his girls.
We hear him saying, " Well, child," " Ay, my girl,"
and we hear them reply, " Nay, sir," " Oh, sir," " You
speak truly, sir," in the charming, stiff, old, respectful
way with which the youth of the last century addressed
their seniors.

75.—THE MAN OF GOD.

Then, again, "Religious Courtship" forces once more upon our recollection that Defoe was, above all things, the Man of God. The dialogues that form the greater part of it might have been written by Bunyan, Rowland Hill, Dr. Watts, Legh Richmond, or Hannah More. The following, for example, is not from " The Shepherd of Salisbury Plain," but from the incident of the "poor labouring man" of Hampshire ("Religious Courtship") who taught the way of salvation to the rich young gentleman who had been refused the hand of the merchant's youngest daughter :—

"In his way, he necessarily went by a poor labouring man's door, who, with a wife and four children, lived in a small cottage on the waste, where he (the gentleman) was lord of the manor ; as he passed by he thought he heard the man's voice, and stepping up close to the door, he perceived that the poor, good, old man was praying to God with his family; as he said afterwards, his heart sprung in his breast for joy at the occasion, and he listened eagerly to hear what was said. The poor man was, it seems, giving God thanks for his condition, and that of his little family, which he did with great affection, repeating how comfortably they lived, how plentifully they were provided for, how God had distinguished them in his goodness, that they were alive, when others were snatched away by disasters ; in health, when others languish with pain and sickness ; had food, when others were in want; at liberty, when others were in prison ; were clothed and covered, when others were naked and without habitation ; concluding with admiring and adoring the wonders of God's providence and mercy to them, who had deserved nothing."

The young squire who heard this " was confounded and struck, as it were, speechless." "What's this man thus thankful for ? " he asked. " Why, my dogs live better than he does in some respects, and is he

T 2

on his knees adoring infinite goodness for his enjoyments!"

Three things, says Defoe, ought not to be wanting in any man—to wit, "a reverence of God, a sense of religion, and a profession, at least, of the duty we all owe to our Maker."

The following are a few more of his shorter sayings, taken haphazard :—

"To compare what we receive with what we deserve will make anybody thankful."

"As the Spirit of God will assist those whose hearts are towards Him, so we must pray that we may be taught to pray."

"Earnest desires are really prayers in their nature; sincere wishes of the heart for grace are prayers to God for grace; prayer itself is nothing but those wishes and desires put into words."

"Mental petition is prayer as well as words, and is, perhaps, the best-moved prayer and the best-expressed in the world."

"A little religion makes a man a churl, but a great deal teaches him to know himself, and to be a gentleman."

"A religious life is the only heaven upon earth."

It is interesting likewise to learn that the Scriptures which gave Defoe most comfort were : "Blessed are they that hunger and thirst after righteousness," etc. ; and "The longing soul shall be satisfied."

As a guide to conduct in life, he also recommends such texts as Phil. i., 9, 10: "That your love may abound in knowledge and all judgment. That ye may approve things that are excellent. That you may be sincere without offence"—a text which, as he points out, combines wisdom and learning, solid judgment, and the honesty and open-heartedness of a true gentleman ; and Col. iv., 8 : "Whatsoever things are honest, just, pure, lovely, and of good report, think of these things." The practice of such advice, says

Defoe, results in a gentleman and a Christian ; and it was by endeavouring to carry out such precepts that Defoe became what he actually was—a true Christian and a real gentleman.

The incidental references to the ladies drinking chocolate in a morning, etc., and the bustle that surrounds one of maids, footmen, and chariots, suggests that at the time Defoe was writing this book his worldly circumstances still continued to be easy.

The appendix concerns servants, and to judge by its contents Defoe and his wife must have been plagued with cooks who couldn't cook a potato, and chambermaids who couldn't "make mantuas, cut hair, or clear-starch"—with a set, in fact, of "very scoundrel, idle jades." If, thought Defoe, the custom prevailed for mistresses to give signed certificates when servants left them, a much better state of things would inevitably ensue.

76.—"THE JOURNAL OF THE PLAGUE" AND "CARTOUCHE."

WORKS : 213.—A Journal of the Plague. 17th March, 1722.
    213 (a).—Due Preparations for the Plague. 1722. (Omitted from Mr. Lee's List.)
    214.—Cartouche. 27th April, 1722.

As we have noticed, there was only a space of twenty-four days between the publication of " Moll Flanders" and " Religious Courtship " ; and now only twenty-five days were to intervene before the issue of another work—and that a work of the first order—namely, the " Journal of the Plague Year," suggested by the pestilence which had just been ravaging France. The full title of this particular publication is : " A

Journal of the Plague Year: being observations or
memorials of the most remarkable occurrences, as well
public as private, which happened in London during
the last great visitation in 1665. Written by a citizen
who continued all the while in London." Of personal
reminiscences Defoe could have furnished only few,
seeing that at the time of the Great Plague he was no
more than five years old; but he must have conversed
with many who had witnessed its horrors; he must
often have listened open-mouthed to the stories of its
speaking sights and moving sounds—of the cross-
marked houses and the tumbrils of corpses, the dread
cries of, "Throw out your dead!" the rakers with
their horns, the conjurers with their fantastical dresses,
the grass growing in the kennels; of the faithful
ministers who remained to tend their flocks, "charging
death itself on his pale horse." In order to give a
vraisemblance to the narrative—or rather the history,
for that it is veritable history there is not the least
doubt—it is put into the mouth of a worthy saddler,
who lived " without Aldgate, midway between Aldgate
Church and Whitechapel bars, on the left hand or
north side of the street." Defoe is nothing if not
precise.

Another work of Defoe's on the same subject
is the "Due Preparations for the Plague," a small
volume of two hundred and eighty-two pages, published the same year (1722). It was this narrative,
part of which describes the vicissitudes of two
families exposed to the Great Plague, that formed
the basis upon which Mr. Harrison Ainsworth
erected his well-known story, "Old St. Paul's."

The " Due Preparations for the Plague" was omitted by Mr. Lee from his catalogue by accident. (See *Notes and Queries*, 1st May, 1869, and after.)

For some time previous, Defoe's articles on foreign affairs in several of his journals had dealt with a subject which was just then on the lips of everyone—the trial and execution of the notorious French robber and murderer, Cartouche; and on the 27th of April (1722) he issued a thick pamphlet entitled " The Life and Actions of Lewis Dominique Cartouche, etc. Translated from the French." What "translated from the French" precisely means, it is not of much use to conjecture. Possibly Mr. Lee is right in supposing that Defoe's only authorities were the French News-Letters which he translated for the journals, in " which case" it would have been more correct had he stated that it was trans-lated *with licence*, "the way in which Defoe did almost everything."

Lewis Dominique Cartouche, the Jack Sheppard of France, began his rogueries at an early age, and soon gathered round him a gang of accomplices, one of the most desperate of whom was a scoundrel called La Magdalene.

Among the more original of their devices, one was to attend church, where "they picked pockets of watches with their real hands, whilst they held up counterfeit hands made of wax with gloves on them, pretending to be saying their prayers."

La Magdalene, who was the first to pay the penalty for his crimes, died by the water-ruff—that is to say, "he had a kind of ruff tied about his neck, which went up above his eyes, and was so contrived as to hold water. They poured water into this ruff by pints at a time, which he was obliged to swallow as fast as he could to prevent his being suffocated. He was overcome by the eighth pint he had drunk."

The punishment reserved for Cartouche was to be broken on the wheel; but meantime the romance of his career had drawn upon him the curiosity of all Paris. Ladies visited him in prison, the "gravers went to work on his portrait," and—here comes a pleasant Defoe-ism—"little poets made ballads upon him." His end is thus described :—

"When Cartouche arrived at the fatal place and beheld four wheels and two gibbets surrounded by soldiers on foot and on horseback, he looked stedfastly upon the tragical spectacle without speaking a word. But when he turned about and saw the hangman and his servants preparing themselves for the work, and disposing the instruments of his execution in order, it startled him, and he could not forbear saying so as to be heard, ' 'Tis a dismal prospect.'"

77.—THE PROPERTY AT COLCHESTER (1722).

Defoe seems to have been in some way or other connected with Colchester for several years past. As we have seen, the early scenes in "Moll Flanders" are laid in this town. It was at Colchester she was left by a "crew of those people they call gipsies or Egyptians." Here she was taught "to spin worsted, which is the chief trade of that city"; here she grew up into womanhood, and married—first the younger son of the lady of the house, and afterwards "an amphibious creature," a gentleman draper. Thirty years later, when " Moll " visits the town in the capacity of an "artist," she remarks—" It was with no little pleasure that I saw the town where I had so many pleasant days; and I made many inquiries after the good friends I had once had there"; nor would it be rash to conclude that Colchester had pleasant memories for Defoe too.

FACSIMILES OF THE THREE SIGNATURES TO A DEED CONCERNING DEFOE'S ESTATE AT COLCHESTER.

The Rev. William Smithies, Rector of St. Michael's, Mile End, within the liberties of the borough of Colchester, and a valued friend, now negotiated, on behalf of Defoe, a lease for ninety-nine years of an estate called "Severallo, or Kingswood Heath," which included Tubbiswick and Brinckley Farms, the whole of it the property of the Mayor and commonalty of the town. The rent of it was to be £120 yearly. The estate, however, was purchased not for Defoe himself, but for his daughter, Hannah, whom a few months previous he had temporally endowed with stock in the South Sea Company,

"purchased when it was depressed below its intrinsic
value, after the bursting of the bubble." The lease
of Kingswood Heath was granted on August 6th,
1722, and for it Defoe was to pay £1,000, namely,
the first moiety of £500 at Michaelmas, 1722, and
the second moiety at Michaelmas, 1723; but when
the second moiety became due, Defoe was short of
cash, consequently the lease had to be mortgaged to
one Mary Newton for £200, which, with its interest,
was not paid off till four years later, on the 13th of
November, 1727. The investment turned out a good
one, for the value of the estate improved rapidly, and
" Hannah Defoe lived upon her income in respectable
gentility until her death, in 1759, when she left her
property to a son of her sister Henrietta." What
Defoe did for his other children we do not know.
Maria, his eldest daughter, was about this time
married to a person of the name of Langley, Henrietta and Sophia, his other daughters, were as yet
unmarried, the latter being only twenty-one.

78.—"COLONEL JACK," "PETER THE GREAT," AND "ROB ROY."

WORKS: 215.—Colonel Jack.
216.—Peter the Great.
217.—Rob Roy.

Next makes his bow, the truly honourable Colonel
Jack, who was born a gentleman, put 'prentice to a
pickpocket, was six-and-twenty years a thief, and
then kidnapped, etc. Just as Defoe had in "Moll
Flanders" portrayed the life of a female convict, so
now he did the same for a male convict, and again
he mingles instruction with amusement. The book was

written—and in this, too, there was a resemblance to "Moll"—with the hope that it would come into the hands of even the vilest, "Every wicked reader," runs the preface, "will here be encouraged to a change, and it will appear that the best and only good end of a wicked and misspent life is repentance. That in this, there is comfort, peace, and oftentimes hope ; and, that the penitent shall be returned like the prodigal, and his latter end be better than his beginning."

"Colonel Jack" is an unequal book. Says Mr. Saintsbury :—

"There is hardly in 'Robinson Crusoe' a scene equal, and there is consequently not in English literature a scene superior, to that praised by Lamb—the scene where the youthful pickpocket first exercises his trade, and then for a time loses his ill-gotten (though, for his part, he knows not the meaning of the word ill-gotten) gains. But great part of the book, and especially the latter portion, is dull."

As we have seen, Defoe had published four works relating to the history of Sweden, namely, "Charles XII." (1715), "Count Patkul" (1717), "Baron Goertz" (1719), and "Memoirs of a Cavalier" (1720), all of which, though on the whole impartial, exhibit a bias in favour of the interests of Sweden; but in this year, 1723, we find him producing a "Life of Peter the Great," the King of Sweden's great rival, which is decidedly Russophile. The hero is now the Czar, whose good qualities are extolled, and whose excesses and cruelties are for the most part passed over. The publication of this book is one of the strongest proofs that Defoe did, as he said he did, compile

his works from original manuscripts. "Charles
XII." is represented as being written by "a Scots
gentleman in the Swedish service," "Count Patkul" by the Lutheran minister who assisted him
in his last hours, "The Memoirs of a Cavalier," by an English gentleman who served in the
army of Gustavus Adolphus. The manuscripts
of these three would naturally exhibit a bias in
favour of Sweden; and Defoe, with whom verisimilitude was the first law of literature, would not
be the man to remove this bias. On the other
hand the "British officer in the service of the
Czar," whom Defoe credits with having written his
"Life of Peter the Great," would, not unnaturally,
see things chiefly from a Russian point of view.
"The Wars of Charles XII.," in short, is the
Swedish version, "The Life of Peter the Great"
the Russian version, of the great conflict between
these mighty potentates.

From Peter the Great to the Scottish Rob
Roy the cry is not a far one; both were un-
principled thieves, and though the former has a
more respectable reputation, the latter, from all
accounts, was the more righteous man. "The
Highland Rogue, or the memorable actions of the
celebrated Robert Mac Gregor, commonly called
Rob Roy," was published on 5th October, 1723.
Defoe's own life was a romance; and in the actions
of this daring devil, he saw resemblance to the
dash and rush of his own strange career. Defoe himself was but a Rob Roy, a Jack Sheppard, with
more grace. But everyone is, or ought to be, an

adventurer. In a world that is all turmoil, change, unrest, war, every man must dare ; and though we may deprecate the crimes of great rogues, it is not in human nature not to admire their audacity.

According to the preface, " it is not a romantic tale that the reader is here presented with, but a real history; not the adventures of a 'Robinson Crusoe,' a 'Colonel Jack,' or a 'Moll Flanders,' but the actions of the Highland Rogue; a man that has been too notorious to pass for a mere imaginary person." And in the *Daily Post* for the 8th of February of the same year, the expression appears "as mere a romance as 'Robinson Crusoe,'" from which it may be concluded that now that his Crusoe was a success, Defoe took as a compliment rather than otherwise the popular verdict that it was a romance. We would notice, however, that it was a peculiarity of Defoe to speak disparagingly of his recently published fictitious or semi-fictitious narratives, yet to assert that the book that was being given to the public was itself real history. Sir Walter Scott's famous novel of the same name was considerably indebted to Defoe's pamphlet.

79.—"ROXANA" (14TH MARCH, 1724).

WORK: 218.—Roxana.

In " Moll Flanders " Defoe had depicted the courtesan of middle-class life, in " Roxana," published on March 14, 1724, we have the portraiture of a courtesan flourishing among the aristocracy; but the aim of the writer continues the same, namely, "to describe human nature as it is, for the purpose of contrasting it with what it should be."

The complete title of the work is : "The Fortunate Mistress : or a History of the Life and vast Variety of Fortunes of Mademoiselle de Beleau, afterwards called The Countess de Wintselsheim, in Germany. Being the Person known by the Name of the Lady Roxana, in the time of King Charles II."

"'Roxana,'" says Mr. Saintsbury, "is, on the whole, the least good of Defoe's minor novels, though there are good things in it; and it is one of the most puzzling. Its title-page speaks of the heroine as having-been known as Roxana 'in the time of Charles the Second,' and there are passages which directly point to the king and to the Duke of Monmouth ; yet the opening words tell us that she only came to England in 1683, and the next page that she was then but ten years old. Moreover, in the latter part there are huge episodes and digressions which square very ill with the rest. Roxana is a cold-blooded creature, the most disagreeable of Defoe's heroines, without a touch of the natural and healthy animalism which redeems Moll Flanders, and with much more than Moll's scheming and calculation."

The latter portion of the book, owing to the numerous digressions (possibly interpolations), is "nearly unreadable, and the bad ends to which both maid and mistress come, though sufficiently well-deserved, are deferred too long, and brought on without dramatic propriety." Charles Lamb considered the best part of "Roxana" to be the story relating to her daughter Susannah, which according to tradition was left out of the second edition owing to a "foolish hypercriticism" of Defoe's friend Southerne. It appears, however, in most subsequent editions.

It was upon this part of Roxana's history that

The Famous ROXANA.

(Frontispiece to Defoe's Novel.)

Godwin founded his tragedy of *Fawkener*, acted and printed in 1807, with a prologue by Lamb.

The following is a brief outline of the story. The daughter of a French refugee of fortune who had fled to London, Roxana was beautiful and accomplished. With a dowry of two thousand pounds, she married an "eminent brewer," a handsome man, a good sportsman, but a fool ; and her unhappy experiences lead her to give very sensible advice to marriageable girls : " No fool, ladies, at all, no kind of fool, whether a mad fool or a sober fool, a wise fool or a silly fool ; take anything but a fool ; nay, be anything, be even an old maid, the worst of nature's curses, rather than take up with a fool." "With this thing called a husband " she lived in good fashion for eight years, and became the mother of five children. Having " no genius to business," her husband permitted himself to be ruined, and then left her to do as she could. The children she sent to their father's relations, " who were very substantial people," and then poverty was her snare, "dreadful poverty !" Besides this, she was young, handsome, and vain of her beauty ; consequently, the landlord of her house, a man of wealth, found her a comparatively easy conquest. Says Roxana : " As it was a new thing, so it was a very pleasant thing to be courted, caressed, embraced, and high professions of affection made to me, by a man so agreeable and so able to do me good." In short, Roxana's husband was more to blame than Roxana herself. He had never been to her the husband that a woman yearning for affection required ; he had been only a fool. Up to this point Roxana has our sympathy, but no further.

Her "gentleman" and she and her maid, Amy, go to
France, where the gentleman gets killed. Though
she really loved him and her distress was unfeigned,
nevertheless she soon found consolation in a Parisian
prince whom she knew as the Count de Clerac, and
with whom she lived in great splendour. Some years
after, seized with compunction on account of his irregu-
larities, the prince severed his connection with her.
Meantime she had accumulated wealth, and taking the
advice of a Paris merchant, who rendered her valuable
assistance, she quitted France. Off the coast of
Holland, she and Amy experience a terrific storm—
one of the best scenes in the book. At Amsterdam
she again meets her Paris merchant, who wishes to
marry her; but, preferring freedom to matrimony, she
refuses. Crossing over to England, she sets up a fine
establishment, gives banquets to distinguished companies, including King Charles II. and the Duke of
Monmouth, and excites universal admiration by her
dancing in a rich Turkish costume. Breaking up her
fine establishment, she lodges with a Quakeress who
lived in a court in the Minories. She marries her
Paris merchant, who had followed her to England.
He purchases a foreign title, and salutes her as the
Countess de Wintselsheim. But, though prosperous,
she is ever accompanied by the torments of a guilty
conscience.

"At length, in the decline of life, the children she
had so long deserted trace her out, by a chain of
events as singular as they are delightfully told," and
establish their relationship. Roxana's whole life is
laid bare, her husband becomes alienated from her,

and after his death she loses her all in speculation. She dies in jail.

Mr. Saintsbury thus happily compares "Roxana" with "Moll Flanders":

"Both are triumphs of novel writing. Both have subjects of a rather more than questionable character, but both display the remarkable art with which Defoe handles such subjects. It is not true, as is sometimes said, that the difference between the two is the difference between gross and polished vice. The real difference is much more one of morals than of manners. Moll is by no means of the lowest class. Notwithstanding the greater degradation into which she falls, and her originally dependent position, she has been well educated, and has consorted with persons of gentle birth. She displays throughout much greater real refinement of feeling than the more high-flying Roxana, and is at any rate flesh and blood, if the flesh be somewhat frail and the blood somewhat hot. Neither of the two heroines has any but the rudiments of a moral sense; but Roxana, both in her original transgression and in her subsequent conduct, is actuated merely by avarice and selfishness—vices which are particularly offensive in connection with her other failing, and which make her thoroughly repulsive. The art of both stories is great; and as regards the episode in 'Roxana' of the daughter Susannah is consummate; but the transitions of the later plot are less natural than those in 'Moll Flanders.' It is only fair to notice that while the latter, according to Defoe's more usual practice, is allowed to repent and end happily, Roxana is brought to complete misery; Defoe's morality, therefore, required more repulsiveness in one case than in the other."[*]

80.—"THE GREAT LAW OF SUBORDINATION CONSIDERED"
(4TH APRIL, 1724).

WORK: 219.—The Great Law of Subordination Considered. 4th April, 1724.

Only three weeks after the publication of "Roxana" the press was turning out another extensive work of Defoe's, "The Great Law of Subordination

[*] "Encyclopædia Britannica."

U

considered : or, the Insolence and Unsufferable
Behaviour of Servants in England duly inquired
into," a subject that he had already touched upon
in the appendix of "Religious Courtship." "The
Great Law," though only a book to be skimmed,
contains some very passable anecdotes, and flings
interesting light on the manners and customs of
the times.

Defoe throws off with some remarks on the
treatment of women. He was not of opinion, he
says, "that if there was a bridge over the narrow
seas all the women in Christendom would run over
into England." The indifferent treatment women
then met with he attributes to the recent spread
of drunkenness, which made so many men "grow
rigid, surly, cruel, tyrannic, and outrageous." Among
the meaner sort, wife-beating had grown quite common. "To hear a woman cry murther now, scarce
gives any alarm ; the neighbours scarce stir at it,
and if they do, and if they come out in a fright
and ask one another what's the matter, the common
answer is only thus : ''Tis nothing, neighbour, but
such a one beating his wife.' ' Oh, dear,' says the other,
' is that all ? ' and in they go again composed and easy."

But if England was the purgatory of wives it was
the paradise of servants, whose "insolence and unsufferable behaviour" are then dilated upon. Maid-
servants, men-servants, field labourers, all were past
praying for, and Defoe could say with a "late
author"—

"The lab'ring poor, in spite of double pay,
Are saucy, mutinous and beggarly."

"They work till they find a few shillings jingle and chink in their pockets, but then, as if they could not bear that kind of music, away they go to the alehouse, and 'tis impossible to bring them to work again while they have a farthing of it left.

"But servants," he remarks, "go to London. London, like the ocean that receives the muddy and dirty brooks, as well as clear and rapid rivers, swallows up all the scum and filth of the country. It is a common jest put upon country girls, when we see them come up to London in the carriers' waggons and on the pack horses, viz., to ask them if they have been churched before they came from home; nor is there anything unreasonable in the question, as things go now in the country, when work is so plenty and wages so high; for who would come away to London to go to service, if things were all well at home."

Then follows an anecdote :—

"I have for some years been concerned in a large public building in the country, where we kept a great many other servants, as also horses and carts, constantly employed; among the rest we kept an old servant, whose name was Wright, in constant work, though paid by the week. . . . It happened one morning that a cart being broken down upon the road, at some distance from the house, this old man was fetched to repair it where it lay; while he was busy at his work, comes by a countryman that knew him, and at some distance salutes him with the usual compliment, 'Good morrow, Father Wright: God speed your labour;' the old fellow looks up at him, for he did not see him at first, and with a kind of pleasant surliness answered, 'I don't care whether He does or no, 'tis day-work.'"

81.—"TOUR THROUGH GREAT BRITAIN" (22ND MAY, 1724).

WORKS: 220.—Tour Through Great Britain, vol. i.
221.—Tour Through Great Britain, vol. ii.
222.—Tour Through Great Britain, vol. iii.

Most of the material for "A Tour Through the Whole Island of Great Britain" was obtained, not, as Mr. Lee supposed, in 1723, but some forty years previous—during the five years that succeeded

Monmouth's rebellion, 1684—1688.   To the journeys
which Defoe took at that time we have already
alluded (§ 8).   We noticed that with " Camden's
Britannia" as his guide, and "an ancient gentleman"
of his acquaintance as his companion, he travelled " in
three or four several tours, over the whole island,"
critically observing, and carefully informing himself
of everything worth observing in all the towns and
counties through which he passed, and that avoiding
the error of previous travellers, who could see nothing
to admire, except the houses of the gentry, he inquired
into the customs of the common people as well, and
informed himself as to their manner of living and
their employment; and we called him the J. R. Green
of Topography.   But though the notes taken during
these tours, which covered a period of "near four
years," formed the principal material upon which
Defoe founded the present work, still he had
frequently travelled over the island since, and every
journey would necessarily increase his store of knowledge.   In England he had made as many as seventeen large circuits, or separate journeys, and three
general tours through the whole country; and as
regards Scotland, not only had he travelled critically
over a great part of it, but he had lived there.   The
north part of England, and the south part of Scotland,
he had viewed "five several times over; all which is
hinted here, to let the readers know what reason they
will have to be satisfied with the authority of the
relation."

The work was comprised in three volumes, the
first of which contained a plate of the siege of Col-

chester. The second volume, which was not published till 8th June, 1725, contains a map of England and Wales by Herman Moll, the Royal geographer. The third, which relates to Scotland, was issued on 13th August, 1726; thus closing the account "of a tedious and very expensive five years' travel." The editions of this work issued after Defoe's death are much mutilated and spoilt.

These Tours of Defoe are among the most charming of his works. By means of them we are able to transport ourselves to a time when all the great towns were in the south, and when Yorkshire and Lancashire were supplied with their manufactured goods from Norwich; when London was adding unto itself "a little city of buildings, streets, and squares at the west end of Hanover and Cavendish Squares"; when the lace trade was flourishing in Buckinghamshire, the bay trade in Essex, when Stourbridge Fair was "not only the greatest in the whole nation, but in the world," when Wanstead House was in its glory, and ere Dunwich had been swallowed up by the sea; when Bury, Bath, and Tunbridge were health-resorts, and when Norfolk turkeys obligingly came on foot in droves of from three hundred to a thousand to supply the London market.

Some of the stories Defoe tells are rather tall ones, nor does the fact of their reception from hearsay in any way excuse him, for the rogue evidently enjoyed them; as, for example, that about the unwholesomeness of the Essex marshes which carried off the women, "insomuch that all along this country it was very frequent to meet with men that had had from

five or six to fourteen or fifteen wives; nay, and some
more. And I was informed that in the marshes on
the other side of the river, over against Candy, there
was a farmer who was then living with the five-and-
twentieth wife, and that his son, who was but about
thirty-five years old, had already had about fourteen."
Notice the "about." Defoe had this only "by report,

DEFOE'S HOUSE AT STOKE NEWINGTON.

though from good hands, too." "The reason for the
disappearance of the women he learnt was this, that
the men being bred in the marshes themselves and
seasoned to the place, did pretty well with it, but
that the women, whom they obtained from the hilly
country, to which they always resorted when they
wanted a fresh wife, not being used to the damp air,"
presently changed their complexion, got an ague or
two, and seldom held it above half a year, or a year
at most. And then, said Defoe's informer, "we go to
the uplands again and fetch another." It is only fair

to Defoe to say that he found out afterwards, and put
it on record, that one of his informers had "fibbed a
little."

82.—DEFOE AT HOME.—MR. BAKER (1724).

Some years previous Defoe had built himself, in
Church Street, Newington, "a very handsome house,
as a retirement from
London." Had Mr.
Henry Baker, whose
words we are using,
said "a large house,
almost a mansion," it
would have been nearer
the mark. A hand-
some exterior it had
not, though it was no
uglier than the gener-
ality of houses built
under Anne and the
first George. It was
square in plan, the
walls, which were of
red brick and very
thick, being raised, as
the fashion then was,
so as to conceal the roof; it had deep window-seats,
curious cupboards in recesses, and massive bolts and
locks to its doors; and at the side was a spacious
coach-house with stables, Mr. Defoe, like Dick Steele
and other Augustans, having a very great weakness
for "a chariot." The garden, with its "green walk"
and other pleasure grounds, which covered four acres,

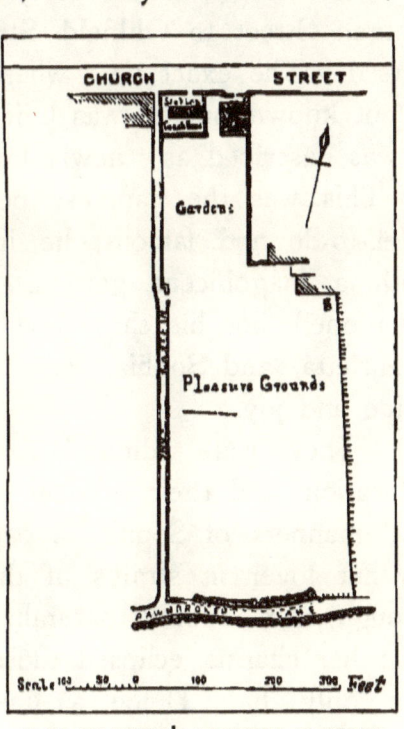

PLAN OF DEFOE'S GROUNDS AT STOKE
NEWINGTON.

were bounded on the south by Pawnbroker's Lane, and on the west by Hussey's Lane. On the site of Defoe's house and grounds is now a street, appropriately called Defoe Road, but the long massive brick wall dividing the grounds from Hussey's Lane is still standing; and Hussey's Lane—running from Church Street to Oldfield Street—can still be traversed. The exact time when this house was built is not known, but he was living in it in 1724, when it was described as "newly built."

This was the happiest period of Defoe's life. Well-to-do and famous, he lived in a fine house with a magnificent garden. His wife is hardly mentioned, but his three lovely daughters, Hannah, Henrietta, and Sophia, were at once their father's pride and joy.

"They were admired for their beauty, their education, and their prudent conduct." The person and manners of Sophia in particular are spoken of by her lover in strains of the highest eulogium— though that is only natural, and does not prove that her charms eclipsed those of her sisters. But not only had Defoe a fine house, a beautiful garden, and three lovely daughters, he had also a magnificent library, and when he was not amusing himself with his garden he was engaged "in the pursuit of his studies, which he found means of making very profitable." Indeed, we are not for a moment to suppose that it detracted from the pleasure of Defoe's reading to know that every half hour so spent was so many portraits of King George in the pockets of his great flapped waistcoat.

A virtuoso, or, as we should now say, an antiquary, Defoe was rarely happier than when studying old MSS., and, like other Georgian bookworms, he delighted to turn up Ave Maria Lane in order to get into Paternoster Row, where "the first shop on the left hand was the famous Mr. Bateman's, a shop well known for old and scarce books of learning and antiquity in most languages."* And they were all fish that came into Defoe's net :—

"The studious geographer and the well-read historian," says he, "travels not with this or that navigator or traveller, marches with not this or that general, or making this or that campaign, but he keeps them all company ; he marches with Hannibal over the Alps into Italy, and with Cæsar into Gaul and into Britain; with Belisarius into Africa, and with the Emperor Honorius into Persia. He fights the battle of Granicus with Alexander, and of Actium with Augustus; he is at the overthrow of the great Bajazette by Tamerlain, and of Tomombejus and his Mamalukes by Selymus; he sees the battle of Lepanto with Don John, the defeat of the Spanish Armada with Drake ; with Adrian he views the whole Roman Empire, and, in a word, the whole world ; he discovers America with Columbus, conquers it with the great Cortez, and re-plunders it with Sir Francis Drake.

"Nothing has been famous or valuable in the world, or even the ruins of it, but he has it all in his view ; and nothing done in the world but he has it in his knowledge, from the siege of Jerusalem

* "The Compleat English Gentleman."

to the siege of Namur, and from Titus Vespasian
to the greater King William: he has it all at the
tip of his tongue."

It is true that Defoe was sixty-five years of
age, and it is also true that he was troubled with
the gout and the stone, which sometimes obliged
him to absent himself from company, but, as the
poet Cowper says, "a man must have something,"
and, all things being taken into consideration, Defoe
might fairly look upon himself in that year (1724)
as a decidedly happy man.

In the cultivation of his garden he took particular
pleasure, garden planning and horticulture having
always been favourite pursuits of his. It will be
remembered that Queen Mary consulted him when
she laid out the garden at Hampton Court.

His "servant," Friday—his supposed collaborator—"a savage, and afterwards a Christian," had
been dead for some time. He was taken from
Defoe by force, and "died in the hands that took
him." Nor had he now his parrot, which used to
sit upon his finger, lay its bill close to his face, and
talk, calling him by his name. Jonathan, however,
Defoe's gardener, seems to have been very much in
his master's confidence.

When the great man walked abroad, he carried
a "little stick not strong enough to correct a dog,
a sword sometimes, perhaps, for decency," which,
"can do no hurt anywhere but just at the tip of it,
called the point. And what's that in the hand of a
feeble author?"

On his finger he wore a mourning ring, "given

at the funeral of Mr. Christopher Love, a Presbyterian minister, beheaded *anno* 1653, for the horrid phanatic plot, contrived for the bringing in, as they then called him, Charles Stuart, and the restoring of Monarchy." Mr. Love was possibly a friend of Defoe's father.

Of the minor troubles of life, Defoe had about the same share as any other mortal. Sometimes his neighbour's horses broke into his grounds ; and once, which was worse, he caught his neighbour's servant turning them in, with the result that he put the horses into the pound. This caused Defoe's neighbour to swear both at Defoe and Defoe's man, William. When the quarrel was made up, a difficulty arose with William, who, enraged at being sworn at, resolved to have the law of the neighbour. Defoe having declared that ·the matter should be proceeded with no further, and William proving obstinate, nothing remained but dismissal ; and concludes Defoe : " I would not stir from him till he had stripped my livery off and put on his frock, and went off " (" Great Law of Subordination "). And serve him right, thought Defoe ; but the unprejudiced reader will sympathise just a little with William.

The only relic of Defoe, besides the manuscripts of some of his books, known to be in existence is his seal, which is in the possession of the Rev. H. Defoe Baker, Rector of Thruxton, Hants. On it are engraved the arms which appear under Defoe's portrait in " Jure Divino" : Per chevron engrailed, gules and or, three griffins passant counterchanged.

In some engravings of Defoe, the arms are represented slightly different.

Defoe's character we have already pretty minutely
sketched, but one or two features of it still remain
to be mentioned or dilated upon further.   His
charitableness is again impressed upon us by the
grateful words of a certain Thomas Webb, who, in
1724, had lost his wife. "And poor distressed I,
left alone," says Webb, "and no one to go and
speak to save only Mr. Defoe, who hath acted a
noble and generous part towards me and my poor
children. The Lord reward him and his with the
blessings of upper and nether spring, with the
blessings of his basket and store."

Defoe was temperate in his habits : unlike so
many of his contemporaries, he never drank to
excess. He did not smoke or take snuff. He
considered smoking as "conducive to intemperate
drinking"; and in his younger days, thanks to a
fine constitution, he rarely troubled the doctor. The
theatre, the ball-room, and the card-table were to
him the very devil. In manly sports and athletic
exercises he had always found an attraction ; nor
was there wanting in him the Puritan love of horse-
play ; and his reputation for swordmanship was
always a protection to him. In that "frenzy of the
tongue," as he puts it, called swearing he could see
"neither pleasure nor profit." He loved a good
tale and a merry jest ; but "low-prised wit," indulged in at the expense of decency and morals,
his soul abhorred. His talk, when he was excited,
was pungent with witticisms ; but he was in the

habit of repeating favourite quotations with too great frequency, as, for example, the passage from Rochester—

> " A woman's ne'er so ruined but she can
> Revenge herself on her undoer, man."

Defoe had not been settled long in his new house before Mr. Henry Baker came on the scene : a young man of twenty-six, who, from a bookseller's apprentice, had risen to be a teacher of deaf mutes, and was making himself famous.

Born in 1698, and at an early age "left by an unhappy father to a relentless world," there was a time when Henry Baker "knew not which way to turn for bread, destined," it seemed to him, "to all the ills of poverty, to pining want, and ill-endured contempt, to misery and ruin." At the age of fourteen he was placed with Mr. John Parker, bookseller, in Pall Mall, with whom he stayed seven years. On April 26th, 1720, after he had left Mr. Parker, he went to stay with a relative named Mr. John Forster, an eminent attorney who lived at Enfield. "This gentleman," says Baker, "having a daughter, Jane, born deaf and dumb, and at that time eight years old, Heaven put into my thoughts a method of teaching her to read, write, understand, and speak the English language." Upon hearing the proposal that his daughter should be taught, Mr. Forster begged Baker to make a trial, and the result exceeded the expectations of both. Another daughter, Amy, and a son of Mr. Forster's— who were likewise deaf and dumb—were afterwards placed under Mr. Baker's care, and received

the same benefits. Subsequently, other pupils were ....
placed under his charge, a number of them being
children of the nobility; and having in his youth
felt the pinch of poverty, he acted with prudence
and foresight, and took care of his money. He
was more than prudent, however, he was over
anxious. But those who have known poverty often
are. An enthusiastic lover of nature, he prosecuted
his studies of animal and plant life with unwearied
diligence, as the manuscripts, illustrated with elabor-
ate drawings, left behind him, abundantly testify;
and two volumes of verse published in 1725 and
1726 remind that he was also ambitious for the
laurels of the poet. Such was the young man who
now became intimate with the Defoes, and found
the society of Mr. Defoe's daughters, especially the
youngest, so very agreeable.

83.—THE CALAIS MURDERS AND JACK SHEPPARD (AUG.—OCT., 1724).

WORKS: 223.—A Narrative of the Proceedings in France, &c. (Bizeau and Le
     Febvre).
   224.—History of the Remarkable Life of John Sheppard.
   225.—A Narrative of all the Robberies, Escapes, etc., of John Sheppard.

Defoe's tract, "A Narrative of the Proceedings in
France for Discovering and Detecting the Murderers
of English Gentlemen, September 21, 1723, near
Calais," etc., etc., may be regarded as a supplement
to "Cartouche." After that great thief had paid the
penalty of his crimes, the band of miscreants of which
he was the head was broken up into a number of
smaller parties, which carried on their rascalities in
different parts of France, and earned for them-

selves the name of Cartoucheans. One of these gangs, under the leadership of two robbers, named Joseph Bizeau and Peter Le Febvre, set upon and murdered, near Calais, four Englishmen, named Lock, Seabright, Mompesson, and Davies, together with their servants. One of the servants, however, Robert Spindelow, though pierced through with many wounds and left for dead, recovered, and not only so, but furnished evidence sufficient to bring two of the murderers to justice. Defoe, ever on the alert for the unusual and the tragic, seems to have had an interview with Spindelow, and wrote, as if from Spindelow's mouth, a full account of the affair—in *Applebee's* for November 2, 1723. The statements in the tract so correspond with those in *Applebee's* that Mr. Lee considers Defoe "had no reason for saying it was a translation, except that it might thus appear better authenticated." It must be noted, however, that the account of the murders at Calais occupies only a small portion of the book, the rest being taken up with a general history of the Cartoucheans.

Whilst the exploits of Cartouche were still fresh in the memory of Frenchmen, the English were put into excitement with the escapades of a still more extraordinary robber—the notorious Jack Sheppard—to whose credit, however, be it mentioned, that, unlike Cartouche, he was not a murderer. The earlier feats of Sheppard, his escapes from the round-house in St. Giles's and the new prison in Clerkenwell, may be passed over.

Being retaken by Jonathan Wild, he was committed to Newgate, where he was visited, among

others, by the representative of *Applebee's*, namely,
Mr. Defoe, who, apparently, "seconded the efforts of
the ordinary to impress his mind with a proper sense
of religion." This, at any rate, is certain, Sheppard
felt himself under great indebtedness to Mr. Applebee
(Defoe). Having made his escape from the Condemned Hold of Newgate, on the 31st of August,
Sheppard was thenceforth the talk of London. This
extraordinary feat was managed in the following way.
From the Condemned Hold in which Sheppard had
been incarcerated, to the lodge of the prison—the
part to which the public were admitted—communicated
a dark passage by means of which prisoners could
approach to the lodge and converse through a hatch
with any they pleased. The hatch was protected by
long thick spikes set six inches apart. At the end of
the day, while the turnkeys and some friends were
drinking together at a table at the far end of the lodge,
there entered two of Sheppard's female associates,
Edgworth Bess and Mrs. Maggot, who, as they talked
with Jack, were hidden from the turnkeys by a pro-
jection of the wall. Whilst this precious pair, as had
been arranged, made great cries and lamentations,
Jack busied himself with a watch-spring saw, and with
such good will that the spike was presently in twain.
The women, still keeping up their lamentations, pulled
his slender form through; and slipping on a "night-
gown, which concealed his irons," Jack escaped. Five
days after he had the impudence to write a letter
to the hangman, to which he added, as a postscript,
"Pray my service to Mr. Ordinary and Mr. Applebee."
Captured again, however, he was once more placed in

durance ; and owing to more attempts to escape, was "carried up to an apartment called the Castle, in the body of the jail ; a place of equal, if not superior strength to the Condemned Hold, and there chained to the floor." Then occurred the most extraordinary feat of all.

"On Thursday night," writes Defoe (*Applebee's*, Saturday, October 17th), "John Sheppard found means to unchain himself from the staples fixed in the strong room called the Castle, in Newgate, twisting and breaking some of the small irons, and unlocking a great horse padlock. He got off his hand-cuffs, and then, with the help only of an iron bar, which he found in the chimney, broke through a nine-foot wall into a strong room, the locks whereof (having not been opened in ten years) he broke and got farther to another door belonging to the chapel, then forced the locks and bolts of that also. In all, he broke through six strong rooms where people had formerly been confined, but had not of late been in use, and got up to the top of the jail, then descended from thence, by two blankets tied together, on the top of a turner's house next to Newgate, broke through without being heard by any therein, let himself out at the street door, at about one yesterday morning, and so made an entire escape."

On the 19th of October Defoe published " The History of the Remarkable Life of John Sheppard," a pamphlet which passed through three editions in three weeks ; and a few days later Sheppard, who was still at large, wrote Defoe a letter, which was left at Mr. Applebee's house in Blackfriars "by a person like an ostler." It ran as follows :—

"Mr. Applebee,—This with my kind love to you, and pray give my kind love to Mr. Wagstaff (the Ordinary) ; hoping these lines will find you in good health, as I am at present ; but I must own you are the loser for want of my dying speech ; but to make up your loss, if you think this sheet worth your while, pray make the best of it. So no more, but your humble servant, JOHN SHEPPARD."

V

With all its cheerfulness, however, the letter contains a foreboding of ill : "And," runs the post-script, " I desire you would be the postman to my last lodging," from which it may be judged that " the writer had fears of recapture, in which case he still wished Mr. Applebee to write an account that should be published immediately after his death." And Sheppard's presentiment was destined to be fulfilled, for only a week later (October 31) he was re-taken. Hogarth, who painted his portrait, Sir James Thornhill, and a host of other celebrities visited him; and an attempt was made to obtain a pardon for him on account of his youth, for he was only twenty-two, but without success.

The crowds of people in the streets of London on the day of Sheppard's execution were greater than had ever been known. When he had reached the fatal tree he beckoned Defoe (or Mr. Applebee, as he called him) into the cart, "and in view of several thousands of people, delivered to him a pamphlet" containing a narrative of all his robberies and escapes. Thus Defoe, as had been requested, became "the postman" to Sheppard's last lodging. This theatrical event proved a magnificent adver-tisement for the new pamphlet on Sheppard which Defoe published next day, " A Narrative of all the Robberies, Escapes, etc., of John Sheppard. Giving an exact description of the manner of his wonderful escape from the castle in Newgate, and of the methods he took afterwards for his security. Written by himself, etc., etc." Prefixed to the volume was "a true representation of his escape from the Con-

The manner of
John Shepherd's Escape
out of the Condemn'd Hole in Newgate.

(*Frontispiece to Defoe's Pamphlet. 1724.*)

demned Hold, curiously engraven on a copper plate," the whole being declared to be published "at the particular request of the prisoner." In less than a month it was in its seventh edition.

84.—THE SO-CALLED DUEL WITH MIST (NOV., 1724).

In June, 1723, Mr. Mist had once more got into trouble. His *Journal* for the 8th of that month having contained a libel against the Government, he was again apprehended, and though liberated on bail, was tried and found guilty. On the 18th of May, 1724, being brought up to receive judgment at the King's Bench Bar, he was sentenced to pay a fine of one hundred pounds and to suffer a year's imprisonment. Mist having kicked against the traces, Defoe, as on former occasions, abandoned him ; but, as on former occasions too, Mist, when pining in prison, and by "frequent trials, fines, and absence from business," being reduced to the verge of ruin, again had recourse to his "judicious, learned, and merry friend," and this judicious, learned, and merry friend again consented to resume duties in connection with the *Journal.* This seems to have been at the end of July, for an article by Defoe appears in *Mist's* for August 1st. The connection with the *Journal* was continued till October 24th, about which time Mist seems to have been liberated, and between that date and November 25th occurred the so-called duel between Mist and Defoe. It was a duel, however, only in the sense that it was a combat between two.

V 2

There had been no formalities. Mist, in a sudden
fury and without any warning, attacked Defoe, and
Defoe defended himself. A regular duel Defoe
would not have fought, for though an accomplished
swordsman, who in earlier life had been concerned
in an affair of honour, nevertheless in the latter part
of his life he deprecated duelling, which he considered a sin against God (*Review* vii. 451), and
looked back with regret that he had himself in that
count been guilty.

As regards Mist's affair, it was, says Defoe, a
case of "save a thief from the gallows and he will
cut your throat." Three times he had fetched Mist
out of prison, had saved him "from the utmost distress, and the immediate danger of life"; and what
was the result? Mist used Defoe basely, insulted,
and provoked him, and at last drew his sword upon
him, and put forth his "utmost endeavour to destroy him." Mist, however, was "disarmed fairly at
his weapon"; whereupon, Defoe "gave him his life,
embraced him, sent for a surgeon to dress a wound
he had, in his own defence, been obliged to give
him," and after this showed him "several acts of
friendship and kindness." Nevertheless, even then
Mist returned only evil for good, "returning abuses
of the worst and grossest nature." Such is the
Roman version; the Carthaginian unfortunately does
not exist. "I can conceive," says Mr. Lee, and
probably he is right, "no other cause of the out-
rage than that Mr. Mist had learnt, in some way,
that during all the time Defoe was connected with
his *Journal* he was holding an appointment under

government but concealing the fact; and, as Mist was now under prosecution of the same government, he may have erroneously conceived that Defoe's censorship was the cause of his present and past troubles."

Thus terminated the connection between these two men, which had continued, with interruptions, more than seven years. Defoe, though employed in the dirty work of the government, had evidently acted again and again with true kindness to Mist. He honoured the man, but abhorred his principles. With Mist, however, it was a case of "Hate my principles, hate me." That he had long been suspicious of Defoe is certain; and, as we have seen, had tried several times to do without him. It was natural in a man so hot-headed as Mist to fly into a furious passion when the whole truth came out; and it was natural in a man so diplomatic as Defoe, when he had frustrated Mist's design, to turn round and figure before the onlookers—that is to say, the readers of *Applebee's*—as the injured saint. But when Defoe strikes that attitude, we need not necessarily conclude that there is nothing whatever to be said on the other side.

85.—"A NEW VOYAGE ROUND THE WORLD" AND "EVERYBODY'S BUSINESS" (MAY AND JUNE, 1725).

WORKS: 226.—A New Voyage Round the World.
227.—Everybody's Business is Nobody's Business.

On the 8th of May, 1725, Defoe published another work which exhibits his extraordinary geographical knowledge, especially concerning parts of

the world then little known. It is entitled "A
New Voyage Round the World, by a Course never
sailed before. Being a Voyage undertaken by some
Merchants, who afterwards proposed the setting up
an East India Company in Flanders." Mr. Lee
terms it "one of the most instructive and best-
written of Defoe's imaginary voyages"; and Mr.
Saintsbury observes that it is full of Defoe's peculiar
verisimilitude, "and has all the interest of Anson's
or Dampier's voyages, together with a charm of
style superior even to the latter." I can only say,
that to me the book seems a very dull one. There
is no particular person in the narrative in whom
we can take any lively interest. There is too much
geography, and too little human nature. You
wouldn't catch a boy reading it. For the man,
however, who can enjoy a gallery of landscapes and
seascapes it is the very thing, and he would be
particularly delighted with the wonders of the
extraordinary journey across Chili and Patagonia.

Defoe now turned again to the subject he had
touched upon in "Religious Courtship," and treated
so lengthily in "The Great Law of Subordination,"
namely the domestic servant question. He entitled
his new production "Everybody's Business is No-
Body's Business" (5th June, 1725), by which is
meant that while everybody is crying out against
the insolence and idleness of servants, nobody
makes it his business to attempt means to lessen
the evil.

First, as to wages. Formerly women servants
took forty shillings a year and were thankful, but

now, complains Defoe, they want "six, seven, nay, eight pounds per annum and upwards ; insomuch that an ordinary tradesman cannot well keep one." If a decent girl does come up from the country and is willing to take fifty shillings a year, other servants soon spoil her by advising her to raise her wages or give warning, "to encourage her to which the herb-woman or some other old intelligencer provides her a place of four or five pounds a year ; this sets madam cock-a-hoop, and she thinks of nothing now but vails and high wages, and so gives warning from place to place till she has got her wages to the tip-top. Her neat's leathern shoes are now transformed into laced ones with high heels; her yarn stockings are turned into fine woollen ones with silk clocks; and her high wooden pattens are kicked away for leathern clogs. She must have a hoop, too, as well as her mistress, and her poor scanty linsey-woolsey petticoat is changed into a good silk one, four or five yards wide at the least. Not to carry the description farther, in short, plain country Joan is now turned into a fine London madam; can drink tea, take snuff, and carry herself as high as the best."

The apparel of our women servants, thought Defoe, ought certainly to be regulated, so that we might know the mistress from the maid. "I remember I was once put very much to blush, being at a friend's house, and by him required to salute the ladies, I kissed the chamber-jade into the bargain, for she was as well dressed as the best. But I was soon undeceived by a general titter, which gave me the utmost confusion.; nor can I believe myself the only person who has made such a mistake."

And the ignorance of servants was likewise intolerable. One who was told that her duties in a small house would be to wash, to dress a common family dinner, to do needlework, and to keep the place tidy, opened her eyes in astonishment, said that she could neither wash, dress a dinner, nor do needlework, and suggested that the mistress required four servants. Were a servant to do her work with cheerfulness, Defoe would not "grudge five or six pounds per annum," nor would he be "so unchristian as to put more upon a girl than she could bear; but to pray and pay too is the devil," and he thought it hard that one must keep four servants or none.

Defoe is obliged, too, to administer a gentle admonition and reproof to some of his own sex— namely, "those gentlemen who give themselves unnecessary airs, and cannot go to see a friend, but they must kiss and slop the maid; and all this done with an air of gallantry, and must not be resented." "This makes the creature pert, vain, and impudent, and spoils many a good servant."

"If I must have an intrigue," he continues, "let it be with a woman that shall not shame me. I would never go into the kitchen when the parlour door was open. We are forbidden at Highgate to kiss the maid when we may kiss the mistress; why, then, will gentlemen descend so low, by too much familiarity with these creatures, to bring themselves into contempt?"

Besides his reforms of domestic servants, Defoe would revolutionise the race of "wicked, idle, pilfering vagrants, called the blackguard, who black your honour's shoes and incorporate themselves under the title of the Worshipful Company of Japanners." "Their profession," he insists, "is gaming and thieving; japanning but the pretence." He would make a clean sweep of' them, compelling them to work in mines, at wool-combing, and agricultural labour, leaving the shoe-cleaning to respectable old women. This book went through four editions in a fortnight.

86.—JONATHAN WILD AND THE DEATH OF SAMUEL TUFFLEY (SUMMER 1725).

WORKS : 228.—Life of Jonathan Wild.
229.—An Account of the Conduct and Proceedings of John Gow, the Pirate.

It was not long after Sheppard had been hanged that Jonathan Wild, the thief maker and thief taker, through whose means Sheppard forfeited his life, was brought to justice. For years he had been in the habit of getting hold of idle young men and encouraging them to become thieves, he himself profiting by their roguery. At the same time he was receiving Government pay for thief catching. Much of his knavery was done under the cloak of religion. To one person who had paid the sum required for returning the goods of which she had been robbed, and who asked Wild what she must give him for himself, he replied, "Good woman, I desire nothing of you but your prayers." On another occasion, when somebody applied to him on a Sunday, he said that he never did business on the Lord's Day; and his favourite maxim was "Honesty is the best policy." Jonathan was arrested on February 15th, 1725, and, after examination, was committed to Newgate, for taking money to restore some goods that had been stolen in his presence by his own men. Defoe had an interview with Wild in prison, and on the 8th and 14th of May lists were published in *Applebee's* of persons whom Jonathan had really brought to justice. These were doubtless inserted at Wild's request, in order that an impression might be made upon the court by the services he had rendered for his country, but no word of comment was added. Wild's efforts, however, were unsuccessful, and on the 24th, amid a vast concourse of people, he was carried to Tyburn.

"In all that innumerable crowd," says Defoe, "there was not one pitying eye to be seen, not one compassionate word to be heard; but, on the contrary, wherever he came, there was nothing but hallooing and huzzas, as if it had been a triumph; nay, so far had he incurred the resentment of the populace that they pelted him with stones." Defoe's "True, Genuine, and Perfect Account of the Life and Actions of Jonathan Wild" appeared on 8th June, 1725; and three days later was issued his account of the conduct and proceedings of another miscreant, John Gow, "Captain of the late Pirates, executed for murther and piracy, committed on board the *George* galley, afterwards the *Revenge.*"

Probably in 1725 died Mrs. Defoe's brother, Samuel Tuffley, "late of St. John's, Hackney," for, on the 23rd of August in that year, probate was granted to Mary, wife of Daniel Defoe; Pettit, the executor, having died before the testator. In the bond the sureties are Daniel De Foe, the elder, of Newington, gentleman; Daniel De Foe, junior, of St. Michael's, Cornhill, merchant; and Aaron Lambe, of St. Mary's, Islington, scrivener. The penal sum was £3,000, and this would be considerably in excess of, perhaps double, the value of the personal estate. One of the trustees appointed by Tuffley was a Mr. Henry Langley, salter, probably the husband, or related to the husband, of Defoe's daughter, Maria. As before mentioned, all Mr. Tuffley's property was left to his sister, Defoe's wife.

CHAPTER XIII.

BUSINESS AND MAGICAL SERIES.

87.—THE COMPETE ENGLISH TRADESMAN (SEPT. 1725).

WORKS: 230.—Complete English Tradesman, vol. i.
231.— Do. vol. ii.
232.—The Friendly Daemon [*see* § 64].

DEFOE had already written much on the subject of trade, both in newspaper and pamphlet; and he now set himself to compose a complete manual or *vade mecum* on the subject, for the use of everyone, but especially the young. It was first published in one volume on the 11th of September, with the following title: "The·Complete English Tradesman, in familiar letters directing him in all the several parts and progressions of trade, etc." It dealt with apprenticeships, industry, over-trading, expensive living, indiscreet marriages, credit, partnerships, book-keeping, and the dignity and honour of trade in England. The second edition, published on the 10th of September, 1726, has a supplement which relates to borrowing of money, and discounting bills, with directions concerning accounts.

On the 18th of May, 1727, was issued a second volume of the "Complete English Tradesman," intended for the use of the more experienced tradesman, who had already thriven; with notes concerning both the home and foreign trade of the country. Defoe closes the preface of the first volume by saying :—

"What I have spoken of, I have endeavoured to do fully and pertinently ; and I think I may say of the following sheets, that they contain all the directions needful to make the tradesman thrive; and, if he pleases, to listen to them with a temper of mind willing to be directed, he must have some uncommon ill-luck if he miscarries."

The general trend of the work can very well be judged by the following :—

"A tradesman behind his counter," writes Defoe, "must have no flesh and blood about him, no passions, no resentment ; he must never be angry—no, not so much as seem to be so, if a customer tumbles him five hundred pounds worth of goods, and scarce bids money for anything; nay, though they really come to his shop with no intent to buy, as many do, only to see what is to be sold, and though he knows they cannot be better pleased than they are at some other shop where they intend to buy, 'tis all one ; the tradesman must take it, he must place it to the account of his calling, that 'tis his business to be ill-used, and resent nothing; and so must answer as obligingly to those who give him an hour or two's trouble, and buy nothing, as he does to those who, in half the time, lay out ten or twenty pounds. The case is plain ; and if some do give him trouble, and do not buy, others make amends, and do buy ; and as for the trouble, 'tis the business of the shop."

Shop, in short, is to come first, and every other consideration is to be subordinated to it. We can only say that had Defoe, when he kept shop himself, put into practice the precepts which he so kindly offers here, he would, at the moment of writing it, have been worth thousands, where he was only worth hundreds ; but we should have had no "Robinson Crusoe"! Defoe, happily for posterity, excellent as is the advice he gives in the

"Complete English Tradesman," was not himself good at minding shop. His advice, however, is none the less valuable; and many a young man has profited by it.

Chadwick calls it the best book written by Defoe; Charles Lamb, who did not like it, considered that "the bent of the book is to narrow and to degrade the heart"; but Chadwick had kept shop (for selling tiles amounts to the same thing), and Charles Lamb had never kept shop, which makes all the difference.

88.—"HISTORY OF THE DEVIL."—MILTON.—PETER THE WILD BOY
(7TH MAY, 1726).—THE GREAT DANIEL TABOOED.

WORKS: 233.—History of the Devil.
　　　234.—Mere Nature Delineated (" Peter the Wild Boy ").
　　　235.—An Essay upon Literature.
　　　236.—A General History of the Principal Discoveries and Improvements in
　　　　　　Useful Arts.
　　　237.—The Protestant Monastery.

The complete title of the book we are now to consider is as follows: "The Political History of the Devil, as well ancient as modern: In Two Parts. Part I., containing a state of the Devil's circumstances, and the various turns of his affairs, from his expulsion out of Heaven to the Creation of Man; with remarks on the several mistakes concerning the reason and manner of his fall. Also his proceedings with mankind ever since Adam, to the first planting of the Christian religion in the world. Part II., containing his more private conduct, down to the present times; his government, his appearances, his manner of working, and the tools he works with.

" Bad as he is, the devil may be abused,
Be falsely charged, and causelessly accused,
When men, unwilling to be blamed alone,
Shift off those crimes on him which are their own."

In the preface to the second edition Defoe affirms " that the whole tenor of the work is solemn, calculated to promote serious religion, and capable of being improved in a religious manner"; but he does not think " that we are bound never to speak of the devil but with an air of terror, as if we were always afraid of him."

In " The Political History of the Devil" Defoe again expresses his belief in the existence and operation of good and evil spirits—a belief to which, in common with very many other good men of his time, he clung, as we have seen, all his life with extraordinary tenacity. Defoe believed in a personal devil, but for the popular idea of the devil — a creature with bats' wings, cloven feet, a hooked nose, and a forked tail — he had nothing but ridicule. " Really," says Defoe, " it were enough to fright the devil himself to meet himself in the dark, dressed up in the several figures which imagination has formed for him in the minds of men." Nor does he think that the devil would terrify people " half so much if they were to con-verse face to face with him." The vulgar notions of hell as a place where tormented souls broiled on gridirons, hung upon hooks, he utterly repudiated; and he ridicules the old pictures of its entrance " represented by a great mouth with horrible teeth gaping like a cave on the side of a mountain, with a stream of fire coming out of it, and smaller devils going and coming continually in and out to fetch and carry souls the Lord knows whither, and for the Lord knows what."

Many human beings, held Defoe, are only devils with a case of humanity about them, called flesh and blood. Bad men are not scarce, but "how many hoop-petticoats complete the entire mask that disguises the devil in the shape of that thing called a woman ?" And this is the more to be lamented because bad mother, bad child ; "the child, you know, has always most of the mother in it." A lady devil is about as dangerous a creature as one could meet. She can kill at a distance : "the poison of her eyes (basilisk-like) is very strong," and she has strange influence over even the wary. She talks like an angel, sings like a syren, does everything and says everything that is taking and charming. No woman, it seems, is perfect ; every one has within her a devil more or less malignant. "*Non rosa sine spinis*, not a beauty without a devil. Lord ha' mercy ! and a -+- may be set on the man's door that goes a-courting."

We have, in short, in this book Defoe's usual dish of fooling, with a strong admixture of the intensely serious, the whole served up with an *olla podrida* of history, literary criticism, and Defoe-an anecdote.

We must keep, however, firmly in the mind, whilst reading it, first that Defoe is an intensely religious man, and secondly that he always believed himself to be accompanied, as we have before pointed out, by a good spirit—a friendly Daemon—upon whose advice he implicitly relied. The first of his references to his Daemon was, as we noticed, just after his bankruptcy (1692), when he refused to go to Cadiz because an impulse told him that " Providence had other work for him to do." Another occasion on which the Daemon helped him was in in his trouble of 1715, when it suggested that he should write to the judge. In the preface to the " Family Instructor," written the same year, "the spirit of God "—that is, his Daemon—"directed his hand in the work." We have also seen that " Robinson Crusoe" and " Serious Reflections " are saturated with the idea, which drew upon him the taunts of Gildon; and the subject of the converse of spirits occupies much of " Duncan Campbell." Defoe had read that God had sent forth "ministering spirits to minister to those who should be heirs of salvation"; and living in an age when people believed in the literal inspiration of the Bible, his views must be pronounced not extravagant, but moderate. On supernatural questions he was not behind his age, but in advance of it; and his ideas on witchcraft, astrology, second sight, fortune-telling, etc., must by many have been regarded as simply revolutionary.

Round the subject of demonism and its adjunct, witchcraft, a furious strife had raged for sixty or seventy years. In the Middle Ages, and up till the time of the Commonwealth, almost everybody in England had believed in the orthodox devil and the orthodox witch, among the last of the defenders of

w

the old theory being dear old Glanvil, who put his
views into that treasury of delights, his famous
"Saducismus." Then arose the body of doubters
(among the best known of whom was the gentle and
amiable Dr. Cotta, of Northampton), who held that
though there might be witches, yet it is impossible
for man to point with certainty to one ; and that, in
consequence, witch-persecutions should cease. These
gentlemen were assailed with the howl of " Sadducee,
witch-advocate, Hobbist, purblind prattlers, profane
drolls, inblown buffoons puffed up with nothing but
ignorance, vanity and stupid infidelity—ignorant objectors." The teachings of the "witch advocates," however, made headway, and after 1705, when Elinor Shaw
was burned at Northamptom, no witches were executed
in England. The teaching of Defoe merely marks
another advance. He held that not only were the
mediæval notions of witches erroneous, but the
mediæval notions of hell and the devil were wrong
too—that they were mere relics of the Pagan notions
of the Greeks and Romans, and figments that have
emanated from the brains of poets. The vulgar idea
of the devil and his den is, he declares, "little more
or less than the old story of Pluto, Cerberus, and
Charon"; only not so well told. There is a devil,
and a personal one, though his "personality is
spirituous"; there is a hell, or place of punishment for
the wicked, but what it is like no man knoweth. So
far had Defoe, one of the chief exponents of what was
then "modern thought," gone in the year 1726. At
the present day, "modern thought" has struggled
on a little further. In my story, "The Blue Fire-

drake " (London : Simpkin and Marshall, 1892), I
have dealt with this subject exhaustively.

In " The History of the Devil " it transpires that
Defoe's favourite poet and his master in satire was
the gifted but licentious Earl of Rochester, whom he
calls "that incomparable noble genius." It is true
that Defoe lashed his countrymen for their *penchant*
for this poet, and said that

"One reads Milton, forty Rochester " ;

but he himself studied both Milton and Rochester.
On the "beautiful thoughts" of Rochester's "fine
poem upon 'Nothing'" he is particularly eulogistic.
At the present day everything that Rochester wrote
is forgotten, with the exception of three or four choice
love songs, and the charming letters to his wife.
Other favourite poets of Defoe were Andrew Marvel,
Sir John Denham, and Buckhurst (Earl of Dorset).

In this book, too, he criticises at considerable
length, and advisedly, the matter—though not the
poetry—of the "majestic poem " of Milton. " Though
I admire Mr. Milton as a poet," says Defoe, " yet he
was greatly out in matters of history, and especially
the history of the devil." Milton, it seems, has
charged Satan falsely in several particulars, and done
him "manifest injuries," and Defoe, who was anxious
to give even the devil his due, felt it his duty to
expose Milton's fallacies. He points out that the
prototype of the war in Heaven was the war of the
Titans against Jupiter, so finely described by Ovid
in his " Metamorphoses " ; and that many other of
Milton's notions have no foundation except the very

W 2

frail one of Pagan fable. Milton's poem, in short, he
considers to be a fine piece of work—the fancy is
good, the strokes are masterly, and the beauty of the
workmanship is inimitably curious and fine, yet it has
some unpardonable improprieties which mar the whole,
and he compares it to a picture of the Magi wor-
shipping the infant Christ, painted by a famous painter
of Toledo, "who, unhappily, when he drew the latter
part of them kneeling, their legs being necessarily a
little intermixed," made three black feet for the negro
king, and but three white ones for the two white kings,
and yet never discovered the mistake till the piece
was hung up in the church. That this book of
Defoe's is ingenious, and in part witty, cannot be
denied, but much of it is only chaff. As in everything else that he wrote, he strains his arguments to
snapping point. If he has a good argument he must
always spoil it by spinning it thinner than it ought to
go. The absurdity of this habit is seen to the greatest
perfection in the "Use and Abuse," but it is exhibited
clearly, too, in his "History of the Devil." Who but
Defoe, for example, would have argued that a man
who in a dream commits a theft is guilty of sin?

From "The History of the Devil" we are to
turn to "Peter the Wild Boy." In July, 1724, was
found in a field near Hamelin, in Hanover, in the
act of sucking a cow, a naked, brownish, black-
haired boy, apparently about twelve years old, who
could not speak. Being enticed into the town he
was placed for safety in a hospital, and called Peter.
In 1726, by order of Queen Caroline, then the
Princess of Wales, he was brought to England and

put under the care of Dr. Arbuthnot; but though masters of every kind were provided for him, he could never be taught to say more than two or three words, and even these he pronounced very indifferently. Instead of concluding that the boy was a mere idiot, escaped perhaps from some home where his loss was not particularly regretted, the naturalists and philosophers of the day advanced the most extraordinary theories to explain the phenomenon; and Defoe, seeing a chance to turn an honest penny, not only paid a visit to the boy, but published an eighteenpenny pamphlet upon him, entitled: "Mere Nature Delineated; or, a Body without a Soul. Being Observations upon the Young Forester lately brought to Town, from Germany, etc." Taking a more common-sense view of the subject than his contemporaries, Defoe argued that Peter could not have lived long in the forest, and that the stories about his going upon his hands and knees were most likely untrue. On the other hand, he was not disposed to admit that the boy was an idiot. "He seems," says Defoe, "to be the very creature which the learned world has, for many years past, pretended to wish for, viz., one that being kept entirely from human society, so as never to have heard anyone speak, must therefore either not speak at all; or, if he did form any speech to himself, then they should know what language nature would first form for mankind." This was, of course, a little bit of fooling; but people liked being fooled. They would have been sadly disappointed had they discovered that the lion of the day was a common idiot; and Defoe's pamphlet, had it contained such a statement, would scarcely have obtained popularity. After narrating Peter's history, Defoe takes upon himself to moralise upon it. He makes many, sarcastic allusions to the men and manners of the time, raps the knuckles of his old enemy Swift, descants on education, and speculates ingeniously upon the possibility of thinking without a knowledge of words. He was also good enough to put in a word for his friend and prospective son-in-law Mr. Baker, speaking of him as one "who is eminently known for a surprising dexterity in teaching such as have been born deaf and dumb, both to speak and understand what is said when others speak to them"; and says that Peter should have been put with Mr. Baker.

"Education," says Defoe, "seems to me to be the only specific remedy for all the imperfections of nature. The difference in souls, or the greatest part at least, is owing to this." He regarded the human mind as a lump of soft wax, capable of receiving whatever impressions are fixed upon it; and he held that "as wisdom and virtue are their own reward, so vice and ignorance are their own punishment."

The latter portion of Peter's life was spent at a farmhouse at Northchurch, near Berkhamstead, with the family of a Mr. Fenn. So that he should not get lost, he wore a leather collar with a brass rim, on which was inscribed: "Peter the Wild Man from Hanover. Whoever will bring him to Mr. Fenn, at Berkhamsted, Hertfordshire, shall be paid for their trouble." He died at Northchurch in 1785, at the age of 72.

On the 19th of November, 1726, appeared Defoe's pamphlet, "The Protestant Monastery; or, a Complaint against the Brutality of the Present Age. Particularly the pertness and insolence of our youth to aged persons. With a caution how they give the staff out of their own hands, and leave themselves to the mercy of others. Concluding with a proposal for erecting a Protestant monastery, where persons of small fortune may end their days in plenty, ease, and credit, without burthening their relations, or accepting public charities."

Respecting this pamphlet, we are especially to notice two things. First the preface, from which we learn that the great Daniel Defoe, the famous pamphleteer, the much-sought-after writer of "Letters Introductory," has outlived his reputation, is no longer in request; nay, is shown the cold shoulder to, and distinctly snubbed, by the whole journalistic world.

"Assure yourself, gentle reader," he says, "I had not published my project in this pamphlet, could I have got it inserted in any of the journals without feeing the journalists or publishers. I cannot but have the vanity to think they might as well have inserted what I send them, *gratis*, as many things I have since seen in their papers. But I have not only had the mortification to find what I sent rejected, but to lose my originals, not having taken copies of what I wrote."

How came it about that the man who, a few months previous, would have gladly been offered payment for anything he had pleased to communicate was now insulted by the proposal that his tract should be treated as an advertisement and be paid for? And this proposal was made not by one journalist, but by all. Why was Defoe tabooed? Mr. Lee's interpretation of the position is that " Defoe's connection with the Government became generally known to the proprietors of the public papers, through the malignant agency of Mr. Mist, and that this caused the termination of the connection between Defoe and Applebee, on the 12th of March, 1726."

" I hope," says Defoe, touchingly, " the reader will excuse the vanity of an over-officious old man, if, like Cato, I inquire whether or no, before I go hence and be no more, I can yet do anything for the service of my country."

The action of the journalists had cut him to the quick.

" It has been the fate of much better men than myself, to be despised when living, though revered when dead."

But most touching of all is the following—

" Alas ! I have but small health, and little leisure to turn author, being now in my sixty-seventh year, almost worn out with age and sickness. The old man cannot trouble you long ; take, then, in good part his best intentions, and impute his defects to age and weakness."

Mr. Lee's interpretation of the conjuncture is, of course, conjecture, and I have given it only for what it is worth. Defoe himself seems to intimate that the reason his communications were refused was because the publishers did not consider them up to the mark, and he as good as admits that, owing to age and weakness, the palmy days of his writing were over.

The second point that we are to notice is the matter of the pamphlet itself. " Particularly the pertness and insolence of our youth to aged persons

With a caution to people in years how they give the staff out of their own hands, and leave themselves to the mercy of others." Whether Defoe's own case is here concerned we need not inquire, but it is deeply touching to remember that the very snare against which he cautioned others he himself ran into. As we shall see, Defoe, owing to harassment by some enemy, unwisely handed over his property to his eldest son ; this son abused the confidence placed in him, and Defoe's grey hairs were brought down with sorrow to the grave.

On March 15th, the *Daily Courant* advertises for the recovery of a small pocket-book, lost a few days previous near Blackwell Hall Bag-gate. It contained eighteen notes and bills on several persons, the second note being "A note of Daniel Defoe to John Clarke, £18," and the fifth bill, "A bill by Joseph Brookes on De Foe, £50." There was to be "half-a-guinea reward, and no questions asked." This reminds us that Defoe continued to be engaged in commercial transactions (*see* § 43). "In all probability," says Mr. Lee, "he purchased broad cloths for merchants residing abroad ; paying for them with his own bills ; and the lost pocket-book was that of a West of England cloth manufacturer or his factor." In his "Plan of the English Commerce," after observing that the master clothier does not know to what part of the world his goods are ultimately shipped, Defoe says, "He sends them up to London to the factor, that sells them, whether at Blackwell Hall, or in his private warehouse, and when sold he draws bills for the money ; there his circle meets."

89.—THE HISTORY OF MAGIC.—"'TWAS NOT THOSE SOULS THAT
FLED IN PAIN."—A TILT AT ALEXANDER POPE (19TH DEC., 1726).

WORKS : 238.—A System of Magic.
239.—The Evident Approach of a War.

The second of Defoe's supernatural treatises,
" A System of Magic ; or, a History of the Black
Art," was published 19th December, 1726, but
dated 1727. The frontispiece represents a magician
practising his tricks in a library, and a merry-look-
ing fiend popping his head in at the door. The
first title is a misnomer, for the book is not a
system of magic at all ; that is to say, it is not a
book of rules for instruction in the Black Art, but
simply a history of it. The earliest magicians, says
Defoe, were "wise and honest"; those of the middle
ages, "madmen and rogues"; modern practitioners
are "wicked fools." To illustrate his subject, he
gives a number of amusing anecdotes ; and, like
almost everything else that he wrote, much of
it is a satire on his own times. Amongst those
whom he chastises is William Whiston, the eminent
philosopher and colleague of Sir Isaac Newton, to
whom he insinuates mercenariness ; and—as in his
former work—he pokes fun at the devil in " Paradise
Lost." Among his stories are some of the Kentish
magician Dr. Boreman, and one is of his own experiences with a countryman with whom he rode
to Northampton, and who subsequently visited
Defoe at the George Inn there, and told him the
sayings and doings of two magicians he (the
countryman) had been consulting, one at a village two

miles from Northampton, and one at Oundle.
Where people have been mostly in error, thinks
Defoe, has been in ascribing all phenomena to
Satanic influence. That there are evil spirits abroad
he admits, but he insists that good spirits are much
more numerous; and he bade those whose breasts
were perturbed because they had seen apparitions to
be at ease. We get an echo of the idea in one of
the most striking stanzas in Coleridge's "Ancient
Mariner":

> "Be calm, thou Wedding-Guest.
> 'Twas not those souls that fled in pain,
> Which to their corses came again,
> But a troop of spirits blest."

We read in the Bible that God conversed with
man; but says Defoe: "Did the great Being of
beings converse with man, and not the smaller and
lower degrees of spirits? Do you think the servants did not converse, if the master did? God
spoke to Noah, and gave him general directions
about building the ark," but He would not furnish
all the minutiae. He would not instruct Noah concerning such matters as how the beams and the
timbers, etc., were to be put together, how the
bottom was to be shaped for swimming, and the
head and the stern for breaking off the force
of the water. Noah's knowledge concerning these
things must have been derived from "good and
beneficent spirits." "It seems," Defoe goes on to
say, "that men, by a differing conduct and a way
of life too gross for so excellent and sublime a
converse, have rendered themselves unworthy and

unqualified since the Flood ; so that the angelic train seem to have forsaken the earth, and only communicate themselves to such as render themselves acceptable and worthy by a life of earnest application to the study of divine science, and who seek after the high illumination."

The question naturally follows : " Then there are some who enjoy this extraordinary society still ? "

To which Defoe answers, " Why not, pray ? The good spirits are the same ; they change not, neither is their goodwill towards men abated." In short, there are good spirits ; and those who seek after the high illumination receive their assistance.

Towards the end of the book, Defoe laments the decadence of poetry. He would be glad to know "whether any of the good spirits or bad spirits, the white devils or black devils, or whatever spirits they were which formerly inspired the Rochesters, the Dorsets, and the Drydens of the last ages, are yet in being ; and if they are, what has been the occasion that they have withdrawn the spirit of poetry from the English world." He satirises the practice of giving pensions and places to poetasters. If this sort of thing goes on, ministers, he believes, will have more dedications and laudatory verses than they can possibly endure. They " are in danger of dying the death of Edward V., and being smothered with feather-beds."

There is no doubt that the passage respecting the withdrawal of the spirit of poetry was a direct thrust at Alexander Pope, at whom Defoe, on more than one occasion, discharged the shafts of adverse criticism. In an article in *Applebee's Journal* for July 31st, 1725, he had written a satirical paper "On Pope's Translation of Homer," in which he insinuates that instead of being the author of the work, Pope, like "Sir Dick Steele with the Tatlers" had abundance of *Aid de plumes* * under him. Homer himself, according to a fellow of Defoe's acquaintance (as Defoe thinks proper to put it), was a plagiarist. "This Homer, in process of Time, when he had gotten some Fame—and perhaps more money than poets ought to be trusted with—grew lazy and knavish, and got one Andronicus, a Spartan, and one Dr. S——l, a Philosopher of Athens, both pretty good poets, but less eminent than himself, to make his songs for him; which, they being poor and starving, did for him for a small matter. And so the poet never did much himself, only published and sold his ballads still in his own name, as if they had been his own; and by that, *got great subscriptions, and a high price for them.*" (For the italicising we are ourselves responsible.) "Now, Mr. Applebee, if my friend be in the right, was not Cousin Homer a knave for imposing thus upon the Grecian world? In a word, it seems to me that old Homer was a mere Mr. P(ope), and Mr. P(ope), in that particular, a mere Homer." No doubt it was this sort of thing that caused Pope to retaliate, by putting Defoe in the "Dunciad."

* *Sic.*)

90.—"THE USE AND ABUSE."—SPECIMENS OF DEFOE'S ANECDOTES.
—THE MAN WHO WAS TOO HARD UPON HIS LADY.—OF
THE OLD WOMAN WHO MARRIED A LITTLE BOY.

WORK : 240.—Conjugal Lewdness : or, Matrimonial Whoredom (30th Jan., 1727).
Reissued 10th June, 1727, with the new title of A Treatise
concerning the Use and Abuse of the Marriage Bed.

This is no place to dilate upon the merits and
demerits of what is to-day called Neo-Malthusianism,
but the best comment on this work of Defoe's is
to point the finger at his son Benjamin. Read the
heart-rending and grovelling letters to Lord Newcastle preserved in the British Museum, and then
inquire whether Benjamin Defoe would not have
found himself more flourishing in this world and
whether he would not have stood a better chance
of finally reaching a happier one had he thought fit
to limit his family. He had seventeen children !

Much of the book, which was begun thirty
years previous, is excellent. Its commencement is
a paean in honour of modesty : "Modesty in Discourse," avast both lewd talk and ribaldry of the
press ; "Modesty in Behaviour," act at all times
with decorum ; "Modesty in regard to Sexes," after
marriage as well as before—which brings us to the
subject of the book.

To write such a work at all was a delicate
business. Says Defoe : "The difficulty before me is
to know how to reprove with decency offences
against decency ; how to expose modestly, things
which 'tis hardly modest so much as to mention."
Whether Defoe ought to have written such a book
is not for me to answer ; some will say yes, others

no. Defoe's defence was "Evil be to him who evil thinks." "The healing, fructifying dews, and the gentle, sweet refreshing showers, which are God's blessing upon earth, when they fall into the sea are all turned salt . . . but the fault is not in the showers of refreshing rain." "The warm, cherishing beams of the sun shining upon the stagnant waters of an unwholesome marsh, or upon a corrupted dunghill, exhale noxious vapours and poisons, but who would blame the blessed sun?"

Very few marriages, observes Defoe, are happy ones. Many take place without love on either side, and are caused by the desire of the ladies for "a good settlement," of the men "for money." But a contract such as that, Defoe will not allow to be really marriage at all; "I should call it," says he, "matrimonial whoredom."

The book teems with anecdotes, one of which, illustrating the folly of perpetually making one's wife the subject of ridicule and jest, may be quoted as a sample.

"I had in friendship several times gently hinted to Mr. M——, that I thought he was too hard upon his lady. However, he went on, and putting one time very hard upon something in her behaviour, which he pretended not to like, though really without cause; she coloured at his words, which showed she resented them, and was moved; but she immediately recovered herself, and keeping back all her resentment, she, with an inexpressible goodness in her face, and a smile, said to him: '*My dear, you would like it in anybody but your wife.*'"

It is satisfactory to know that this sweet and gentle answer had the effect of curing Mr. M—— of his complaint.

The book is studded with excellent aphorisms.

" A cheerful affection is the beauty of a conjugal state."

" 'Tis a wise man's business after matrimony, by all means possible to preserve the affection of his wife entire, to engross her to him, and to make and keep himself the single and entire object of her best thoughts."

" Marriage without love, is the completest misery in life."

" Love is the only pilot of a married state."

Dryden, or to quote Defoe, " Mr. Dryden, a lewd poet," paints rosily the time when polygamy was in vogue—

" 'Ere one to one was cursedly confined."

Defoe, on the other hand, advances a host of arguments to demonstrate that the present condition of things is a decided improvement.

But if some of the book is admirable, that cannot be said about all. Much of it is a great pother about nothing, or next to nothing, and his arguments are some of them drawn out so fine as to make them downright ridiculous. Far better advice than much that Defoe gives is the simple injunction, " Recognise the laws of nature, and use your common-sense."

One chapter is in condemnation of the practice of marrying children; and among the anecdotes is one of an old lady, who, in order that her nieces should not succeed to her money, proposed to a father that he should let her marry his little boy, aged ten. " He is so young," she added, " that nobody can raise any objection against it; for to be sure, I shall be in my grave before he will be grown up to man's estate." After some demur the father consented, and the pair were united. The sequel of the story, which is told in Defoe's daintiest style, is as follows :—

" But even this unsuitable match did not prove so satisfactory as might have been expected ; for it pleased God this woman lived to such a prodigious age, that the little boy was seventy-two years of age when he followed her to the church to bury her, and she was one hundred and twenty-seven years old.

" This story I had attested to me by a person of an unquestioned veracity, who told me he was himself at her funeral : she was sixty-five when she married, and lived sixty-two years with her husband ; she indeed made him some amends for the disparity of years by this, that she was a most excellent person, of an inimitable disposition, preserved the youth of her temper, and the strength of her understanding, memory and eyesight to the last ; and, which was particularly remarkable, she bred a whole new set of teeth, as white as ivory, and as even as a youth, after she was ninety years old."

Defoe's didactic works are besprinkled with anecdotes of this kind as liberally as a birthday pudding with plums, and it is impossible not to notice the boyish glee with which he tells them.

In conclusion, he declares that "the whole tenour of the work is calculated to bear down vice, vicious practices, and vicious language." That he thoroughly enjoyed writing it is patent. Dancing among broken bottles was a business that ever had charms for him, and the fact that here he had more bottles than usual could have only added to the zest with which he went about it.

91.—THE HISTORY OF APPARITIONS. — THE SPIRITS WHO "BE-TWEEN SOMEWHERE AND NOWHERE DWELL" (18TH MARCH, 1727).

WORKS : 241.—An Essay on the History and Reality of Apparitions. 18th March, 1727.
242.—A New Family Instructor. 1727.

The "History of Apparitions," the third and last of Defoe's treatises on supernatural subjects,

X

was published 23rd November, 1728. The full title
is "An Essay on the History and Reality of
Apparitions. Being an account of what they are,
and what they are not. As, also, how we may
distinguish between the Apparitions of Good and
Evil Spirits, and how we ought to behave to them.
With a great variety of surprising and diverting
examples, never published before.

> " By Death transported to th' Eternal Shore,
> Souls so removed re-visit us no more :
> Engrossed with joy of a superior kind,
> They leave the trifling thoughts of life behind."

On the 23rd of November the work was republished with a fuller title ; but the sheets were
those of the first edition. Instead of the verse
just quoted was the following from Milton :—

> " Spirits in whatsoever shape they choose,
> Dilated or condensed, bright or obscure,
> Can execute their airy purposes,
> And works of love or enmity fulfil."

As in his work on magic, Defoe expresses
himself a firm believer in the presence of good and
evil spirits, and in the converse "between our
spirits cased up in flesh, and the spirits unembodied ; who inhabit the unknown mazes of the
invisible world ; those coasts which our geography
cannot describe ; who between somewhere and nowhere dwell, none of us know where, and yet we
are sure must have locality, and for aught we know,
are very near us." He considers them to be an
intermediate order of beings between angels and .

HENRY BAKER, THE NATURALIST, DEFOE'S SON-IN-LAW.

(From a painting in the possession of the Rev. Henry Defoe Baker, Rector of Thruxton, Hants.)

men, and that they are the immediate agents in
dreams and premonitions, "calling upon men to
seek for direction and counsel from that hand who
alone can both direct and deliver." He denies, as
contrary to the teaching of the Bible, that ghosts
and apparitions are the departed souls of human
creatures. They are simply unembodied spirits.

We don't worry ourselves about things of that
sort, now-a-days; but in the eighteenth century,
they occupied no small portion of people's thoughts.
He who imagines that our forefathers did not
really believe in witchcraft and apparitions; that it
was only their fun, as Charles Lamb would say,
had better read Glanvil, or if Glanvil be unattain-
able, the author's story, "The Blue Firedrake."

92.—THE COURTSHIP OF HENRY BAKER.—"*AUGUSTA TRIUMPHANS.*"
    —"THE FINEST JULAP UPON EARTH" (17TH AUG., 1727—30TH
    APR., 1729).

WORKS: 243.—Parochial Tyranny. 9th Dec., 1727.
    * 244.—*Augusta Triumphans.* 16th Mar., 1728.
    245.—A Plan of English Commerce. 23rd Mar., 1728.
    246.—*Universal Spectator.* 12th Oct., 1728.
    247.—Second Thoughts are Best: or a Further Improvement of a late
        Scheme to Prevent Street Robberies. 12th Oct., 1728.
    248.—Street Robberies considered. 12th Nov., 1728.
    249.—Fog's Weekly. 11th Jan., 1729.
    250.—An Humble Proposal. 15th Mar., 1729.
    251.—Reasons for a War. Mar., 1729.

The admiration of Henry Baker for Sophia
Defoe had now developed into ardent love, and on
August 17th, 1727, he declared his passion. Fortunately for us, Mr. Baker took the trouble in after
years to copy out all the letters that, during the
period of his courtship, had passed between him
and Sophia and Defoe, and this volume has been

placed in my hands. Its contents have never before been made public, and none of Defoe's previous biographers have even seen the book. The following, in the handwriting of Mr. Baker, appears on the first page:—

"Letters that passed between me and my dear wife Sophia during the time of courtship, viz., from Aug. 17th, 1727, to April 30th, 1729, when we were happily married, and likewise the letters that passed between us afterwards when we happened to be separated. These letters are all genuine and strictly exact, being carefully copied from the originals which are still in being."

The idea of the match gave satisfaction to Defoe, and this alone is a sufficient guarantee of the excellence of Mr. Baker's character. Defoe was very particular in the matter of marriages, and he had a rather poor opinion of the young men of the day. There were ten rakes, he says, to one sober man, and among sober men there were ten Atheists to one religious man; "and, which is worse than all the rest, if a woman finds a religious man, it is three to one whether he agrees with her in principles." (" Religious Courtship.")

Did these letters bear reference only to Mr. Baker and Sophia Defoe, we should have given them only passing notice; but teeming as they do with references to Defoe, and throwing strong light both on his character and his relations with Mr. Baker, they are invaluable. We get from them word-pictures of Defoe such as could be found nowhere else. If the book itself should ever get printed, I would suggest as a title " The Complete

Lover "; for it is the history of a passion from beginning to end—or rather from incipiency to marriage, for with marriage, strange as it may appear, the infatuation of Mr. Baker for Sophia Defoe did not cease. The first letter, which is dated " Newington, Aug. 27th, 1727," runs as follows :—

" How shall I make you sensible of what I feel for you ? How shall I express the uneasiness of absence? or the no less torment of being restrained from speaking to you when I see you ? I love your sisters ; I love them for your sake, next you, the best of all things. And yet I hate them for your sake, whenever they interpose between my bliss and me ; but I forgive them, for though they do me the greatest injury, they ignorantly do it. O how I now repent the hours I have lost, those unhappy happy hours ! when all alone with you, but overawed, I durst not tell my flame. And yet I hope they were not wholly lost ; surely then, my eyes, my silence, my confusion told it : for even silence speaks, and love declares itself a thousand ways without the help of words. Ah ! how can I bear this absence ! Absence did I say ? How lovers rave ! No, you are always with me ; your lovely image haunts me day and night, where'er I go, whatsoe'er I do ; O give me leave to think of nothing but yourself. By what strange means this comes to pass, I cannot tell ; but sure you must be something more than woman, since from all my frequent converse with that charming sex I never found the like effect before."

An unwearied student, and a man of ambition, who sought to distinguish himself both as a scientist and a poet, Henry Baker found even more delight in the beauties of Sophia's mind than in the beauties of her face. " I liked you when first I saw you, but I loved you not till I found in you perfections few of your sex are blest with." From Saturday till Wednesday evening was the unhappy part of the week when he could not see

her; and this distressing period—all lovers, and all
who have been lovers, will sympathise—was "wholly
filled up with anxious hopes and desires," which it
was impossible to satisfy. "Ah, my dearest," he
continues" (Nov. 26, 1727), "how long must more
than half my days be miserable? When will your
father declare his intentions for us, and when will
you be mine!"

Like every other courtship, it was lighted up
with the ridiculous. For example, Baker spends
his Sundays reading the Song of Solomon, and
sends Sophia such extracts from it as "Thou hast
doves' eyes." In reply to this "borrowed rapturous
letter," Sophia cruelly told him "it cost you little
pains to copy words. Is the subject grown so dull
that you are fain to be beholding to so antiquated
a lover?" In this same letter (4th Dec., 1727),
Sophia refers to an illness of her father's. "Since
I sat to write you this, I was alarmed by my
father's complaining of a violent sudden pain, which
spreads itself all over him, but is, I hope, not dangerous, though I fear it is a messenger from that
grand tyrant which will, at last, destroy the (to me)
so-much-valued structure."

Judging from appearances—*e.g.*, the "very genteel"
way of Defoe's living—Mr. Baker supposed that
Defoe "must be able to give his daughter a decent
portion; he did not suppose a large one." But all
that could be got out of Defoe was that "he hoped
he should be able to give her a certain sum
specified," and "when urged to the point some time
afterwards, his answer was, that formal articles he

thought unnecessary; that he found he could not
part with any money at present; but at his death,
his daughter's portion would be more than he had
promised; and he offered his own bond as a guarantee for the payment." With this, Baker was not
satisfied, and the relations between them became
strained. Here note we three facts: first, that
Defoe, though in comfortable circumstances, was not
so well off as Mr. Baker imagined; secondly, that
Defoe's affairs were, as they had ever been, in a
muddle; and thirdly, that mystification was Defoe's
supreme delight. No one could understand him, no
one could lay hand on him and say he had got
him, and no one could tell what he was driving at.
We might also add a fourthly: he was a great
man—and he never forgot that he was a great man—
he would have his way. That Mr. Baker had parts
he admitted, but Henry Baker was not Daniel
Defoe; and Daniel Defoe was not to be bullied into
what he had objections to.

Writing to Sophia (31st Dec., 1727), Mr.
Baker says :—

"I think your father's objections are of much less weight than
mine. To have his affairs known can be but an imaginary evil, but
for me to act myself in what I am wholly ignorant may prove a real
one."

To Defoe he writes :—

"I can't help objecting to that part of your paper which provides
that in case your daughter dies without issue her portion shall revert
to your executors. Will you consent if I die childless that what I
leave shall go among my relations. I know you won't. And is not
your negative a good argument for my objection?"

This was on Jan. 7th, 1728, and two days later Sophia writes:—

"Your letter, sir, to my father seems to have much of the air of barter and sale. My fortune, though not great, fully answers yours, which is less than I need accept of, and which I think does not justify such nice demands."

Mr. Baker, it seems, was ready to make over to Sophia, for her sole benefit, immediately on their marriage, the sum of £1,500. Mr. Defoe, however, would not give way, and "Sophy" sided with her father. "What strange kind of illness have you," Mr. Baker enquires of her, "that will at your command be gone on Friday, but not before?" Baker then made himself uneasy about the lease of Defoe's house at Newington, which was to be the security for the dowry; and he worried Defoe to try and obtain another lease. Defoe unwillingly consented; and we find him writing to Baker on Jan. 21st, 1728, as follows:—

"The sending me to Sutton to mend a title which I have no reason to think precarious has had the effect I expected, to put vain conceit in his head of his power, which, however . . . no weight may yet puff him up to refuse what I have really no occasion to ask, and you will see, if you please to judge impartially, that I was not wrong when I said it was harassing me and without cause, too."

In reply, Baker said that as a new lease could not be obtained, they "must make the best of things without it. I shall never expect impossibilities, but, indeed, wondered at your unwillingness to attempt it, but I never intended it as a *sine qua non*."

Baker's conduct in insisting on an attempt to

obtain a new lease ; and now, after putting Defoe to so much trouble, coolly observing that its obtainment was not of supreme importance, exasperated Defoe to the last degree.

"I am very much surprised," he writes (25th January, 1728), "that now you plainly see the difficulties which I foresaw would occur in this affair have happened accordingly, you drop them as things which may be let alone, after they had been insisted upon before as absolutely necessary, and after you have by this brought me into a labyrinth which I do not see my way out of, and like some other people ventured to rouse a devil they cannot lay. What you expect next I know not, or what, from having been so handled, you desire me to do, and therefore desire you will please to let the lease be left with my son in Finch Lane, where I will also leave your receipt for it. I am sorry my poor child has the misfortune to have no better treatment, after so long being exposed, but I hope God will provide for her his own way.—I am, Sir, your friend and humble servant,

"De Foe."

The more coldness, however, Sophia exhibited, the more fervent grew Baker's passion.

" My former pleasures are displeasing to me, company becomes tiresome, books insipid, and the muse impertinent."

This was on February 14th (1728), and a week later he writes—

"Whilst I sit by my Sophy and gaze upon her I'm all ectsasy, my body trembles, my soul rejoices, and my tongue falters with pleasure not to be described, but soon as e'er I leave her I'm in a state of wretchedness, and, like one of the false angels, find myself greatly miserable for having been greatly happy."

On February 27th he is more passionate still—

"My Sophy, ah, how I languish for thee ! What soft sensations seize me ! What fondness inexpressible possesses me whene'er I think of thee ! This very moment my soul is stretching after thee with ardent longings. Methinks I fold thee in my eager arms, and bask and pant and wanton in thy smiles ; and now I hold thee off and gaze upon thy charms with infinite delight, and now all ecstasy I snatch thee to me, and devour thy lips, strain thee with breathless raptures to my bosom, till feeble mortal nature faints, unable to endure bliss so excessive, and sinks with joys celestial."

In a subsequent letter he says, "Whatever disregard your father shows me can never destroy my love or shake my constancy ; he may go on to slight me" ; in another, "Your father is greatly angry with me for no other reason but because he has misused me" ; and in a third he refers to "Mr. Defoe's contempt of me." "To be in love," says Baker, "is a state of madness," a madness, however, not incurable ; "there is a drug called marriage which is a sure specific in this disease." In another saying, he betrays the scientist : "Melancholy," says he, "avails nothing, but only like a microscope serves to magnify misfortunes and show them in their most hideous forms." Some of his letters are in verse, and he several times addresses Sophia under the poetical name of Amanda.

"I love you," he writes, June 3, 1728, "more than life, nor does my resenting your father's ungenerous conduct and my rejecting his chimerical offers at all contradict this true assertion." But Baker had another difficulty ; his mother was opposed to the match, and had quarrelled with him on account of his persistency in it. "I hope, my dearest," he writes to Sophia (August 4, 1728), "neither you nor I are like our parents." A little later Defoe declares that he has made as good proposals as his affairs will admit. "If you desire my daughter, you must take her as I can give her;" this is followed on August 23 (1728) by his ultimatum ; and then there was some haggling as to whether four per cent. or five per cent. should be paid by Defoe upon Sophia's dowry, as long as it remained in his hand.

From the foregoing we see that Defoe was at this time not rich, but neither was he poor. He had a comfortable income, and the one desire of his life now was to see his children provided for. In a letter to Mr. Baker, of September 4, 1728, he speaks of "being arrived at an age when, if ever, it is needful to settle what little I have among my children. This is so settled and so engaged, and no otherwise. I cannot think it a breach of honour that I do not think it proper to expose, no not to my own children, all the particulars of my family settlement while I am still living."

During the period we are now considering, Defoe's pen had been almost as busy as ever ; "Parochial Tyranny" (9th Dec., 1727), a tirade against the corruption of "select vestries," and "the abuses committed in the distribution of public charities," was succeeded on 16th March, 1728, by the interesting pamphlet "Augusta Triumphans: or, the Way to make London the most flourishing city in the Universe." To bring this about, Defoe had six proposals : (1) The establishment of a University ; (2) and of a Foundling Hospital ; (3) The suppression of Private Madhouses ; (4) The clearing of the Streets of gay women ; (5) The formation of an Academy of Music ; (6) A prevention of the "immoderate use of Geneva."

This pamphlet, like some of its predecessors, was published under Defoe's *nom - de - plume*, "Andrew Morton, Esq." Of the six proposals four of them—the first three and the fifth—are now *faits accomplis*. Defoe here makes further allusion to his age and infirmities. "I have but a short time to live," he says, "nor would I waste my remaining thread of life in vain; but having often lamented sundry public abuses, and many schemes having occurred to my fancy, which to me carried an air of benefit, I was resolved to commit them to paper before my departure."

Among the customs condemned, one is that of Sabbath-breaking; but if Defoe is severe on dese-crators of the Lord's Day, he is ten times more severe on the "extravagant use, or rather abuse, of that nauseous liquor called Geneva" among the lower sort.

Not only, he argues, does this Geneva so in-fatuate the common people, that half the work is not done now as formerly, but it debilitates and enervates them, and makes them "incapable of getting such lusty children as they used to do." The women, too, spoil their milk by it, "so that in less than an age, we may expect a fine spindle-shanked generation."

Having looked on that picture, look on this: "On the contrary, our own malt liquor, especially common draught beer, is most wholesome and nourishing, and has brought up better generations than the present. It is strengthening, cooling, and balsamick; it helps digestion, and carries nourishment with it. And, in spite of the whims of some physicians, is most pertinent to a humane, especially a good wholesome English constitution. Nay, the honest part of the faculty deny not the use of small beer well brewed, even in fevers. I myself have found great benefit by it ; and if it be good in its kind, 'tis the finest julap upon earth."

We note, too, that Defoe takes the opportunity here to give his old antagonist Gay a good hearty slash. " Our Rogues," says he, " are grown more wicked than ever, and vice in all kinds is so much winked at, that robbery is accounted a petty crime. We take pains to puff 'em up in their villainy, and thieves are set out in so amiable a light in the *Beggars' Opera* that it has taught them to value themselves on their profession, rather than be ashamed of it." No wonder that Gay and his friends did not like Defoe. The charge that the *Beggars' Opera* had demoralised the town was always a sore point with them ; and Dean Swift well cudgelled even the Archbishop of Canterbury (Dr. Herring) for taking such a view.

Defoe now harks back to trade, and writes " A Plan of the English Commerce " (23rd March, 1728), in which he handles the subject as it concerned the general interest and prosperity of the nation ; just as formerly, in his " Complete English Tradesman " he had had in view the interest and prosperity of the individual tradesman.

In October, 1728, Henry Baker, Defoe's prospective son-in-law, floated a new periodical, *The Universal Spectator and Weekly Journal*, and this happening at a time when the quarrel about the dowry was being patched, Defoe, at Baker's request, wrote the first number (October 12th). It is chiefly valuable for Defoe's clear definition of what in his opinion constitutes a good writer :—

"The character of a good writer, wherever he is to be found, is this, viz., that he writes so as to please and serve at the same time. The writer that strives to be useful, writes to *serve* you, and at the same time, by an imperceptible art, draws you on to be pleased also. He represents truth with plainness, virtue with praise ; he even reprehends with a softness that carries the force of a satire without the salt of it ; and he insensibly screws himself into your good opinion, that as his writings merit your regard, so they fail not to obtain it."

Defoe wrote nothing for Baker's paper besides this first number.

The feasibility of many of the projects of Defoe's in the "scheme to prevent street robberies," inserted in "*Augusta Triumphans*," so commended itself about this time to the intellect of another literary gentleman, that he coolly claimed the whole scheme as his own, and announced in the public journals his intention of laying it before Parliament "for their approval during the next session."

The plagiarist of George the Second's day went in for none of your petty prigging of a thought here and a paragraph there : he "lifted" the whole concern.

To be jockeyed out of his labours, however, piqued Defoe not a little, especially as all the reward he had asked was a "Thank-ye," so he wrote a letter to *Applebee's* and exposed the little trick of this "second-hand schemist"; and, not to be behindhand with him, "I determine," says Defoe, "next sessions to present copies of my aforesaid book to divers honourable worthy members of both Houses, unto whom I have the honour to be known, and then we shall see whose scheme shall have the precedence." But Defoe did more than that. He recast his whole scheme, and extended it into a distinct pamphlet, with the title "Second Thoughts are Best ; or, a further improvement of a late scheme to prevent street robberies. In which our streets will be so strongly guarded, and so gloriously illuminated, that any part of London will be as safe and pleasant at midnight as at noonday, and burglary totally impracticable " : a title illustrating at least one thing — the extraordinary sanguinity of Defoe's temperament when once his passions were roused. If to prophesy such a state of affairs would argue an enthusiast even nowadays with our electric light, what must it have argued in the era of oil ? This pamphlet was presented both to the King and Queen at Windsor, and to the Lord Mayor of London. It must be remembered that the pseudonym of Andrew Moreton was by this time well known to belong to Defoe. An advertiser in *Read's Journal* for October 26, 1728, refers to the scheme as "'Squire Moreton's, *alias* D——l Def—e's, Scheme." "Second Thoughts are Best" was quickly followed by another pamphlet on the same subject : "Street Robberies Considered" (12th November, 1728), which contains, among other things, warnings to travellers, with rules how to know a highwayman, observations on housebreakers, and a "description of shoplifts, how to know 'em, and how to prevent 'em," etc. "Written by a converted thief. To which is prefixed some memoirs of his life. Set a thief to catch a thief."

An article in *Fog's Journal*, the successor of *Mist's*, for January 11th, 1729, recommending "The Complete English Tradesman," which had lately passed into a second edition, points to the fact that Defoe was now writing again for the public journals, and suggests that the strong feeling against him among journalists had in part passed away. The 15th of March shows him returned once more to the subject on which he was so great an authority—the subject of trade. "An Humble Proposal," he calls his pamphlet, "to the People of England, for the increase of their trade and encouragement of their manufactures; whether the present uncertainty of affairs issues in peace or war." "The following sheets," he says, "are as one alarm more given to the lethargic age, if possible to open their eyes to their own prosperity. If the trade of England is not in a flourishing and thriving condition, the fault and only occasion of it is all our own, and is wholly in our own power to amend, whenever we please." He tells Englishmen "that they live by trade, that their commerce has raised them from what *they were* to what *they are*, and may, if cultivated and improved, raise them yet further to what *they never were;* and this," he exclaims, "in a few words is an index of my present work."

The next production of Defoe's was the last political effort of his of which we have any knowledge, a tract entitled "Reasons for a War, in order to establish the tranquillity and commerce of Europe" (March, 1729). He argues that the protracted uncertainty of diplomatic proceedings only injures trade; and that a short sharp war followed by peace would be decidedly better than to be constantly on tenter-hooks.

93.—MARRIAGE OF SOPHIA DEFOE.—"BE AT THE PARSON'S BY FARTHEST AT TEN O'CLOCK" (APRIL, 1729).

On January 27th, 1728-29, the quarrel between Defoe and Baker had reached its highest point. "You," says Baker to Sophia, "are my good genius, and your father is my evil one. He, like a curst infernal, continually torments, betrays, and overturns my quiet; you, like a divinity, allay the storm he raises and hush my soul to peace. Ruin and wild destruction sport around him and exercise their fury on all he has to do with, but joy and happiness are your attendants and bless where'er you come." On February 1, Baker proposes that he and Sophy should take poison and die in each other's arms: "The world telling with wonder our amazing story, pitying our youth and our too cruel fate. It might be, some brother bard with monumental verse would celebrate our memory and give us down with praise to future times." Sophia, however, instead of consenting, very properly castigates. In different letters Baker thus refers to Defoe: "I am persuaded he is all deceit and baseness"; "What your father now designs to do with us I won't pretend to guess, for his purposes are always dark and hideous"; "Your father loves

Y

to hide himself in mists, and if he pleases may enjoy his fancy, but for my part, I will ever breathe the clear and wholesome air of truth and honesty"; "One who is under the necessity of being crafty, ungenerous, dishonest"; "Him I abhor as much as I love you, for to his baseness I owe all the misery I am brought to, and he will be my certain ruin." Poor Sophia felt the situation very keenly. Deeply as she loved Baker, she persisted that her father was and would be just. "Your suspicions of my father," she says, "I think wholly unjust and groundless, He has not one thought I am assured of, that you so rashly charge him with." At last the health of the poor girl utterly broke down, and a dangerous fever ensued. But the distress of both the father and the lover at this critical moment put an end to the quarrel. They came to terms, and at Defoe's desire the marriage articles were at once drawn up. All anxiety being removed, Sophia speedily recovered, and the marriage was appointed for April 30.

"I beg the favour of you," writes Baker on April 27, "to be at the parson's by farthest by ten o'clock. There I myself shall be at nine, and I expect you with great impatience."

A month later Baker told a friend, "I do not yet repent, and what is more wonderful, believe I never shall." Nor did he, for no marriage ever turned out happier.

The question of Sophia's dowry, however, continued from time to time to be a bone of contention between Defoe and Baker; and it was never really settled till Defoe's death.

94.—A TOUCHING LETTER.—THE DEATH OF SIR RICHARD STEELE
(1ST SEPTEMBER, 1729).

WORK : 252.—Servitude, a Poem [only the prose introduction by Defoe].

In a letter of Defoe's hitherto unpublished, which is dated 9th June, and was probably written in 1729, we are again touchingly reminded of his deep affection for his children, and particularly for Sophia. She had inadvertently caused him pain—and from the way in which Mr. Baker and Mr. Forster, Mr. Baker's friend, are alluded to, in all probability it was in connection with the interminable dowry squabble; as soon, however, as she discovered that her father's feelings had been wounded, she hastened to make reparation, and the following is his reply :—

"*June* 9.

" MY DEAREST SOPHIE,—Allow me to begin with a little philosophy. Where affections are strongest they are always most sensible of a shock, and unkindness (nay, though but seeming such) makes the deepest impressions. Hence Cæsar, though of a spirit invincible, gave up to death when he felt a stroke from his adopted Brutus, and said no more but (*et tu quoque mi fili ; tu Brute !*) What ! and thou, too, Brutus ? my son ! Nay, hence the wise man says, A brother offended is harder to be won than the bars of a castle. Love is of so nice a nature that, like the heart, it faints at the least touch. Where it is not so, it must be because such know not how to love.

" If I have been more sensibly grieved at what I thought un-kind in my Sophi (say it was only that I thought so) if I took fire more than another would have done, it was because I loved you more than ever any loved or will or can love you (he that has you excepted). Had Deb, the hussy, though rash and so far weak, said ten times as much to me, it had made no impression at all : but from Sophi ! thee, Sophi, whose image sits close to my affection, and whom I love beyond the power of expressing, I acknowledge it wounded my very soul, and my weakness is so much more as that affection is strong, so that I can as ill express the satisfaction I

Y 2

have from your letter as I could the grief of what I thought an unkindness. Perhaps I do not write like a father, but perhaps I do too, if it be considered that love is the same, let the relation be what it will ; besides, as a father I hope I may be allowed even to love in a less exalted, sublimer manner, but a greater : so the same affection doubles the satisfaction I have at my dear Sophy's return : I view your letter, my dear, with a joy not to be described but in the deepest silence, or expressed but in tears.

" From hence I forbear to enter upon the subject of this irruption, and shall only hint that you mistake it : and be it that you mistake it, yet as on that mistake you are so generous as to make this reparation, I believe you would with same filial goodness have made the like and more if you had been sensible in what tender part you gave the wound.

" But you have healed it. One word can wound where love is, and one word can heal where sincerity joins the affection. You have healed it at once, and since you do not yet see where the hurt was, I choose to leave it concealed, because, whatever I say, I would have you feel no grief.

" I would say more, but hope I need not. Let this tell you I am satisfied, and rejoice that you think your father's affection worth preserving. I am persuaded I shall never give you room to lessen your value for it, human frailty excepted. I shall conclude only with letting you see with what a sincere heart I was acting when this happened, and how little I thought of disobliging you or Mr. Forster ; and this I cannot do better than in sending you the letter (unopened) which I had written to Mr. Baker, and had had in my hand to give you. Let this speak for me, and believe it to be the very meaning and intent of my heart, and I am sure you will continue your affection to your father upon the very conviction of it. All the penance I shall enjoin you, on this whole affair, is that you will give Mr. Baker the letter, let him know when I wrote it, and desire him to lend me a kiss of peace to Sophi, and I'll pay it him in kind.

" My dearest Sophi, I am and ever shall be

" Your most affectionate father,

" D. F.

" (But very much tormented with pain ever since)."

About this time occurred that pleasing incident —the seeking-out of Defoe by Robert Dodsley, afterwards the eminent bookseller, with its slight resemblance to the subsequent and better-known meeting of Boswell and Dr. Johnson. Robert Dodsley, who was born in 1703, at Mansfield, Notts, and had for some years followed in London the occupation of a footman, had written a short poem called " Servitude," and the person to whom he ventured to show it made the observation that he wondered Dodsley had not "taken notice of a late pamphlet entitled ' Everybody's Business is Nobody's Business,' done by one who writes himself Andrew Moreton, Esq." Dodsley replied that he had never seen it, upon which the "person" observed that it would be worth Dodsley's while; so the book was bought. It took Dodsley very little trouble to find out that Andrew Moreton and the great Daniel Defoe were one and the same, for all the bookselling world, and a good many outside it, had for at least twelve months, as we have already observed, been aware to whom the pseudonym belonged; and, seeking the great man out, Dodsley begged his advice. Defoe was now in his seventieth year, worn with age and infirmities; Dodsley a sprightly young fellow of twenty-six. Ever ready to lend a helping hand to struggling merit, Defoe good-naturedly not only gave Dodsley the advice required, but revised the poem, and wrote for it a preface, an introduction, and a postscript. It is rather amusing to hear of a poem being consigned to Defoe's care for revision. Even in his palmy days Defoe sang oddly, and his note in his seventieth year was probably even less bird-like. However, the effusion was of such a nature that it couldn't very well be spoilt, so no harm was done; and Dodsley, who soon found out that his calling was not poetry, took up with something more profitable.

On September 1st, 1729, died in King Street, Carmarthen, in his fifty-eighth year, Defoe's great contemporary and fellow-penman, Sir Richard Steele.

CHAPTER XIV.

HIS LAST DAYS.

95.—THE "COMPLEAT ENGLISH GENTLEMAN."—NE'ER A BLOCKHEAD IN THE FAMILY BUT ME.

WORKS: 253.—The Compleat English Gentleman. Begun to be printed in 1729. Published in full, 1890.
254—An Effectual Scheme for the Immediate Preventing of Street Robberies. 1731.

AT the time Dodsley was putting to press his poem on "Servitude," Defoe was employed upon another important work, "The Compleat English Gentleman," the last book but one that he is known to have written. As a letter of Defoe's to Mr. J. Watts, of Wild Court, shows, Mr. Watts was about to begin to print it on September 10th, 1729. Defoe apologises for not having sent the manuscript before, and gives as his reason that he had been "exceedingly ill."

Only two or three pages of the book, however, were printed in Defoe's lifetime. After his death the manuscript found its way into the possession of the Baker family, and it is now in the British Museum. In 1890, one hundred and sixty years after the book was written, it was published for the first time by Mr. David Nutt, of London, who, with the editor, Karl D. Bülbring, M.A., Ph.D., and Mr. Francis B. Bickley, of the British Museum,

who performed the arduous task of making the copy
for the printer, deserve the hearty thanks of all
lovers of Defoe.

The manuscript, a small quarto of one hundred
and forty-two leaves, comprises, besides "The Compleat English Gentleman," a supplement to it
entitled "On Royall Education," which is also to
be published by Mr. Nutt.

The MS. is well preserved, but the close and
hurried writing, the indistinct characters, the great
number of emendations, additions, and deleted passages, the extensive use of contractions and of
shorthand and other abbreviations, and the uncommon, irregular, and often curious and faulty spelling,
make it difficult and sometimes perplexing to read.

Defoe uses a short thick horizontal stroke for
and, a similar one from left to right for *the*, o with
a horizontal stroke means either *which* or *what ;* if
crossed obliquely from right to left it means *particular ;* oo = *good* ; xdome = *Christendom ;* D, *Providence ;* a long stroke with an o = *notwithstanding ;*
and there are many other abbreviations. He puts very
few commas, capitals at random, and often begins a
sentence with a small letter.

The MS. is all in Defoe's own firm, small, and
close writing. As a rule only one side of the paper
is written on, but many insertions and notes are
added on the opposite page, and the book is
evidently not quite finished.

He commences by adopting the then current
acceptation of the word "gentleman" as a "person
born of some known or ancient family"; and adds,

"I have the honour to be ranked, by the direction of Providence, in the same class." He affects throughout the whole book to write as a gentleman for gentlemen.

The principal aim of the book is to make the gentry ashamed of their want of culture, and to induce them to give their children a better education. The distinction between the "man of polite learning" and the "mere scholar" is everywhere insisted upon. "The former," he says, "is a gentleman, and the latter a mere bookcase." These and other similar passages betray the bitter feeling left in his mind by the scornful treatment he had formerly received from University men.

The gentry of Defoe's time did not hold schoolmasters in much honour.

Says Defoe's sample of a mother :—

"Shall my son be sent to school to sit bareheaded and say a lesson to such a sorry diminutive rascal as that ; be brow-beaten and hectored and threatened with his authority, and stand in fear of his hand ! My son ! that a few years after he will be glad to cringe to, cap in hand, for a dinner ! No, indeed ; my son shall not go near him. Let the Latin and Greek go to the Devil. My son is a gentleman ; he shan't be under such a scoundrel as that."

The lament of a gentleman on account of his lack of learning is touching :—

"I have no learning. I was an unhappy dog : I was born to the estate, or else I had been taught ; but I must be a blockhead forsooth, because I was to be the gentleman. There's Jack, my youngest brother, they gave him Latin and Greek as much as he could carry upon his back, and the devil and all of other learning besides, and now he's a pickpocket—a lawyer, I would say ; and there's Will, my second brother, now he's commander of a man-of-war,

and knighted a'ready, and all by his being a mathematical dog.
There's ne'er a blockhead in the family but me."

Deficiency of education Defoe looked upon as a
disease, but he entered his "caveat against the
patient's being given over by his physicians." That
any man could in his heart of hearts be proud of
ignorance he refused to believe. "Was ever a
crooked man proud of a hump-back?" he asks,
"or a cripple proud of his wooden leg? Was ever
a man proud of the small-pox in his face, or vain
of being squint-eyed?"

An interesting book, except to students of Defoe,
"The Compleat English Gentleman" is not; but it
is instructive, and in parts amusing.

96.—IN HIDING AT GREENWICH.—*ET TU! BRUTE.*—THE LAST
TE DEUM.

In 1730, the machinations of his enemies proving
too powerful for him, Defoe, in order to avoid their
malice, first of all legally conveyed his property,
during the remainder of his life, to his son Daniel,
for the benefit of Mrs. Defoe and Hannah and
Henrietta, his two unmarried daughters, and then
went into hiding.

The person who delivered him the blow that
led him to take this course he describes as a
"wicked, perjur'd, and contemptible enemy"—probably, thinks Mr. Lee, Nathaniel Mist, who may
have made mischief between Defoe and the Government—perhaps by producing documents written by
Defoe when he was a spy in the Jacobite camp,

and managing to lead the Government to put a wrong construction on them.

This blow of Mist's, if it was Mist's, was bad enough, but the action of the son to whom Defoe had confided his property was still worse. Instead of proceeding according to his father's desires, Daniel Defoe, *fils*, converted the property to his own use, and thereby occasioned great inconvenience, if not suffering, to his mother and sisters. So much did the poor father feel this conduct, that his mind gave way; and it was whilst in this condition that he wrote the last letter of his that has been preserved, one of the most touching in the language. It was written to his son-in-law, Mr. Baker, from "About two miles from Greenwich, Kent," and is dated Tuesday, August 12th, 1730 :—

"DEAR MR. BAKER,—I have your very kind and affectionate letter of the first; but not come to my hand till the 10th; where it had been delayed I know not. As your kind manner, and kinder thought, from which it flows (for I take all you say to be, as I always believed you to be, sincere and Nathaniel-like, without guile), was a particular satisfaction to me; so the stop of a letter, however it happened, deprived me of that cordial too many days, considering how much I stood in need of it, to support a mind sinking under the weight of an affliction too heavy for my strength; and looking on myself as abandoned of every comfort, every friend, and every relative, except such only as are able to give me no assistance.

"I was sorry you should say at the beginning of your letter, you were debarred seeing me. Depend upon my sincerity for this: I am far from debarring you. On the contrary, it would be a greater comfort to me than any I now enjoy, that I could have your agreeable visits with safety, and could see both you and my dearest Sophia, could it be without giving her the grief of seeing her father *in tenebris* [in prison], and under the load of insupportable sorrow. I am sorry I must open my griefs so far as to tell her, it is not the blow I received from a wicked, perjur'd, and contemptible enemy, that has

broken in upon my spirit ; which, as she well knows, has carried me
on through greater disasters than these. But it has been the injustice, unkindness, and I must say, inhuman dealing of my own son
which has both ruined my family, and, in a word, has broken my
heart; and as I am at this time under a weight of very heavy illness,
which I think will be a fever, I take this occasion to vent my grief
in the breasts who I know will make a prudent use of it, and tell you,
that nothing but this has conquered or could conquer me. *Et tu!
Brute.* I depended upon him, I trusted him, I gave up my two dear
unprovided children into his hands ; but he has no compassion, and
suffers them and their poor dying mother to beg their bread at his
door, and to crave, as if it were an alms, what he is bound under
hand and seal, besides the most sacred promises, to supply them
with : himself, at the same time, living in a profusion of plenty. It
is too much for me. Excuse my infirmity. I can say no more : my
heart is too full. I only ask one thing of you as a dying request.
Stand by them when I am gone, and let them not be wronged while
he is able to do them right. Stand by them as a brother ; and if
you have anything within you owing to my memory, who have bestowed on you the best gift I have to give, let them not be injured
and trampled on by false pretences and unnatural reflections. I
hope they will want no help but that of comfort and council ; but
that they will indeed want, being too easy to be managed by words
and promises.

"It adds to my grief that it is so difficult to me to see you. I
am at a distance from London, in Kent, nor have I a lodging in
London, nor have I been at that place in the Old Bailey, since I
wrote you I was removed from it. At present I am weak, having
had some fits of a fever that have left me low. But those things
much more. I have not seen son or daughter, wife or child, many
weeks, and know not which way to see them. They dare not come
by water, and by land there is no coach, and I know not what to
do. It is not possible for me to come to Enfield, unless you could
find a retired lodging for me, where I might not be known, and
might have the comfort of seeing you both now and then; upon
such a circumstance, I could gladly give the days to solitude, to
have the comfort of half an hour now and then, with you both, for
two or three weeks. But just to come and look at you, and retire
immediately, 'tis a burden too heavy. The parting will be a price
beyond the enjoyment. I would say (I hope) with comfort, that
'tis yet well. I am so near my journey's end, and am hastening to

the place where the weary are at rest, and where the wicked cease
to trouble ; be it that the passage is rough, and the day stormy, by
what way soever He please to bring me to the end of it, I desire
to finish life with this temper of soul in all cases : *Te Deum
Laudamus.*

"I congratulate you on the occasion of your happy advance in
your employment. May all you do be prosperous, and all you meet
with, pleasant ; and may you both escape the tortures and troubles
of uneasie life. May you sail your dangerous voyage of life with a
forcing wind, and make the port of heaven without a storm.

"It adds to my grief that I must never see the pledge of your
mutual love—my little grandson.* Give him my blessing, and may
he be to you both your joy in youth, and your comfort in age, and
never add a sigh to your sorrow. But, alas ! that is not to be
expected. Kiss my dear Sophy once more for me ; and if I must
see her no more, tell her this from a father that loved her above all
his comforts to his last breath.

"Your unhappy

"D. F.

"*About two miles from Greenwich, Kent.*

"P.S.—I wrote you a letter some months ago, in answer to one
from you about selling the house ; but you never signified to me
whether you received it or not. I have not the policy of assurance ;
I suppose my wife or Hannah may have it.

"*Idem,* "D. F."

So runs the last preserved letter of Defoe's, written
eight months before his death, and in moments of the
greatest anguish—a letter sad in the extreme, but
brightened up with that grand refrain which we have
heard resounding in this situation and that situation
and all through his life—*Te Deum Laudamus.*

Mr. Minto regards this letter as a clever evasion
of Mr. Baker's attempts to make sure of his share of
the property to be left by Defoe. It is easy, he
says, to make out what the guilt of Defoe's son
consists in. Defoe had assigned certain property to

---

* David Erskine, Mr. Baker's eldest son, born that year, 1730.

the son to be held in trust for his wife and children. The son had not secured them in the enjoyment of this provision, but maintained them, and gave them words and promises, with which they were content, that he would continue to maintain them. It was this that Defoe called making them "beg their bread at his door, and crave as if it were an alms" the provision to which they were legally entitled.

"Baker had written to his father-in-law making inquiry about the securities for his wife's portion," Defoe in reply tells a long story of his son's treachery, and dismisses the inquiry about the securities in a postscript. He will not sell the house, and he does not know who has the policy of assurance. "One thing," continues Mr. Minto, "and one thing only shines clearly out of the obscurity in which Defoe's closing years are wrapt—his earnest desire to make provision for those members of his family who could not provide for themselves. The pursuit from which he was in hiding was in all probability the pursuit of creditors. His income must have been large from the year 1718 or thereabouts, till his utter loss of credit in journalism about the year 1726; but he may have had old debts. It is difficult to explain otherwise why he should have been at such pains, when he became prosperous, to assign property to his children."

97.—"DANIEL DEFOE, GENTLEMAN. TO TINDALL'S (LETHARGY)," 26TH APRIL, 1731.

At the time he wrote the letter to Baker of August 12, 1730, Defoe, with health broken down, and mind enfeebled, looked forward only to the grave. Of his history between that date and the date of his death we know only two facts. The first is that he returned to London and took lodgings in Ropemaker's Alley, Moorfields, then a pleasant part of the town, containing, to use the language of an advertisement of that day, very sweet and large houses, standing in the midst of pleasant gardens; the other that he published one more work—his last—the title-page of which runs: "An Effectual Scheme for the Immediate Preventing of Street Robberies, and suppressing the other disorders of the night; with a brief history of the night-houses, and an appendix relating to those sons of hell, called incendiaries. Humbly inscribed to the Right Honourable the Lord Mayor of London. London: Printed by J. Wilford, at the three Flower-de-Luces, behind the Chapter House in St. Paul's Churchyard. Price one shilling." This pamphlet, which is an 8vo of seventy-two pages, was published in 1731, but the day and month are not known.

His death occurred at his lodging in Ropemaker's Alley on the 26th of April, 1731, in the seventy-second year of his age; but concerning the circumstances of his last hours history is silent: he seems to have died as he had lived—alone. Ropemaker's Alley was hard by what is now Finsbury Pavement (there is still a Ropemaker Street), into which runs Fore Street, so he died only a few yards from the spot where he was born. The entry in the parish register runs as follows:

"Daniel Defoe, gentleman. To Tindall's (Lethargy)
April 26," which is so far satisfactory, for it
describes him, as he had always wished to be
described, as a gentleman. This entry, despite its
baldness, is sufficient to bring before us the lordly
air of the portrait in front of the "Jure Divino."·
"Daniel Defoe, gentleman": we see him gorgeous
in military accoutrements in the train of King
William; we note his laced coat and sword when
down on his luck at Bristol; we hear the rumble
of his "chariot" when "The True-born Englishman" and King William's favour had put money
into his purse again; we remember his seal with
coat of arms; his servants in livery; and we feel
that it was distinctly kind of fate to humour him
even after his decease, and to write him down in
the Cripplegate register as "Daniel Defoe, gentleman." Of the death of so distinguished a man,
however, we should have been glad to learn more
than that he died of a lethargy. The contemporary
press referred to his decease, but only briefly. "A
few days ago," says the *Daily Journal*, "died Mr.
Daniel Defoe, sen., a person well known for his
numerous and various writings." The *Grub Street
Journal* speaks of him as "The Great Author
deceased."

In 1737 Mr. Rivington, the publisher, issuing a
third edition of the "Plan of English Commerce,"
announces it to be "By the late ingenious Mr.
Daniel Defoe."

From the lodging in Ropemaker's Alley they
bore him to Tindall's burying-ground, now Bunhill

Fields. The entry in the register of Tindall's was evidently written by some ignoramus who had never even heard of the great man's name ; who didn't even trouble to spell it properly : " 1731, April 26, Mr. Dubow, Cripplegate."

THE OLD TOMBSTONE OF DANIEL DEFOE.

Over the remains of the literary giant they placed a mean stone with the following inscription :

DANIEL DEFOE
Author of
Robinson Crusoe
who died April 24 1731
in his 70th* year.

In 1858, when Mr. Chadwick visited the grave, the stone was lying " broken, and the inscriptions were obliterated." He was told that the lightning had done it.

* Doubtless an error. *See* § 2 and elsewhere.

z

In 1870 a more worthy monument was placed
on the spot, the result of an appeal, and an appropriate one, in the columns of the *Christian World*,
"to the boys and girls of England." The inscription is as follows :

(*On shaft*)

DANIEL DE-FOE
Born 1661
Died 1731
Author of
ROBINSON CRUSOE.

(*On pedestal*)

This monument is the result of an appeal,
in the " Christian World " newspaper,
to the boys and girls of England, for funds
to place a suitable memorial upon the grave
of
DANIEL DE-FOE
It represents the united contributions
of seventeen hundred persons.
Septr. 1870.

— —

The monument consists of an Egyptian or Cleo-
patric pillar, eight feet four inches at the base,
tapering to a height of seventeen feet, and is constructed out of two massive blocks of pure marble.
It is surrounded by a low iron railing.

On July 5th of the same year that Defoe died,
Mrs. Defoe, his widow, made her will according to
the powers of disposition given by the last will of
her brother, Samuel Tuffley. She gave to her
sons, Daniel and Benjamin, £1 each to buy a ring ;
and to her daughter, Maria Langley, one-third of
the profits from her three houses in White Cross

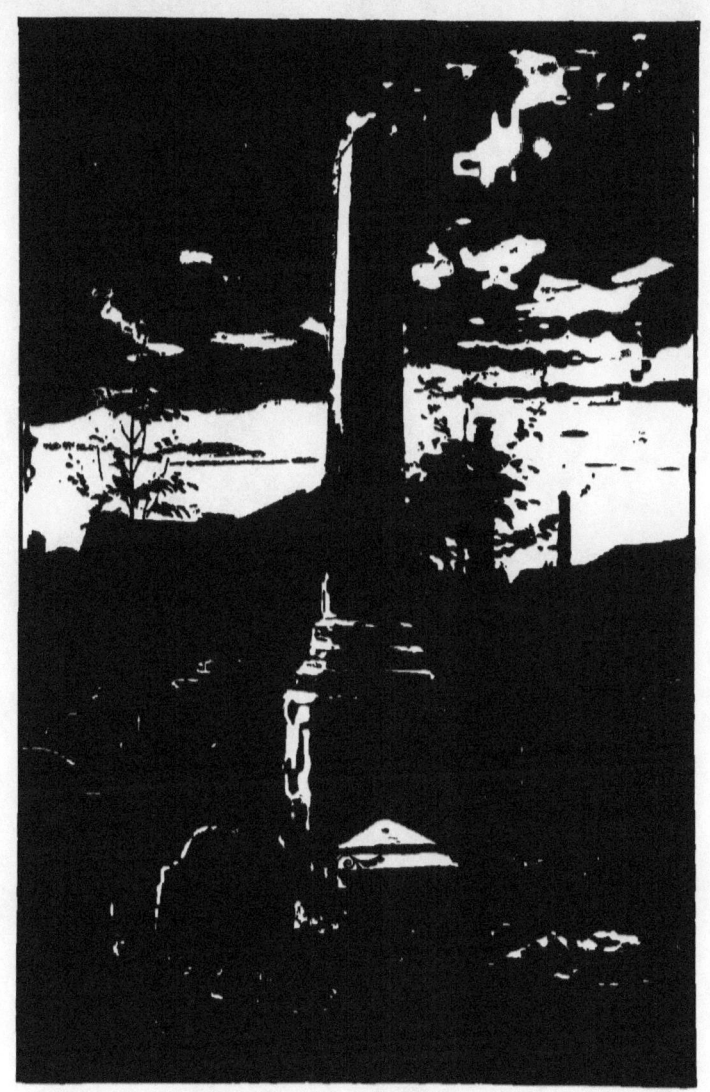

DEFOE'S TOMB IN BUNHILL FIELDS BURIAL-GROUND.

(*From photograph by York and Son, Notting Hill, W.*)

Alley, Moorfields, to be paid as long as the executors enjoyed the same. The remaining two-thirds
was left to her daughters and executors, Hannah
and Henrietta equally ; but if Maria died before
the houses were out of the possession of the
executors, her share was to go to the other
daughters and to their heirs. Her daughter Baker
was to have £1 equal with her brothers. To
Hannah and Henrietta, equally, and to their heirs,
was left a farm at Dagenham, Essex, then in the
possession of Henry Camping, tenant, as well as
all the rest of the estate, including all plate and
wearing apparel.

Mrs. Defoe died in December of the following
year, and was buried with her husband, whom she
had survived only a little over eighteen months.

In September, 1733, according to an entry in
the books of Doctors' Commons, letters of administration on the goods and chattels of Daniel Defoe
were "granted to Mary Brooks, widow, a creditrix,
after summoning in official form the next-of-kin to
appear."

Mr. Lee's explanation of this is that Mrs.
Brooks was the person with whom Defoe lodged
in Ropemaker's Alley, and that his children, to
whom he had left fortunes, were so abominably
mean, that they would not even settle the small
sum owing at the time of his death for lodgings ;
and that Mrs. Brooks, in order to recoup herself,
seized those of Defoe's goods that were in her house.

One is always curious regarding the library of
a man of genius, and Defoe's was a fine one.
About six months after his death, the greater part
was sold to Mr. Oliver Payne, the bookseller in
Round Court, in the Strand, who published a catalogue of it, together with a catalogue of the books
of the Rev. Philip Farewell, D.D. ; and advertised
the same in the *Daily Advertiser*, 13th November,
1731. The advertisement calls our author the "Ingenious Daniel De Foe, Gent., lately deceas'd" ;
and speaks of the library as "containing a curious
collection of Books relating to the History and Antiquities of divers Nations, particularly England, Scotland, and Ireland." Further on, the description says :
" N.B. Manuscripts. Also several hundred Curious,
Scarce Tracts on Parliamentary Affairs, Politicks,
Husbandry, Trade, Voyages, Natural History, Min-
erals, &c. Several Curious Prints, Medals, &c."
The books are stated to be "in very good condition, mostly well-bound, Gilt and Lettered." The
lowest price was marked in each book : they were
to be sold on the 15th of November, and afterward, until disposed of. Eight booksellers' shops,
etc., are specified, where catalogues were to be had
gratis.

Unfortunately, this catalogue has been searched
for in vain, and it is to be feared that no copy
exists. One of the books on Defoe's shelves, it is
pleasing to note, was Charles Lillie's collection* of

* Published in 1725.

"Original and Genuine Letters sent to the *Tatler* and *Spectator*," in two volumes, for on the subscription list are the names of "Mr. Daniel De Foe," and "Mr. Daniel De Foe, Junior."

99.—SUMMARY OF DEFOE'S WORK.

Of the life work of no author is a summary more needful than of that of Daniel Defoe. Careful as I have been in proceeding with these pages to bring into prominence his great works, to throw into the shade his minor ones, and to refer by only a passing word to those that the world has long lost all interest in, nevertheless the question may not unreasonably be asked: Which out of this mass of productions ought one to read—which are Defoe's masterpieces? Much as he might admire Defoe, no man on earth would attempt to read all Defoe's two hundred and fifty odd books. No one would be so insane. There are other authors to read beside Defoe, and the years of a man's life are only three-score and ten. Hence the need for a general summing up.

We will begin with his works of History, Biography, and Fiction, for on them hangs his chief claim to fame.

His two masterpieces are "Robinson Crusoe" and "Moll Flanders." These are not only the greatest works of Defoe, but among the greatest works the world has produced. In them his art is at its highest. By "Robinson Crusoe" is meant, of course, the original work, what we now call Part I.

In the second rank stand the fine " Memoirs of a Cavalier" and the inimitable " Journal of the Plague Year."

To the third belong " Captain Singleton," " Colonel Jack," and " Roxana."

He who reads these seven, together with " The Apparition of Mrs. Veal," will have the *crême de la crême* of Defoe ; and he will read every one, with the exception of portions of " Singleton" and " Roxana," without weariness. Most, he will devour with passionate delight.

For the busy man of the world this is enough ; but the student, or any who has more time on his hands, should read also " The Complete English Tradesman," " Robinson Crusoe," Parts II. and III., and " The Tours Through Britain " ; and he should skim " The History of the Devil," " The System of Magic," " The Use and Abuse," " The Reality of Apparitions," " Duncan Campbell," " Dickory Cronke," " The Family Instructor," " Religious Courtship," and " The Essay on Projects," but in all these, though there is abundance of toothsome and nutritious food, there is also a large quantity of chaff.

Of Defoe's poetry, the man of the world need not read any. The student even need concern himself with nothing except " The True-born Englishman."

The best of Defoe's political pamphlets are " The Shortest Way," " An Argument showing that a Standing Army, etc.," and the three tracts dealt with in § 44 ; but much as these productions are praised, it would be untrue to say that at the present day they

are extensively read. Some of them are contained in
vol. iv. of the " Pocket Library of English Literature,"
published by Percival and Co.

100.—DEFOE'S DESCENDANTS.

At Defoe's death in 1731, six of his children were
living : Hannah, who seems to have been the eldest,
Daniel, Benjamin, Maria (married to a Mr. Langley),
Henrietta, and Sophia (married to Henry Baker).

(1).—_Hannah_, who died single in 1759 (April 25),
and is buried at Wimborne, Dorset. She left her
property to her nephew, John Burton.

(2).—_Daniel_, born probably about 1785. We
know that he was not of age in 1705. He seems
to have married about 1707, for in the Clerkenwell
registers is the entry, " January 1, 1708-9, Daniel, son
of Daniel De Foe, and Dorothy his wife." His first
wife must have died rather young, for, as we have
seen, in 1720, he married Mary Webb. The child
Daniel must also have died young, for in 1724 we
read of another Daniel, " an infant and nursed child,"
who was buried at Hackney, June 14, 1724. Thus
two children of Daniel Defoe the second were named
Daniel, and both died young.

Second Generation.—A third child, _Samuel_, born
about 1730, was on April 1st, 1743, put apprentice
to a calico-printer, in London. His apprenticeship
indentures are in my possession. He afterwards
followed the business upon his own account. In the
American war he lost a fortune. He died at Pedlar's
Acre in November, 1783, and was buried in Lambeth

Churchyard. By his first wife, who kept the Royal Inn at West Ham, in Essex, he had three sons, Samuel (died young), Richard, bred a carpenter, and Joseph ; and by his second wife one son, James, and three daughters.

Third Generation. — *James*, a box-maker and undertaker, in Hungerford Market, had fourteen or fifteen children, six of whom are buried in the churchyard of St. Martin's-in-the-Fields.

Fourth Generation.—Two of the children of James Defoe are still living, namely, *James William* (of Bishop's Stortford) and *Mary*, the latter of whom is in enjoyment of a small government pension. With this lady, who is now sixty-six years of age, I have long had the pleasure of being personally acquainted, and she has helped me much in getting material for this book. For James William Defoe, who is in the receipt of parish relief, I in 1892, as stated in the preface of this book, started an assistance fund. It is still open.

Fifth Generation.—James William has a large family of daughters but only one son, *Daniel*, a young man of eighteen. He is now (1894) an apprentice at sea, "and," continued his aunt, as she finished the story of the family, "we hope some day to see him ship-captain," a hope, need it be said, that we heartily endorse.

(3).—*Benjamin Norton*, married in 1718 to Hannah Coates of Norwich. They had seventeen children, the eldest of whom, Benjamin, was baptised at Norwich, 6th June, 1719. Mrs. Defoe "was brought from Hackney, and buried in Bunhill Fields," in

1737. The letters of Benjamin Defoe, in 1739, to the Earl of Newcastle, show that he was then in great poverty. He seems to have inherited a little of his father's genius, and all his father's faults. Subsequently he emigrated to Carolina. Only three out of his seventeen children were living in 1737. Their descendants are scattered about the earth. One cropped up in a Melbourne post-office a year or two back, but nothing could be got out of him except that he hugged the tradition that he was descended from the great Daniel.

According to a ridiculous scandal of the time, Benjamin Norton Defoe was the son of Daniel Defoe and an oyster-wench. Savage, in the Preface to his "Author to be let," is primarily responsible for propagating this precious legend; and Pope, whom Benjamin Defoe had abused in the *Flying Post*, patted it into rhyme and inserted it in his "Dunciad."

> "Norton, from Daniel and Ostrœa sprung,
>   Blest with his father's front and mother's tongue."

Among Benjamin Defoe's works were: "A Compleat English Dictionary" (1735), the "Memoirs of the Princes of the House of Orange," and "The Life of Alderman Barber."

(4).—*Maria*, married to a Mr. Langley.

(5).—*Henrietta*, married, subsequent to her father's death, to John Boston of Much-Hadham, Herts. She died March 5th, 1760, and was buried at Wimborne, Dorset. John Boston, her son, inherited the property of his aunt, Hannah Defoe. John's son William died at sea in 1784, aged fifteen.

(6).—*Sophia* married to Henry Baker. She died
in 1772, at the age of seventy-one; her husband
died in November, 1774, leaving £20,000 to his
son. They were buried in St. Clement Danes,
Strand, but there is no memorial to them. There
ought to be a memorial, for Baker left a name that
will ever be honoured in the scientific world; and
I would suggest, as an accompaniment to its
wording, the sensible epitaph which he wrote for
himself :—

> " Of all my cares and all my pains
> If aught commendable remains
> Be that my epitaph ; if not,
> May I for ever be forgot."

By his wife Sophia, Henry Baker had two sons:
David Erskine (1730–1767), who died without issue,
and Henry (1734–1776). Henry left an only son,
William (1762–1828), who became Rector of Lyndon
and South Luffenham. The Rev. William Baker
left issue Henry Defoe Baker (Vicar of Greetham,
Rutland) and William Baker, M.D. (died, 1850).
The eldest son of Henry Defoe Baker, the Rev.
Henry Defoe Baker, is now (1894) Rector of
Thruxton, Hants; the eldest son of Dr. William
Baker is the Rev. William Defoe Baker, now Rector
of Welton, Linc.

APPENDIX A.

SOME OF THE EVENTS CONNECTED WITH DEFOE AND
HIS WORKS, FROM 1733 TO THE PRESENT YEAR 1894.

1733.—Sept. 7 : Administration of the goods, etc., of Daniel Defoe. Granted to Mary Brooke, widow, principal creditrix. Dec. 11 : Note from Benjamin Norton Defoe (British Museum).

1736.—In this year Daniel Defoe, *fils*, was one of nine candidates for the office of secretary to the Million Bank, vacant through the death, by suicide, of Mr. Robert Harle. Twenty directors voted, the result being that Mr. Nathaniel Neal was elected by a majority of one vote (ten to nine) over Mr. George Wallis. "Mr. Daniel Defoe" appears to have been in the good graces of one director only, as he received but a single vote.

1737.—A Mrs. Deffoe buried in Bunhill Fields. This was Hannah Coates, wife of Benjamin Defoe. [*See* 1739.]

1738.—May 12 : Letter from Daniel Defoe, *fils*, to his cousin Miss Cornwall. Written in London. His age was about 53. Oct. 2 : Benjamin Defoe writes to Duke of Newcastle. He has had seventeen children in less than seventeen years. Says his wife died "last Christmas."

1739.—Nov. 11 : Letter of Benjamin Norton Defoe to Duke of Newcastle. Nov. 24 : Another of ditto to ditto. He is in great poverty, and speaks of having been recently connected with "*The Craftsman*." He expresses a desire to serve the Government, therefore he was then in England. His age was about 52.

1744.—The Apprenticeship Indenture of Samuel Defoe, Defoe's grandson, signed. It runs :—"This Indenture Witnesseth, that Samuell Deffoe doth put himself apprentice to William Walker, Callicoe printer of Westham, in the county of Essex, to learn his Art, and with him after the manner of an apprentice, to serve from the first day of Aprill last past 1744 unto the full end and term of Six years from thence following, etc., etc. . . . . And the said Master in considera- tion of Thirty pounds being the money given with ye said apprentice to instruct, etc., etc." The Indenture is signed April 19th, in the 18th year of George II. by 'S. Deffoe.' Witnesses—Wm. Sale, Robert Browne." Sideways is written (ink now very indistinct) "1st April, 1743, to serve by his Indenture 7 years, 1750." He had served one year before this indenture was made.
This interesting relic is in my possession. It was given to me by Mr. James William Defoe in 1892.

1747.—Biographia Britannica. Life of Defoe by Dr. Towers.

1761.—Henrietta (Defoe's daughter), wife of John Burton, died (Mar. 5).

1762.—Sophia, wife of Henry Baker, died. Buried at St. Mary-le-Strand. She was Defoe's youngest daughter.

1765-6.—The church of Presbyterians, founded by Defoe, erected the "Defoe Presbyterian chapel" at Tooting, Surrey.

1786.—Life of Defoe by George Chalmers.

1820.—Issue of a number of Defoe's works with Chalmers's Life.

1830.—Life and Times of Defoe by Walter Wilson. 3 vols.

1831.—Robinson Crusoe, with Life of Defoe by Roscoe.

1840.—"Defoe's Works," with Memoir by William Hazlitt.   3 vols., 1840–43.

1840-41.—"Novels and Miscellaneous Works of Defoe."   20 vols.   Oxford.

1858.—Historical and Biographical Essays, by John Forster.   Vol. II.

1859.—Life of Defoe by William Chadwick.

1869.—"Daniel Defoe: his life, and recently discovered writings," by William Lee, 3 vols. (Vol i., the life ; vols. ii. and iii., the writings.)

1870.—September.   A monument to Defoe, placed over his grave, was unveiled in Bunhill Fields, by Mr. Charles Reed, M.P., in the presence of a great concourse of people.   It was the gift of the subscribers of *The Christian World*.

1892.—A Building fund started for the erection of a Defoe Presbyterian Church at Tooting for the congregation that formerly worshipped at the Defoe Presbyterian Chapel.   Pastor, Rev. William Anderson, D.D., Defoe Manse, Tooting, London, S.W.

APPENDIX B.

LIST OF THE LETTERS OF DEFOE.

To whom Written.	Date.	Where to be Found.
John Fransham	1704–1707 ...	*Notes and Queries*, April 3 and April 10, 1875.
Lord Halifax	1705, April 5	Lee, p. 106.
Do.	1705, July 16	Lee, p. 114.
Do.	1705... ...	Lee, p. 117.
Harley	1705, Aug.	Wilson ii., p. 358.
Lord Wharton	1710, April 7	Wilson iii., p. 121.
Dyer	1710, June 17	Wilson iii., p. 185.
Keimer	(No date) ...	*Notes and Queries*, May 8, 1869.
Earl of Buchan	1711, May 29	*Notes and Queries*, Jan. 26, 1884.
De la Faye	1718, April 12	Lee, Introduction.
Do.	1718, April 26	*Id.*
Do.	1718, May 10	*Id.*
Do.	1718, May 23	*Id.*
Do.	1718, June 4	*Id.*
Do.	1718, June 13	*Id.*
Henry Baker	1728, Jan. 9	Unpublished. Appendix.
Do.	1728, Jan. 21	Do. Do.
Do.	1728, Jan. 25	Do. § 92.
Do.	1728, Aug. 23	Do. Appendix.
Do.	1728, Aug. 27	Do. Do.
Do.	1728, Sept. 9	Do. Do.
Do.	1729, April	Do. Do.
Sophia Defoe	1729, June 9	Do. § 94.
Watts the Printer	1729, Sept. 10	Wilson iii.
Henry Baker	1730, Aug. 12	§ 96.

Of the eight unpublished letters of Defoe, one is given in § 92 and one in § 94. The following are the other six—all of which refer to the dowry squabble:—

(1.)

"Newington, January 9th, 1728.

"SIR,—I must acknowledge I am very Sorry we should break at last upon a Point so very nice and yet so important as This, and I am the more concerned because I think we have been both wrong in omitting a more early Debate about it.

"After the Frankness with which I at first treated your proposal, and the Kindness with which I always treated you personally, I should be very sorry to offer anything now that should seem less kind than at first. Nor can I see the least room to have it thought so; but at the same time that I desire to be thought kind, you will not, I hope, offer anything that shall look like unkind.

"The Thing proposed, I confess, is in my Opinion consistent not wth kindness only, but with Justice. And, indeed, Justice to the rest of my little Family commands it from Me: It is a little hard to put a Father to express himself upon it, but at the same time that You argue your Case as an Husband, with what Horror (excuse the Word) must I suppose the case before I can argue upon it as a Father. I must suppose My Child lost, dead, childless. Mr. Baker, who now I value and shall (before that) say I value and love, lost to me; the Relation sunk out of Nature and embarked perhaps in another Family, how can I look on the rest of my Children disinherited and impoverisht by the double Loss of their Sister and their Fortune! Make the Case your own if that be possible.

"I can say no more! 'tis my Weakness: I would hope for long Life and a Family between you. God in his mercy grant it if you come together: but how can You (and I much less) enter upon the melancholy and mornful Negative and suppose me deprived doubly and made miserable, and yourself supported at the expence of the Family.

"Besides what Necessity as well as what Justice to lay such a dead weight always on a Father's Thoughts ready to sink with hut the mention of it.

"If you live and encrease, the Thing is at an end; if not, the Occasion is at least lessened. I hope the odds is in your Favour: may it be to you and yours for ever; and if there is so apparent Hopes, why should you lay so much more weight on the melancholy part: I run the Risque Equally and indeed much more than you, for upon the whole you run no Risque at all. If you lose your Wife you have all your own with its encrease, and I can not call it a maintaining her in the mean time; if she will not more than merit her maintenance, She will be a worse Wife than I would wish Mr. Baker to have, and much worse than I hope she will make.

"I am very sorry my Family circumstances make it needful to me to say this, but as it is nothing but what is consistent with my first offer, and with the Nature of the Thing customary in like Cases, and which I yielded to myself on the like occasion, I can not be chargeable with taking the least step aside, from what I proposed and what you had accepted.

"I am, with the same kindness and sincerity as before,

"Y^r. Friend affectionately,

"D. F.

"P.S.—Pray reflect on the risque on my Side if my Child should drop off in a year or two or less, as often happens. The very Thought afflicts me so I cannot go on writing upon it. Suppose again you should be taken from her in a few Years before you had encreased sufficiently for the support of a Family which may be left: Where would that dead weight lye?

"God avert these melancholy Things! but they are all possible."

The following was written after Baker had worried Defoe to try to obtain another lease for the house at Newington (*see* p. 360):—

(2.)

"*January* 21*st*, 1728.

"SIR,—I believe you will now be convinced that what I suggested in this affair was right Judged, tho as I was not sure you might then think me mistaken. The sending me to Sutton, to mend a title which I have not the least reason to think precarious, has had the effect I expected, and put vain conceits in his head of his power, which, however, I see no weight in, puff him up to refuse what I have really no occasion to ask; and you will see, if you please to judge impartially, that I was not wrong when I said it was hard upon me, and without cause, too.

"However, nothing shall move me to any dispute with Mr. Baker, or lessen my respect for him, and for that reason circumstances allow me not to offer anything that he thinks fit to accept (I can only say I am sorry for it), I shall make no remark upon it here. If you please to let my lease be returned either to my daughter or to my son in Finch Lane I shall leave your receipt with either of them as you shall direct.

"I am,

"Sir, Your very Humble servant,

"Dr Foe."

Mr. Baker's Answer.

"Sir,—I never supposed you could force Sutton, but presumed I might without offence desire your endeavours towards another lease. You have tried, it seems, in vain ; if then it can't be done, we must make the best of things without it. I never shall expect impossibilities, but indeed wondered at your unwillingness to attempt it, but I never intended it as a *sine qua non.* To have the house is not my wish, and if you please, as yourself proposed, to secure the yearly payments, I shall not only be well contented, but be in the sincerest (manner ?)

"Your Most obliged

"Humble servant."

Defoe now sends his ultimatum :—

(3.)

"*London, August 23rd, 1728.*

"I cannot but say I am concerned on many Accounts, to see an Affair of this Nature hang thus in suspence ; and you will not take it ill that I add, It is more than I expected, and that it is highly reasonable it should be brought to an Issue.

"As I said to you at first, that if you design'd to ask my Daughter, you must take her as I could give her, so I think it is far from being out of the Way to repeat it : adding with it that I also think I have endeavoured to shew the Respect I profess'd for you, by making as good proposals as my affairs will admit.

"The first Proposal you have rejected, and also a second ; You and I will no more debate the Reasons of it, because whether I think it fair or kind or otherwise, Yet as I resolve to take nothing ill from You, so I choose to say no more of it, I think my Offer was fully consistent with my first proposal as it is with my Ability.

"You have since plac'd the Affair in another Situation demanding [word or sum scratched out] down, which I said I would consider of. Many intervening Accidents have made the Time much longer than I intended to take in giving my Answer. I have now drawn it up and sent it herewith to my Daughter, to show you : I have only to add, that as this is my *Ultimatum,* not that I shall but that I can make an Offer of, I intreat, that you will consider of it so effectually, that your answer may put an end to the whole affair, one way or other ; which I think highly necessary, as well for yourself, who have much trouble in it, as for my child, who I am too heartily concerned for to think it proper to leave it longer in Suspence.

"I am (and shall be which way soever this matter may issue) always

"Your sincere Friend

"and Servant."

Mr. D. F.'s Proposal.

"*August 23rd, 1728.*

"Mr. B—r's last Demand   as of [   ]* down, and my Return is thus—

"My Affairs do not permit me to advance the money presently, but I offer this as Equivalent.

* Scratched out.

"1. That I will pay [   ]* at a certain Term, or sooner if it may be.
"2. That till it be paid I will pay the Interest annually at £4 per cent., which is the ordinary Interest of Money.
"3. That in Case of Mortality, Hannah will oblige herself to pay the [   ]* out of the Essex Estate, which shall be legally vested in her to enable her to perform it, and to come immediately upon my Decease into her Hands.
"This I take to be paying the Money down, seeing Mr. B—r does not pretend to want the Money otherwise than to put it out to Interest."

Now they haggle as to whether four per cent. or five per cent. shall be paid upon Sophia's dowry as long as it remains in Defoe's hands. (*See* p. 563)

(4.)

"*Newington, August 27th,* 1728.

"S^{R.}—I am sorry there should be any manner of room for an objection when we are so near a Conclusion of an Affair like this. I should be very uneasy when I give you a Gift of so much value (and I hope I do not over rate her neither), there should be any reserve among us that should leave the least room for un-kindness or so much as thinking of unkindness, no, not so much as of the Word.

"But there is a Family Reason why I am tyed down to the words of four per cent., and I cannot think Mr. Baker should dispute so small a matter with me, after I tell him so (viz.) that I am so tyed down. I can, I believe, many ways make him up the little sum of [   ]* a year, and when I tell you thus, under my Hand, that I shall think myself obliged to do it *durante vita*, I shall add that I shall think myself more obliged to do so, than if you had it under hand and seal.

"But if you are not willing to trust me on my Parols, for so small a sum and that according to the great Treaties abroad there must be a seeret Article in our Negotiations : I say if it must be so, I would fain put myself in a Condition to deny you nothing which you can ask, believing you will ask nothing of me which I ought to deny.

"When you speak of a Child's Fortune, which I own you do very modestly, you must give me leave to say only this, you must accept of this in bar of my Claim from the City Customs, and I doubt you will have too much Reason, seeing I can hardly hope to do equally for all the rest as I shall for my dear Sophia ; but after that, you shall only allow me to say, and that you shall depend upon, whatever it shall please God to bless me with more shall have a deeper share in it, and you need do no more than remem-ber that she is, ever was, and ever will be, my dearest *and* best beloved. And let me add again I hope you will take it for a Mark of my Singular Esteem, and Affectionate Concern for you, that I thus give her to you, and that I say too, if I could give her much more it should be to you with the same affection.

"Yours without Flattery,
"D. F."

As further security for the dowry, Baker wants Defoe to mortgage the Essex property.● Defoe declines.

(5.)

"*Newington, September 9th,* 1728.

"I am very Sorry to hear that Mr. Forster should say I have not acted with Honour in this Affair. I must ask your Leave to think quite otherwise, and that I am not well used at all.

"From the beginning, I said, both to you and Mr. Forster, that I would never Mortgage the Triffle (*sic*) I have in Essex for the Security of this Affair. I did not speak ambiguously in it at all, but in Words at length and explicit such as were capable of no other meaning, so as an honest Man ought always to speak.

"Mr. Forster concludes from hence, that it is already Mortgaged, which is something hard. I told him it was at first indeed engaged for £200, which is since paid off. ·
But that I may more fully explain it, if it must be so, the Case is this and

* Scratched out.

nothing else (viz.), that being arrived to an Age when, if ever it is needful to Settle what little I have among my Children, this is so settled and so engaged and no otherwise, and I cannot think it a Breach of Honour, that I do not think it proper to expose, no, not to my own Children, all the particulars of my Family Settlet. while I am still living; and as this is the only reason, and that no Mortgage or other Engagement is made on the Estate but this, and yet, that this binds me not to make any other Disposition of it, I cannot see how I act dishononrably, and I think ought not to be told so. I am sorry I am obliged to say this, but since this is Truth, and that the Circumstances oblige me to speak it, I hope you will excuse my Freedom. I shall still be with respect as before,

"Your humble Servant,

"D. F."

(6.)

No date. Apparently just before the marriage of Mr. Baker, i.e., April, 1729.

(See pp. 369-370.)

"SIR,—I have perused the writing and see nothing amiss with it, if you think the security against the lost writings is sufficient, but I thought Mr. Curryer, in whose possession they were left and by whom they are lost (or by persons intrusted by him), should have given something under his hand obliging him to deliver up the old deed and Assignment to be cancelled, if it should come to his hand, and should have indemnified D. F. from all Claims or pretensions which might hereafter be made by any person on the foot (?) of those writings, nothing of which is mentioned in this deed.

"There is a small objection which occurs to me against a clause in the draft of the marriage contract which I perused but hastily and in disorder that night on account of our family being so discomposed, I suppose it is not too late. The payment of the £200 is made to take place within a month after my decease, which is sooner than can be supposed executors can be in readiness after such a revolution in the family. Such things have usually twelve months time allowed, and as my effects will be much abroad I think it cannot be expected in less. This is a matter so reasonable that I hope you cannot scruple the alteration.

"I am your Friend and servant,

"Friday night.'

"DEFOE."

A A

APPENDIX C.

THE MEETING OF DEFOE AND SELKIRK.

In connection with the meeting of Selkirk and Defoe, mentioned in § 42, I received from Mr. Richard Champion Rawlins two statements from separate and original sources. These were sent to Mr. Hugh Owen, the antiquary, by the late Francis Fry, who, like Mr. Owen, was an enthusiastic and painstaking member of the Society of Antiquaries.

The first statement consists of an undated letter to the Editor of the *Bristol Mirror*, and runs as follows :—

"SIR,—Have accidentally taken up an old paper of yours, Oct. 20, 1849. I found it stated in a very interesting account of the *Duke* and *Duchess* Privateers that my grandfather, Alderman Harford, was the first person who proved that 'Defoe composed "Robinson Crusoe" from papers given him by Alex. Selkirk, and that you would be glad of any further information on the subject.' I have much pleasure in confirming the account there given, having often heard my father say 'that an old lady, Mrs. Daniel, a daughter of the celebrated Major Wade, told my grandfather that Selkirk had informed her that he had placed his papers in Defoe's hands.' My grandfather purchased many of the things which were sold on the return of the Duke and Duchess with the rich prize of the Manilla Ship (mentioned by Woodes Rogers in his account of the voyage in which Selkirk was found on the Island of Juan Fernandez. They are now in my possession, and consist principally of very handsome china, which was given to the Queen of Spain, with curious articles in tortoise shell and Indian ink.

"Captain Rogers, who commanded the *Duke* and *Duchess*, lived at Frenchay in the house near the residence of Mrs. Brice.

"Frenchay."   "H. C. HARFORD."

The preceding, as stated, has been published, but the following, which belongs to a date fifteen years previous, has not been published. It is in the handwriting of Francis Fry, and runs as follows :—

"Mem^m. after a conversation with W. P. Lunell, 5th month, 1834.

"Joseph Beck, the father of Joseph, the husband of the well known Mary Beck, built the house at Frenchay. The wife of the elder Joseph Beck, survived him. She had three husbands, Jos. Beck, Coysgarne, and lastly Daniells, This Mrs. Daniells lived at a corner house in James Square, Bristol, the corner originally opposite the entrance from the Barton. Here she was visited by Alexander Selkirk, then recently returned from his solitary abode in the Island of Juan Fernandez. There also she was accustomed to entertain Daniel De Foe. It was in her house that Selkirk gave De Foe an account of his adventures, etc., from which De Foe drew up a narrative of Selkirk which was published. Many years later Defoe wrote and published his romance of Robinson Crusoe, the notion of which was suggested by Selkirk's narrative. The Romance speedily supplanted the genuine work, and while the existence of the latter is now hardly known the former is still among the most popular of books.

"A gentleman (name forgotten) who was accustomed to meet Selkirk at Mrs. Daniells' sent a paper to the *Gentleman's Magazine* containing a very specific account of what he heard from him.

"W. P. Lunell died 30 or 40 years since. His sons are living. The foregoing has been copied by some few but never published just as here given. Who the conversation was with I do not know, but it is quite authentic. It works in with J. Harford's account, and the gentleman alluded to as sending to the *Gent. Mag.* was no doubt Joseph Harford. Use this as you like as original,

"Cotham, 1868."   "(Sd.) FRANCIS FRY."

"The conversation as copied was given to me by a friend of mine who knew all the parties."

PAGE FROM "THE COMPLEAT ENGLISH GENTLEMAN."

PAGE FROM "THE COMPLEAT ENGLISH GENTLEMAN."

APPENDIX D.

MR. LEE'S LIST OF DANIEL DEFOE'S WORKS, WITH A FEW ALTERATIONS BY THE AUTHOR.

NOTE.—*The Works underlined are in verse.*

1.—Tract on the Turks. (Lost.) 1683.

2.—A *New Discovery* of an *Old Intreague*. A Satyr level'd at *Treachery* and *Ambition:* Calculated to the Nativity of the Rapparee Plott, and the Modesty of of the Jacobite Clergy. Designed by Way of Conviction to the 117 Petitioners, and for the Benefit of those that Study the Mathematicks, &c. Printed in the Year 1691. (4to. pp. 36.) 1691.

3.—The *Englishman's Choice*, and *True Interest:* In a Vigorous *Prosecution* of the *War* against *France* and Serving *K. William* and *Q. Mary*, and acknowledging their Right. London. Printed in the Year 1694. (4to. pp. 32.) 1694.

4.—The *Character* of the late *Dr. Samuel Annesley*, by Way of Elegy. (Folio.) 1697.

5.—Some *Reflections* on a Pamphlet lately Published, entitled, "An Argument showing that a Standing Army is Inconsistent with a Free Government, and absolutely Destructive to the Constitution of the English Monarchy." London. Printed for *E. Whitlock*, 1697. (4to. pp. 28.) 1st Edition, 1697.—(4to. pp. 28.) 2nd Edition, 1697.

6.—An *Enquiry* into the *Occasional Conformity* of *Dissenters* in Cases of Preferment. With a *Preface* to the *Lord Mayor*, Occasioned by his carrying the *Sword* to a *Conventicle*. London. Printed Anno Dom. 1697. (4to. 4 leaves & 28 pages.) 25 Jan. 1698.

7.—An *Essay* upon *Projects*. London. Printed by *R. R.* for *Tho. Cockerill*, at the Corner of Warwick Lane, 1697. (8vo. Title, pp. xiv & 336.) 1st Edition, 29 May, 1698.—With a New Title, 2nd Edition, 23 May, 1702.

8.—The *Poor Man's Plea*, in Relation to all the *Proclamations, Declarations, Acts* of *Parliament*, &c., which have been or shall be made or published for a Reformation of Manners, and suppressing Immorality in the Nation. London. Printed in the Year 1698. (4to. 2 leaves, pp. 31.) 1st Edition, 31 Mar. 1698.— 2nd Edition, 24 May, 1698.—3rd Edition, 26 Mar. 1700.

9.—An *Argument* showing that a *Standing Army*, with *Consent of Parliament*, is not *Inconsistent* with a *Free Government*. London. *E. Whitlock*. (4to. 2 leaves & pp. 26.) 1698.

10.—The *Pacificator*, a Poem. London. Sold by J. Nutt near Stationers' Hall. Folio. (Title & pp. 14.) 20 Feb. 1700.

11.—*The Two Great Questions Consider'd.* I. What the French King will do, with respect to the Spanish Monarchy. II. What Measures the English ought to Take. London. Printed in the Year 1700. (4to. 2 leaves & pp. 28.) 15 Nov. 1700.

12.—An Enquiry into the Occasional Conformity of Dissenters in Cases of Preferment. With a Preface to Mr. How. London. Printed, Anno Dom. 1701. 20 Nov. 1700.

13.—The *Two Great Questions further Consider'd.* With some Reply to the Remarks. *Non licet hominem Muliebriter Rixari.* London. (4to.) 2 Dec. 1700.

14.—The *Six* distinguishing *Characters* of a *Parliament Man ;* address'd to the good People of England. London. Printed in the Year 1700. (4to. 2 leaves & pp. 22.) 4 Jan. 1701.

15.—The *Danger* of the *Protestant Religion* Considered, from the present *Prospect* of a *Religious War in Europe.* Printed in the Year 1701. (4to.) 9 Jan. 1701.

16.—The *True-Born Englishman.* A Satyr. Printed in the Year 1700. (4to. 2 leaves & pp. 71.) 1st Edition, Jan. 1701.—With an Explanatory Preface. (4to. 5 leaves & pp. 60.) 9th Edition, 1701.—" A *New Edition* Neatly Printed on a Superfine Paper with an Elzevir Letter *very much enlarged* of the *True-Born Englishman.* Just Published. London. J. Roberts. (8vo. .) With a New Preface." 22 March, 1716.—" A *Neat* and *Correct Edition* (on an Elzevir Letter) of the True-Born Englishman. A Satyr. To which is prefixed a *New Preface* by the Author, adapted to the Present Reign. Price 6d." 9 Oct. 1719. —" A *Neat Pocket Edition* (Corrected and *Enlarged* by the Author) of the *True-Born Englishman.* A Satyr. Price 6d." 2 Nov. 1721.

17.—*Considerations* upon *Corrupt Elections of Members* to serve in *Parliament.* London. Printed in the Year 1701. (4to. 2 leaves & pp. 24.) Jan. 1701.

18.—The *Freeholders Plea* against *Stock-Jobbing Elections* of *Parliament-Men.* London. Printed in the Year 1701. (4to. 2 leaves & pp. 27.) 1st Edition, 23 Jan. 1701.—2nd Edition, 4 Feb. 1701.

19.—A *Letter* to Mr. *How* by Way of Reply to his Observations on the *Preface* to the Enquiry into the *Occasional Conformity of Dissenters* in Case of *Preferment.* By the *Author of the Preface* and the *Enquiry.* Printed 1701. By *A. Baldwin* in Warwick Lane. 24 Jan. 1701.

20.—The *Villainy* of *Stock-Jobbers* detected, and the Causes of the late Run upon the Bank and Bankers Discovered and Considered. London. Printed in the Year 1701. 1st Edition, 11th Feb. 1701.—(4to. Title & pp. 26.) 2nd Edition, 17 Feb. 1701.

21.—The *Succession* to the *Crown of England Considered.* London. Printed in the Year 1701. (4to. pp. 38.) About 1 March, 1701.

22.—Legion's Memorial to the House of Commons (2 leaves quarto) presented. 14 May, 1701.

23.—The *History* of the *Kentish Petition. London. Printed* in the Year 1701. (4to. Title & Preface 3 leaves & pp. 25.) August, 1701.

24.—The *Present State* of *Jacobitism* Considered, in two *Queries.* I. What Measures the *French King* will take with respect to the *Person* and *Title* of the *P. P. of Wales?* II. What the *Jacobites* in *England* ought to do on the same *Account?* London. *A. Baldwin.* (4to. Title & Preface 3 leaves, pp. 22.) Before Oct. 1701.

25.—*Reasons* against a *War* with *France ;* or, an Argument shewing that the *French King's* Owning the *Prince of Wales* as King of *England, Scotland,* and *Ireland,* is no Sufficient Ground of a *War.* London. Printed in the Year 1701. (4to. Title & pp. 30.) October, 1701.

26.—The *Original Power* of the *Collective Body* of the *People* of *England,* *Examined* and *Asserted.* With a double Dedication to the King, and to the Parliament. *London.* (Folio, Title and Dedications 4 leaves & p. 24.) Printed in the year 1702. 27 Dec. 1701.

27.—Legion's New Paper: Being a Second Memorial to the Gentlemen of a late House of Commons. With Legion's Humble Address to His Majesty. London. Printed and are to be Sold by the Booksellers of London and Westminster. (4to. pp. 18.) 1 Jan. 1702.

28.—The *Mock Mourners,* a Satyr, by way of Elegy on *King William.* By the Author of the True-born Englishman. London. W. Gunne. 1st Edition, about May, 1702.—Corrected. (4to. 2 leaves & pp. 20.) Price 6d. 2nd Edition, 1702.—Corrected. (4to. 2 leaves & pp. 32.) 3rd Edition, 1702.—Corrected. (8vo. pp. 16. Corrected by the Author. London. Printed 1702.) 7th Edition. 23 Feb. 1703.

29.—*Reformation* of *Manners*. A Satyr. *Væ Vobis Hypocritæ.* Printed in the year 1702. (4to. 2 leaves & pp. 64.) 1702.

30.—A *New Test* of the *Church* of *England's Loyalty* : or, Whiggish Loyalty and Church Loyalty Compared. *Printed* in the year 1702. (4to. Title and pp. 34.) June, 1702.

31.—*Good Advice* to the *Ladies :* shewing, that, as the World goes, and is like to go, the best way for them is to keep Unmarried. By the Author of the True-born Englishman. Printed in the year 1702. (4to. Title & Preface 4 leaves pp. 16.) 1st Edition, 3 Sept. 1702.—(The Second Edition corrected) with the Character of a Beau. London. Printed for R. Smith, without Temple Bar, and are sold by J. Nutt, near Stationers' Hall. (4to. Title and Preface 3 leaves & pp. 16.) 2nd Edition, 1705.

32.—The *Spanish Descent.* A Poem. By the Author of the True-born Englishman. London. Printed in the year 1702. (4to. pp. 27.) Nov. 1702.

33.—An *Enquiry* into *Occasional Conformity.* Shewing that the Dissenters are in no Way Concerned in it. By the Author of the Preface to Mr. How. London. (4to. pp. 31.) 1st Edition, Nov. 1702.—In his collected Writings, 2nd Edition, 1703.—(The same with the following Title) an Enquiry into the Occasional Conformity Bill. By the Author of the True-Born Englishman. London. (4to. pp. 14.) 3rd Edition, 1704.

34.—The *Shortest Way* with the *Dissenters :* or, *Proposals* for the *Establishment* of the *Church.* London. Printed in the year 1702. (4to. Title & pp. 29). 1 Dec. 1702.

35.—A *Brief Explanation* of a late *Pamphlet,* entitled The *Shortest Way* with the *Dissenters.* 1703.

36.—*King William's Affection* to the *Church* of *England,* Examined. London. (4to. pp. 26.) 1st Edition, 25 March, 1703.—2nd Edition, 1703.—(4to. Title & pp. 26.) 3rd Edition, 3rd April, 1703.—(4to. Title & pp. 36.) 4th Edition, 13 April, 1703.

37.—An *Ode* to the *Athenian Society,* signed D. F. In the second volume of the Athenian Oracle. (8vo. 1 leaf.) 6 May, 1703.

38.—A True Collection of the *Writings* of the Author of the *True-Born Englishman,* corrected by himself. London. (8vo. Portrait 12 leaves pp. 465.) A Spurious Edition had been published about six months before. 1st Edition, July, 1703.—2nd Edition, 1705.

39.—A *Second Volume* of the *Writings* of the *Author* of the *True-Born Englishman.* Some whereof never before Printed, Corrected and Enlarged by the Author. London. Printed and Sold by the Booksellers. 1705. Price 6s. (8vo. Portrait, Title, Preface and Contents 8 leaves pp. 479.) Beginning of 1705. —The *Collected Works* of the *Author* of the *True-Born Englishman,* containing &c., with a Key. 2 Vols. 8vo. 3rd Edition. 28 December, 1710.—A True Collection of the Writings of the True-Born Englishman. 2 vols. 8vo. 4th Edition, 1 July, 1713.

WRITTEN DURING HIS FIRST IMPRISONMENT IN NEWGATE.

40.—A *Hymn* to the *Pillory.* London. Printed in the year 1703. (4to. 2 leaves & pp. 24.) 29 July, 1703.—(Reprinted and sold in the Streets.) 25 Feb. 1721.

41.—*More Reformation.* A Satyr upon *himself.* By the Author of the *True-Born Englishman.* London. Printed in the year 1703. (4to. 4 leaves & pp. 52.) 16 July, 1703.

42.—The *Shortest Way* to *Peace* and *Union.* By the *Author* of the *Shortest Way with the Dissenters.* London. (4to. pp. 26.) 28 July, 1703.

43.—The *Sincerity* of the *Dissenters Vindicated* from the *Scandal* of *Occasional Conformity.* With some Considerations on a late Book, entitled, *Moderation a Virtue.* London. Printed in the year 1703. Price 6d. (4to. pp. 27.) 18 Sept. 1703.

44.—An *Enquiry* into the *Case* of Mr. *Asgil's General Translation :* shewing that 'tis not a nearer way to Heaven than the Grave. By the *Author* of the *True-Born Englishman.* London. J. Nutt. (8vo. 4 leaves & pp. 48.) 4 Nov. 1703. —Reissued 1704.

45.—A *Challenge* of *Peace*, addressed to the whole *Nation*, with an Enquiry into Ways and Means for bringing it to pass. London. (4to. 4 leaves & pp. 24.) 23 Nov. 1703.

46.—Some *Remarks* on the First Chapter in Dr. *Davenant's* Essays, concerning *Appeals* to the *People* from their *Representatives*. Printed and Sold, by A. Baldwin. London, 1704. (4to. Title & pp. 29.) 1st Edition, 10 Dec. 1703.— Reissued with Title of " *Original Right*," &c. (4to. pp. 30.) 2nd Edition, 1704.

47.—The *Liberty* of *Episcopal Dissenters* in *Scotland* truly *Stated*. By a Gentleman. 4to. 1703.

48.—*Peace* without *Union*. By way of *Reply* to Sir H— M—'s Peace at Home. London. (Folio, Title & pp. 14.) 1st Edition, Dec. 1703.—(4to.) 2nd Edition, 5 Jan. 1704.—3rd Edition, 7 March, 1704.—To which is added a Preface. (8vo. pp. 24.)—4th Edition, 1704.

49.—The *Dissenters' Answer* to the *High Church Challenge*. London. (4to. pp. 55.) 5 Jan. 1704.

50.—An *Essay* on the *Regulation* of the *Press*. Sold by the Booksellers of London and Westminster. Price 6d. (4to.) 7 Jan. 1704.

51.—A *Serious Inquiry* into this *Grand Question :* Whether a *Law* to prevent *Occasional Conformity* of *Dissenters* would not be Inconsistent with the Act of *Toleration*, and a Breach of the Queen's Promise. London. Printed in the year 1704. (4to. pp. 28.) Early in 1704.

52.—The *Parallel :* or, *Persecution* of *Protestants* the shortest Way to prevent the Growth of Popery in Ireland. (4to.) About Feb. or early in 1704.

53.—The *Layman's Sermon* upon the late *Storm*. Held forth at an honest Coffee-House Conventicle. Not so much a Jest as 'tis thought to be. (4to. Title & pp. 24.) 24 Feb. 1704.

54.—*Royal Religion*. Being some Enquiry after the *Piety* of Princes. With Remarks on a Book, Entitled a Form of Prayers used by King William. (4to. pp. 27.) Price 6d. 1st Edition, 18 Mar. 1704.—2nd Edition, 1704.

55.—*Legion's Humble Address* to the *Lords*. (One leaf folio.) About April, 1704.

56.—*More Short Ways* with the *Dissenters*. London. (4to. pp. 24.) 28 April, 1704.

57.—The *Dissenters Misrepresented* and *Represented*. (4to.) May, 1704.

58.—A *New Test* of the *Church of England's Honesty*. London. Printed in the year 1704. (4to. Title & pp. 24.) 16 July, 1704.

59.—The *Storm :* or, a *Collection* of the *Most Remarkable Casualties* and *Disasters*, which happened in the late Dreadful *Tempest*, both by *Sea* and *Land*. London. G. Sawbridge. 1704. Price 3s. 6d. (8vo. Title and Preface 8 leaves & pp. 272.) 17 July, 1704.

WRITTEN AT BURY.

60.—An *Elegy* on the *Author* of the *True-Born Englishman*. With an *Essay* on the late *Storm*. By the Author of the *Hymn* to the *Pillory*. London. (4to. Title and Preface 2 leaves & pp. 56.) 15 Aug. 1704.

61.—A True State of the Difference between Sir George Rooke, Kt., and William Colepeper, Esq , together with an Account of the Trial of Mr. Nathaniel Denew, Mr. Robert Britton, and Mr. Merrian ; before the Right Hon. Sir John Holt, Kt., Lord Chief Justice of England, on an Indictment for the Designs and Attempts therein mentioned against the Life of the said Wm. Colepeper, on behalf of the said Sir George Rooke. Sold by the Booksellers of London and Westminster. London. (Folio pp. 44.) 22 Aug. 1704.

62.—A Hymn to Victory. By the Author of the True-Born Englishman. London. Printed for John Nutt, near Stationers' Hall. (4to. 4 leaves & pp. 52.) 1st Edition, 29 Aug. 1704.—Three Spurious Editions. 1, a Half-sheet. 2, a Sheet, 3, a Sheet and a half. Aug. 1704.—(With Latin Epigrams behind Title.) (4to. 4 leaves & 52 pages.) London. Printed for J. Nutt, near Stationers' Hall. 2nd Edition, 9 Sept. 1704.

63.—The *Protestant Jesuite Unmasked*. In answer to the two Parts of *Cassandra*. Wherein the Author and his Libels are laid open, with the True

Reasons why he would have the Dissenters Humbled. With my service to Mr. Lesley. London. Printed in the year 1704. (4to. 2 leaves & pp. 52.) 12 Sept. 1704.

WRITTEN AFTER HIS RETURN TO LONDON.

64.—*Giving Alms no Charity,* and *Employing* the *Poor* a *Grievance* to the *Nation.* Being an *Essay* upon *this Great Question.* Whether *Workhouses, Corporations,* and *Houses* of *Correction* for *Employing* the *Poor,* as now practised in *England,* or Parish Stocks as proposed in a late Pamphlet, Entitled, *A Bill for the better Relief, Imployment and Settlement of the Poor,* &c., are not mischievous to the Nation, tending to the Destruction of our Trade, and to Encrease the Number and Misery of the Poor, Addressed to the Parliament of England. London. (4to. pp. 28.) 18 Nov. 1704.

65.—The *Double Welcome.* A *Poem* to the *Duke of Marlborough. London.* Printed in the year 1705. (4to. Title & pp. 30.) 9 Jan. 1705.

66.—*Persecution Anatomized :* or an *Answer* to the following *Questions,* viz. I. What *Persecution* for *Conscience Sake* is? II. Whether any *High Church* that Promote the *Occasional Bill,* may not properly be called *Persecutors ?* III. Whether any *Church* whatever, whilst it *Savours* of a *Persecuting Spirit,* is a true *Church ?* IV. Who are the greatest *Promoters* of a *Nation's Welfare,* the *High Church* or *Dissenters ?* London. Printed in the year 1705. (4to. Title and Dedication 2 leaves & pp. 23.) 22 Feb. 1705.

67.—A *Review* of the *Affairs of France,* and of all Europe as influenced by that Nation, &c. &c. (4to. pp. 424. Five Supplements of Scandal Club, pp. 140, and Appendix, pp. 32.) Vol. I. London. 24 Feb. 1705.

68.—The *Consolidator :* or *Memoirs* of Sundry *Transactions* from the *World* in the *Moon.* Translated from the *Lunar Language.* By the Author of the *True-Born Englishman.* London. Printed and are to be sold by Benj. Bragg. (8vo. 2 Titles, pp. 360.) 26 Mar. 1705.—With Additions. 2nd Edition, 17 Nov. 1705.

69.—A Journey to the World in the Moon, &c. By the Author of the True-Born Englishman. Printed at London and Reprinted at Edinburgh by James Watson in Craig's Closs. (4to. pp. 4.) 1705.

70.—A Letter from the Man in the Moon to the Author of the True-Born Englishman. Printed at London and Reprinted at Edinburgh by James Watson in Craig's Closs. (4to. pp. 4.) 1705.

71.—A Second Journey to the World in the Moon, &c. By the Author of the True-Born Englishman. London. (4to. pp. 4.) 1795.

72.—The Experiment ; or, the Shortest Way with the Dissenters Exemplified. Being the Case of Mr. Abraham Gill, a Dissenting Minister in the Isle of Ely, and a full Account of his being sent for a Soldier by Mr. Fern (an Ecclesiastical Justice of the Peace) and other Conspirators. To the Eternal Honour of the Temper and Moderation of High Church Principles. Humbly Dedicated to the Queen. London. Printed and Sold by B. Bragg. (4to. 3 leaves & pp. 58.) 1st Edition, 27 March, 1705.—The Modesty and Sincerity of those worthy English Gentlemen commonly called High Churchmen, exemplified in a Modern Instance. Most humbly dedicated to her Majesty and her High Court of Parliament. London. B. Bragg. (4to. 3 leaves & pp. 58.) 2nd Edition, 19 Oct. 1706.

73.—Advice to all Parties. By the Author of the True-Born Englishman. London. Printed and are to be sold by B. Bragg. (4to. 2 leaves & pp. 24.) 30 April, 1705.

74.—The *Dyet of Poland.* A Satyr. Printed at Dantzick in the year 1705. (4to. 2 leaves & pp. 60.) May, 1705.

75.—The High Church Legion : or, the Memorial Examined. Being a New Test of Moderation, as 'tis recommended to all that love the Church of England and the Constitution. London. (4to. 3 leaves & pp. 21.) 17 July, 1705.

76.—A Declaration without Doors. By the Author of the True-Born Englishman. Sold by the Booksellers of London and Westminster. (4to.) 24 Oct. 1705.

77.—Party Tyranny : or, An Occasional Bill in Miniature ; as now Practised in Carolina : Humbly offered to the Consideration of both Houses of Parliament. London. (4to. Title and pp. 30.) About Nov. 1705.

78.—An Answer to Lord Haversham's Speech. By Daniel De Foe. (Reprinted from the Review of 23 Nov. 1705.) (4to. pp. 4.) At the end is "London. Printed 1705." About 1 Dec. 1705.

79.—A Hymn to Peace. Occasioned by the two Houses joining in one Address to the Queen. By the Author of the True-Born Englishman. London. Printed in the year 1706. (4to. pp. 60.) 10 Jan. 1706

80.—A Reply to a Pamphlet, entitled the L—d Haversham's Vindication of his Speech, &c. By the Author of the Review. London. (4to. pp. 32.) 15 Jan. 1706.

81.—A *Review* of the *Affairs of France* ; with *Observations* on Transactions at Home. (4to. 4 leaves & pp. 508.) Vol. II. (including the "Little Review," from 6 June to 21 August, 1805.) 1 Jan. 1706.

82.—The *Case* of *Protestant Dissenters* in CAROLINA ; shewing how a LAW to prevent *Occasional Conformity* there, has ended in the *Total Subversion* of the Constitution in *Church* and *State*. Recommended to the serious Consideration of all that are true Friends of our present Government. *Mutato nomine de te Fabula narratur*. London. Printed in the year 1706. (4to. pp. 42.) Early in 1706.

83.—*Remarks* on the *Bill* to prevent *Frauds* committed by *Bankrupts*. With *Observations* on the *Effect* it may have upon TRADE. *London*. (4to. Title & pp. 29.) 18 April, 1706.

84.—An *Essay* at *Removing National Prejudices* against a *Union* with SCOTLAND. To be continued during the Treaty here. LONDON. Printed for *B. Bragg*. (4to. Title & pp. 30.) PART I. 1st Edition, 4 May, 1706.

85.—PART II. (The Title as before.) 1st Edition, 28 May, 1706.—*Edinburgh, Parts I. & II.* reprinted in one. (4to. pp. 51.) 2nd edition, 1706.

86.—An *Essay* at *Removing National Prejudices* against a *Union* with ENGLAND. By the Author of the two First. [Edinburgh.] Printed in the year 1706. (4to. pp. 35.) PART III. Nov. 1706.

87.—A Fourth Essay at Removing National Prejudices ; with some Reply to Mr. *H—dges*, and some other Authors, who have Printed their Objections against a Union with England. [Edinburgh.] Printed in the year 1706. (4to. pp. 44.) PART IV. Dec. 1706.

88.—A FIFTH *Essay* at *Removing National Prejudices* ; with a *Reply* to some *Authors*, who have Printed their Objections against a *Union* with ENGLAND. [Edinburgh.] Printed in the year 1707. (4to. Title and Preface 4 leaves, pp. 35.) PART V. Jany. 1707.

89.—Two Great Questions Considered—I. What is the Obligation of Parliaments to the Addresses or Petitions of the People, and What the Duty of Addressers ? II. Whether the Obligation of the Covenant, or other National Engagements, is concerned in the Treaty of Union ? Being a SIXTH Essay at Removing National Prejudices against the Union. [Edinburgh.] Printed in the year 1707. (4to. pp. 31.) PART VI. Jan. 1707.

90.—A *Plea* for the *Non Conformists :* Shewing the true State of their Case, &c. &c. By *Thomas de Laune*. With a *Preface* by the *Author* of the *Review*. London. Printed and Sold by W. & J. Marshall, at the Bible in Newgate Street. (4to. Title [Preface by Defoe, pp. xi.] pp. 66.) 1st Edition, 6 June, 1706.— Another Edition (8vo. Title [Preface by Defoe: pp. xvi.] Witness & Contents 3 leaves. Plea pp. 144.) 1712.

91.—A *Sermon* preached by *Mr. Daniel De Foe*, on the Fitting up of *Dr. Burgess's Meeting House*. (Taken from his *Review* of the 20th June, 1706.) (4to.) June, 1706.

92.—A *True Relation* of the *Apparition* of one Mrs. *Veal*, the next *Day* after her *Death*, to one Mrs. *Bargrave* at *Canterbury*, the 8th of September, 1705. Which *Apparition* recommends the *Perusal* of *Drelincourt's* Book of *Consolations against the Fears of Death*. London. Printed for B. Bragg, at the Black Raven. 1st Edition, 5 July, 1706.—(8vo. Title and Preface 2 leaves & pp. 12.) 11th Edition.

93.—*Jure Divino :* a *Satyr*. In Twelve Books. By the *Author* of the *True-Born Englishman*. London. Printed in the year 1706. [8vo. SPURIOUS

EDITION. Port. Title and Dedication, 2 leaves. Preface, pp. xlii. Contents, 1 leaf. Poem to the Author, pp. 2. Introduction, pp. 5. Book I. pp. 25. Book II. pp. 24. Book III. pp. 19. Book IV. pp. (68 to 93). Book V. pp. 26. Book VI. pp. 15. Book VII. to the end pp. (135 to 278). 20 July, 1706.— *Jure Divino*: a *Satyr*. In Twelve Books. By the *Author* of the *True-Born Englishman*. London. Printed in the year 1706. (Folio. GENUINE EDITION. Portrait. Title & Dedication, 2 leaves. Preface pp. xxviii. Contents and Poem to Author, 2 leaves. Introduction, pp. vii. The 12 Books separately paged Together, pp. 346.) 20 July, 1706.

94.—A *Letter* to a *Friend*, giving an *Account* how the *Treaty* of *Union* has been received here. With remarks on what has been written by Mr. H(odges) and Mr. R(idpath). Edinburgh. (4to.) 1706.

95.—The *Dissenters* in *England Vindicated* from *some Reflections* in a late *Pamphlet*, called " Lawful Prejudices," &c. &c. *Edinburgh*. 1706. (4to. pp. 8.) 1st Edition, Jan. 1707.—Reprinted, *London*. 2nd Edition, 1707.

96.—*Caledonia*, &c. A *Poem*, in Honour of *Scotland*, and the *Scots Nation*. EDINBURGH. Printed by the Heirs and Successors of Andrew Anderson, Printer to the Queen's Most Excellent Majesty. (Folio. Title, Dedication, and Preface 5 leaves. Poem, pp. 60.) 1st Edition, 1706.—*London*: Printed by J. Matthews, and Sold by John Morphew, near Stationers' Hall. (8vo. Title, Dedication, and List of Subscribers, 4 leaves. Poem, pp. 55.) 2nd Edition, 28 Jan. 1707.

97.—A *Review* of the *English Nation*. *London*. (4to. Title and Preface 4 leaves & pp. 688.) Vol. III., 6 Feb. 1707.

98.—A *Short View* of the Present *State* of the *Protestant Religion* in *Britain*, as it is now profest in the Episcopal Church in *England*, the Presbyterian *Church* in Scotland, and the *Dissenters* in Both. EDINBURGH. Printed in the year 1707. (8vo. pp. 48.) 1st Edition, March, 1707.—The *Dissenters Vindicated*: or, a *Short View* of the Present *State* of *the Protestant Religion* in *Britain*, as it is now professed in the *Episcopal Church* of England, the *Presbyterian Church* in Scotland, and the Dissenters in both. In Answer to some Reflections in *Mr. Webster's* two Books published in Scotland. London. J. Morphew. (8vo. pp. 48.) 2nd Edition, 1 April, 1707.

99.—A *Voice* from the *South*: or, an *Address* from some *Protestant Dissenters* in *England* to the *Kirk in Scotland*. (From his *Reviews* of May 10 and 15, 1707.) (4to. pp. 8.) May, 1707.

100.—A *Modest Vindication* of the *Present Ministry*: From the *Reflections* published against them in a late *Printed Paper*, Entitled, The *Lord Haversham's Speech*, &c. With a *Review* and *Balance* of the *Present War*. Evincing, That we are not in such a Desperate Condition as that Paper Insinuates. Humbly submitted to the Consideration of all, but especially to the Right *Honourable* and the *Honourable*, the *North British Lords and Commoners*. By a Well-wisher to the *Peace* of *Britain*. London. Printed in the year 1707. (4to. Title & pp. 14.) 1707.

101.—An Historical Account of the Bitter Sufferings, and Melancholy Circumstances of the Episcopal Church in Scotland, Under the Barbarous Usage and Bloody Persecution of the Presbyterian Church Government. With an Essay on the Nature and Necessities of a Toleration in the North of Britain. Edinburgh. Printed in the year 1707. (8vo. pp. 40.) 1707.

102.—De Foe's Answer to Dyer's Scandalous Newsletter. [Edinburgh.] (4to. pp. 3.) August, 1707.

103.—The *Union Proverb*, viz., "If *Skiddaw* has a *cap*, *Scruffell* wots full well of that." Setting forth, I. The necessity of Uniting, II. The good consequences of Uniting, III. The happy Union of England and Scotland, in case of a Foreign Invasion. *Felix quem faciunt aliena pericula cautum*. *London*. G. Sawbridge. (8vo.) 13 March, 1708.

104.—A *Review* of the *State* of the *British Nation*. *London*. (4to. Title, Preface 2 leaves & pp. 700.) VOL. IV., 25 March, 1708.

105.—The *Scots Narrative* Examined ; or, the *Case* of the *Episcopal Ministers* in *Scotland* stated ; and the late *Treatment* of them in the *City* of *Edinburgh*, enquired into. With a brief *Examination* into the *Reasonableness* of the *Grievous Complaint* of *Persecution* in *Scotland*, and a *Defence* of the *Magistrates* of

Edinburgh, in their *Proceedings* there. Being some *Remarks* on a late *Pamphlet*, entitled *A Narrative of the late Treatment of the Episcopal Ministers, within the City of Edinburgh*, &c. London. Sold by A. Baldwin, in Warwick Lane. (4to. pp. 41. Postscript x.) 19 Feb. 1709.

106.—A *Review* of the *State* of the *British Nation*. *London*. (4to. Title and Preface 4 leaves & pp. 632.) VOL. V., 31 March, 1709.

107.—The *History of the Union of Great Britain*. *Edinburgh*. Printed by the Heirs and Successors of Andrew Anderson, Printer to the Queen's Most Excellent Majesty. (Folio, Portrait, Title, and Dedication, 8 leaves. Preface, xxxii., and total pp. 694.) 1709.

108.—An *Answer* to a *Paper* concerning *Mr. De Foe*, against the *History* of the *Union*. *Edinburgh*. (4to. pp. 8.) 1709.

109.—A *Reproof* to *Mr. Clark*, and a *Brief Vindication* of *Mr. De Foe*. *Edinburgh*. *John Moncur*. (4to. pp. 8.) A.D. 1710. 1709.

110.—A *Commendatory Sermon*, Preached November 4th, 1709. Being the Birth Day of *King William* of *Glorious Memory*. By *Daniel Defoe*. *London*. Printed by *J. Dutton*, near Fleet Street. (8vo. pp. 8.) From the *Review*. Nov. 1709.

111.—A *Review* of the *State of the British Nation*. *London*. (4to. Title and Preface, 4 leaves & pp. 600.) VOL. VI., 23 March, 1710.

112.—A *Letter* from *Captain Tom* to the *Mob*, now Raised for *Dr. Sacheverell*. *London*. Printed for J. Baker at the Black Boy in Paternoster Row. (8vo. pp. 8.) 11 March, 1710.

113.—A *Speech* without *Doors*. *London*. Printed for A. Baldwin, near the Oxford Arms in Warwick Lane. Price Two Pence. (8vo. pp. 20.) 19 April, 1710.

114.—*Instructions* from *Rome* in Favour of the *Pretender :* Inscribed to the most Elevated *Don Sacheverillio*, and his Brother *Don Higginsco*. And which all *Perkinites, Non-Jurors, High-flyers, Popish Desirers, Wooden-shoe Admirers*, and *Absolute Non-resistance Drivers* are obliged to pursue and maintain (under pain of his *Unholiness Damnation*), in order to carry on their intended subversion of a *Government*, fixed upon *Revolution Principles*. London. Sold by J. Baker, at the Black Boy in Paternoster Row. Price 2d. (8vo. pp. 16.) 11 May, 1710.

115.—An *Essay* upon *Publick Credit :* Being an Enquiry ; How the *Publick Credit* comes to depend upon the Change of the *Ministry* or the Dissolutions of *Parliaments :* and whether it does so or no. With an Argument, Proving that the *Publick Credit* may be upheld and maintained in this Nation ; and perhaps to a greater Height than it ever yet arriv'd at ; Tho' all the Changes and Dissolutions already made, pretended to, and now Discoursed of, should come to pass in the world. London. Printed and Sold by the Booksellers. Price 3d. (8vo. pp. 28). 23 Aug. 1710.

116.—A *Word* against a *New Election ;* that the *People* of *England* may see the *Happy difference* between English *Liberty* and French *Slavery :* and may consider well before they make the Exchange. (8vo. pp. 23.) Oct. 1710.

117.—A *New Test* of the *Sense* of the *Nation :* Being a *Modest Comparison* between the ADDRESSES to the late *King James*, and those to her present *Majesty*. In order to observe how far the *Sense* of the *Nation* may be judged of by either of them. *London*. (8vo. Title and pp. 91.) 12 Oct. 1710.

118.—An *Essay* upon *Loans :* or, An *Argument* proving That Substantial FUNDS, settled by Parliament, with the Encouragements of *Interests*, and the Advances of *Prompt Payment* usually allowed, will bring in *Loans* of *Money* to the *Exchequer*, in spite of all the *Conspiracies* of *Parties* to the Contrary ; while a *Just, Honourable*, and *Punctual Performance* on the Part of the *Government*, supports the *Credit* of the *Nation*. By the Author of the *Essay upon Credit*. *London*. Printed and Sold by the Booksellers. (8vo. pp. 27.) 21 Oct. 1710.

119.—The *Edinburgh Courant*. 1 Feb. 1711.

120.—*Atalantis Major*. Printed in *Olreeky*, the Chief City of the Northern part of Atalantis Major. Anno Mundi 1711. (8vo. Title and pp. 46.) Early in 1711.

121.—A *Review* of the *State* of the *British Nation*. London. (4to. Title and Preface, 4 leaves & pp.   .) Vol. VII. 22 March, 1711.

122.—*Eleven Opinions* about *Mr. H(arle)y ;* with *Observations.* London. J. Baker. (8vo. pp. 89.) 14 May, 1711.

123.—The Secret History of the October Club: From its Original to this Time. By a Member. London. Printed in the year 1711. Price 1s. (8vo. Title & pp. 86.) 1st Edition, 21 April, 1711.—2nd Edition, 10 May, 1711.

124.—The Secret History of the October Club. From its Original to this Time. By a Member. Part II. London. Printed for J. Baker, at the Black-boy in Paternoster Row (Price 1s.), where may be had the first Part. (8vo. Title, pp. 93.) About Aug. 1711.

125.—An *Essay* on the *South Sea Trade :* With an *Enquiry* into the *Grounds* and *Reasons* of the present *Dislike* and *Complaint* against the *Settlement* of a *South Sea Company.* By the *Author of the Review.* London. J. Baker. (8vo. pp. 47.) 1st Edition, 6 Sept. 1711.—(8vo. pp. 47.) Printed on Title 1712. 2nd Edition, 29 Nov. 1711.

126.—*Reasons* why *this Nation* ought to put a *Speedy End* to this *Expensive War.* With a *Brief Essay* at the probable *Conditions* on which the *Peace* now *Negociating* may he *Founded.* Also an *Enquiry* into the *Obligations* Britain lies under to the *Allies,* and how far she is obliged not to make *Peace* without them. *London. J. Baker.* (8vo.) 1st Edition, 6 Oct. 1711.—(8vo. pp. 47.) 2nd Edition, 11 Oct. 1711.—3rd Edition, 13 Oct. 1711.

127.—*Armageddon :* or, the *Necessity of Carrying on the War* if *such a Peace* cannot be obtained as may render *Europe safe* and *Trade secure.* London. J. Baker. Price 6d. (8vo. pp. 47.) 30 Oct. 1711.

128.—The *Balance of Europe ;* or, an *Enquiry* into the respective *Dangers* of giving the *Spanish Monarchy* to the *Emperor,* as well as to *King Philip.* With the *Consequences* that may be expected from either. Printed for John Baker. (8vo. pp. 48.) 1 Nov. 1711.

129.—An *Essay* at a *Plain Exposition* of that *difficult Phrase a Good Peace.* By the Author of the *Review.* London. J. Baker. Price 6d. (8vo. pp. 52.) About 27 Nov. 1711.

130.—*Reasons* why a *Party* among us, and also among the *Confederates,* are obstinately bent against a *Treaty* of *Peace* with the *French* at this *Time.* By the Author of *Reasons for putting an End to this Expensive War.* J. Baker. Price 6d. (8vo.) 1st Edition, 29 Nov. 1711.—2nd Edition, 8 Dec. 1711.

131.—The *Felonious Treaty :* or, an *Enquiry* into the *Reasons* which Moved his late Majesty *King William* of *Glorious Memory,* to enter into a *Treaty* at two Several *Times,* with the *King of France,* for the *Partition* of the *Spanish Monarchy.* With an Essay proving that it was always the sense of *King William,* and of all the *Confederates,* and even of the *Grand Alliance* itself, that the *Spanish Monarchy* should never be united in the *Person* of the *Emperor.* By the *Author of the Review.* London. J. Baker. Price 6d. (8vo. pp. 48.) Dec. 1711.

132.—An *Essay* on the *History* of *Parties* and *Persecutions* in *Britain,* be-beginning with a brief *Account* of the *Test Act* and an *Historical Enquiry* into the *Reasons,* the *Original,* and the *Consequences* of the *Occasional Conformity* of the *Dissenters ;* with some *Remarks* on the several *Attempts,* already made and now making, for an *Occasional Bill.* Enquiring how far the same may be esteemed a *Preservation* to the *Church,* or an *Injury to the Dissenters. London.* Printed for J. Baker, at the Black Boy, in Paternoster Row. Price 6d. (8vo. pp. 48.) 22 Dec. 1711.

133.—The *Conduct* of *Parties in England,* more especially of those Whigs, who now appear against the new Ministry and a Treaty of Peace. (8vo. pp. 42.) 24 Jan. 1712.

134.—The *Present State* of *Parties* in *Great Britain :* Particularly an *Enquiry* into the *State* of the *Dissenters* in *England,* and the *Presbyterians* in *Scotland,* their *Religious* and *Public Interests* considered as it respects their *Circumstances* before and since the late *Acts* against *Occasional Conformity in England,* and for *Toleration* of *Common Prayer* in *Scotland. London.* Printed and Sold by J. Baker. Price Five Shillings. (8vo. Title and Preface 4 leaves & pp. 352.) 17 May, 1712.

135.—*Reasons* against *Fighting ;* Being an *Enquiry* into this *Debate* whether it is *Safe* for her *Majesty,* or her *Ministry,* to *Adventure* an *Engagement* with the *French*, considering the present *Behaviour* of the *Allies*. Printed in the year 1712. Price 6d. (8vo. Title and pp. 38.) 7 June, 1712.

136.—A *Review* of the *State of the British Nation*. *London*. (4to. pp. 848.) VOL. VIII., 29 July, 1712.

137.—An *Enquiry* into the *Real Interest* of *Princes* in the *Persons* of their *Ambassadors ;* and how far the Petty Quarrels of Ambassadors, or the *Servants* and *Dependants* of *Ambassadors*, one among another, ought to be Resented by their *Principals*. With an Essay on what *Satisfaction* it is Necessary to Give or Take in such *Cases*. Impartially applied to the affair of *Monsieur Mesnager*, and the *Count de Rechteren*, *Plenipotentiaries* at *Utrecht*. London. J. Baker. (8vo. pp. 23.) 18 Sept. 1712.

138.—A Seasonable Warning and Caution against the Insinuations of Papists and Jacobites in favour of the Pretender. Being a letter from an Englishman at the Court of Hanover. Printed by J. Baker, at the Black Boy. (8vo. pp. 24.) 1712.

139.—*Hannibal* at the *Gates ;* or, the *Progress of Jacobitism* and the *Danger* of the *Pretender*. London. J. Baker. (12mo. pp. 40.) 1st Edition, 30 Dec. 1712.—With remarks on a Pamphlet now Published Intituled Hannibal not at our Gates, &c. (8vo. pp. 48.) 2nd Edition, 1714.

140.—*A Strict Enquiry* into the *Circumstances* of a *late Duel*, with some *Account* of the *Persons* concern'd on both *Sides*. Being a *Modest Attempt* to do *Justice* to a Noble *Person* DEAD, and to the *Injured Honour* of an *Absent Person* LIVING. To which is added the substance of a *Letter* from *General McCartney* to his *Friend*. London. (8vo. pp. 30.) 1713.

141.—*Reasons* against the *Succession* of the *House* of *Hanover*, with an *Enquiry* how far the *Abdication* of *King James*, supposing it to be *legal*, ought to affect the *Person* of the *Pretender*. London. J. Baker. Price 6d. (8vo. Title & pp. 45.) 1st Edition, 21 Feb. 1713.—4th Edition, April, 1713.

142.—And *What* if the *Pretender* should *Come ?* or some *Considerations* of the *Advantages* and real *Consequences* of the *Pretender's* possessing the *Crown* of *Great Britain*. *London*. J. Baker. (8vo. pp. 44.) 1st Edition, 26 March, 1713.—2nd Edition, April, 1713.

143.—An *Answer* to a *Question* that *nobody* thinks of, viz., *What if the Queen should die ?* London. J. Baker. (8vo. pp. 44.) April, 1713.

144.—An *Essay* on the *Treaty of Commerce with France*, with *Necessary Expositions*. 1st Edition, May, 1713.—London. J. Baker. (8vo. pp. 44.) 2nd Edition, 1713.

WRITTEN DURING HIS SECOND IMPRISONMENT IN NEWGATE.

145.—Considerations upon the 8th and Ninth Articles of the Treaty of Commerce and Navigation. Now published by Authority. With some Enquiries into the DAMAGES that may accrue to the English Trade from them. London. J. Baker. (8vo. pp. 40.) 2 June, 1713.

146.—The *Review* (each Number a single leaf) (4to. pp. 212.) 2 Aug. 1712 to 11 June, 1713. Vol. IX., 11 June, 1713.

147.—*Some Thoughts* upon the *Subject* of *Commerce* with *France*. By the *Author of the Review*. London. J. Baker. (8vo. ——). June, 1713.

148.—A General History of Trade, and especially considered as it respects British Commerce, &c. Four fortnightly Numbers. London. J. Baker. (8vo. each No. about pp. 40). Aug. & Sept. 1713.

149.—*Whigs* turned *Tories* and *Hanoverian Tories* from their avowed *Principles* proved *Whigs ;* or each side in the other Mistaken. Being a plain proof that each party deny that *Charge* which the others bring against them ; and that neither side will disown those which the other profess. With an *Earnest Exhortation* to all *Whigs*, as well as *Hanoverian Tories*, to lay aside those uncharitable heats among such *Protestants*, and seriously to consider, and effectually to provide, against those *Jacobite*, *Popish*, and *Conforming Tories*, whose principal *Ground* of *Hope* to ruin all *sincere Protestants* is from those *Unchristian* and violent *Feuds* among ourselves. *London*. *J. Baker*. (8vo.) 1713.

150.—*Union* and no *Union*. Being an Enquiry into the Grievances of the Scots and how far they are right or wrong, who alleged that the Union is dissolved. J. Baker. (8vo. pp. 24.) 1713.

151.—A *Letter* to the *Dissenters. London. Printed* for *J. Morphew* near Stationers' Hall. Price 6d. (8vo. pp. 48.) 3 Dec. 1713.

152.—The *Scots Nation* and *Union Vindicated* from the *Reflections* cast on them in an *Infamous libel* entitled the *Public Spirit of the Whigs*, &c. In which, the most *Scandalous Paragraphs* contained therein are fairly *quoted* and fully *answered.* London. Printed for A. Bell. (4to. pp. 28.) March, 1714.

153.—A *View of* the *Real Danger* of the *Protestant Succession. London. J. Baker.* Price 6d. (8vo. pp. 15.) April, 1714.

154.—*Reasons* for Im(peaching) the L(or)d H(ig)h Treasurer, and some others of the P(resen)t M(inistr)y. Printed and Sold by J. Moore, near St. Paul's. Price 6d. (8vo. pp. 39.) End of April, 1714.

155.—The Remedy worse than the Disease ; or, Reasons against passing the Bill for preventing the Growth of Schism. To which is added a brief Discourse of Toleration and Persecution, shewing their Unavoidable Effects Good or Bad ; and Proving that neither Diversity of Religions, nor Diversity in the Same Religion are Dangerous, much less Inconsistent with good Government. In a Letter to a Noble Earl. London. J. Baker. (8vo. pp. 48.) 9 June, 1714.

156.—*Mercator :* or, *Commerce* Retrieved, Being Considerations on the Subject of British Trade ; particularly as it respects Holland, Flanders and the Dutch Barrier ; the Trade to and from France, the Trade to Portugal, Spain and the West Indies, and the Fisheries of Newfoundland and Nova Scotia : With other Matters and Advantages accruing to Great Britain, by the Treaties of Peace and Commerce lately Concluded at Utrecht. The whole being founded upon just Authorities, faithfully Collected from Authentick Papers, and now made Publick for General Information. 26 May, 1713, to 20 July, 1714.

157.—The *Flying* Post and *Medley* (Hurt's). [Written by Daniel Defoe, a small leaf folio published thrice a week, continued to the 21st of Aug. 1714, if not later.] 27 July, 1714 to 21 Aug. 1714.

158.—Advice to the People of Great Britain, as to what they ought to expect from the King, and how they ought to behave to him. London. J. Baker. 1st Edition, 7 Oct. 1814.—Reprinted in Dublin for G. Risk, Bookseller. (8vo. pp. 30.) 2nd Edition, 1714.

159.—A Secret History of One Year. London. J. Baker. (8vo. Title & pp. 40.) 1714.

160.—The Secret History of the White Staff. Being an Account of Affairs under the Conduct of Some late Ministers ; and of what might probably have happened if her Majesty had not died. J. Baker. (8vo. pp. 71.) 1st Edition, Oct. 1714.—(8vo. pp. 71.) 2nd Edition, 7 Oct. 1714.—(8vo. pp. 71.) 3rd Edition, Oct. 1714.—(8vo. pp. 71.) 4th Edition, 27 Oct. 1714.

161.—(8vo. pp. 71.) Part II. 1st Edition, 27 Oct 1714.—2nd Edition, 1714.—(8vo. pp. 71.) 3rd Edition, 1714.

162.—(8vo. pp. 80.) Part III. 1st Edition, 29 Jan. 1715.

163.—An *Appeal* to *Honour* and *Justice*, tho' it be of his *Worst Enemies*, by *Daniel Defoe. Being a True Account of his Conduct* in Publick Affairs. London. Printed for J. Baker. (8vo. Title & pp. 58.) January, 1715.

164.—A *Reply* to a *Traitorous Libel* entitled, *English Advice* to *the Freeholders of England.* J. Baker. (8vo. pp. 40.) 29 January, 1715.

165.—A *Friendly Epistle* by Way of *Reproof*, from one of the People called *Quakers* to *Thos. Bradbury*, a Dealer in many Words. *London.* Printed and Sold by S. Keimer, Paternoster Row. Price 6d. (8vo. pp. 39.) 19 Feb. 1715.

166.—The *Family Instructor :* in three Parts. 1. Relating to Fathers and Children. II. To Masters and Servants. III. To Husbands & Wives. By Way of Dialogue, With a Recommendatory Letter by the Rev. Mr. S. Wright. London. E. Matthews. (12mo. 3 leaves & pp. 444.) 31 March, 1715.—Corrected by the Author. (Title and Preface 3 leaves, & pp. 414.) 2nd Edition, 17 Sept. 1715.—Corrected by the Author. (12mo. Title and Preface 3 leaves, & pp. 385.) 8th Edition, 1720.—(12mo. pp. 384.) 16th Edition, 1766.

167.—A *Sharp Rebuke* from one of the *People* called *Quakers* to *Henry Sacheverell, the High Priest of Andrews, Holborn.* By the Same Friend that wrote to Thos. Bradbury. London. Printed and Sold by S. Keimer, Paternoster Row. Price 6d. (8vo. pp. 35.) 1715.

168.—A *Seasonable Expostulation*, and *Friendly Reproof* unto *James Butler*, who by the Men of this *World* is styled the Duke of O——d, relating to the *Tumults* of the *People.* · By the same *Friend* that wrote to *Thos. Bradbury*, the Dealer in many *Words*, and *Henry Sacheverell*, the *High Priest of Andrews, Holborn.* London. S. Keimer. (8vo. pp. 31.) 1st Edition, 31 May, 1715.— (8vo. pp. 24.) Reprinted in Dublin by Thos. Humes. 2nd Edition. 1715.

169.—*History* of the *Wars* of his present Majesty *Charles XII. King of Sweden;* from his first Landing in Denmark, to his Return from Turkey to Pomerania. By a Scots Gentleman in the Swedish Service. London. A. Bell. (8vo. 2 leaves & pp. 400.) 1st Edition, 6 July, 1715.—With a continuation to his Death. (Portrait. Title and Preface, 2 leaves. Hist. pp. 1 to 248. Continuation, pp. 249 to 402.) 2nd Edition, 21 May, 1720.

170.—A *Hymn* to *the Mob*. London. Printed and Sold by S. Popping, &c. Price 6d. (8vo. Title and Preface, 3 leaves & pp. 40.) 14 July, 1715.

171.—A *View* of the *Scots Rebellion.* With some Enquiry into what we have to fear, from the Rebels? and what is the properest method to take with them? London. R. Burleigh, in Amen Corner. Price 6d. (8vo. pp. 40.) 15 Oct. 1715.

172.—A *Trumpet, Blown* in the *North*, and sounded in the Ears of JOHN ERESKINE, called by the Men of the World, DUKE OF MAR. By a Ministering Friend of the People called Quakers. With a word of Advice and Direction to the said JOHN ERESKINE and his followers. Sold by S. Keimer, at the Cheshire Coffee House in King's Arms Court, in Ludgate Hill. Price 6d. (8vo. pp. 38.) 10 Nov. 1715.

173.—An *Account* of the *Great* and *Generous Actions* of *James Butler* (late Duke of Ormond). Dedicated to the Famous University of Oxford. London. Printed for J. *Moore.* Price 6d. (8vo. pp. 48.) Dec. 1715.

174.—Some *Account* of the *Two Nights Court* at *Greenwich;* wherein may be seen the Reason, Rise, and Progress of the late Unnatural Rebellion, against his Sacred Majesty, King George and his *Government.* London. J. Baker. (8vo. Title, & pp. 72.) 1716.

175.—*Some Considerations* on a *Law* for *Triennial Parliaments;* with an *Enquiry.* I. Whether there may not be a Time, when it is necessary to suspend the Execution of Such Laws as are most essential to the Liberties of the People? II. Whether this is such a Time or No? London. J. *Baker.* (8vo. pp. 40.) April, 1716.

176.—The *Alteration* in the *Triennial Act Considered. London.* R. *Burleigh.* Price 3d. (8vo. pp. 22.) April, 1716.

177.—*Mercurius Politicus:* Being Monthly Observations on the Affairs of Great Britain; With a Collection of the Most Material Occurrences. [For the Month of May.] By a Lover of Old England. *London.* Printed and Sold by J. *Morphew.* Price one Shilling. (8vo. pp. 96.) [Continued probably later than Sept. 1720.] May, 1716, to Sept. 1720.

178.—*Dormer's News Letter* (conducted by Daniel Defoe for some time. I have found no Copies of this Journal, and, therefore, can give no farther particulars.) *Each Number one Sheet Small Folio.* June, 1716, to Aug. 1718.

179.—*Memoirs* of the *Church* of *Scotland*, in 4 Periods. I. The Church in her Infant State, from the Reformation to Queen Mary's Abdication. II. The Church in its Growing State, from the Abdication to the Restoration. III. The Church in its Persecuted State, from the Restoration to the Revolution. IV. The Church in its Present State, from the Revolution to the Union. With an Appendix of Some Transactions since the Union. *London. Eman. Matthews.* (8vo. Title and Preface 2 leaves, pp. 232 and 196. Appendix, pp. 9.) 26 April, 1717.

180.—A *Short Narrative* of the *Life* and *Death* of *John Rhinholdt*, Count *Patkul*, A NOBLEMAN of *Livonia*, who was broke Alive upon the Wheel in *Great Poland*, anno 1707. Together with the manner of his Execution. Written by the Lutheran Minister, who assisted him in his last Hours. Faithfully

Translated Out of a High Dutch Manuscript; and now published for the Information of Count Gyllenborg's English Friends. By L. M. The Second Edition. London. Printed For T. Goodwin, Fleet Street. Price 1s. (8vo. 2 leaves, & pp. 59.) April, 1717.

181.—*Minutes* of the *Negociations* of Mons. *Mesnager*, at the Court of England, Towards the Close of the last Reign. Wherein some of the Most Secret Transactions of that Time, relating to the Interest of the PRETENDER, and to a Clandestine Separate Peace are detected and laid open. Written by himself. Done out of French. London. S. Baker. (8vo. pp. 326.)—1st Edition, 17 June, 1717.—2nd Edition, 1717.—3rd Edition, 8 July, 1731.—4th Edition, 1736.

182.—A *Declaration* of *Truth* to *Benjamin Hoadley*, one of the *High Priests* of the *Land*, and of the Degree whom Men Call *Bishops*. By a Ministering *Friend* who writ to *Tho. Bradbury*, a Dealer in Many Words. London. Printed for E. Moore. Price Six Pence. (8vo. pp. 31.) 1717.

183.—The *Weekly Journal*; or, *Saturday's Post* (Mist's). [*Defoe* first found in it at No. 37, and Continued to No. 101, 15 Nov. 1718. *Defoe* again connected with *Mist's Journal*, 31 January, 1719, and continued its Management, writing Letters introductory until the beginning of July 1720; after which he only Watched the Paper, and translated the Articles on Foreign Affairs, and Occasionally Contributed Articles.] (Each Number 1½ Sheets. Small Folio.) 24 August, 1717, to 15 Nov. 1718. 3 Jan. 1719, to July, 1720; and Occasionally afterward, until 24 Oct. 1724.

184.—A Curious Little Oration, Delivered by Father Andrew. concerning the Great Quarrels that divide the Clergy of France. Translated from the Fourth Edition of the French, by Dan. D. F——e. (8vo. pp. 20.) 1st Edition, 1717. —2nd Edition, 1717.

185.—Memoirs of Publick Transactions in the Life and Ministry of his Grace the D. of Shrewsbury. In which will be found much of the History of Parties, and especially of Court Divisions, during the last Four Reigns; which no History has yet given an Account of. *Plus valet occulatus Testis quam Aurite Decem.* London. Printed for Tho. Warner, at the Black Boy, in Paternoster Row, 1718. Price Two Shillings. (8vo. Title and Preface 2 leaves & pp. 139.) 6th May, 1718.

186.—The Case of the War in Italy Stated. Being a Serious Enquiry, how far Great Britain is Engaged to concern itself in the Quarrel between the Emperor and the King of Spain. *Pax Quæritur Bello.* London. T. Warner. Price 6d. (8vo. Title & pp. 34.) 1718.

187.—Memoirs of the Life and Eminent Conduct of that Learned and Reverend Divine, Daniel Williams, D.D. With some Account of his Scheme, for the Vigorous Propagation of Religion, as well in England as in Scotland, and several other Parts of the World. Address'd to Mr. Pierce. London. Printed for E. Curll. Price 2s. 6d. Bound. (8vo. Title & pp. 86.) 1718.

188.—The Family Instructor. In Two Parts. I. Relating to Family Breaches, and their obstructing Religious Duties. II. To the Great Mistake of Mixing the Passions, in the Managing and Correcting of Children. With a great Variety of Cases of Setting Ill Examples to Children. Vol. II. (12mo. Title & Pref. vi. pp. 404.) 1st Edition, 1718. (12mo. pp. viii. & 384.) 8th Edition, 1766.

189.—The Whitehall Evening Post. (Commenced and Edited by Defoe, Published every Tuesday, Thursday, and Saturday. He continued to write in it occasionally until June 1720.) (2 leaves small 4to.) 18 Sept. 1718 to June, 1720.

190.—A Friendly Rebuke to One Parson Benjamin; Particularly Relating to his Quarrelling with his own Church, and Vindicating Dissenters. By one of the People called Quakers. London. Printed for *E. Moor*, near St. Paul's. Price 6d. (8vo. pp. 32.) 10 Jan. 1719.

191.—The Life and Strange Surprizing Adventures of Robinson Crusoe, of York, Mariner; Who lived eight and twenty Years all alone, on an uninhabited Island on the Coast of America, near the Mouth of the Great River of Oroonoque; Having been Cast on Shore by Shipwreck, wherein all the Men perished

B B

but himself. With an Account how he was at last Strangely delivered by Pyrates. Written by Himself. London. Printed for W. Taylor, at the Ship, in Paternoster Row. (8vo. Frontispiece. Title and Preface 2 leaves & pp. 364. 1st Edition, 25 April, 1719. (8vo. Frontispiece. Title and Preface 2 leaves & pp. 364.)—2nd Edition, 12 May, 1719—3rd Edition, 6 June, 1719—4th Edition, 8 Aug. 1719.

192.—The *Farther Adventures* of *Robinson Crusoe.* Being the *Second* and *Last Part* of his *Life,* and of the *Strange Surprizing Accounts* of his *Travels* Round three *Parts* of the *Globe.* Written by Himself. To which is added a Map of the World, in which is Delineated the *Voyages of Robinson Crusoe.* *London.* Printed for W. Taylor, at the Ship in *Paternoster Row.* (8vo. Map, Title, Preface and Advertisements, 4 leaves & pp. 373.) 1st Edition, 20 Aug 1719.

193.—*Serious Reflections* during the Life and Surprizing Adventures of Robinson Crusoe. With his Vision of the *Angelick World.* Written by Himself. *London.* Printed for *W. Taylor* at the Ship in Paternoster Row. (8vo. Frontispiece. Title, Preface, and Introduction 8 leaves & pp. 270, and 84.) 1st Edition, 6 Aug. 1720. 1st and 2nd Vols. Reprinted in the *Original London Post* or Heathcote's Intelligencer. 7 Oct., 1719, to 19 Oct., 1720. 1st Vol. spuriously abridged, and published by T. Cox at the *Amsterdam Coffee House* in *London* before the 7th August, 1719. 5. First Abridgement in 1 Vol (8vo.) 5th Edition, 19 Nov. 1720. 6. In 2 Volumes. 6th Edition, 28 Oct., 1721. 7. An Abridged Edition in 1 Vol. 28 Feb. 1722. 8. Another Edition in 2 Volumes with 14 Copper Plates called 6th Edition. 5 June, 1722. 9. In 2 Volumes, called 7th Edition. 27 Aug. 1726.

194.—Some *Account* of the *Life* and most *Remarkable Actions* of *Henry, Baron de Goertz, Minister* to the late *King* of *Sweden. London.* Printed for *T. Bickerton.* (8vo. Portrait, Title, & pp. 46.) About May, 1719.

195.—A *Letter* to the *Dissenters. London. J. Roberts.* Price 6d. (8vo. pp. 27.) About May, 1719.

196.—The *Anatomy* of *Exchange Alley ;* or a System of Stock-Jobbing; proving that Scandalous Trade, as it is now carried on, to be knavish in its private Practice, and Treason in its Publick. Being a Clear Detection. I. Of the private Cheats, used to deceive one another. II. Of their Arts to draw Innocent Families into their Snare, understood by their new Term of Art, viz., being let into the Secret. III. Of their Raising and Spreading false News, to ground the Rise or Fall of Stocks upon. IV. Of the Dangerous Consequences of their Practices, and the necessity there is to Regulate or Suppress them. To which is added some Characters of the most Eminent Persons concern'd now, and for some Years past, in carrying on this pernicious Trade. By a Jobber. Printed for E. Smith near Exchange Alley, and Thomas Warner in Paternoster Row. Price 1s. (8vo. Title & pp. 64.) 1st Edition, 11 July, 1719. 2nd Edition, 26 Mar. 1720.

197.—*The Daily Post.* [Commenced and Edited by *Daniel Defoe.* Continued connected with it, writing occasionally, until 27 April, 1725.] (Each Number one Leaf small folio.) 4 Oct. 1719 to 27 Ap. 1725.

198.—*The Dumb Philosopher ;* or Great Britain's Wonder, containing I. A Faithful and very Surprising Account, how Dickory Cronke, a Tinner's Son, in the County of Cornwall, was born Dumb, and continued so for 58 years ; and how, some Days before he Died, he came to his Speech. With Memoirs of his Life, and the manner of his Death. II. A Declaration of his Faith and Principles in Religion ; With a Collection of Select Meditations composed in his Retirement. III. His Prophetical Observations upon the Affairs of Europe, more particularly of Great Britain, from 1720 to 1729. The whole extracted from his original Papers, and confirmed by unquestionable authority. To which is annexed, His Eelgy, written by a young Cornish Gentleman, of Exeter Coll. in Oxford. With an Epitaph by another Hand. London. Printed for T. Bickerton. Price one Shilling. (8vo. pp. 64.) 1st Edition, 14 Oct. 1719—2nd Edition, 27 May, 1720.

199.—Charity still a Christian Virtue : or, an Impartial Account of the Tryal and Conviction of the Reverend Mr. Hendley, for Preaching a Charity Sermon at

Chisselhurst. And of Mr. Campman, and Mr. Harding, for Collecting at the same Time the Alms of the Congregation. At the Assizes held at Rochester, on Wednesday. July 15th, 1719. Offer'd to the Consideration of the Clergy of the Church of England. London. Printed for T. Bickerton, at the Crown in Pater-Noster Row, 1719. (Price One Shilling.) (8vo. *Frontispiece.* Title and Preface 2 leaves & pp. 72.) 16 Oct. 1719.

200.—The King of Pirates : Being an Account of the Famous Enterprizes of Captain Avery, the Mock King of Madagascar ; with his Rambles and Piracies, wherein all the Sham Accounts formerly published of him are detected. In two Letters from himself, one during his Stay at Madagascar, and one since his Escape from thence. London. A. Bettesworth. Price 1s. 6d. (8vo. Title and Preface pp. vi. and 93.) 1st Edition, 10 Dec. 1719—(Collation the same). 2nd Edition, 1720.

201.—The Chimera : or, The French ¡Way of Paying National Debts Laid Open. Being an Impartial Account of the Proceedings in France for Raising a Paper Credit, and Settling the Mississippi Stock. London. T. Warner. Price One Shilling. (8vo. Title & pp. 76.) About Jan. 1720.

202.—The History of the Life and Adventures of Mr. Duncan Campbell. A Gentleman, who though born Deaf and Dumb, writes down any Stranger's Name at First Sight ; and their Future Contingencies of Fortune. Now living in Exeter Court, over against the Savoy in the Strand. London. E. Curll. (8vo. Portrait, Title, Dedication, and Contents xxiv. & pp. 320. 4 Plates.) 1st Edition, 30th April, 1720.

203.—Mr. Campbell's Pacquet, for the Entertainment of Gentlemen and . Ladies, Containing, I. Verses to Mr. Campbell, Occasioned by the History of his Life and Adventures. By Mrs. Fowke, Mr. Phillips, &c. II. The Parallel, a Poem comparing the Poetical Productions of Mr. Pope, with the Prophetical Predictions of Mr. Campbell. By Capt. Stanhope. III. An Account of a Most Surprising Apparition ; sent from Launceston in Cornwall. Attested by the Rev. Mr. Ruddle, Minister there. London. Printed for T. Bickerton, at the Crown in Paternoster Row. (8vo. Title, & pp. 33.) [Section III., by Defoe.] 18 June, 1720. The History of the Life and Adventures of Mr. Duncan Campbell (with the Pacquet included). London. E. Curll. (8vo. Portrait & Plates. Title, &c. xxiv. Pacquet pp. 33. Life pp. 320.)—2nd Edition, 4 Aug. 1720.—2nd Edition reissued 14th Mar. 1721. The Supernatural Philosopher : or, the Mysteries of Magick, in all its Branches clearly unfolded, Containing, I. An Argument proving the Perception, which Mankind have by all the senses, of Demons, Genii, or Familiar Spirits ; and of the Several species of them, both Good and Bad. II. A Philosophical Discourse, concerning the Second Sight, demonstrating it to be Hereditary to some Families. III. A full Answer to all Objections that can be brought against the existence of Spirits, Witches, &c. IV. Of Divination by Dreams, Omens, Spectres, Apparitions after Death, Predictions, &c. V. Of Enchantment, Necromancy, Geomancy, Hydromancy, Æromancy, Pyromancy, Chiromancy, Augury, and Aruspicy. All Exemplified in the History of the Life and Surprizing Adventures of Mr. Duncan Campbell, a Scots Gentleman, who though Deaf and Dumb writes down any Stranger's Name at first Sight, with their Future Contingencies of Fortune. Collected and Compiled from the most approved Authorities, wherein is inserted that most celebrated Tract written by Dr. Wallis, The Method of Teaching Deaf and Dumb Persons to read, write, and understand a Language. By William Bond, of Bury St. Edmund's, Suffolk. London. E. Curll. (8vo. Collation as 2nd Edition, except New Title and the Portrait omitted.) 3rd Edition, 1728 (This was again reissued as a 2nd Edition). 4th Edition, 21 Dec. 1728.

204.—*Memoirs* of a *Cavalier* : or, a Military Journal of the Wars in Germany, and the Wars in England. From the Year 1632, to the Year 1648. Written threescore years ago, by an *English* Gentleman, who served first in the Army of *Gustavus Adolphus*, the Glorious King of *Sweden*, till his Death, and after that in the Royal Army of King Charles the First, from the Beginning of the Rebellion to the End of the War. London. Printed for *A. Bell*, at the *Cross Keys* in *Cornhill, J. Osborn*, at the *Oxford Arms* in *Lombard Street, W. Taylor*, at the

Ship and Swan, and. *T. Warner*, at the *Black Boy*, in *Paternoster Row*. 1st Edition, 21 May, 1720.—(Leeds, James Lister.) (8vo. Title, and Preface, 6 leaves, & pp. 338). 2nd Edit.

205.—The Life, Adventures, and Piracies of the Famous *Captain Singleton* : Containing an Account of his being set on Shore in the Island of *Madagascar*, his Settlement there, with a Description of the Place and Inhabitants : Of his Passage from thence in a Paraguay, to the Main Land of Africa, with an Account of the Customs and Manners of the People : His great Deliverances from the Barbarous Natives and Wild Beasts : Of his meeting with an *Englishman*, a citizen of *London*, amongst the *Indians*. The great Riches he Acquired, and his Voyage Home to *England*. As also Captain *Singleton's* Return to Sea, with an Account of his many Adventures, and Pyracies with the famous Captain *Avery*, and others.   London.   Printed for *J. Brotherton* at the *Black Bull*, in *Cornhill*, *J. Graves*, in *St. James's Street*, *A. Dodd*, at the *Peacock*, without *Temple-bar*, and *T. Warner*, at the *Black Boy* in *Paternoster Row*. (8vo. Title & pp. 344.) 1st Edition, 4 June, 1720.—Reissued in the Post Master or Loyal Mercury, Exeter. 4 Nov. 1720, and following weeks.—Printed and Sold by Nath. Mist, in Great Carter *Lane*.   2nd Edition, 9 Sept. 1721.

206.—*Applebee's Original Weekly Journal*. [Established in 1714. *Daniel Defoe* began to write weekly articles, and to assist in the management, and continued to do so nearly six years. The Journal continued long afterward.] 25 June, 1720, to 12 March, 1726.

207.—The Director. [Defoe wrote Leading Articles in it, but whether he was the responsible Editor or not I cannot say.] No. I. published 5 Oct. 1720.

208.—The Compleat Art of Painting. A Poem. Translated from the French of M. Du Fresnoy. By D. F., Gent.   London.   T. Warner.   Price One Shilling. (8vo. Title & pp. 53.) 1720.

209.—A Vindication of the Honour and Justice of Parliament against a most Scandalous Libel, Entituled the Speech of John A—— Esq. London.   Printed for A. Moore, near St. Paul's, and Sold by the Booksellers of London and Westminster.   Price Six Pence. *n. d.* (Title and Preface 2 leaves & pp. 36.) Feb. 1721.

210.—A Collection of Miscellany Letters, selected out of Mist's *Weekly Journal* [12mo. (Vol. I. Title and Dedication 4 leaves, Preface xiv., Contents 4 leaves & pp. 310.) (Vol. II. Title, &c., xii. pp. 332, Contents 4 leaves.)] * Contains many Letters written by Defoe.   9 Jan. 1722.

211.—The Fortunes and Misfortunes of the Famous Moll Flanders, &c., who was born in Newgate, and during a Life of continued Variety, for Threescore Years, beside her Childhood, was Twelve Years a Whore, Five Times a Wife (whereof once to her own Brother), Twelve Years a Thief, Eight Years a Transported Felon in Virginia, at last grew Rich, liv'd Honest, and died a Penitent. Written from her own Memorandums.   London. ` W. Chetwood, 1721. (8vo. pp. xiii. & 424.) 1st Edition, 27 Jan. 1722.—London. J. Brotherton. (8vo. 4 leaves & pp. 366.) 2nd Edition, 23 July, 1722.—London. W. Chetwood. (8vo. 4 leaves & pp. 366) 3rd Edition, 21 Dec. 1722.—An Abridged Edition (for the Pocket). London. J. Read. 4th Edition, 13 July, 1723.—A Reissue of the 3rd Edition. 2nd Nov. 1723.

212.—Religious Courtship : Being Historical Discourses on the Necessity of Marrying Religious Husbands and Wives only.   As also of Husbands and Wives being of the same Opinions in Religion with one Another.   With an Appendix of the Necessity of taking none but Religious Servants, and a Proposal for the better Management of Servants. London. E. Matthews. (8vo. 4 leaves & pp. 358.) 20 Feb. 1722.

213.—A Journal of the Plague Year : Being Observations or Memorials of the most Remarkable Occurrences, as well Publick as Private, which happened in London during the last Great Visitation in 1665. Written by a Citizen, who continued all the while in London. Never made publick before.   London. Printed for E. Nutt, &c. (8vo. 3 leaves & pp. 287.) 1st Edition, 17 Mar. 1722. —The History of the Great Plague in London, in the Year 1665. Containing Observations and Memorials of the most remarkable Occurrences, both Publick and Private, that happened during that dreadful period. By a Citizen who lived the Whole Time in London. To which is added a Journal of the Plague at Marseilles, in the Year 1720. London. T. and J. Noble. (8vo. Title and pp. 376.) 2nd Edition, 1754.

213A.—Due Preparations for the Plague 1722. Omitted accidentally by Mr. Lee. A separate work from 213.

214.—The *Life* and *Actions* of *Lewis Dominique Cartouche*, who was broke alive upon the wheel at Paris, Nov. 28, 1721, *N.S.*, Relating at large his remarkable *Adventures, Desperate Enterprises*, and Various *Escapes*. With an Account of his Behaviour under Sentence, and upon the Scaffold, and the Manner of his Execution. Translated from the French. *London. J. Roberts.* Price 1s. 6d. (8vo. pp. 88.) 27 April, 1722.

215.—The *History* and *Remarkable Life* of the truly Honourable *Colonel Jacque*, vulgarly called *Col. Jack*, who was born a *Gentleman;* put 'Prentice to a *Pickpocket;* was six and twenty years a *Thief*, and then kidnapped to *Virginia;* came back a *Merchant;* was five times married to four *Whores;* went into the Wars, behaved bravely, got Preferment, was made Colonel of a *Regiment;* came over, and fled with the *Chevalier*, is still abroad Completing a life of *Wonders*, and resolves to die a *General. London. J. Brotherton*, &c. &c. (8vo. Title and Preface, pp. vii. & pp. 399.) 1st Edition, 20 Dec. 1722.—(8vo. Title and Preface 4 leaves & pp. 399.) 2nd Edition, 19 Jan. 1723.—(8vo. Title and Preface 4 leaves & pp. 399.) 3rd Edition, 1724.

216.—An *Impartial History* of the *Life* and *Actions* of *Peter Alexowitz* the present *Czar* of *Muscovy:* From his *Birth* down to this present *Time*. Giving an Account of his *Travels* and *Transactions* in the *Several Courts* of *Europe*. With his *Attempts* and *Successes* in the *Northern* and *Eastern Parts* of the World. In which is intermixed the *History* of *Muscovy*. Written by a *British Officer* in the Service of the *Czar. London.* Printed for *W. Chetwood*, at *Cato's Head* in *Russel Street*, Covent Garden; *J. Stagg* in Westminster Hall; *J. Brotherton*, at the Bible, near the Royal Exchange; and *T. Edlin*, at the Princes Arms, over against Exeter Exchange in the Strand. Price bound 5s. (8vo. Title & pp. 420.) 1723.

217.—The *Highland Rogue*, or the Memorable *Actions* of the celebrated *Robert Macgregor;* commonly called *Rob Roy*. Containing a Genuine *Account* of his Education, *Grandeur*, and sudden *Misfortune;* his commencing Robber, and being elected *Captain* of a formidable Gang; his exploits on the Highway, breaking open *Houses*, taking *Prisoners;* commencing Judge, and Levying Taxes; his Defence of his Manner of Living; his Dispute with a Scotch Parson upon Predestination; his joining with the *Earl of Mar* in the *Rebellion;* his being decoy'd, and imprison'd by the Duke of ——, with the Manner of his Escape, &c. Introduced with the Relation of the Unequall'd Villainies of the Clan of the Macgregors several Years past. The whole impartially digested from the Memorandums of an Authentick Scotch M.S. *London. J. Billingsby*, &c. &c. Price 1s. (8vo. pp. 63.) 5 Oct. 1723.

218.—The *Fortunate Mistress:* or, a *History of the Life and Vast Variety of Fortunes of Mademoiselle de Belau;* afterwards called the Countess of Wintselsheim, in Germany. Being the person known by the name of the *Lady Roxana*, in the Time of King Charles II. *London. T. Warner*, &c. (8vo. Frontispiece, Title, and Preface 3 leaves, & pp. 407.) 1st Edition, 14 March, 1724.

219.—The *Great Law* of *Subordination* Consider'd; or, The Insolence, and Unsufferable Behaviour of Servants in England, duly enquired into. Illustrated with a great Variety of Examples, Historical Cases and Remarkable Stories of the Behaviour of some particular Servants, Suited to all the Several Arguments made use of as they go on. In Ten Familiar Letters. Together with a Conclusion, being an Earnest and Moving Remonstrance, to the Housekeepers and Heads of Families in Great Britain, pressing them not to cease using their Utmost Interest (especially at this Juncture), to obtain sufficient laws, for the effectual Regulation of the Manners and Behaviour of their Servants. As also a Proposal, containing such Heads, or Constitutions, as would effectually answer this great End, and bring Servants of every Class to a just (and yet not a Grievous) Regulation. *London. S. Harding*, and other Booksellers. *Price Three Shillings and*

Six Pence. (8vo. Title and Preface 2 leaves & pp. 302.) 1st Edition, 4 April, 1724.—The *Behaviour* of *Servants* in *England,* Inquired into. With a Proposal containing Such Heads or Constitutions as would effectually answer this Great End, and Bring Servants of every Class to a Just Regulation. *London.* H. Whittridge, under the Royal Exchange. Price, 2s. Stitcht, or 3s. Bound. (8vo. Title & pp. 302. In fact the sheets of the previous Edition, with suppression of Preface, and Change of Title.) 2nd Edition, no date.

220.—A *Tour* thro' the *whole Island* of *Great Britain;* divided into Circuits or Journies. Giving a Particular and Diverting Account of whatever is Curious and worth Observation, viz. :—I. A Description of the Principal Cities and Towns, their Situation, Magnitude, Government, and Commerce. II. The Customs, Manner, Speech ; as also the Exercises, Diversions, and Employment of the People. III. The Produce and Improvements of the Land, the Trade and Manufactures. IV. The Seaports and Fortifications, with the Course of Rivers, and the Inland Navigation. V. The Publick Edifices, Seats and Palaces, of the Gentry and Nobility. With useful observations on the whole. Particularly fitted for the Reading of Such as desire to travel over the Island. By a Gentleman. *London.* G. *Strahan.* (8vo. Plate of the Siege of Colchester in 1648. Title and Preface vii. & pp. 140, 121, and 127.) Vol. I., 1st Edition, 22 May, 1724.

221.— ———— With a Map of England and Wales, by Mr. Moll. (8vo. Map, Title, and Preface, viii. & pp. 192 and 200. Index to Vols. 1 and 2, pp. xxxvi.) Vol. II., 1st Edition, 8 June, 1725.

222.— ———— Which completes this Work, and contains a Tour thro' Scotland, &c. With a Map of Scotland, by Mr. Moll. (8vo. Map, Title, and Preface, 3 leaves & pp. 232 and 230. Index, 2 leaves.) Vol. III., 1st Edition, 13 Aug. 1726. – Complete, 3 Vols., 2nd Edition, 15 June, 1727.

223.—A *Narrative* of the *Proceedings* in *France,* for Discovering and Detecting the Murders of the English Gentlemen, September 21, 1723, near Calais. With an Account of the Condemnation and Sentence of Joseph Bizeau and Peter Le Febvre, Two Notorious Robbers, who were the principal Actors in the said Murder ; particularly in the Killing Mr. Lock. Together with their Discovery and manner of perpetrating that execrable Murder ; and also large Memoirs of their Behaviour during their Torture, and upon the Scaffold; their impeaching Several other Criminals, and a brief History of their Past Crimes, as well in Company with their former Captain, the famous Cartouche, as since his Execution. In which is a great Variety of Remarkable Incidents, and Surprising Circumstances, never yet made Publick. Translated from the French. *London.* Printed for *J. Roberts,* in Warwick Lane. Price 2s. (8vo. pp. 108.) 17 Aug. 1724.

224.—The *History* of the *Remarkable Life of John Sheppard.* Containing a Particular Account of his Many Robberies and Escapes, &c. &c. Including his last Escape from the Castle, at Newgate. Printed and Published by John Applebee, in Black Friars. Price one Shilling. (8vo. pp.   .) 1st Edition, 19 Oct. 1724.—2nd Edition, 26 Oct. 1724.—3rd Edition, 12 Nov. 1724.

225.—A *Narrative* of all the *Robberies, Escapes,* &c., of *John Sheppard,* Giving an Exact Description of the Manner of his Wonderful Escape from the Castle in Newgate, and of the Methods he took afterward for his Security. Written by *himself* during his Confinement in the *Middle Stone Room,* after his being retaken in Drury Lane. To which is Prefix'd a true Representation of his Escape, from the condemned Hold, Curiously Engraven on a Copper Plate. The whole Published at the particular request of the Prisoner. London. Printed and Sold by *John Applebee,* &c. in Black Friars. Price 6d. (8vo. front. pp. 31.) 1st Edition, 17 Nov. 1724.—2nd Edition, 18 Nov. 1724—3rd Edition, 19 Nov. 1724—4th Edition, 20 Nov. 1724.—5th Edition, 21 Nov. 1724.—6th Edition, 28 Nov. 1724.—7th Edition, 12 Dec. 1724.

226.—A *New Voyage Round* the *World.* By a *Course* never Sailed *before.* Being a Voyage undertaken by some Merchants, who afterwards proposed the setting up of an East India Company in Flanders. Illustrated with Copper Plates. *London.* A. *Bettesworth.* (8vo. Plates. Title & pp. 208 and 205.) 8 May, 1725.

227.—*Everybody's Business* is *Nobody's Business:* or Private *Abuses, Publick Grievances.* Exemplified in the Pride, Insolence, and Exorbitant Wages of our Women Servants, Footmen &c. By Andrew Morton, Esq. 1st Edition, 5 June, 1725.—2nd Edition, 9 June, 1725.—(8vo. pp. 34) 3rd Edition, 14 June, 1725.— 4th Edition, 19 June, 1725.—(With an addition of a Preface) 5th Edition, 24 July, 1725.—Reprinted 1767.

228.—The *True, Genuine,* and *Perfect Account* of the *Life* and *Actions* of *Jonathan Wild.* Taken from good Authority, and from his own Writings. Printed and Published by J. Applebee, in Black Friars. (8vo.) 1st Edition, 8 June, 1725.—2nd Edition, 10 June, 1725.—3rd Edition, 12 June, 1725.

229.—An *Account* of the *Conduct* and *Proceedings* of the late *John Gow*, alias Smith, Captain of the late *Pirates*, executed for Murther and Piracy, committed on Board the *George Galley*, afterwards called the *Revenge ;* with a Relation of all the horrid Murthers they Committed in Cold Blood.. As also of their being taken at the Islands of Orkney, and sent up prisoners to London. *London.* Printed and Sold by J. *Applebee*, in *Black Fryers.* Price 1s. (8vo. Title, &c. viii. pp. 62.) 11 June, 1725.

230.—The *Complete English Tradesman*, In Familiar Letters, Directing him in all the several Parts and Progressions of Trade—viz. I. His acquainting himself with Business during his Apprenticeship. II. His Writing to his Correspondents, and obtaining a general Knowledge of Trade, as well what he is not as what he is employ'd in. III. Of Diligence, and Application, as the Life of all Business. IV. Cautions against Over-Trading. V. Of the ordinary Occasions of a Tradesman's Ruin : such as Expensive Living,—Too early Marrying,— Innocent Diversions,—Giving and Taking too much Credit,—Leaving Business to Servants,—Being above Business,—Entering into Dangerous Partnerships, &c. VI. Directions in the several Distresses of a Tradesman, when he comes to fail. VII. Of Tradesmen Compounding with their Debtors, and why they are so particularly severe. VIII. Of Tradesmen ruining one another, by Rumour and Scandal. IX. Of the Customary Frauds of Trade, which even honest Men allow themselves to practise. X. Of Credit, and how it is only supported by Honesty. XI. Directions for Book-keeping, punctual paying Bills, and thereby maintaining Credit. XII. Of the Dignity and Honour of Trade, in *England*, more than in other Countries ; and how the Trading Families in *England* are mingled with the Nobility and Gentry, so as not to be separated, or distinguished. Calculated for the Instruction of Our Inland Tradesmen, and especially of Young Beginners. London. Charles Rivington. (Title & Preface xv. Contents 1 leaf & pp. 447.) 1st Edition, 11 Sept. 1795—Reissued, 1726. (Title as before to Section XII.) The Second Edition. To which is added a Supplement, Containing—I. A Warning against Tradesmen's Borrowing Money upon Interest. II. A Caution against that destructive Practice, of drawing and Remitting, as also discounting Promissory Bills, meerly for a supply of Cash. III. Directions for the Tradesman's accounts, with brief but plain Examples, and Specimens for Book-keeping. IV. Of keeping a Duplicate, or Pocket Ledger, in Case of Fire. London. Printed for Charles Rivington, at the Bible and Crown in St. Paul's Churchyard. (Title, Preface, and Contents xx, & pp. 368. Supplement, 148.) 2nd Edition, 10 Sept. 1726. (*Supplement may be had alone. Price 1s.) Reissued, 1727.

231.—The *Compleat English Tradesman.* Volume ii. In two Parts. Part I. Directed chiefly to the more Experienc'd Tradesmen ; with Cautions and Advices to them after they are thriven, and supposed to be grown rich, viz. I. Against Running out of their Business Projects, and Dangerous Adventures, no Tradesman being above Disaster. II. Against Oppressing one another by Engrossing, Underselling, Combinations in Trade, &c. III. Advices, that when he leaves off his Business he should part Friends with the World ; the great Advantages of it ; with a Word on the Scandalous Character of a Purseproud Tradesman. IV. Against being litigious and Vexatious, and apt to go to Law for Trifles ; with some Reasons why Tradesmen's Differences should, if possible, all be ended by Arbitration. Part II. Being useful Generals in Trade, describing the Principles and Foundation of the Home Trade of Great Britain, with Large Tables of our Manufactures, Calculations of the Product, Shipping,

Carriage of Goods by Land, Importation from Abroad, Consumption at Home, &c. by all which the infinite number of our Tradesmen are employ'd, and the General Wealth of the Nation rais'd and increas'd. The whole calculated for the use of our Inland Tradesmen, as well in the City as in the Country. London. Printed for *Charles Rivington* at the Bible and Crown in St. Paul's Churchyard. (Title, Preface and Contents xiv. & pp. 298 and 176.) 1st Edition, 13 May, 1727—Compleat. In 2 Volumes. 2nd Edition, 10 Aug. 1728.

232 —The *Friendly Dæmon;* or, the Generous Apparition. Being a True Narrative of a Miraculous Cure newly performed upon the famous Deaf and Dumb gentleman, Dr. Duncan Campbell, By a familiar Spirit, that appeared to him in a white surplice, like a Cathedral Singing boy. *London. J. Roberts.* (8vo. pp. 39. Pp. 14 to 48, by Defoe.) 1726.

233.—The *Political History* of the *Devil, As* well *Ancient* as Modern. In two Parts. I. Containing a State of the Devil's Circumstances, and the Various Turns in his affairs, from his Expulsion out of Heaven, to the Creation of Man. With remarks on the Several Mistakes concerning the Reason and Manner of his Fall. Also his Proceedings with Mankind, ever since Adam, to the first planting of the Christian Religion in the World. Part II. Containing his more Private Conduct down to the present Times; his Government, his Appearances, his Manner of Working, and the Tools he Works with. *London. T. Warner.* (8vo. Frontispiece, Title, Dedication and Contents, 4 leaves & pp. 408.) 1st Edition, 7 May, 1726.—(8vo. Frontispiece, Title, Preface and Contents 4 leaves pp. 408.) 2nd Edition, 20 April, 1727.—Westminster. J. Brindley (8vo. Front. Title, Ded. & Preface 4 leaves & pp. 408). 3rd Edition, 1734.

234.—*Mere Nature Delineated;* or, a *Body* without a *Soul.* Being Observations upon the young Forester lately brought to Town from Germany. With Suitable Applications. Also a Brief Dissertation upon the Usefulness and necessity of Fools, whether Political or Natural. Price 1s. 6d. *London. T. Warner.* (8vo. 2 leaves & pp. 123.) 23 July, 1726.

235.—An *Essay* upon *Literature;* or, an Enquiry into the Antiquity and Original of Letters. Proving that the two Tables, written by the Finger of God in Mount Sinai, was the first Writing in the World; and that all other Alphabets derive from the Hebrew. With a short view of the methods made use of by the Ancients to supply the want of Letters before, and improve the use of them, after they were known. *London. Thos. Bowles.* (8vo. Title & pp. 127.) 1726.

236.—A *General History* of the *Principal Discoveries* and *Improvements* in *Useful Arts.* Particularly in the Great Branches of Commerce, Navigation, and Plantation in all Parts of the known World, &c. London. J. Roberts. (Complete in Four Monthly Parts. 8vo. Title and Preface viii., pp. 307, and General Index & pp. 5.) Oct. 1726 to Jan. 1727.

237.—The *Protestant Monastery,* or, a Complaint against the Brutality of the Present Age. Particularly the Pertness and Insolence of our Youth to Aged Persons. With a Caution to People in Years how they give the Staff out of their own Hands, and leave themselves to the Mercy of others. Concluding with a Proposal for Erecting a Protestant Monastery, where Persons of small Fortune may End their Days in Plenty, Ease and Credit, without Burthening their Relations, or accepting Publick Charities. By *Andrew Moreton,* Esq., Author of "Everybody's Business is Nobody's Business." London. W. Meadows, 1727. Price 6d. (8vo. Title and Preface viii., and pp. 31.) 19 Nov. 1746.—Reissued, 1727.

238.—A *System* of *Magick;* or, a History of the *Black Art.* Being an Historical Account of Mankind's most early Dealings with the Devil, and how the Acquaintance on both Sides first began. *London. J. Roberts.* (8vo. Front. Title, Preface & Contents 5 leaves & pp. 403.) 1st Edition, 19 Dec. 1726.— With Additions. 2nd Edition, 16 Jan. 1731.

239.—The *Evident Approach* of a *War:* and Something of the Necessity of it, in order to Establish Peace and Preserve Trade. *Pax Quæritur Bello.* To which is added an Exact Plan and Description of the Bay and City of Gibraltar. *London,* J. Roberts. Price 1s. 6d. (8vo. Plan. 2 leaves & pp. 52.) Jan. 1727.

240.—*Conjugal Lewdness:* or, *Matrimonial Whoredom,* &c. &c. *London.*

T. Warner. (8vo. Title, Preface, & Contents 4 leaves & pp. 406.) 30 Jan. 1727.—[Reissued with the following Title, but collation as befoie.]—A Treatise concerning the Use and Abuse of the Marriage Bed. Shewing—I. The Nature of Matrimony, its Sacred Original, and the True Meaning of its Institution. II. The gross abuse of Matrimonial Chastity from the wrong Notions which have possessed the World, degenerating even to Whoredom. III. The Diabolical practice of attempting to prevent Childbearing by Physical Preparations. IV. The Fatal Consequences of Clandestine, or forced Marriages, thro' the Persuasion, Interest, or Influence of Parents and Relations, to wed the Person they have no love for, but oftentimes an Aversion to. V. Of Unequal Matches as to the Disproportion of Age ; and how such many Ways occasion a Matrimonial Whoredom. VI. How married Persons may be guilty of *Conjugal Lewdness*, and that a Man may, in *effect*, make a Whore of his own Wife. Also many other Particulars of Family Concern. *London.* *T. Warner.* (8vo. Title, Preface, & Contents 4 leaves & pp. 406.) 10 June, 1727.

241.—An *Essay* on the *History* and *Reality of Apparitions.* Being an Account of What they are, and What they are not ; Whence they Come, and Whence they Come not ; As also how we may distinguish the Apparitions of Good and Evil Spirits, and how we ought to behave to them. With a great Variety of Surprising and Diverting Examples, never published before. London. J. Roberts. (8vo. Front. and Plates. Title, Preface, and Contents 6 leaves, & pp. 395.) 1st Edition, 18 March, 1727.—The *Secrets* of the *Invisible World Disclos'd :* or, An *Universal History* of *Apparitions, Sacred and Profane,* under all *Denominations ;* whether *Angelical, Diabolical,* or *Human Souls Departed.* Shewing—I. Their Various Returns to this World ; with sure Rules to know, by their *Manner* of *Appearing,* if they are *Good* or *Evil Ones.* The *Differences* of the *Apparitions* of *Ancient* and *Modern* Times ; and an Enquiry into the *Scriptural Doctrine* of *Spirits.* III. The many Species of Apparitions ; their real Existence and Operations by Divine Appointment. IV. The *Nature* of Seeing Ghosts before, and after Death, and how we should behave towards them. V. The *effects* of Fancy, Vapours, Dreams, Hyppo, and of real or imaginary Appearances. VI. A Collection of the most Authentic Relations of Apparitions, particularly that surprizing One attested by the learned Dr. *Scott.* By *Andrew Moreton, Esq.* Adorned with Cuts. *London.* Printed for *J. Peele.* (8vo. Plates, Title, Preface and Contents 6 leaves, & pp. 395. Only the Title altered.) 23 Nov. 1728.—(Printed for John Clarke & A Millar, &c.) Reissued. 2nd Edition, 13 Feb. 1729.

242.—A *New Family Instructor ;* in *Familiar Discourses* between a *Father* and his *Children,* on the most Essential *Points* of the *Christian Religion.* In Two Parts. Part I. containing a *Father's* INSTRUCTIONS to his *Son* upon his going to *Travel* into *Popish Countries ;* and to the rest of his Children, on his Son's turning *Papist ;* confirming them in the *Protestant Religion,* against the *Absurdities* of *Popery.* Part II. Instructions against the *Three Grand Errors* of the *Times ;* viz. 1. Asserting the *Divine Authority* of the *Scriptures ;* against the *Deists.* 2. Proofs, that the *Messias* is already come, &c. ; against the *Atheists* and *Jews.* 3. Asserting, the *Divinity* of *Jesus Christ,* that he was really the *same* with the *Messias,* and that the *Messias* was to be really,GOD ; against our *Modern Hereticks.* With a *Poem* upon the *Divine Nature* of JESUS CHRIST, in *Blank Verse.* By the Author of the *Family Instructor. London, T. Warner.* (8vo. Title and Pref. xv. & pp. 384.) 1st Edition, 1727.—With an altered Title. 2nd Edition, 1732.

243.—*Parochial Tyranny :* or, the *Housekeeper's Complaint,* against the insupportable *Exactions* and partial *Assessments* of *Select Vestries.* With a plain *Detection* of many Abuses committed in the *Distribution* ol *Public Charities.* Together with a *Practical Proposal* for *Amending* the *same :* which will not only take off great *Part* of the *Parish Taxes* now subsisting, but ease *Parishioners* from Serving troublesome *Offices,* or paying exorbitant Fines. By *Andrew Moreton, Esq. London. W. Meadows.* (8vo. Title & pp. 36). 9 Dec. 1727.

244.—*Augusta Triumphans :* or, the Way to make *London* the most Flourishing *City* in the *Universe.* I. By Establishing a *University* where Gentlemen may have Academical Education under the Eyes of their Friends. II. By an

Hospital for *Foundlings.* III. By forming an Academy of Sciences at *Christ's Hospital.* IV. By Suppressing pretended *Mad-Houses,* where many of the fair Sex are unjustly confined, while their Husbands keep Mistresses, &c., and many Widows are locked up for the sake of their Jointure. V. To Save our Youth from *Destruction,* by Clearing the Streets of impudent *Strumpets,* suppressing *Gaming Tables,* and *Sunday Debauches.* VI. To Save our lower Class of People from utter *Ruin,* and render them useful, by preventing the immoderate use of Geneva. With a frank Exposition of many other Common Abuses, and incontestable Rules for Amendment. Concluding with an Effectual Method to prevent *Street Robberies,* and a Letter to Col : Robinson, on Account of the Orphan's Tax. By *Andrew Moreton, Esq. London. J. Roberts.* (8vo. pp. 63). 1st Edition, 16 Mar. 1728.—(Collation the same). 2nd Edition, 1729.

245.—A *Plan* of the *English Commerce.* Being a Compleat *Prospect* of the *Trade* of this *Nation,* As well the *Home Trade* as the *Foreign.* In three Parts. Part I. Containing a view of the present *Magnitude* of the *English Trade,* as it respects, 1. The *Exportation* of our own Growth and Manufacture ; 2. The *Importation* of Merchant Goods from Abroad ; 3. The *Prodigious Consumption* of Both at Home. Part II. Containing an Answer to that Great and Important Question now depending, Whether our Trade, and especially our Manufactures, are in a declining Condition, or No? Part III. Containing several *Proposals* entirely new, for *Extending* and *Improving* our *Trade,* and *Promoting* the *Consumption* of our *Manufactures* in *Countries* wherewith we have hitherto had no *Commerce.* Humbly offered to the Consideration of the *King* and *Parliament: London. C. Rivington* (8vo. pp. 368). 1st Edition, 23 March, 1728.—A *Plan* of the *English Commerce,* Being a *Compleat Prospect* of the *Trade* of this *Nation,* as well the *Home Trade* as the *Foreign.* Humbly offered to the Consideration of the King and Parliament. The Second Edition. *To which is added,* an APPENDIX, containing A View of the *Increase of Commerce,* not only of *England,* but of all the Trading *Nations* of *Europe,* since the Peace with *Spain.* The whole Containing several *Proposals,* entirely new, for *Extending,* and *Improving* Our *Trade ;* and *Promoting* the CONSUMPTION *of our Manufactures* in *Countries,* wherewith we have *hitherto* had no *Commerce. London.* Printed for *C. Rivington,* 1730. (8vo. Title and Pref. xvi. Contents, &c., 4 leaves & pp. 368, and Append. pp. 40). 2nd Edition, 13 Jan. 1761.

246.—The *Universal Spectator.* No. 1. (Impl. 4to. one sheet.) 12 Oct. 1728.

247.—*Second Thoughts* are *Best:* or, a Further Improvement of a late *Scheme* to Prevent Street Robberies. By which our Streets will be so strongly Guarded, and so gloriously illuminated, that any part of London will be as safe and pleasant at Midnight, as at Noonday, and Burglary totally impracticable. With some Thoughts for Suppressing Robberies in all the Publick Roads of England, &c. Humbly offered for the good of his Country, Submitted to the Consideration of the Parliament, and Dedicated to his Sacred Majesty George II. By Andrew Moreton, Esq. London. W. Meadows. Price 6d. (8vo. pp. 24). 12 Oct. 1728,

248.—*Street Robberies* considered. The reason of their being so frequent, with probable means to prevent 'em. To which is added, three short Treatises:— 1. A Warning for Travellers : with Rules to Know a Highwayman, and Instructions how to behave upon the occasion. 2. Observations on Housebreakers. How to prevent a Tenement from being broke open. With a Word of Advice concerning Servants. 3. A Caveat for Shopkeepers : with a Description of Shoplifts, how to know 'em, and how to prevent 'em ; also a Caution of Delivering Goods : With the Relation of several Cheats, practised lately upon the Publick. Written by a Converted Thief. To which is prefix'd some Memoirs of his Life. *Set a Thief to Catch a Thief. London.* Printed for J. Roberts, in Warwick Lane. Price 1s. (8vo. pp. 72). 12 Nov. 1728.

249.—*Fog's Weekly Journal.* (An Article by Defoe.) 11 Jan. 1729.

250.—*An Humble Proposal,* to the People of *England,* for the Encrease of their Trade and Encouragement of their Manufactures; whether the present Uncertainty of Affairs issues in Peace or War. By the *Author of* the *Compleat English Tradesman.* London. C. Rivington. (8vo. Title and Preface, 2 leaves & pp. 59.) 15 March, 1729.

251.—*Reasons* for a *War*, in Order to Establish the Tranquility and Commerce of Europe. *Pax Quæritur Bello.* London. Printed for A. Dodd, and R. Walker, without Temple Bar; E. Nutt and F. Smith, at the Royal Exchange, and Sold by the Booksellers, and Pamphlet Shops, Mercuries and Hawkers of Londor and Westminster. Price 6d. (8vo. pp. 32.) Mar. 1729.

252.—*Servitude:* a Poem. To which is prefix'd an Introduction, humbly submitted to the Consideration of all Noblemen, Gentlemen, and Ladies, who keep many Servants. Also, a Postscript, occasioned by a late trifling Pamphlet, entitled, *Every Body's Business is Nobody's Business.* Written by a Footman. In Behalf of Good Servants, and to excite the Bad to do their Duty. London. *T. Worrall. Price* 6d. [The Prose, comprising the larger part, written by *Defoe;* the Verse by Robert *Dodsley.*] (8vo. pp. 32.) 20 Sept. 1729.

253.—The *Compleat English Gentleman:* Containing useful Observations on the general Neglect of the Education of English Gentlemen, with the Reason and Remedies. The Apparent Differences between a well-born, and a well-bred Gentleman. Instructions how Gentlemen may recover a Deficiency of their Latin, and be Men of Learning, though without the Pedantry of Schools. First printed in 1890 by David Nutt of London. 1729.

254.—An *Effectual Scheme,* for the immediate *Preventing* of *Street Robberies,* and suppressing the other Disorders of the Night; With a Brief History of the Night-Houses, and an Appendix relating to those Sons of Hell, called Incendiaries. Humbly Inscribed to the Right Honourable, the Lord Mayor of London. *London.* Printed by *J. Wilford,* at the three Flower-de-Luces, behind the Chapter House in St. Paul's Church-Yard. Price 1s. (8vo. pp. 72.). 1731.

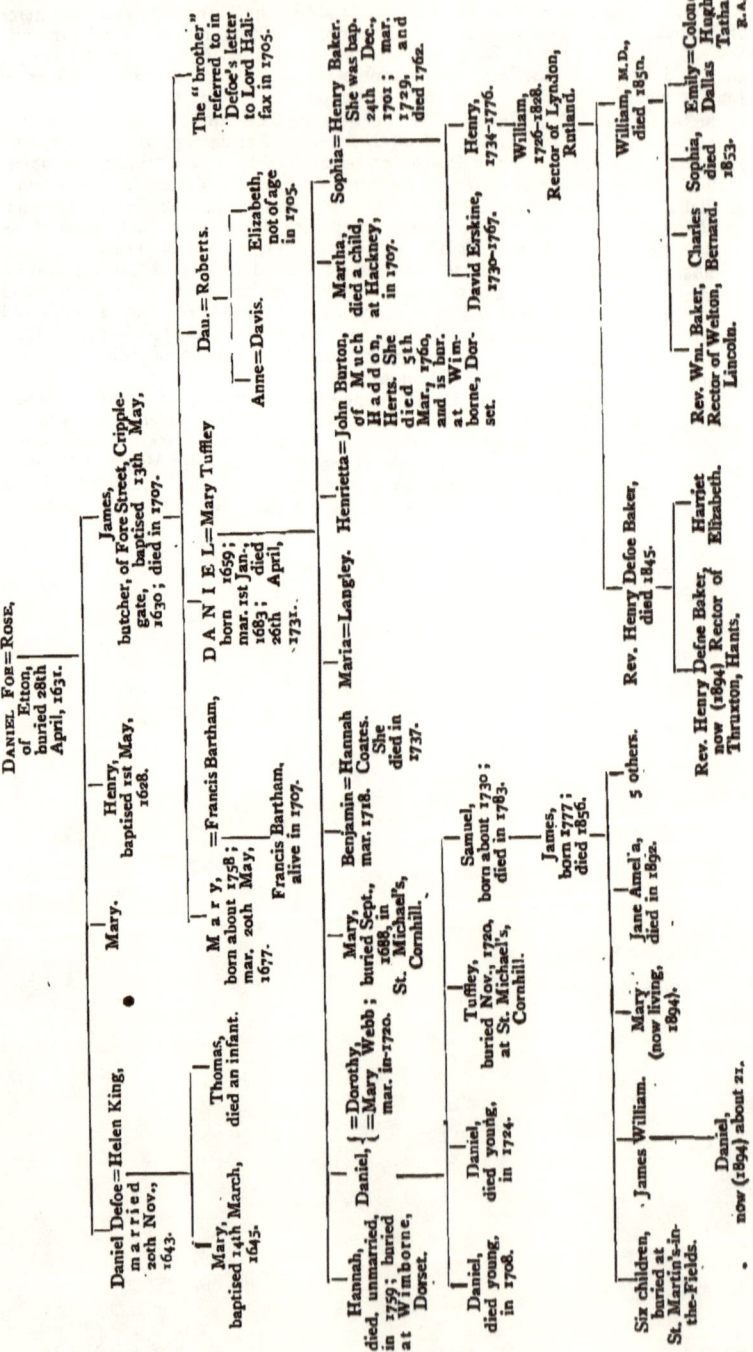

INDEX.

THE END.

PRINTED BY CASSELL & COMPANY, LIMITED, LA BELLE SAUVAGE, LONDON, E.C.

www.ingramcontent.com/pod-product-compliance
Lightning Source LLC
Chambersburg PA
CBHW032016110726
47901CB00004B/1111